THE SECOND ACT COMEBACK

By Jamie Norton

Valenza Publishing

More from Valenza Publishing

<u>Andrew Valenza</u>

Empire of the Void
Lost World of the Void

Three Short Horror Stories

<u>J.T. McGee</u>

Thrall

Praise for Jamie Norton

"An often-compelling story about trauma recovery and personal empowerment... Get it!"

-Kirkus Reviews

"You will pull your hair out and no matter how much these characters drive you mad, you will NOT put the book down... It was beautifully done. I loved this book."

-Jade Nimoa, author of "Fate's Tether"

"Incredibly witty, well written and the perfect amount of humor. I honestly couldn't stop reading..."

-Goodreads Review

"Recommended to: People who wonder what would have happened, People who love theater, People who love the Red Sox, and anyone who enjoys reading a compelling tale that feels real and fully fleshed out."

-Goodreads Review

"A relatable tale of the lasting impact childhood trauma can have on a person's life."

-Goodreads Review

Valenza Publishing
Hadley, NY 12835

"The Second Act Comeback" first published in 2024

Edited by Dr. Stephen Hull

ISBN: 979-8-9891368-9-6 (paperback)
ISBN: 979-8-9904945-0-3 (ebook)

For Mom and Justin, both of whom have always believed
in me way more than I believed in myself. And for Lisa,
who gave me the courage and encouragement to try.

I think it's a mistake to ever look for hope outside of one's self.

--Arthur Miller
After the Fall (1964)

CURTAIN UP

A herpes scare wasn't even the worst part of my day.

To my left, a turtle-shaped lady with wrinkly cheeks and short, stringy hair knitted a baby sweater out of pink yarn. By the window, a slouching twenty-year-old fuckboy with a backwards Celtics hat and faded neck tattoo played *Fortnite* with his phone at full volume. Next to the receptionist's desk, a fourteen-year old blond girl with doe eyes and a baby bump thumbed through a pamphlet about contraceptives. Toward the back of the room near the exit sat Beth and me—a late-twenties couple comprised of a tallish-but-burly strawberry blonde dude with an unkempt beard and a tight-fitting *Phantom of the Opera* T-shirt and a fantastically fit, freckle-faced redhead wearing black Adidas jogging pants and neon green Asics. Our paths, as disparate as they were, had all led us to the same little cornflower blue waiting room on a busy Tuesday morning to sit in awkward, judgmental silence, exchange side-eyed glances, and wonder, *I wonder what these people are here for.*

While Beth filled out her paperwork, I pulled out my phone, closed the "Hey You" text from Kay, and Googled "genital herpes." The images that flooded my feed twisted my stomach into a painful knot. Nasty shit like bulbous discs on bright red labia and half-erect penises oozing pus. I almost gagged, but at the same time, I was (slightly) relieved, because the "little white spots" Beth had noticed in the shower an hour earlier didn't sound nearly as bad as the disgusting clusters of blisters on my screen.

"Bethany Patrick?"

My heart paused. Beth and I looked at each other, stood up, and walked toward a salty-haired nurse with heavy eyelids and ruby red lipstick.

"Please," Beth said, "just call me Beth."

"Fine," the nurse said. "This way."

Solemnly, we approached the heavy steel door that led toward the little room with the exam table and the crinkly sanitary paper and the tongue depressors and the unflattering fluorescent light—the room that would seal our fate. I hadn't been too nervous before, but the moment we heard Beth's name, I began biting down on the callus inside my cheek, and my mind began to race: *What if it IS herpes—what do we do then? Can you catch herpes if you use condoms? Should I get tested, too? How will I keep her calm when I'm here freaking out?*

But just as we got to the door, Beth put her hand on my forearm and said, "Actually, Mick, I'm just going to go in myself right now, okay?"

"Oh. O.....K."

We'd gone to appointments together before, like when we'd had pregnancy scares, or when we wanted to collaborate on another medication that would surely curb my depression "this time." So, when she sprung this on me, I was curious. Nevertheless, if this was how she wanted me to support her—by giving her privacy— that's what I'd do. So I went back to my seat, and Beth went away.

Moments to myself were seeping cracks for my mental health. Anytime I daydreamed about what my life would've been like if I'd had the guts to go to the right college, take the big job, or chase The Goose, those cracks would widen just enough to drain me of whatever faux happiness I'd managed to find in the trivial: My sugar-saturated caramel latte. A lazy single in my slow-pitch softball game. A *Zits* comic strip that made me snicker for a second. Those were all welcome distractions from the self-loathing I'd otherwise mired myself in. Had I chosen this path? Sure. Did I regret it? You bet your ass I did. Could I alter course? I guess. But was it worth disrupting everything with a colossal decision that would inevitably bring the Red-Faced Banshee out of its slumber to vanquish my soul anew?

Ehh. Packing up all my shit would be a lot of work.

I sat in my cold wooden chair, my right heel bouncing up and down as it does when it's bursting with nervous energy, while the population in the waiting room continued to thin out. One by one, they all went out back. Neck Tattoo Fuckboy. Doe-Eyed Teen Slut. Wrinkly Turtle Lady. Before long, I was all alone with my destructive thoughts, "Genital Herpes" in my search history, and an "HPV is Not Your Friend" poster gawking at me from the opposite wall. *How long does this shit take?* I thought.

I pulled out my phone to text Kay back when the door opened. It was the salty-haired nurse with heavy eyelids and ruby red lipstick. But Beth wasn't with her.

"Mister Patrick, come back here with me, please."

I stood up, put my phone in the back pocket of my jeans, and followed her through the heavy steel door, down twisty hallways, and into the exam room with the unflattering fluorescent light. Beth was on the exam table wearing a hospital gown and in full-on blubbers. Her face was a radish, her eyes were clamped shut, and her mouth was cracked open and bellowing loud, desperate sobs, unable to form a coherent word.

Shit. Maybe it is herpes. Or something worse.

"What's going on?" A ball of emptiness spun in my gut.

"You wanna tell him?" The nurse had a flatness and disconnect in her voice she'd clearly developed from years of like encounters with hysterical young women and distressed young men on her crinkly-papered table; this was just another boring day at the office for her. "Or do you want me to tell him?"

Still unable to speak, Beth just shook her head. The nurse hesitated long enough for me to say, "Can *someone* just tell me?"

"Mister Patrick, your wife is pregnant," the nurse said impatiently, failing—or, perhaps, not caring—to recognize the magnitude of the statement she'd blurted out with such indifference.

"For real?" I said, incredulous. I glanced at my wife's scrunched-up face. Beth nodded and wiped a thin film from under her nose, then she looked away and fixed her narrow, bloodshot eyes on a "Hang in There" poster of a tiny gray kitten dangling from a clothesline. I fixed my own eyes on that freckle in the middle of her forehead I used to think was so cute.

"For real," Nurse Salty Hair said.

My frazzled brain searched frantically for the right response while my eyes popped out of my face and my jaw hung helplessly on its hinges. All I could force my mouth to say was, "How far along?"

"About six weeks," the nurse said.

"And the…spots?"

"Bartholin's cysts. They're harmless." She slipped her pen behind her ear. "I'll give you two a minute to talk."

She left abruptly, leaving a void in the room Beth and I could only fill with awkward tension.

"Hey," I said to her forehead freckle after what felt like an hour of silence (it was probably only about two minutes). She continued peering at the little gray kitten.

I leaned against the exam table and took her hand. She was still trembling from the unexpected news, and I hoped my "big ol' bear paws," as she used to call them, would calm her a little.

"I know this isn't exactly what we wanted," I said, "but this might actually be a good thing."

My brother always gave me crap for trying to sugar-coat everything. But Beth knew I'd been depressed and desperate for a sense of purpose for longer than either of us could remember. She knew our relationship had begun to crumble, pebble by pebble, as a result. So, I couldn't help but consider that a child in our lives, as twisted as the thought may seem to an emotionally stable person, might give me what I'd been missing for so long. And it might provide us that connection to each other that had long been lost.

Instead, Beth shot me a look of irritated confusion. Or confused irritation or something. She never wanted kids, and she knew I knew that. So, the dream that she would carry this child to term was as fantastical as those I'd had years ago when I used to dream big.

Predictably, she blurted, "I'm not keeping it, man."

"What?" I wasn't surprised, but I still wanted to hear her reasoning out loud.

"I'm not going to let it, like, wreck my body! I'm not going to let it ruin my life! I'm not going to be one of those moms who just live for their kids! I don't want this, man!"

I took a deep breath, chewed the inside of my cheek the way I do when I want to say something but can't, and nodded. The little gray kitten was looking at me now.

"Well," I said with a tight-faced shrug. "At least you don't have herpes. That's good news."

The bad news?

We hadn't had sex in six months.

ACT I

1

The drive home felt like it took about forty-seven years; it was probably only about ten minutes. Muted rays of sunlight were trapped behind somber gray clouds that spread into eternity, and the chill of the day's early air held steadfast at something just above freezing. Words between Beth and me were few, eye-contact non-existent; we flaccidly held hands while she stared out the passenger-side window and I guided our clunky black Jetta through the aggressive morning traffic in a listless fog. Cars and trucks of every shape and size scuttled along in each direction as glaze-eyed drivers juked through gobs of traffic, typical of any weekday morning here in our coastal New Hampshire hometown of Rockingham, but this morning had been anything but typical for us. Beth had been so desperate to get to the clinic and so bullheaded about how she intended to proceed once we got the news, that I'd never had time to digest the gravity of the words that blubbered out of her mouth when she'd first gotten out of the shower.

"Mickey—I'm sorry! I had sex with Brad and the condom broke and now I have these little white spots on my junk and they don't feel right. I gotta go to the doctor!"

Still rubbing the grogginess out of my crusty eye sockets, I thought to myself, *Did she just say she had sex with that Brad guy?*

It hadn't bothered me much when she started hanging out with Brad again. If she hung out with him more often, I figured, she'd have someone to party with so she wouldn't drag me to those noisy, crowded bars where she loved to hang out. I hated the smell of beer, hated the way the smoke stung my eyes, and hated drunk, sloshy people. Simply put, the bar scene was not my scene.

But it was Brad's scene.

Beth and her sister went to Funky Knuckler, a sports bar downtown, the night before Thanksgiving, and I didn't go. I had to get up wicked early to work my minimum-wage job at Charlie Mart, because working in retail means twelve-hour battles with these abominable beasts known as "Black Friday shoppers," and for some reason, Black Friday now included most of Thanksgiving Day, too. If I missed the biggest shopping day of the year, I'd be initialing my own pink slip, which I couldn't afford to do. Without this job, I wouldn't be able to make late payments on my student loans again or buy microwavable chicken nuggets to mush down for dinner.

Besides, if I went to Funky Knuckler, I'd have to talk to people. It had been years since I enjoyed talking to people. So, Beth put on her favorite Seven Jeans and that black Calvin Klein sports bra that always got me hot, straightened her scarlet locks, contoured her eyes, and forged ahead without me; I remained firmly planted in my comfort zone—sunken into our oversized, cushy couch wearing my favorite oversized, cushy blue sweatpants and dominating the World Series with my greasy PlayStation controller.

She sent me a few texts early in the night when she was bored. But honestly, they just annoyed me. I didn't need to put this thriller between the Cubs and the Red Sox on pause to hear about some drama. Luckily for me, as the night wore on and she became more inebriated, I heard from her less and less frequently.

9:32 p.m. No one here. This is lame.

9:57 p.m. OMG we saw Brie's ex. He got fat. Loser!

11:13 p.m. Yaaaaaay Meg's here! She has some guy with her. I think it's her ex. Weird.

11:15 p.m. O wait, it's Brad! He has a beard now. Din't recognize him.

12:36 a.m. No need 2 pik me up, Meg nd Brad said theyd brng me home

1:40 a.m. Woo hoo! gtettng drnk!

I woke up to Beth crawling into bed a little after 4 a.m. Her eyes were glassy, the contour had mostly rubbed off, her hair had relaxed to its natural wispiness, and the smell of rum seeped from her pores.

"Hey," I grumbled. I leaned over and pecked her on that freckle in the middle of her forehead. "Did you have a good time?"

"Had a great time, yeah," she said, still beaming from her night of mass consumption. She didn't get to party much anymore, so I was glad she was in a good mood. She was much easier to deal with when she was in a good mood. "But I'm beat, man."

She turned away from me and closed her eyes. My own were still quite heavy, but I scooted over toward her, nestled my thighs up against her backside, and draped my arm around her. "Didn't the bar close at two?"

"Yeah, but we were hungry, so we just went to Goldy's."

Ah, yes. There were two places in Rockingham where hungry boozers could line their stomachs after last call. They could go to Kwickfiks if they wanted to scarf down something quick and salty for the drunken drive home, or they could go to Goldy's Diner if they wanted to sit in a greasy booth and try to line up a fork with their mouth holes. Beth loved to snarf when she was hammered, so I'd experienced both on separate nightcaps when all I wanted to do was get home and go to bed.

"Oh, okay," I said as I drifted back into my world of fantasy. "Love you."

"Love you," she told me.

****

The six weeks since Thanksgiving had been a blizzard of busy-ness. I'd been murdering my knees for fifty hours a week trying to satisfy the relentless queues of "happy" holiday shoppers. Beth had been dividing her time between waitressing at the Shrimp Bucket, coaching basketball at St. Mary's, and teaching CrossFit classes at Body Flex. In between, we were force-feeding ourselves all the obligatory holiday traditions—buying gifts for people who didn't need them, watching painfully sentimental movies about how perfect the world is that time of year, pretending to be impressed by the elaborate light displays in our neighbors' yards—all that sappy crap.

Meanwhile, as the lights, love, and lunacy of the season kept me distracted and exhausted, that Brad guy was entrenching himself in our lives, little by little. First, he was hanging out with Beth at the bar. Then, he was bringing over heaping plates of holiday cookies. Next thing I knew, he was fixing our frozen pipes and not charging us for it. I never thought weeds could grow during the winter.

I didn't say anything about it. Because of course I didn't. Sure, it seemed like something about it was a bit off, but questioning Beth would make it a whole thing, and after standing on concrete and faking Christmas cheer for weeks on end, I didn't have it in me to start a whole thing. Besides, Brad was just in town for the holidays visiting his sister Meg (Beth's bestie) and their parents, so he'd go back to California soon to run his little sporting goods shop and be out of our lives forever. He was a nice guy (but nothing to look at with that sloppy mop, big honker, and beady eyes), and that thing between Beth and him back in the day was ancient history. She was just happy to have a drinking buddy, something I didn't want to be.

Now, after finding out he was more than a drinking buddy, I still didn't want to start a whole thing. So, I kept quiet about it on the way to the clinic, at the clinic, and on the way home from the clinic. Sure, I wanted to know more—*When did she fuck him? Where did they do it? Did Meg know about this? If she did, why didn't she tell me? Does that Brad guy have feelings for Beth, or does he just want to fuck her again? Have they been fucking the whole time he's been here?*—but I didn't ask those questions. I didn't say a thing until we got home from the clinic and could go to separate rooms if we had to. All I asked was, "Are you going to tell—"

"No way, man," she snipped before I could finish. She'd anticipated that question and had a response loaded, cocked, and ready to fire off. "He doesn't need to know. I just want to get this thing out of me and get back to my life."

My life, she called it.

It didn't even phase me that she called the unborn child a "thing," because I knew a baby was not a person to her—it was a burden. When Beth and I had gotten married three years prior, we agreed we'd have kids "someday," but we never agreed on what "someday" meant. Then, as the newlywed glow dimmed and we began getting crushed by some of the thirty-ton boulders life drops on you— marital problems, miserable jobs, mountains of debt, and more—a future with children got much foggier.

In fact, as Beth grew wearier and more cynical, she began to think of children as just another cruel, demanding burden in an already cruel, demanding world.

"Kids suck the life out of you," she said when her over-zealous former party pal became an overtired stay-at-home mom.

"Kids destroy your body," she said after her former size-four gym partner gained forty pounds of baby weight.

"Kids ruin everything," she said after her sister's toddler cried through the entirety of *Toy Story 3* so Beth couldn't enjoy it.

I, on the other hand, still clung to "someday." I knew I'd be a great dad; I used to be animated, silly, and charming, and I could tap into that again if given the chance. And while my own dad was never around, my mom took it upon herself to instill kindness and empathy in my brother and me, and I wanted to share those traits with my own lit-tle people. That way I would know there would be at least one or two kind, empathetic people out there who could sprinkle a little bit of happiness, humor, and warmth on this cruel, demanding world.

But when we found out Beth was pregnant, it didn't feel the way it should have. I wasn't excited. I wasn't nervous. I wasn't engorged with some kind of parental instinct to protect and provide. I didn't feel closer to my wife than ever before. More than anything, I was stunned. Frazzled. Numb. So, when Beth said, "Just get rid of it," and Nurse Salty Hair looked at me for confirmation, all I could do was shrug limply and say to Beth, "It's your body."

My life, she'd just said. Not *our* life. Not *our* marriage. Not even *our* decision.

I couldn't get past the way she'd scorched me so casually, fully disregarding how I thought this "thing" could affect our lives together, regardless of whether or not she wanted to keep it, nor whether she wanted that Brad guy involved. Did she not see the irreparable damage this situation could cause? Or worse, was she aware of it and just didn't care?

But just as the word "life" slipped off Beth's tongue, her shoulders sunk, her face soured, and tears and snot burst from her orifices. The tension that had steadily thickened throughout this strange and horrible morning exploded from every fiber of muscle in her body, and she began sobbing with the innocence of a three-year-old who'd been bowled over in the sandbox.

"I'm sorry, Mickey! I didn't mean to hurt you!"

I guess she *did* care.

As she leaned toward me, my throat filled with mucous and my eyes began to water. With those words, she yanked my heart back to simpler, more innocent times, like when she covered her face with a pillow after she told me she loved me for the first time, or when we shared our perfectly imperfect first kiss. We'd been together since we were teenagers, basically grown up together, and discovered as a young couple how this insane world could be both magically uplifting and heartlessly cruel at the same time. And all I ever wanted to do in those tender moments was protect her and make her smile. Now—again—on this strange and horrible morning, as I had a million times before, all I could do was pull her head onto my shoulder and wrap her in my arms. It didn't matter that I was crushed by what I'd just learned. It didn't matter that I was questioning our marriage, how we got here, and what was going to happen next. My pain didn't matter—it never had. My job was to make Beth feel better.

That's why, when she bawled, "I'll understand if you want a divorce," all I could do was pull her toward me and say, "No, stop. We'll get through this. I love you."

We would get through this because we always had. And we always had because I didn't have the balls to battle it out. She could do or say whatever she wanted to me and get away with it. She'd learned to take advantage of my debilitating fear of confrontation way back in Year One. In those early days when I used to stand up to her, or at least tell her when something was on my mind, she discovered that all she had to do was yell and cry a little and I'd let her win. So that became standard practice—I bailed on scholarships, job offers, even friends and family—all because I was frozen in fear of the Red-Faced Banshee. After a while, I stopped aspiring to anything that didn't fit into Beth's narcissistic little world, because it wasn't worth a fight I couldn't win anyway.

But now, after years of submission, this should've been the biggest blowout of our lives. It was a no-brainer: She'd cheated on me, lied to me, and gotten pregnant with another dude's baby. If there were ever a time to leave her and this dehumanizing dumpster of a marriage—and be totally justified—this should've been it. After all the times I had taken a dive and let her win, this would be an easy and defining victory for me. This relationship was destined to end ugly eventually anyway, so why not now? Just pull the trigger. Rip off the Band-Aid. Power through. She'd even given me an out.

I still couldn't do it.

The reasons this time were wicked different from the other times. It's not like I was afraid to see her cry. She was already crying. There wasn't someone else this time—hadn't been in about four thousand years. And it wasn't like I had a great thing going in my career now, either. In fact, those were both long-evaporated memories at this point. Dead dreams. This time, I couldn't break up with her for one simple reason.

I didn't know who the hell I was anymore.

I wasn't "Mack-Pack" the baseball star. I wasn't "Big Ol' Bear Paws," the cutesy romantic, or "Mickey-Mack," charismatic rising theater star. These days, my identity—or what was left of it—had been eroded to "Beth's Husband." I wasn't a real person, just an extension of Beth. A sidekick. Arm candy. Beth's Husband craved the familiar—the cushy old couch and his cushy blue sweatpants. Beth's Husband would rather live in his own little fantasy PlayStation baseball world, because that was the only thing that made him feel like a winner these days. Beth's Husband had no conviction, no passion, no self-respect. He was fine with his wife doing whatever (or whomever) the hell she wanted, because it was easier than fighting the fight.

Beth's Husband was a doormat.

MASON PATRICK, Age 12

October 4, 1997

Dear Daddy,

I miss playing He-Man with my little brother.

We used to play it like every day when we were little. Soon as we woke up, whoever got dressed and found the magic sword first got to raise it up in the air and say, "I have the power," and be He-Man. The other one had to be Skeletor, the ugly skeleton-faced bad guy who always tried to beat He-Man and take over the world. But He-Man always won. He was the most powerful man in the universe—nobody could beat him—and he wasn't afraid of anything. So, even though it was just a skinny little tree branch, whoever had the He-Man sword felt strong. Powerful. Maybe even invincible.

Then Raymond ruined everything.

Mickey got in trouble at school one day a couple years ago because he showed his butt to Torey Rizzo. Torey and some other kids had been picking on him a lot that year. One time they pushed him down in the mud and threw one of his shoes on top of the baseball dugout. Another time they splattered paint on him and ruined his favorite Power Rangers shirt. Mickey never got to learn some of the stuff I did. Like man stuff. Like how to shoot a BB gun, or how to play hockey, or how to fish. Or how to stick up for yourself. Kids never pick on me very much, and if they do, I just yell in their face and then knock them down. Mickey always runs away and hides when kids tease him.

I really was just trying to help my little brother. When

Torey Rizzo started making fun of him, I told Mickey he had to act tough and not run away. He isn't scared of me, and Torey Rizzo isn't that much bigger than me, so he shouldn't be afraid of him. I told Mickey to push Torey back next time he picked on him. But he didn't push him. He threw a bunch of rocks at him and called him "Banana Brains" and he mooned him. I didn't tell my brother to do all that, but I still feel like it was my fault Raymond got so mad at him.

When we got home from school that day, Mama sat Mickey down on the couch and said it was not okay to throw rocks at people or show them his butt at school. He was crying, but Mama asked him if he understood. He said yes, and then she made him promise not to do it again, and then she gave him a hug and sent him to his room. She always says it's okay to mess up, as long as we learn our lesson and promise not to do it again.

Raymond got wicked mad when Mama told him what Mickey did. Mama said it was okay, because she talked to Mickey and he said he wouldn't do it again. But then Raymond stood up and said, "You're damn right he isn't going to do it again" (sorry about the swear word). Mama tried to stop him, but he pushed her into the bookcase and then slammed Mickey's bedroom door wicked hard in front of her, which made one of our happy family photos fall off the wall and break. Then he yelled, "Show me what you did on the playground!"

I bet the whole neighborhood can hear it when Raymond starts yelling. Like sometimes I see cars slow down a little in front of our house when he's being really loud. And my brother was only seven back then, so it was probably wicked scary for him when Raymond was in his bed-

room yelling at him like that.

"Show me," he kept yelling. "Show me."

The Ninja Turtles were on TV and they were making jokes and eating pizza, but I turned down the volume because what was happening at my house wasn't funny at all. I could hear Mickey begging and crying through the wall, just like he was in the same room. Raymond kept telling Mickey to show him what he did on the playground, but Mickey kept squealing "I don't wanna" and "I'm sorry" and "please don't."

The pasta Mama was cooking on the stove was burning and smelled like charcoal. She got up off the floor and went into the kitchen to shut off the stove, then into her and Raymond's room and closed the door. She never yelled at us like that, and she never, ever spanked my brother as hard as Raymond did. Sometimes he would spank him with his belt or a newspaper rolled up really tight. One time Mickey had to sit on pillows for two days after Raymond spanked him with a yardstick.

Raymond finally said, "Fine I'll do it for you," and Mickey started yelling for Mama and crying louder than I ever heard him cry before. But then I heard something smacking his butt like a million times, and he started crying even louder. I curled up on the couch like a little kid and put two pillows over my head. My heart was beating wicked fast because I felt like I was in a monster movie.

Soon, Raymond came out of my brother's bedroom and threw something in the trash, and then he went into the main bedroom to talk to Mama. I heard her crying too, but there were no smacking noises this time. I was shaking, but I got up to put the trash out because it was my turn and I didn't want to get spanked like my brother just did. When I lifted the lid to the kitchen trash can, I saw what Raymond had hit my brother with so hard, so many times. It was our He-Man sword, and it was broken in two pieces. Then I started crying, too. I went into Mickey's room and gave my brother a hug.

I stayed in Mickey's bed with him, and we sobbed together for like an hour until he fell asleep. But I could not sleep for the rest of the night. I am not afraid of the dark, but ever since then, I've been having bad dreams, like there's an evil ghost or a demon or a spirit that lives right inside my own house. But nothing is scarier than Raymond when he gets angry (he looks like a hungry mountain lion or something). So I always do my homework right after school, and I always clean my room and do my chores without being asked, and I always eat what we're having for dinner, even if I don't like it. I never want Raymond to break a tree branch on my butt, so I always make sure I stay out of trouble. And I do my best to also make sure my brother always does the right thing so he doesn't get spanked like that again, either.

It's been two whole years now, but Mickey has never been the same. He never jokes around like he used to, and he never even talks when Raymond is home unless him or Mama ask him questions. When kids pick on him now, he hides in the baseball dugout and cries until me or a teacher chase them away. After school, he goes right into his room and works on his homework, and then he stays in there the rest of the night, except for dinner. And we never play He-Man anymore. After Raymond broke our "sword" on Mickey's butt, Mickey never wanted to be He-Man again. Now I'm scared that my little brother won't ever come back.

Just like you.

Forever yours,
Mason

2

There was no flaccid hand holding on the way home from the clinic this time. There were no blubbery tears, not even any sniffles, just a cold stare out the passenger window as I guided "The Jet" through dirty ice and slush.

The whole thing was so fast and blurry, like an old MTV video. I wasn't sure who was who or what was happening as I stood next to Beth with my hand on her shoulder. I just knew that there were numerous people looking between my wife's legs, the grating sound of a vacuum cleaner, and a lady with sandy blond hair saying, matter-of-factly, "You're all set." And then we were alone.

We stayed there until Beth said she felt okay to leave, then they gave her some painkillers and told her to take it easy for the rest of the day. When we got home, she grabbed a granola bar and crawled into bed, and I grabbed my green vest to head off to Charlie Mart.

"What time will you be home?" she asked as she turned on the TV, only half-listening for my answer.

"Probably 10 since I'm going in so late. I had to switch

shifts so I could go to this."

"Okay, well, I don't know if I'll be back by then. Game's way up in Colebrook."

"You're still going? They told you to take it easy."

"I'm the head coach, Mick—I can't just, like, skip out because I feel a little crampy."

"Okay, well, see you whenever you get home, I guess."

"Thanks for coming to my appointment with me."

"Yeah."

I didn't want her to feel like I'd done her some big favor; I went with her out of obligation, because that's what good husbands do. They stick around. They support their wives. They drive to the clinic. I didn't go because I was on board with her decision, nor the circumstances surrounding it. I went because if I hadn't, it would've been a whole thing. And I didn't have the energy for another whole thing.

I put on my grungy old Spyder jacket and my tattered-but-tough Columbia boots to trudge back out into the icy air. I'd been wearing the same Spyder jacket and Columbia boots since college, and even though the jacket was a little too tight now and the boots scuffed up the backs of my heels, they still worked well enough, and they reminded me of times that were bigger, better, and brighter. Besides, I couldn't afford to replace them on a Charlie Mart sala-ry—even a full-time one. Maybe if I got the promotion they'd been dangling in front of me—Front End Lead—I could get over the $26,000-per-year hump and at least go on eBay to look for a newish North Face jacket and some gently-used Timberlands. But that wasn't going to happen if I missed another shift due to Beth's not-so-secret sexual misadventures.

By now, we were far from the only people who knew

about her little fling with Brad. Beth told her sister Brie, who in turn told Meg, who in turn talked to Brad himself. Brad, who was back in San Bernadino now, tried to deny it at first, saying he was "fixed," but once Beth told him she and I hadn't done it since her birthday in June, he was suddenly on the phone with her every day trying to "help." He even texted me once to say how sorry he was and ask if he could do anything, and instead of blasting him and telling him what a piece of shit he was and to never talk to me or my wife again, I just responded with, "No, thank you." That's right, I practiced proper politeness with my wife's manstress.

And I told people, too. Beth had told me not to because she was embarrassed, so I only did so with the verbal disclaimer that they were not allowed to tell anyone (does that ever work?). So, I told Mason, who I'm sure told Mom, and I told Torey, who I'm sure told Luci. And I told Kay during one of our late-night text conversations, and who knows who she told?

Mason and Torey said I should leave her. Kay said I deserved better. I didn't hear from Luci, but I knew the others were right. I could do better—well, could have done better (the old, fun me could have). It was far too late now. I had nothing of substance to offer anyone new. But even though I knew I wasn't going to actually do anything about it, it was nice to know I had people in my corner. That had grown less apparent in the years since I'd devolved gracelessly into the lifeless droid I was now.

Of course, Beth had people in her corner, too. Brie was much less civil with me these days, calling me Beth's "fat loser husband" behind my back and "Big Mack" to my face. She seemed to take some kind of sadistic joy in pointing out that I'd gained sixty pounds since they met me and that I was a retail cashier making minimum wage now, but she always left out the part where I gave up my "real job," as she put it, so I could live in this shithole town with her asshole sister. Beth told me Brie was thrilled about her "gettin' some strange" from a guy Brie had said (in front of me, many times) was super cute. Meg, Beth said, was a little more tactful but nonetheless supportive of how Beth dealt with our dead bedroom. Apparently, Meg's position was, *if your husband isn't having sex with you, instead of talking to him about it, you should just go screw someone else. Like my single brother in California who you made out with in college that one time.*

It didn't matter anymore, anyway. Beth had gotten away with it, and I had let her get away with it. All I said to her when this all came to light a few weeks ago was, "Please just don't do this again," to which she responded with an assuring nod. But even as that crossed my lips I knew deep down in my bowels that, even if it did happen again, I probably still wouldn't do anything about it. Because leaving would be too hard, and I had no place to go. A fight would take energy and conviction, and I had none left of either. It was easier to slog through each dreary day, wait until she went to bed, and slip into my colorful fantasy world of PlayStation baseball stardom and texting with girls who used to like me (well, *a* girl who used to like me).

It reminded me of when I used to like myself.

3

Alright, Mickey the Mouse, let's see what ya got."

There he was—Torey Rizzo—the kid who'd gotten my ass beaten with a tree branch. He squished his cleats into the muddy batters' box on this brisk late-March afternoon, waving his bat at me with that cocky, crooked grin of his. I stood on the mound, looking past him to the circle on the backstop I was supposed to hit, gripping the dingy old baseball with grit. This was just some light preseason batting practice to an onlooker, but for me and this d-bag, it was personal.

"Please stop calling me that," I said.

"What? Mickey the Mouse?" He laughed. "Nah, it's fun. C'mon—pitch."

I hadn't pitched since Little League, ever since Raymond got pissed about me not eating my cauliflower or something and yanked my ten-year-old arm so hard he tore a bunch of ligaments in my shoulder. But during warm-ups, it felt pretty damn good. In fact, I stung my partner's hand so bad, Coach Gutierrez wanted me to try pitching some batting practice.

Coach didn't want me throwing at full speed, but even at reduced effort, it took me five or six pitches to find the strike zone. I finally gave the first batter enough passable pitches to get him through a serviceable early-season round. With the second batter, as I got more comfortable, I found I was able to put the ball where I wanted it, and he got in some pretty good rips.

The third batter was Torey Rizzo.

I'd become somewhat of a silent recluse since Ray Slater, my stepdad, had come into my life and shown his true colors. It was only about six months after we moved in with him that I stood up to Torey—the same kid who was grinning and waving his bat at me now. I didn't know how to make the kid leave me alone back then—I was only seven—so, after a pep talk from my brother, I threw some rocks at him, called him "Banana Brains," and mooned him. That night, when Ray heard about it, he hit my bare ass so hard with a tree branch—the same tree branch Mason and I had used to pretend we had superhuman He-Man strength—that it snapped, and so did my spirits.

I tossed an easy one down the middle. Rizzo ripped it down the third base line.

"There ya go. Nice," he said.

So, I became a model student, never getting lower than an A-minus, and teachers would rarely hear a peep from me. I sat front-and-center in every class, took notes until my fingers cramped, and spent all my free time studying, because staying in my bedroom and memorizing world capitals or mastering the Pythagorean Theorem kept me safe. If I got good grades, did all my chores, and kept quiet, Raymond would have no reason to snap another tree branch across my ass.

I gave him another softy. Fly ball to center.

"Yes," Rizzo grunted.

Ray grew up in the 50s with parents who subscribed to the antiquated belief that "Children should be seen and not heard," and anytime he broke that code, he was beaten by anything his father could swing—leather belts, ping pong paddles, canes. Ray made sure Mason and I knew he endorsed the same, so I grew accustomed to not saying much at home. I carried that with me to school, and I became "Mickey the Mouse" because I was quiet and meek, and I always ran away and hid. I spoke only to teachers during classes. During lunch, I holed myself up in a closet or an empty classroom. After school, I spent every day in my bedroom doing homework and entertaining myself, sometimes by acting out scripts from old plays Mom had tucked away in her scrapbook, sometimes by reading my father's old sports almanacs and memorizing stats and scores from decades before I was born. I didn't have any friends except some kid named Tucker, and the only thing he liked to do was steal his uncle's Penthouses and draw caricatures of our female teachers with cartoonishly large boobs. While that became more interesting to me when puberty encroached on my innocence, at fourteen I decided I wanted more out of life than memorization and masturbation.

I threw the next one a little harder. Missed up and away. Rizzo snickered.

I knew what I might face when I showed up to baseball try-outs. The world of athletics, while fun and family-friendly during my abbreviated Little League tenure, was at the high school level inhabited by the very people who used to push me down on the playground. I could avoid them when I was home in my room learning about Millard Fillmore and the 1850 Compromise or comparing the '89 Oakland A's to the '27 Yankees. But joining this world would inevitably bring me face to face with some of the dickheads who pushed me around—including Torey Rizzo.

I gave him another meatball. He smoked it to the left-center gap.

"Alright, Mouse-Man can pitch!"

I inhaled sharply, paused, and said, "Please stop."

"Oh, don't be such a girl, you're fine." He snickered again.

I stood, stoic, and began chewing the inside of my cheek. There he was. The asshole who'd gotten my ass blistered, had never seen the ramifications of that confrontation, had never really stopped harassing me, and had never paid the price. Now he was staring at me from just sixty feet, six inches away, calling me that stupid name, and I had a different kind of rock in my hand.

I inhaled slowly, set my feet, and wound up. His face froze as he watched a full-speed fastball zip across the plate for a perfect strike.

"Oh, is that what we're doing?" he said. He stood up straight and puffed his chest out. "Let's see that shit again, when I'm actually ready for it."

I just nodded as he squared back into his batting stance. I wound up and fired one right over the heart of the plate; he took a huge hack, grunted, and missed.

"Again," he demanded.

Wind up. Fastball down the middle. Big swing. Not even close.

He yelled "FUCK!" and slammed his bat on the plate.

"Enough," Coach Gutierrez said from the dugout. "Slow it down, Mick. Batting practice. Don't throw your arm out. Let him hit."

"One more!" Rizzo said. "I can hit this weak-ass shit."

"Fine," Coach said. He held up his index finger and said, "One more."

Rizzo dug in, looked at me, and said, "Let's go, Mickey the Mouse. Pitch."

I looked at the sky and shook my head. I'd asked nicely. Twice. Even said please—both times. But this fucking douchebag needed a wake-up call. So, I spun into my wind-up, kicked my knee up extra high, and rifled one squarely between his shoulder blades.

Before I knew it, Torey Rizzo was charging toward me with blind fury, the coaches were yelling at us to stop, and our teammates were closing in on us from every direction.

"Little bitch, I'll fucking wreck you," Rizzo said as he entered my bubble and lunged toward me. I spun away to dodge him, then grabbed the back of his shirt and, using his forward momentum, forced him face-first to the squishy, wet grass. Then I got on his back, pushed down with my forearms and pinned his legs with mine until he stopped struggling.

"Get off me," he grunted.

I dipped my face toward his ear and whispered, only loudly enough for him to hear me, "It's not my dad's fault your dad's dead."

The moment I said that the rage in his eyes loosened, and his face whitened. He looked back at me with an initial confusion that quickly melted into calm, quiet solidarity. I said nothing else, just kept him subdued for another several seconds before he half-whispered, "We're cool. You can let me up."

I got off him, stood back up, and offered my hand. He gripped my forearm, I gripped his, and I pulled him back to his feet. Then, with red eyes and pursed lips, he came in for a hug and said, "Sorry."

"All good," I said as we exchanged back slaps. "Just—please no more Mickey the Mouse."

"Got it," he said with a nod. And for the first time in my life, I saw kindness on Torey Rizzo's face.

***

I made the starting rotation by the fifth game of the season. By the tenth, I was the team's second-best pitcher. And after my two-hit shutout in the state championship game, the same kids who once pushed me down on the playground now lifted me up on their shoulders. I was no longer "Mickey the Mouse." I was "Mack-Pack." And "Mack-Pack" was a winner.

Torey and I had come a long way since our skirmish. He was a phenomenal catcher with a sky-high 'Baseball IQ,' (I don't know, it's a term coach Gutierrez borrowed from *Baseball Tonight,* I think), and he helped me develop into a pretty damn good pitcher for a freshman. I could already throw hard, but he helped me learn how to control and locate my pitches, and he stayed after practice with Coach G and me three times a week so I could work on my curveball. And when I used that curveball to strike out the final batter to win the Division II title, we ended the season the same way we began it—in a sweaty, adrenaline-fueled embrace—but this time as friends instead of rivals.

I got home late the night we won the championship.

And by late, I mean 9 p.m. It was the first title our school had won in thirty years—so Coach G took us out to celebrate with pizza, soda, and ice cream (it wasn't like we were out snorting lines and throwing back shots until 3 a.m.). But I'd been so entranced by the euphoria of victory that I'd forgotten to call home and check in. Raymond wasn't at the game because he had some "big project" over in Manchester, and Mom was taking night classes at the Rocks to try to get her associates degree, so she couldn't make it either. And I didn't have a cell phone with which to text because texting wasn't a big thing in '03.

I was still floating on a cloud when I opened the front door, and I could hear the feint sound of *Cheers* reruns coming from the living room. As the door clicked closed behind me, whatever Sam and Diane were bickering about was muted, and the only sound I could hear was Raymond clearing his throat. He did that whenever he was about to say something he thought was important.

"Hi Dad," I said cautiously. We were calling him Dad to his face now, but behind his back, we called him "Ray-Hole."

"How are you?" That's what he always said after clearing his throat. It meant he didn't care how I was; he had something to say, but the formalities his parents had beaten into him were automatic—robotic even.

I was so excited I didn't care that he didn't really care.

"Good! We won! We won the whole thing!"

I plucked the "NHIAA Division II State Champs" medallion from around my neck and gestured it toward him. I couldn't wait to pin it in mom's scrapbook with the article from the *Daily Record* the next day.

"Congratulations," he said with artificial enthusiasm.

"Did you get your homework done?"

I hadn't. Because A.) We'd gone directly from school to Holman Stadium in Nashua to B.) play the biggest game of our lives and then C.) went to celebrate afterward. And besides, D.) it was Friday night. I wanted to explain all of this to him, but more than that, I wanted him to be happy for me and proud of me. But I didn't say any of that to him. All I could force myself to say was, "No, not yet."

"Go get that done, and then we can talk about the game."

Even for him, this struck me as odd. I was a good student, so he'd always given me the option to do my Friday homework during the weekend. So, I wasn't sure if he was joking.

"But it's Friday."

"And?" he said sharply. He wasn't joking.

I didn't know what to say. My frazzled brain searched frantically for the right response while my eyes popped out of my face and my jaw hung helplessly on its hinges.

"I'm glad you had a good time at your ballgame." He came closer. "What time is it?"

He knew what time it was. And he knew I knew what time it was.

"It's ni—"

"Nine 'o clock." He took another step toward me, lowered his chin, and peered at me through his wispy eyebrows. In an instant, his meaty pointer finger and craggy yellow teeth were inches from my nose. Then, like a hungry mountain lion preparing to devour its prey, he flattened me with a mighty roar.

"You're fourteen years old. You know you're supposed to call if you're going to be out past dinnertime. I shouldn't have to get a phone call from your coach telling me you're at Pizza Hut."

So, he wasn't upset that he didn't know where I had been. He knew the whole time. But Raymond wasn't the type to let someone off the hook. It was still my responsibility to check in, and I hadn't done my part.

"Now it's nine 'o clock and you're telling me your homework isn't done." He pointed toward the stairs. "Get your ass to your room and do it, and then we can talk about your punishment."

I thought we were going to talk about the game. I began chewing the inside of my cheek the way I do when I want to say something but can't. Then it occurred to me—he didn't care about my game. He just wanted to make sure I remembered he was still in charge. Maybe I was getting too big for him to push around, but he knew if he got in my face and used a loud, aggressive voice, he could still make my jaw snap shut and my head nod up and down at anything he said.

Because children should be seen and not heard.

4

January 2018

Beth got home around 11:30 that night. I heard the back door shut, so I quickly texted: *Gotta go, bye* to Kay and paused my *MLB: The Show* game between the Sox and the Yankees. Beth tossed her keys on the coffee table and plopped down into the old, dilapidated recliner on the opposite side of the room.

"'Sup?" she said.

"Hey, how are you feeling?" I asked. "How was the game?"

"I'm fine. Little crampy, but fine. We lost in overtime."

"That sucks." I didn't need to ask anything else about the game because I knew she would tell me. When they won, it was because her girls played great. When they lost, it was because the referees were trying to screw them.

"Goddamn refs kept calling the gayest fouls on us," she said on cue. I gave her a look that said, *'Gayest'? Really?'*

"Sorry. The dumbest fouls. And then 'Showtime' fouled out with thirty-two seconds left in regulation, so we had to play OT without her. Stupid refs."

"Showtime" was Lindsay Schodak, St. Mary's best play-

46

er, and she was the only player Beth didn't refer to by her full first and last name. Beth was always wicked defensive of her because she could remember what it was like to be "screwed by the refs" from when she herself was St. Mary's best player.

"Welp," I shrugged and then asked rhetorically, "Whaddya gonna do?" as in, *shit happens, life goes on.*

"I know you don't care," she said. "Just sucks."

I rolled my eyes and began chewing the inside of my cheek. I'd learned not to take the bait anymore.

"I'm glad you're home though." I blew her a kiss; she didn't blow one back. Also—as usual—she didn't ask how my day was. But I had nothing to say even if she did ask. Aside from terminating her illegitimate pregnancy first thing in the morning, it had been just another ho-hum day of scanning clothes and groceries, putting them in plastic bags, and telling people I didn't care about to have a nice day. Because that was my place in the universe now.

"Yeah," she said.

I unpaused my game and got ready to pitch to Aaron Judge. He was up with two men on in the seventh, and I was protecting a two-run lead. Mickey Patrick, the All-Star Red Sox hurler, threw a fastball down and on the outside corner for strike one.

Normally, when I turned my attention back to the PlayStation, Beth either pulled out her phone to skim through her Instagram feed or just headed to bed so I could finish my virtual ballgame in peace. But she hadn't moved yet. She was fidgeting with her fingers and looking around the room. She had something on her mind.

I paused the game again, looked at her, and asked, "Everything okay?"

She looked at me for a second, then down at her feet, then at the corner of the couch and said, "Yeah, man. All good."

I squinted, confused. She obviously had something to say, but I wasn't going to drag it out of her. I didn't play those games with her anymore. I turned back toward the television. Mickey Patrick, the Sox' undisputed ace, shook off another fastball from his catcher and tossed a looping curveball that caught too much of the plate. Judge blasted a long fly ball to left that went just foul.

"So, like…" she stopped. I inhaled through my nose and looked up at the ceiling.

After a moment, I looked at her and said, "So, like, what?"

She cracked her knuckles one at a time with her thumb and leaned back in the recliner. She pulled her feet up off the ground and sat cross-legged.

"So, I was thinking about something on the way home tonight." She seemed apprehensive, but I couldn't tell by her tone whether it was something I should be worried about or not. I paused the game and turned toward her.

"Okay?" I tried to stay as even as I could because I had no idea where this was going. Was she about to dump me? Did she cheat on me again? Did she decide she wanted kids after all, just not with That Brad Guy? Were we getting a puppy? I had no idea.

"So, I know I fucked up. Like, real bad," she said.

"Yeah?" I wasn't going to argue with that.

"And I feel like I owe you something."

"Beth, we talked about it, it's fine—like I said, I just don't want it to happen again."

"I know, man. I know. But I still feel really bad about it."

"Just forget it—it's over. We don't need to talk about it anymore."

"C'mon, Mick. Just listen."

I took a deep breath, crossed my arms, and said, "M'kay?" She sat a little more upright in the recliner. What exactly did she think she 'owed' me?

"So, I talked to Meg the other day, and she said—"

"Great, I can't wait to hear what Meg said," I scoffed. "She was basically rooting for you to hook up with Brad the whole time."

"Shut up, no she wasn't," Beth said (yes she was). "Anyway, she said that a lot of couples who get into these funks, like, try something new. To, you know, light the fire or whatever."

I raised my eyebrows. "Try something new? What do you mean? We've tried all the positions. You like cowgirl the best, so we do cowgirl."

"No, not that," she said with the tiniest little smirk.

"Well, you've always told me you did. Sorry, we can switch it up."

"I'm not talking about positions, Mickey!"

"Oh." I was more confused now. "Well, you said your butt was exit-only, so I mean, I've stayed out of there, but we can—"

"Ew, no. God no," she said. "No, what I mean is, Meg said a lot of couples try opening things up."

"Like the doors and windows? Like voyeurs? Beth, there are kids across the street."

She threw her head back and said, "Ughhh—No!"

I looked at the freckle in the middle of her forehead. I knew what she was getting at, but I was trying to keep her from saying it for as long as I could. Finally, I caved.

"Then what, Beth?"

She looked at me and said, "Opening up our marriage, man. Like, seeing other people. Staying together but, like, being able to mess around."

"You mean fuck other people and not get in trouble." I didn't say it as a question because, despite her intentions, she'd failed to adequately sugarcoat it. I wanted it stated without ambiguity.

She hesitated for a moment, looked at the floor, then back up at me, shrugged and said, "I mean... It was a thought."

I stared at her for a moment, then narrowed my eyes. "Are you for real? You want me to have sex with another girl."

"Yes. I mean… Yes." Her eyes shifted back and forth before settling apprehensively back on me. "I mean, I wouldn't want to know the details, but I'd give you a free pass because of how bad I fucked up."

"Beth, don't you think we should talk about *why* it happened instead of—"

"We *know* why it happened, Mick!"

"We do?" I was curious, because we had never actually addressed why it happened, only that it had happened, and then she said she'd understand if I wanted to divorce her, and I told her I wouldn't (not that I didn't want to— just that I wouldn't). So, I had only my assumptions—that she'd done it because she was insecure, that I didn't make her feel sexy anymore, that she didn't find me sexy anymore, and that we'd been married less than three years and had already stopped having sex.

"Yes," she said. "You know I've always had a thing for Brad. And he was here, and you didn't want to go to Funky

Knuckler, and he was macking on me hard."

I sat up and gave her my full attention. I did *not* know that she'd 'always had a thing for Brad.' I knew they made out one time in college, but that was forever ago, so I didn't know she still held a flame for him. I sat there with my jaw hanging on its hinges while my frazzled brain searched for the right response.

"I didn't know that you actually—" I had a hard time saying the next few words, which seeped out meekly. "Had feelings for him."

"Yeah, man, of course," she said gently. "Haven't you ever heard me and Brie talk about how hot he is?"

"Thinking someone is hot and actually *liking* them are two completely different things. I think Sofia Vergara's hot, but I would never want to hang out with her."

"Sofia Vergara? Really? Ew."

I huffed. "My point is, I thought you just found him physically attractive, not that you liked him as—as a person."

She looked at the floor and shrugged. "I do. He's cool. I've always liked him."

And suddenly, it was all so clear; this "little fling" between Beth and Brad was not just a little fling. There was much more to it than I'd ever allowed myself to believe.

***

March 2008

"I need to tell you something."

It was about halfway through the spring semester my freshman year of college, and I'd just passed my mid-term for Middle Eastern Culture in the Modern World. It was a ball-buster for which I'd studied two hours a night for the past week, and I counted myself lucky to have survived it with a B-plus. I was looking forward to a reprieve for the weekend, so I called Beth to talk about how we wanted to celebrate our one-year anniversary when she stopped the conversation dead in its tracks with those six words.

"Oh," I said. "Something wrong, Bethy-Bear?"

I was trying to keep it light. Whenever I asked this and everything was fine, she would respond with a patronizing giggle and say, "We're good, Mick-a-Roni. Stop being paranoid." Whenever I asked this and everything was not fine, there was nothing. No "Mick-a-Roni." No giggle. Just radio silence.

Everything was not fine.

"What is it?" I asked with a grave undertone. I heard Beth sniffle on the other end. It wasn't the throaty, mucus-y sniffle that accompanies the head colds everyone in the northeast gets each winter. It was a lighter, looser sniffle. It was her cry sniffle.

"Beth? What's going on?"

I heard more sniffles, a huff, and suddenly a barely audible, high-pitched sob. I heard her hand slide over the mouthpiece, and suddenly, just the inside of a seashell as I waited for her to collect herself and talk to me again. My forehead got sweaty, and my heart began to palpitate through three minutes of shuffling, sniffling, sobbing, and seashell sounds before she finally spoke.

"So, remember when I told you about Meg's brother on the rugby team?" There was a wobble in her voice.

"Brad?" I said with my fist clenched. She'd told me over Christmas break about some questionable ass-slapping that went on during her co-ed rugby matches, and I let it go at the time. But I knew that Brad guy was bad news. "What about him?"

"I've kinda been hanging out with him a lot this semester."

I didn't like that she'd waited until now to tell me this, and it made me wonder why. It also made me wonder something else.

"What do you mean 'hanging out'?"

"Just, like, in between classes, at lunch, sometimes we shoot hoops. That kind of stuff."

That doesn't sound so bad, I thought. *Nothing wrong with having a friend of the opposite sex. I had one or two of those, too.*

"Is he still smacking your ass?" I was half-joking and knew full well that rugby season had ended in November.

"No," she said, before hesitantly changing her tune to, "Well, sometimes."

My right heel began bouncing up and down as it does when it's bursting with nervous energy.

"Okay…" I said, waiting for her to drop the other shoe. It seemed like there was more to this conversation than Beth saying, "I have a guy friend who smacks my ass sometimes."

"So," she continued delicately, "I hung out with him in his room with a bunch of his friends last night to watch the Syracuse game. We were all, like, on our way out when it was over, and then—he grabbed my hand."

"He grabbed your hand?"

That could mean so many things—*help me clean up the mess from this party; my grandmother just died, and I don't want to be alone; careful not to step on that wasp*—but in the context of horny college guys who don't care if their girl friends are other guys' girlfriends, it probably meant only one thing.

Beth confirmed my assessment.

"Yeah. He wanted me to stay."

I cleared my throat and took a breath. "And did you stay?"

After another momentary pause, she said, "Yeah," with pangs of sorrow in her voice. "But only for, like, a little bit."

'A little bit'? I thought. *How long is 'a little bit'? A lot can happen in just 'a little bit' of time.*

"What were you and Brad doing when you were alone for 'a little bit'?"

"He—he kissed me."

Then, with a long, remorseful howl, she upgraded her statement to, "We made out."

I tried to slow my breathing as I glared at a photo on my desk of Beth and me laughing in a playful, snow-covered embrace on Christmas Eve. She was showing her bright, flashy, carefree smile and wearing one of those winter hats with the little brims on the front. I remembered thinking she looked really cute that day, but now, looking at the photo, she kind of looked like a cheating whore.

"What exactly do you mean you made out with him? Like, specifically what did you guys do?"

Much like the expression "hooking up" does now, the term "making out" encompassed a spectrum of sordid possibilities ranging from playful and flirty to deviously sexual. So, I needed more information.

More sniffles. "We kissed a lot. Like—a lot. I'm sorry, Mickey."

"As in French kissing? With tongue?" For some reason I needed to know, because it would be less bad if it were a puckered-up smooch like a six-year-old would give to her grandfather.

"Yes," she said, more composed. She seemed to realize her crying wasn't going to get her out of this. "He kissed my neck, too."

I picked up a pen and started scribbling vigorously all over my Intermediate Statistics syllabus. Then I pushed pen to paper as hard as I could, tearing through in spots, and wrote *FUCK YOU BRAD* in big, jagged letters.

"Did you touch him?" I asked, fixating on the 'A' in Brad's name. *A is for asshole*, I thought as my brain regressed back to a primitive state of jealous rage. *I knew this asshole wanted to fuck my girlfriend.* But did she want to fuck him, too? "Did you go down on him?"

"No," she said assertively. "God, no. He tried to put my hand on his dick, and I didn't let him."

"What did you do?"

"Just pulled my hand away and said, 'No way, man, you know I have a boyfriend.'"

"Okay. Well, that's good," I said with some relief. "But did he--"

"He touched my boob once. But I took his hand off it and put it around my waist."

"You were still kissing him, though?"

"Yeah. And then . . ."

She stopped and took a breath. I could hear her put down the phone and blow her nose. "Sorry."

"Okay, and then what?"

"Brad—he... he tried to put his hand between my legs."

I started bending the pen between my fingers, slowly, angrily. I held it horizontally with my index finger, middle finger, and ring finger, used my pinkie for leverage, and pushed on the pen as hard as I could with my thumb until it snapped. I threw the two pieces across the room, vaguely in the direction of the Red Sox garbage tin next to my bed, and demanded, through gritted teeth, "What did you do?"

"I shut it down, man," she said with certitude. "I stood up and said, 'Dude, it's not happening,' and when I wouldn't sit back down with him, he like, got all pissed. So I left, and that was it."

"That was it?"

"That was it. I swear."

For some reason, I believed her. Maybe because I didn't have a choice; I wasn't there, so there was no way I could ever know what really happened. Maybe I just didn't want to fight about it because I needed to give my brain a break from what had been an exhausting semester. But the fact that Beth was telling me what had happened when she could've easily kept it a secret until she died meant she deserved the benefit of the doubt.

"It's okay," I said, knowing that this was not actually okay, but if I let her off the hook this time, she surely wouldn't do anything like this ever again.

"Are you going to be okay?" she asked. "Are you still my Mick-a-Roni?"

I responded with my best replication of her patronizing giggle and said, "We're good, Bethy Bear. Stop being paranoid."

***

January 2018

I chewed the inside of my cheek and bounced my right

heel up and down as we sat there in unsettled silence for what felt like an hour; it probably was only about fifty-three seconds.

Beth disrupted it by asking, "So, what do you think?"

I looked at her incredulously. "What do I think about you having feelings for Brad?"

"No!" she responded as if I were ridiculous to suggest that the thing she had just said should still be on my mind. "I mean, what do you think about my proposal? The free pass? The open thing?"

I'd forgotten about the thing she'd mentioned before that could permanently damage our marriage when she introduced this new information that could destroy it.

"I don't know, Bethany, don't you think—"

"Beth."

I gave her a look. Was now really the right time for that? "Don't you think we should start having sex with each other again before we start talking about sex with other people? Wouldn't that make more sense? Work on us? You and me?"

"I'm never going to feel better unless you get a chance to, like, make things even."

Right. We should worry about making you *feel better*, I thought.

"I don't care about making things even," I said with a little more bite. Or maybe I just wanted the conversation to end because I was tired, so I was losing patience. "I just want it to not happen again. *Beth*."

"But I *do* want to make it even! It's only fair! I hurt you! I care about you! I owe you!"

"You care about *Brad*." I couldn't help it.

"Well, yeah." She wasn't denying it. "But I care about you, too. I love you."

"I love you, too," I said despondently. "But this doesn't make sense."

"What doesn't?"

I took a deep breath and then, with an unsteady voice, said, "Why don't you just—"

My voice cracked. I paused to collect myself, then continued.

"Instead of messing around with him behind my back, telling me you have feelings for him, and then giving me a chance to 'even the score' or whatever, why don't you just…" I choked down the lump in my throat. "Why don't you just leave me? That would be a lot simpler than trying this open marriage thing."

"Because, Mickey, you're my husband," she said with a rare softness in her voice that gave me hope for a moment. "We've been together eleven years. I'm not gonna throw that all away."

I looked at my wife with a little smile. This was the kind of thing I'd needed to hear for a long time, since long before this whole cheating/pregnancy thing had happened. We'd wandered so far off the path that we'd started on a decade before, growing further and further apart the longer we'd been together, that hearing her say she wasn't ready to wave the white flag filled me with warmth. Other people had left me, given up on me, abandoned me, but Beth wouldn't. She looked back at me with that bright, off-center smile, the one I'd seen less and less of over the years, then blinked those jade green eyes at me, and I felt like we were finally starting to connect.

And then, just as suddenly, the connection was lost.

"Besides, Brad's way out in California."

My smile evaporated and my eyes shifted sideways. I

found the timing of this statement peculiar.

"Soooo," I wondered if I should press the issue. I proceeded with caution, unsure of whether or not I wanted to hear the answer to my next question. "What if he wasn't in California?"

"You mean if he lived here?"

"Yeah. If he lived here. Or if this were some alternate universe and we lived in San Bernadino. If Brad was nearby, and you could see him whenever, who would be your husband then?"

Beth started looking around the room and fidgeting with her fingers a bit more fervently. She was giving it more thought than I was comfortable with. Finally, she shrugged and said, apologetically, "I don't know."

Whether she knew it or not (I suspected she did), she'd just answered my question. And just like that, I understood my reality. I was competing with another man for my own wife's affection, a brand of affection I wasn't sure I wanted anymore, but one that would hurt to lose anyway. Likewise, Beth loved me out of habit and stayed with me out of convenience and familiarity, but if Brad lived closer, she might have left me for him instead of just fucking him behind my back. So, I had nothing to lose by agreeing to the terms of her 'proposal.' Our marriage was on life support at this point, anyway, so I might as well enjoy some spouse-approved extramarital intercourse.

Knowing she'd won a get-out-of-jail-free card, Beth gave me an open-mouthed kiss and went to bed. I turned back to the television in a daze, and after shaking off reality one more time, I unpaused the PlayStation to reabsorb myself into my fantasy world of video game baseball. I threw a meatball right down the middle to Judge, who belted a soaring bomb ten rows into the stands to give the Yankees the lead. Mickey Patrick hung his head in shame. The one-time phenom just got crushed.

5

Torey Rizzo and I had formed something of a bond as batterymates during our championship run, and he recruited me to throw batting practice to him once a week throughout the summer so he could stay sharp. As the summer wore on, what had once been an antagonistic relationship between "Mickey the Mouse" and his bully began to evolve, first into a symbiotic partnership between two teammates who'd grown to respect each other, and then into something much more meaningful. We practiced together every Sunday starting at the beginning of June. By July, we were hitting the field twice a week and hanging out together until dinner. By mid-August, we were going to movies, talking about our dads, and showing up at each other's houses at random. And by the time school started in September, we'd become much more than batting practice partners. We were friends.

I was never formally introduced to Torey's younger sister, Luciana. She was always just – there. We'd go to his house after baseball, and she was there blasting showtunes on the stereo. We'd be watching the Red Sox game and she'd sing her way into the room and block the TV until he told her to fuck off. We'd be talking about personal stuff, like how aimless he felt without his father or why I'd been quiet at school for so long, and she was there making tuna melts for the three of us. And when we were sitting at the lunch table on the first day of school talking about what I should do with my free time now that I'd discovered the toastiness of freedom and friendship that lived outside the asphalt walls of my self-imposed solitude, Luciana plopped her tray down, scooted in next to me, and nosed her way into the conversation.

"I thought you'd be good on the grid, but you were a girl about it," Torey teased with the maturity of the adolescent he was. He'd talked me into trying out for football, and it was absolute hell. I'd never in my life been pushed so hard physically, been screamed at so much by grown men trying to "motivate" me, nor dreaded anything like I did the three hours of practice I vomited through each of the four days I went before I said, "Nope."

"I don't know," he said. "There's soccer. Cross country. Band. Yearbook. I mean, those are all for dorks, but you might like them."

"Whatever—Torey's the biggest dork in the whole school," Luciana said as she peeled the aluminum foil off her tuna melt. Torey was two years older than his sister but only one grade ahead of her; he'd repeated first grade when his teacher deemed him "not emotionally ready" to advance after what happened with their father. So, being both emotionally stunted and the oldest kid in our class, the bullying he once tortured me and other kids with came very naturally to him. But Luciana was immune to her brother's antics.

Then, as if a light bulb clicked on, she sat up excitedly and gestured to me with her melty fishy sandwich. "Ooh!

You know what you should do?"

"What?" I was curious.

"You should join Drama Club!"

"He's not gonna do Drama, Ass Bag," Torey said. "The kid barely even talks."

"Suck my butt, Hamster Balls," Luciana said. I smirked because it was always entertaining to see her shut her older brother down like that. You could tell they were siblings, both with dark Italian complexions, almost-black hair, and big, round eyes. And their noses, with the tips rounded off and slightly flared nostrils, were all but identical. Luciana sported braces on her teeth, though, while Torey had opted to let his snaggled grin remain snaggled. She turned back to me. "You should try it, Mickey-Mack! I'm in it, my BFF Danica's in it. It's fun. The first meeting is Thursday."

The only acting I'd ever done was in the backyard with Mason when we were little kids—unless you count all the times I acted like I didn't hate Raymond. But I was intrigued; sometimes when I would read through my mom's old scripts, I'd imagine myself up on stage making hundreds—maybe thousands—of people laugh or cry or touch their hearts. But the thought of getting up on an actual stage made my stomach queasy.

"I don't know," I said. "Being around people, talking to people, makes me nervous."

Torey always did the talking when we were around people. He was a popular jock who all the "women" (if you can call fourteen- and fifteen-year-old girls "women") fawned over. And in high school, if you talk loudly, people will listen, whether you have something to say or not. I, on the other hand, was much looser in smaller groups, and Torey and Luciana had both seen a different side of me than most of our peers had.

"Oh, Mickey-Mack," Luciana said with a sympathetic little laugh. "You're just shy."

"You don't have to be nervous, kid. You're hilarious," Torey said. "Why do you think I hung out with you all summer?"

Torey reminded me of the time during batting practice when the bat slipped out of my hand and I yelped, "Oh, Melvin!" as it spun through the air (when he asked, "Who's Melvin?" I shrugged and said, "My twelve-pound guinea pig with pickle toes"). Then Luciana reminded me about Pictionary with our moms, when my hastily drawn Chrysler Building looked like a pointy purple penis; we all laughed so hard I accidentally farted, causing her to blast apple juice out of her nose.

"You're funny and you're smart—just be yourself," the younger Rizzo said. "You're talking to me, right?"

"Yeah, but you're Torey's sister," I said. "Our moms have known each other forever. You're like—a friend."

She jerked her head back, as if bewildered by what I'd assumed was a given. "Dude, you think I'm your friend?"

Disarmed by her reaction and unable to navigate the unforeseen social black hole I'd haphazardly fallen into, I froze. But then her face softened into an "I gotcha" smile and she jabbed me with her elbow.

"If we're gonna be friends, call me Luci."

A breath of sweet relief burst from my lungs.

"Okay," I said with an apprehensive smile. I cleared my throat. "What time Thursday?"

"Right after school," Luci said as a big, bracey grin spread across her face. "Yay! Another recruit!"

Then she squealed and made little, happy claps with her

fingertips.

***

"QUESTION FOR THE GROUP—" I sprung from my seat with no warning and leapt on top of a piano bench. Everyone's faces popped out of their scripts and looked up at me with wide eyes and half smiles like awe-struck six-year-olds wondering what the magician would pull out of his sleeve next.

"What's the difference between a bounced check and an angry jackrabbit?"

Something about Drama Club not only pulled me from my shell but shattered it. Maybe it was because half the people in the club had been labeled nerds and losers by the "cool kids," and the other half were the "cool kids" who didn't care what the other "cool kids" thought, so I didn't have to worry about being bullied, picked on, or judged. Maybe it was because it was an escape from Ray, an escape to a different world, where I could pretend I was somebody bigger, better, more successful, more confident. Or maybe it was because I got my first girlfriend. Whatever the case, here I was, bopping around the auditorium and making terrible jokes.

I looked around at everyone as they cackled at the unusual question; they hadn't even heard the punchline yet. My eyes darted about the room and the corners of my mouth curled into a knowing grin.

"Tell us!" said Darius Duckman. "I can't take it!"

"One is bad money—the other is a mad bunny!"

A mix of sophomoric giggles and light-hearted groans filled the air. I dropped down off the bench and laughed with my full belly, proud of myself, not only for my clever, if cheesy, little joke, but for how far I'd come in just a few short months.

"When life gives you lemons"—I paused for dramatic effect and stroked my chin with mock insightfulness—"shove them back in life's face and say, 'No. Give me apples. You can make better stuff with apples.'"

"Let me do my lines, Mack! You makin' me laugh!" Darius said as we did that thing where you low-five but hook your fingertips together and pull away with a snap. I didn't know what it was called, but I liked it.

"I always aim to please," I said with a smirk. "But sometimes I miss and hit a squirrel."

"Stop it!" He laughed and pushed my shoulder. "I can't! Dani, control your boy!"

I looked over at Danica, who was sitting across the stage with half of her face hiding behind her playscript and the other half fighting to mask a mix of restrained laughter and embarrassment.

"I can't," she said with nervous laughter. She buried the exposed half of her face in her empty hand.

Luciana – sorry, Luci – who had both gotten me involved with the club and helped me to loosen up, also helped facilitate the budding of a romance between her "bestie" and me, the two shiest people in the solar system. Danica was a bit of a pet project for Luci, like I'd been for Torey, so I guess Luci figured it would be good to give her socially timid acquaintance a soft launch with someone of a similar ilk.

She was right. Having spent years as "Mickey the Mouse," I could relate to Dani in ways most guys couldn't. Rather than off-put, I was captivated by her shyness; I wanted to find out who she was, what made her tick, and what she was keeping from the world. So, when I wasn't up on stage, I'd sit next to her and try to make her laugh. When rehearsal was over, I'd walk her home and ask questions about her life, her family, and her past. We grew closer and more comfortable with each other as the days turned into weeks, and soon enough, we were a "thing."

Danica was the first girl who ever smiled at me "like that." The first girl who ever gave me butterflies. The first girl who ever held my hand. The first girl who ever kissed me. And most importantly, she was the first girl who ever made me feel confident. She was blessed with natural beauty that she hadn't yet started sculpting with caked-on foundation and thick, tar-colored eyeliner the way she would by the time she got her reputation a few years later. She had icy blue eyes, big, sleepy-looking eyelids, some baby fat in her cheeks and around her waist, an upturned little nose, and dirty-blond hair that she kept in a messy bun. And for whatever reason, she liked me. She thought I was funny, thought I was sweet, and thought I was cool. Danica helped me find whatever it was that made me the person I became in Drama Club.

And I relished it.

By the time dress rehearsals came around, "Mickey the Mouse" had peaced out. Talking to people (even girls!) no longer scared me. In fact, I learned, it was quite natural for me. It was something that had always been there, like sunlight that had been trapped behind bland gray clouds for centuries. And having rediscovered this long-muted radiance, I became a person I liked. A person everybody liked. People started approaching me with grins in their cheeks instead of sneers on their lips. They started asking me what

I was doing after rehearsal. They started inviting me to parties. Guys started picking me for their teams in gym class. Girls started giving me hugs for no reason.

"Alright," Mrs. Forrester said, trying to get an iota of control over a group of goofy teenagers that just wanted to get through one final three-hour dress rehearsal. "Break time's over. Let's go through Act Two."

We all gulped down our giggles and shuffled to our places. Mine was at a kitchen table in the middle of the stage across from one of the senior girls named Kaylin Bedford. She'd been acting since fourth grade and had won New Hampshire Regional Tony awards at the Pinkerton Academy Theater Festival each of the last three years. Her grandfather had produced off-Broadway shows in Providence in the 50s, and her mother was a lifelong actress whose biggest claim to fame was as one of Jack's improv students on *Will & Grace*. So, this stuff was in Kaylin's blood. Easily the most talented and committed performer in this hodgepodge of amateurs who were mostly just there to fuck around and flirt. She was the Big Leagues. So, whenever I was onstage with her, I was determined not to embarrass myself—or her.

"Okay, Mr. Loman," Mrs. Forrester said. "Go ahead."

She was talking to me.

As it turned out, I was good, too. A sophomore newbie, I'd won the legendary role of Willy Loman over three seniors and a junior. I read for three other parts, but Mrs. Forrester said I "invoke Willy's pain so honestly. But you also capture the spirit of his childlike escapism so naturally." It felt like a backhanded compliment, but she'd given me a shot at the lead, so she clearly saw something in me. And having someone as masterful as Kaylin, who captured

Linda Loman's pained-but-loving disposition with such nuance and professionalism, running lines with me for hours every day only made me better.

I cleared my throat, closed my eyes, and took a moment to let the weight of Willy's world wash over me. I took a deep breath, opened my eyes, exhaled, and began.

"Wonderful Coffee. Meal in itself…"

6

March 2007

It all started because Herb Fitz got stuck.

It was a snowy, late-winter day when Frank Roberts summoned me to his desk and said, "Looks like you're up, kid."

"I'm up?" I said, confused but hopeful.

"Herb doesn't have four-wheel drive, so he's spinning his wheels in his driveway. We need someone to get up to Plymouth, and I know you've got your dad's truck."

Ray had let me borrow his F-150 to get to my seasonal internship at the *Rockingham Daily Record*, but I was only supposed to go to the office to take phone calls and practice a little page design that night. I wasn't supposed to take it to a basketball game sixty miles upstate, even if it was a wicked big one. But it was just a temporary gig and it was ending soon, and I wanted to make a splash before they showed me the door. Now Frank was asking me to do something I'd never done before—cover a state championship game—and I wanted to jump at the opportunity. But before I could say yes, I had to make a call.

"I'll have to ask if I can take it all the way up there." I

70

was embarrassed that Ray still wielded his power over me at age eighteen, and even though Frank's voice said, "Okay, I understand," the look on his face said, "Jesus Christ." But Ray always checked the odometer before I took his truck, and he would see my ByLine at the top of the story if I went to the game, so there was no way I could drive his rig all the way to Plymouth State University without him finding out.

Humility had become a much more familiar friend in recent months than it had been during my years of high school heroics. I'd been accepted into Boston University's College of Communication and invited to try out for its baseball program, but after high school, I'd decided to take a gap year so I could stash away a little cash. As summer dwindled down, my friends went off to their respective colleges, and I suddenly had way too much free time to fill. After a few months working a (temporary!) summer job at Charlie Mart, I responded to an ad for a seasonal internship at the *Daily Record* to help take phone calls from local coaches, type up box scores, and even write brief game summaries. It was a great way to keep my hand in the game before I went all-in with my studies the next fall, but it wasn't without its fair share of humble pie. The old sports writers welcomed me at first with fond memories of my baseball accomplishments ("Hey! It's Mack-Pack!" "How's the ol' pitching arm, Mickey?" "That no-no you chucked in Hanover still gives me goosebumps!"), but once the shine of having one of their star subjects sitting alongside them wore off, there was much more of a "You don't know what you're talking about, kid" vibe. So, it wasn't long before "Mickey the Mouse," a persona I thought I'd smothered long ago, trickled back to the surface to remind me that "children should be seen and not heard."

I was surprised by Ray's response when I called. Well, at first.

"Oh? They want you to cover a championship game? Great!"

I smiled; he didn't often get excited about something going on in my life. Then he added, "How much are they paying you?"

"I don't know."

"Are they paying your mileage?"

"I don't know."

"Find those things out first, then get back to me."

I finally got his blessing when I told him Frank said I'd get $50 plus mileage.

The drive to Plymouth was slightly terrifying between the three inches of packed slush and ice on Interstate 93 and the elephant-sized moose that wandered into the middle of the freeway and caused me to yank the truck into the other lane and squeal like a frightened toddler. The next challenge was trying to convince a pair of grandmotherly ticket takers that I was, in fact, representing the newspaper and not just some shifty teenager in his dad's blazer trying to cheat them out of their $4 admission fee.

It was the Division IV title between Saint Mary's Catholic School—a little private school in Rockingham on the opposite side of town from where I grew up—and Sunapee, a little public school near a small lake on the western side of the state. The big, bright gym at PSU buzzed with twelve minutes to go before tip-off. Eminem's "Lose Yourself" blared through the speakers and bounced off the concrete walls. The crowd, already on its feet and boisterous, donned a festive mix of red and green; red for the top-seeded Cardinals from St. Mary's and green for the fourth-seeded Lakers. Out on the floor, young women of varying heights and hairdos lined up under opposite hoops in contrasting colors and loosened their legs with layups and short-range jump shots. The scent of buttered popcorn saturated the open air.

I recognized Bethany Connelly as soon as I saw her. I'd heard all about her from the *Daily Record's* coverage of her and the SMCS basketball team throughout the season. The first time I'd seen her smile was in a posed picture in the *Record* after she scored her 1,000th career point just a few weeks prior; she was standing next to her coach in her white-and-red Number 16 jersey holding an old, dirty basketball with the date and "BC1K" scribbled on it in Sharpie. Dried sweat had matted her orange bangs to her forehead, her long French braid drooped limply over her left shoulder, and there was an air of pride and mischief in her smile, a smile that seemed to glow through the pixels on the printed page. It glowed even brighter here under the fluorescent gymnasium lights. When the statuesque redhead tugged playfully at a high, bouncy ponytail attached to Number 26—a shorter, smaller-framed version of herself whom I gathered was her lesser-known younger sister, Brianna—her eyes squinted and her cheeks rose to reveal a bright, off-center smile packed with flashy white teeth, and I was instantly mesmerized. And that was before I even saw her play.

I'd only been to two other games during my internship, both as tag-alongs with Herb, one of the *Daily Record's* most seasoned sports reporters. He taught me how to keep score, what statistics to keep track of, and how to shorthand a game in such a way that I could craft an entire eighteen-inch story out of a few pages of notes, symbols, and scribbles. But that was all just practice for me—Herb's game logs were the ones the paper published.

This time, though, I was on my own. I had no safety net; no one to guide me, correct me, teach me, or point things out for me. As an impressionable tenderfoot, it was hard not to get swallowed by the euphoric cheers, the feet pounding on the bleachers, and the heart-thumping sense of dread and hope that ebbed and flowed between team benches with each splash of the basket. But I had to stay focused. Frank was counting on me, and I was counting on myself to prove I could do this. So, my eyes tracked every bounce, every pass, every brick, and every swish of that big orange orb, and my hands etched a glorious masterpiece of chicken scratch that only my adept young mind could ever decode.

During halftime, I took a moment to catch my breath and work out some stat totals. I was disappointed to see that this Bethany Connelly player I'd heard so much about had scored only eight points, and her team was down by five to the No. 4 seed. St. Mary's had never won a state championship before, but this was supposed to be their year. All the local papers had predicted that St. Mary's would cruise to a Division IV title on the backs of the Connelly sisters. Brianna was a speedy sophomore point guard who could get the ball up the court in a hurry and score when she needed to. But it was Bethany Connelly, the senior shooting guard, who had everybody talking. She'd averaged 27 points and 14 rebounds per game throughout a 19-1 regular season.

"She has height, athleticism, ball-handling skills, and the

ability to shoot from anywhere inside the halfcourt line."—
The Concord Monitor

"Brianna Connelly has court vision like few sophomores at this level, but Bethany Connelly is the complete package. If she'd had a good supporting cast her whole career, she might have scored 2,000 points."—*The Portsmouth Herald*

"She's an incredible athlete who, with the right attitude, could've been a key player at bigger nearby schools like Division II's Rockingham or D-I's Winnacunnet, but she's a bona fide superstar in Division IV."—*The Rockingham Daily Record*

It got worse after halftime, though, and the Lakers were smelling an upset when they finished the third quarter with a surprising 61-52 lead. I sensed a nervous energy coming from the patrons in red, who were holding their heads, holding their hands, holding their hearts, holding onto anything they could to try to will the Cardinals to a win. But despite the season-long hype surrounding the Cardinals and the Connelly sisters, they were just eight short minutes from a season of unrealized potential. Meanwhile, as I added up the stats again and saw Bethany Connelly, this supposed "superstar," still only had twelve points, I couldn't help but wonder, *What's so great about this girl?*

Then, as if she'd heard me ask it, she answered my question.

When the fourth quarter got started, so did Bethany Connelly. With her team's back against the wall, she morphed into an invincible beast—a sleek, gray wolf among common household mutts—able to do exactly what she wanted with the ball, when she wanted. She single-handedly began to deconstruct the Lakers' zone defense, moving around the court so smoothly, with precision, calculation, and gritty determination, the ball rolling off her fingertips as if poured from a spout; she was unstoppable. She'd spin through three defenders for an open layup on one possession, then sit back and drain a three-pointer from NBA range on the next. Anytime Sunapee dared foul her to try and slow her down, she made them pay from the free throw line. She racked up 20 points in that stunning fourth quarter and finished with 32. Her finishing touch came at the buzzer, when she knocked down a jumper from the corner to win the game—and the whole damn championship—75-74, and as the crowd erupted and her teammates mobbed her, I stood there, electrified, chills tingling through my pores. I was speechless, entangled in the beauty of this incredible moment, sharing in the exhilaration and joy of this girl I didn't even know.

Bethany always *did* have a flair for the dramatic.

***

I stood next to the scorer's table smiling like a goof as the Saint Mary's coaches and players got their awards, and it brought me back to my freshman year, when I stood at home plate at Holman Stadium and got to hold one of those New Hampshire-shaped wooden-and-gold-plated trophies in my own hands. I still had to grab both coaches for post-game interviews, of course, but I knew if I wanted my story to be worth reading, I had to talk to Bethany Connelly, and the longer the post-game ceremonies went on, the more nervous I became. I'd never interviewed a player before, only coaches, and until this game, only over the phone. So, I waited anxiously, checking my watch every thirty seconds, wondering if I'd be able to make my deadline, as one player after another walked back to the Cardinals' bench in their sweaty white-and-red jerseys. Finally, after all the photos were taken and the crowd had begun to dissipate, she, Brianna, and two other players whose names didn't matter wandered in my direction, and my heart sprung into my throat. Being both outnumbered by the Connelly sisters and their teammates and, admittedly, a little star struck, I wasn't sure how to approach her. So, I just belched out, "Hi—Bethany?"

She stopped and looked at me, her narrow green eyes shifting back and forth, puzzled. Her friends walked a few extra paces but decided to wait for her.

"Hi Bethany—my name's Michael Patrick from the Recordham Daily Rocking—" I caught myself. "Sorry, the *Rockingham Daily Record*. Can I talk to you for a sec?"

She sniggled a bit at my foible and said, "Uhh, sure. Fitzie didn't come?"

Saint Mary's had been one of the schools on Herb's beat for years, so they were accustomed to seeing him at most of their important games.

"No, sorry—he got stuck in the snow. You'll have to deal with me."

She looked me over from head to toe. "Really? Aren't you, like, still in high school?"

"Nah, graduated last year. I'm just an intern, so I won't be around to bug you long."

"Alright, man." She still wasn't sure what to think about the situation. "What's up?"

"So, Bethany—"

"Call me Beth," she chimed in with some immediacy, as if she'd told people that 196 thousand times. "Just Beth."

"Okay—Beth." I was a little perplexed. She was always "Bethany" in the newspaper and on the roster, but if she wanted me to call her Beth, then Beth she would be.

Finally, we proceeded to settle into an amiable interviewer/interviewee rhythm: I'd ask her mundane questions like how it felt to win her school's first title, she'd respond with diplomatic answers sprinkled with overused sports clichés like how they "came together as a team" or that they were just trying to "chip away at the lead" by taking it "one shot at a time" and giving it "110 percent." She gave me enough to work with, but a nervous eighteen-year-old rookie reporter trying to pull teeth from an uncomfortable seventeen-year-old high school athlete isn't exactly what Pulitzer Prizes are made of.

I thanked her and shook her hand; she looked down to the end of her arm and said, "Man, your hand's huge—it's like a big ol' bear paw."

I wasn't sure if I should laugh or be offended. I gave her the benefit of the doubt and let out a fake chuckle. "Thanks, I guess?"

"Just be careful swingin' that thing around is all I'm saying."

"Will do." I gave her a nervous smirk. "Thanks, Bethany."

She pointed at me, half joking (I thought), and said, "What'd I tell you?"

"Sorry," I said, ashamed of my misgiving. "Thanks, Beth."

"That's better," she said, and she aimed her bright, off-center smile at me for the first time. "Later, man."

"Bye."

I turned, walked away, and grinned.

***

"Terrific story, Mick," Frank said to me the next day as he sat me down in the conference room. "I appreciate you helping us in a pinch like that. Good stuff, too."

Inspired both by the rousing Cardinals comeback spearheaded by their star player and by the challenge of writing a full-length game log by myself for the first time, I'd pounded out a twenty-inch masterpiece about Saint Mary's stunning victory in forty-five minutes. It was the kind of story that writes itself once you find your hook, and Bethany Connelly's fourth-quarter heroics made it a no-brainer.

I'd captured it all: The unease of the Christmas-colored crowd as their beloved teams battled through this high-stakes clash between two of Division IV's best; the unsettled excitement on the Sunapee players' faces as they entered the final frame with a nine-point lead; and the heart-stopping half-second of silence that befell an entire gymnasium as the Cardinals' final shot floated through the air and splashed through the nylon net for the winner. I'd written about Bethany Connelly a lot—and deservedly so—the way she single-handedly willed her team to victory, driving the ball through traffic, knocking down threes in the face of desperate defenders, rising head-and-shoulders above the competition in a way rarely seen in prep basketball. By the time I put the finishing touches on my first big story and hit SEND, I knew I'd nailed the assignment.

I'd already cut out the article and plopped it in my mom's scrapbook that morning, and now, this validation from Frank Roberts—a guy who'd covered some of the biggest sporting events in Granite State history—was a gigantic green checkmark for my early-career bucket list.

"Thanks!" I responded with a hyper-happy gawk before he went on to inform me that, with the winter sports season all but wrapped up, my internship would be done the following week. He offered to bring me back as a freelancer for the spring season, but I had something else on my plate coming up soon.

"Actually, I can't," I said with a regretful wince. "I'm auditioning for the spring show at The Silverman."

It had been over a year since I'd been in a production, when I had my last go-round in the regional festival at Pinkerton Academy. So, I was itching to get back onstage, and *Footloose* was calling my name.

"I didn't know you were an actor," Frank said. In a single five-second silence that seemed like five hours, I felt his opinion of me shifting, but I was uncertain which direction his meter was moving. "I thought you were a ballplayer."

With a cheeky smile, I said, "I am. Ballplayer, actor—writer—I'm a man of many talents."

He paused for a moment. Then he cracked a huge grin.

"I knew there was something about you, son," he said with a proud, grandfatherly chuckle. "You've got a spark in your eye."

He got out of his chair, stood up, and extended his hand to me. "You've done well here, Mick. If you ever change your mind and want me to toss you a game for some extra cash, just call me."

I grabbed his hand enthusiastically and shook it. "Thanks, Frank—I really appreciate that."

"I mean it. I've a feeling you're on your way to bigger

things in your life than you'll find in a little place like Rock-ingham. Don't ever let me or anyone else hold you back."

"I won't—thank you so much."

I walked out of the conference room with happy tears in my eyes and sat back down at my desk to finish my day's work, which included fiddling with Photoshop and Quark, reading wire stories about March Madness, and proofreading press releases. A few minutes later, someone said, "Michael?"

I looked up and saw a middle-aged, bottom-heavy woman with a short-cropped mop of curly red hair and a face that seemed familiar; but I'd never met her.

"Yeah, hi. Can I help you?"

"It's nice to meet you—I'm Judy, Beth's mom. I work over in advertising."

Beth? Who's Beth? I thought. But then I remembered the conversation I'd had the night before with a certain statu-esque redheaded basketballer.

"Oh, you're Bethany Connelly's mom?" I was sudden-ly wicked happy to be talking to this bowling pin-shaped stranger. "I didn't know you worked here—great to meet you!"

"I wanted to tell you—Beth absolutely loved your arti-cle. She cut it out and put it right on the fridge this morn-ing."

"I'm glad she liked it," I said. "She deserved it—that was an incredible game."

"It was, wasn't it? She was absolutely thrilled! Nicest thing anyone's written about her all year."

"I doubt that—she's the best player in Division IV."

"No, it's true! Everyone always just talks about her at-titude, but it was nice to have someone write about how good she is as a player and not focus on all that negative stuff."

Her attitude? I thought to myself. *She seemed fine to me—just a little unusual.* But I didn't dig any deeper.

"Well, it was my pleasure," I said. "She was a lot of fun to watch."

"Hey, she wanted to email you and thank you, but we couldn't find your email address on the website. Maybe it's not up yet because you're new?"

"Actually, I'm just an intern—I don't have a company email address. And I'm done next week."

"Oh, you are? Well then you MUST give me your personal email. I mean, if that's okay. I just know she really wanted to thank you."

"Sure!" I scribbled out my email address on a torn piece of notebook paper and handed it to Bethany Connelly's mom. I wasn't sure if that was crossing some kind of professional/personal line or whatever, but in a few days, it wouldn't matter.

After she left, I looked back at my screen for about five seconds before I heard a very low-key "Hey, kiddo." I looked up and it was Herb Fitz.

"Sorry 'bout last night. Two tires caught in a foot of snow—no way I was gettin' to Plymouth," he said. "Great story, though."

I smiled. "Thanks—it was an awesome experience."

Then Herb scanned the room with his droopy old eyes to make sure no one was listening, scratched his bushy gray mustache, and leaned toward me as if he were about to share the nuclear codes at the Pentagon.

"Tread lightly with that one," he said.

"Who?"

"Connelly. Great athlete, piss-poor attitude."

He slid a sun-faded old paper across my keyboard. "Read this."

It was a column he had written a year prior about the middling Saint Mary's basketball team's challenges in finding leadership despite a boatload of talent. One particular paragraph caught my eye:

Junior guard Bethany Connelly, for example, should be the de facto leader of the team based on her statistics and her game-altering physical abilities. But her struggles to control her temper on the court have resulted in various ejections, technical fouls, and even a two-game suspension during her sophomore year. That won't fare well for her should college scouts ever take notice, less so should she hope to bring a trophy to the Cardinals before she graduates.

"Wow, I had no idea," I said. "She seemed cool when I talked to her last night."

"That's 'cause they won, see. If they lost, you would've seen a red-faced banshee, whinin' about the refs, yellin' at the other coach. She probably wouldn't've even shook the other team's hands. And any time we write somethin' that isn't roses and sunshine about'er, Mom is in here carryin' on and givin' Frank a hard time."

"Damn," I said, before I shrugged it off. "Oh well. Glad I got to see a good one."

"Me too, kiddo," he said. Then he patted my shoulder and added, "Ahh, you'll probably never even see'er again."

7

I didn't think Bethany Connelly would actually write to me; surely, she was too famous—even on a small scale—to bother with a lowly intern like me. But the next day, as I waded through endless junk emails about Nigerian princes and penis enlargement pills, wondering if I'd ever force myself to learn how to implement the spam filters in my Inbox, there it was: A message from BethCon1@zmail.com.

Dear Mr. Patrick,
Thank u SOOOOOOOO much for writing such a nice article about me. Sorry if I acted weird. You are a great writer :)
—Beth #16

I laughed to myself at her erratic train of thought, and it was cute that she felt like the article about her team's big win—though she featured prominently—was just about her. But it was nice to get some positive feedback from someone outside of the newsroom, so I wrote back to tell her I appreciated it:

Hi Beth,

Please, just call me Mickey. It was a pleasure covering your game. Congratulations again, and thank YOU for such a nice compliment! You have a bright future ahead of you and can take your talents anywhere you want. Best of luck.

—Mickey Patrick

I figured that would be the end of it, so I closed my browser and went about my day, a routine consisting of watching *SportsCenter* reruns, looking for jobs in the newspaper, and reading about obscure Broadway bombs from the 70s and 80s like *Flahooley* and *Moose Murders*. A few hours later, as I was getting dressed to head to the newsroom, I logged back on for one last look, and there she was again:

Don't worry, I'll be around ;)

My heart palpitated as I re-read the message and tried to interpret the meaning of the semicolon-and-closed-parenthesis combination. It was a troubling time before the emoji exploji, when groups of punctuation that didn't typically go together in a grammatical sense could mean so many different things. I was pretty sure, though, that semicolon-and-closed-parenthesis was known universally as only one thing: A wink.

Was Bethany Connelly flirting with me?

I took a second to consider my response. *Tread lightly with that one*, Herb had told me, and I was compelled to heed his advice at first. But what I hadn't told him was that I was wicked lonely. My friends were all away at college, and Mason had just moved to Boston. Meanwhile, aside from this internship, I had nothing going on and no one to talk to until *Footloose* auditions—and even then, there was no guarantee I'd get a part. So, if someone was tossing me a semicolon-and-closed-parenthesis, regardless of her preceding reputation, I could tread as heavily as I wanted. So, I wrote back:

You know what? I'll be around, too. Maybe we should hang out sometime…

She responded within seconds:

ABSOLUTELY :) :) :)

8

Beth was a cool person to hang out with. She wasn't quite like the showy girls from Drama who wore silly outfits or blurted out random song lyrics, but she wasn't quite like the guys from the baseball team who talked about the Sox and plowing each others' moms. She was definitely a different type of character, but I didn't hate it.

Our first date was on a Saturday night. It was Saint Patrick's Day, so I wore a pine-colored polo shirt and cargo pants that were too baggy, and she wore tight black jeans and an emerald green cable knit hoodie. It was the first time I saw her with her hair down, and it framed her masculine jawline much more nicely than the long French braid she normally sported. The dark eyeliner she wore made her narrow eyes pop a little more, and she had a single, milk chocolate-colored freckle, perfectly centered in the middle of her forehead, that was just adorable. She gave me a modest, unsure smile when I picked her up, and she didn't say a whole lot on the drive to the Shrimp Bucket. Clearly, this girl—the cocky, confident, sleek gray wolf on the basketball court—was but a timid little hamster in the dating world.

I did my best to pull her out of her shell as we drove.

"So, Beth, I'd like to get something off my chest," I said, fighting to suppress my grin.

"What?" She sounded a bit defensive.

"It's this 75-pound chipmunk wizard," I said. "He's been sitting here all day casting spells and he smells like tartar sauce."

I sat there with my hands on the steering wheel, looking back and forth between the road and my date, smiling in anticipation of a guffaw, a giggle, a snicker—anything. But she just smiled politely and rolled her eyes. Strange, that kind of stuff had always killed with my Drama Club friends. Maybe the chipmunk wizard should smell like fudge instead. Fudge is a funnier word.

"Sorry," I said. "Just trying to break the ice a little."

"Don't worry about it, man. Sorry if I'm quiet. I haven't been on many dates."

"No worries—neither have I." I gave a reassuring glance. A half-ounce of tension escaped from her face and shoulders.

Once we arrived at the Shrimp Bucket and got a few sodas down the hatch (we were too young for alcohol), we both relaxed a little. I asked her how she got to be so good at basketball, and she said other girls used to pick on her in junior high because she was tall and lanky and had crooked teeth, so the only way to shut people up was to be good at sports. I said I could relate, because I never had many friends either until I played baseball. Beth said she actually saw me play my junior year when a friend of hers was dating one of the guys on my team, so she knew who I was when I approached her after her championship game.

"That's why I didn't think you were a real reporter. I

thought you were, like, stalking me or something."

"Maybe I was," I said with elevated ostentation so she would know I was joking. Then I scrunched my face into the grossest expression I could make, straining my neck muscles, crossing my eyes, and with a lateral lisp from the left side of my lips, I groaned, "Those were some lovely panties you were wearing this morning."

"Ew!" She retreated and covered her face with her napkin, then half-giggled and said, "Dude, don't talk about my panties!"

I stared at her with my "Goblin Face" for a good five seconds before she pulled the napkin down, pointed her fork at me, and, with restrained laughter, said, "If you don't stop, I will stab you."

My face straightened back to normal; I was happy we finally were having fun. As the evening unfolded, I discovered the way to really make Beth laugh was to do what she called "dorkeling." It was a play on the word "snorkeling," but instead of observing beautiful and mythical underwater species, the goal was to watch strangers, point their flaws out to each other, and privately make fun of them. It wasn't really my style, but I was down to try it, as long as we kept it between us. So, we would casually look around the room talking trash about imperfect people, like the balding thirty-year-old in a Best Buy shirt, the fat kid who looked like the fat kid from *Billy Madison*, and the waitress with a skin tag on her neck and her shirt buttoned wrong. I never knew I could think up such mean things to say about people, but that kind of stuff was right in Beth's wheelhouse. Maybe "big ol' bear paw" wasn't a compliment after all.

As first-date conversations inevitably do, ours eventually drifted toward the future.

"So, if you're not writing for the paper anymore, like, what's your plan?" Beth asked.

"My dream job is to be in movies or on TV," I said. "Even Broadway. There's nothing in the world like acting. It gives me so much energy—such a rush—I love it."

"Cool. So, you wanna go to Hollywood or something?"

"That's the dream. If I had the chance, I'd jump at it, but realistically it's a million-to-one shot. I also love sports, and I think it would be awesome to be a sports anchor on TV."

"Nice, like *SportsCenter*?"

"Exactly—but not one of the boring ones," I said. "I want to bring some flair to the air. I want to be the guy everyone tunes in to see. I want to tell you how the Red Sox did, but make it fun and entertaining, and not cheesy, you know?"

"Well, your article about me was really good; I bet you'd be awesome at that," Beth said. "But how do you even get on *SportsCenter*?"

"I'm going to Boston U in the fall. They have a wicked good program for sports broadcasting; if I do well there, who knows what'll happen."

"That's so good, man—wow!"

"Yeah," I smiled. I'd had this mapped out since my junior year. "What about you? What's 'BethCon1' got planned for next year?"

"Oh," she said, like she wasn't expecting me to ask her the same question. "I don't know. I've been accepted at The Rocks. I'll probably commute and play hoops. We don't have to pick a major until sophomore year."

Rockingham State College (or "The Rocks," as New Hampshirites called it) was one step above a community college. Anybody with a C-minus GPA could get in, and most people just applied to it as a backup school. Its sports offerings consisted of intramurals and a few intercollegiate club teams in rugby, soccer, and co-ed Ultimate Frisbee. RSC wasn't normally a place where elite athletes went to continue their careers.

"I figured D-1 would be calling you," I said, hiding my disappointment that the legendary Bethany Connelly would not be driving Auriemma's Huskies or Summit's Lady Vols to their next national titles.

"Oh, they did," she said, like it wasn't a big deal. "I got scouted by, like, UConn, Pitt, Syracuse. 'Cuse offered me a partial."

My eyes popped open. "And you didn't take it?"

"No way, man—way too far away," she said, as if playing for a D-1 school was an option for anybody who wanted it. "This way, I can stay home, save money, still go to Brie's games, not fly all over the country with bitchy girls who don't even know me."

That's when I realized it. Beth didn't want a big life like I did. I wanted to get out of Rockingham, meet different kinds of people, learn about other cultures, see all the amazing things there were to see in the world. She wanted to stay close to home, close to her family, close to the buildings, streets, and people she knew. She was an incredible basketball player with a unique charisma, but she was also shy and insecure; the emotional scars from the girls in junior high sat just under a thin layer of skin and still stung, and she was petrified of being vulnerable. She could do anything she wanted to—she just didn't want to.

But who was I to judge?

"In that case," I said with a smile as I raised my glass

of Pepsi, "here's to Bethany Connelly tearing it up at The Rocks."

"Fuckin' right," she said as we clinked our soda glasses together. "And remember, man—just call me Beth."

***

When we kissed for the first time that night, it didn't feel the way it should have. I wasn't excited. I wasn't nervous. I wasn't engorged with a sudden and urgent desire to rip her clothes off. I didn't feel closer to finding my soul mate than I ever had before. More than anything, it was awkward.

The drive back to her home was a lot more fun than the drive to the restaurant. We continued "dorkeling" (this time making fun of the jogger whose sports bra was too tight and the old man picking his nose in his rearview mirror). When we arrived at her house, I walked her to her door, and before she could grab the handle, I grabbed her hand.

"What?" she said nervously.

I pulled her toward me, squared up to her, and looked into unsure little jade-green eyes. "Thanks for a nice time."

"You're welcome. I had fun, too."

I leaned in to kiss her on her cheek, and she wrenched her neck so that our noses and mouths suddenly mashed together. I tried to just go with it and act like that was my plan all along, but while I was attempting to kiss her smoothly and gently, her lips were moving up and down on mine like an old lady trying to keep her dentures from falling out. Beth didn't have dentures, though. She had real teeth, and she was smashing them against mine. I wasn't sure before if she had ever kissed anyone, but now I knew she hadn't.

We pulled apart, and she was looking at me with the most genuine smile I had seen on her face all night. She took one hand away to wipe her lips, then gave it back to me and said, "Big ol' bear paws." I smiled, looked at her long, slender fingers and said, "Little string beans."

She laughed, gave me a hug, and said goodnight.

9

April 2007

I started seeing Beth quite a bit after our Shrimp Bucket date. Usually, it was at her parents' house with her sister (who insisted everyone call her "Brie") and Brie's dumb little skateboarder boyfriend Preston. We'd go to movies, shoot hoops in her driveway, watch overplayed sitcom reruns, or just take walks. On the rare occasion when we could be alone, we made out a little—Beth did get better at kissing—but I was in no rush to go any further than that with her. I admired how athletic she was, she put out a laid-back vibe (on the surface), and she did have a nice smile, but I didn't have that burning desire to suck on her neck, feel her boobs, or touch her between her legs. But she liked having a boyfriend, and I liked having someone to spend time with since Torey was playing football at West Virgina, The Goose and The Duck were spending every waking second together, and Mason was living in Boston and training for his upcoming fitness test. Besides, Beth was a cool person to hang out with.

She was helping me run lines the night before my *Footloose* audition when she said the words. We were working through the scene where Ariel shows Ren her "poetry" and tells him what happened to her brother, and Ren professes how much he cares about Ariel; I was really trying to dial in on the emotion of the scene despite Beth's untrained, mechanical readings of Ariel's lines. The romance of the scene wasn't lost on her, though.

She was sitting cross-legged on her bed in black Reebok workout pants and her lime-green spaghetti strap tank top, her hair tied up in a top knot when, after the fourth read-through, she put the script face-down in front of her, looked up at me with her eyebrows arched and her lips curled in an apprehensive smile, and said, after a big exhale, "I love you."

I was facing away from her toward her bookshelf full of stuffed animal bunnies of various colors and sizes, trying to concentrate on my next line. I paused for a second to recalibrate, then looked at her. "That's not in the script."

"Mickey . . ." she whined.

I sat down next to her and put my hand on her shin. "Are you serious?"

"I think so, man." She covered her face with her pillow.

It had only been a few weeks, but I already knew a lot about Bethany Connelly. I knew she always covered her face with something when she was embarrassed. I knew she laughed at other people hitting their heads on things. I knew she and her sister fought like rabid jackals but would literally die for each other. I knew she insisted on being called "Beth" and would correct an offender every time someone called her Bethany—every time. I knew that she loved stuffed animal bunnies and Indiana Jones and basketball. I knew she acted a lot tougher on the outside than she really was on the inside. I knew she was a cool person to hang out with. But I didn't know if I loved her.

"You gonna say anything?" she asked meekly.

"Of course," I said as I ran my hand up her forearm and shoulder, cupped her cheek, and looked into her hopeful eyes.

I felt like I had been here before. *Yes*, I thought to myself. *Three years ago. Death of a Salesman.* But that time, the situation was reversed...

***

December 2003

"The competition at Pinkerton is fierce," Mrs. Forrester said. This was her rallying cry in the weeks leading up to the regional theater festival. She'd say it at the beginning of every rehearsal. She'd say it at the end of every rehearsal. She'd say it any time she thought we were losing focus or having any kind of fun.

Sometimes she would add, "Everyone there is a Kaylin Bedford."

I chewed the inside of my cheek whenever she said that. I'd worked for almost three months directly alongside Kaylin and learned so much from her—nuance, immersion in the character, verbal tempo and inflection, even posture— that if Mrs. Forrester was going to say, "Everyone there is a Kaylin Bedford" as if Kaylin walked alongside Streep and Hanks on Hollywood Boulevard, that she should add, "or a Mickey Patrick."

It ignited my competitive side—which, I suppose, was the point—and motivated me to delve headlong into perfecting my new favorite craft. For almost a month, I poured every ounce of energy into each rehearsal, as if I were performing for a brand-new audience every night. I'd go home exhausted and gaze into the mirror for hours honing my gestural and facial expressions, then I'd get in the shower and, with a head full of shampoo, practice varying versions of my lines. It was actually a good thing Danica and I hadn't spent much time together since our awkward conversation.

As triumphant as I'd been over the past six-plus months, first on the diamond, and now on the stage, I remained stunningly green in the realm of relationships. Like many fifteen-year-olds, everything I knew about relationships came from the amalgamation of gooey romantic comedies I'd seen. *Say Anything. The Princess Bride. Sleepless in Seattle.* In those, I watched handsome men make sweeping romantic gestures to beautiful women, who in turn flung themselves into their arms with big cheeky smiles and joyful tears as the credits began to roll—and I wanted that.

But everything else? All the small, day-to-day stuff that strengthens or weakens a relationship? The understanding that sweeping romantic gestures don't just erase the pain we feel, nor the tears we shed, in real life? The fact that trusting someone with your heart means praying they won't crush it, then figuring out how to put the shattered pieces back together when they do? I had to learn all that on my own.

My first lesson came when I told Danica I loved her.

It was right after our final performance on opening weekend at RHS. I was floating on a cloud after a rousing standing-O from a hometown crowd consisting of parents, teachers, and friends, and as I walked Danica home that night, I was entranced in happy reflection. I thought about how amazing the past few months had been; I'd found a group of people who truly liked me; I'd discovered my talent for acting and developed a thirst for it; I'd made my first true connection with someone of the opposite sex. I was happier than I had ever been in my fifteen years on Earth. So, I went for it.

In the movies, when the handsome male lead professes his love to his beautiful female counterpart, she becomes mindlessly gleeful, slings her arms around his neck, and seals their newfound love with a glorious kiss. Cut to the next scene, and the euphoric couple is scampering down the aisle together and speeding off in a shiny limousine to parts unknown.

When I said it to Danica, though, all she said was, "You do?"

"Yes." I smiled.

"What do you mean? How do you know?"

I couldn't tell whether she was really trying to understand, or if she just didn't want to say it back, so I had no idea how to answer that. I just knew this wasn't how it went in the movies.

"I don't know, I just—"

"It's only been a couple months," she said. "We haven't even had sex."

"So?" My face twisted up. *What does sex have to do with it?* I thought.

"So—I don't think you love me." She paused to make sure I was taking it okay so far. Then she continued. "You were awesome onstage, and you got a standing ovation, and you got all kinds of attention. I think you're just feeling good because everyone loves you right now."

I noticed when she said, "everyone loves you," the part

she didn't say was, "except me." But she didn't have to.

****

April 2007

…I didn't know what to think. Maybe Beth did love me—would she know if she did? Maybe she just loved the idea of being in love. Maybe she was just excited. I knew there was affection there. I knew I loved spending time with her. I knew I at least *liked* her. Then I remembered the moisture in my eyes, the quivering in my bottom lip, and the queasy, empty sensation in my chest from someone not saying "I love you" back. At the very least, I couldn't do that to her.

"I love you, Bethany," I said.

Then she smiled at me, took my hand with both of hers, kissed me on the thumb, and said, "Just Beth."

10

I won the role of Ren in *Footloose* the weekend after Beth and I said those words. And over the following eight weeks, I got to know the real Bethany Connelly.

She wasn't the awkwardly guarded girl I'd met after that basketball game, but she wasn't the "red-faced banshee" Herb Fitz had described her to be, either. She wasn't the pouty little five-year-old she pretended to be when she was upset, nor was she the beaming, affectionate angel she pretended to be when she got her way. She was a complicated mix of all of these versions of herself. She'd look at me with a tender, loving smile one minute, then fart on my lap the next. She'd tell me how much she loved having such a nice guy in her life on Monday, then call me a pussy when I didn't yell at the Kwickfiks cashier for getting my order wrong on Tuesday. She'd jump up and down and giggle with the innocence of a Care Bear when she'd get to pet a bunny, then flip off another driver and call them a "fuck-tard" on the way home. I began to question whether the whole truly was greater than the sum of her parts, or if I really only liked certain parts of her. And if the latter were true, would it be worth dealing with the parts I didn't like in order to enjoy those I did?

The time commitment to my first professional production was a bear; four to six hours per day at rehearsals, one to two hours per day with Anthony, my personal dance instructor, and another hour or two at night studying my lines for the next day. So, time with my girlfriend was limited, and when we did get to hang out, we were constantly at odds about how to spend that time. When I wanted to relax after a marathon session at the studio, she wanted to get out of the house and go for a hike; when I wanted to go see *Shakespeare in Love*, she wanted to watch the Celtics game; when Mom and Ray wanted me to invite her over for dinner, she wanted to go to Red Lobster, just me and her. Three months into our relationship, Beth and I were still trying to get in sync, and it seemed like every single day we became locked in a polite game of tug-of-war. I would always cave, though, because I felt wicked bad about being gone so much — and because I didn't want her to be upset.

Beth had a way about her when she got angry, sad, or disappointed. Her eyebrows would descend, her chin would lower, her bottom lip would slide out into a cute little pout—her face would almost shrink—her arms would fold, and she'd avoid eye contact. If it was something really important to her, like a big sale at Olympia Sports on a pair of Air Jordans, sometimes she'd squirt a tear or two. It was the most dejected, child-like look I had ever seen on a seventeen-year-old, and I learned early on that all I had to do to erase that face was say yes to whatever she wanted. And that harmless three-letter word would transform that gloomy scowl into the sunny smile I said I loved, then she'd throw her arms around me and kiss me on the cheek, and everything would be okay.

The closer we got to opening night, though, the tougher it was finding time to spend with her. We were rehearsing six days a week, sometimes up to ten hours a day, finalizing the music and tech, the choreography, the blocking, and anything else that needed fine tuning before we went live. Beth didn't get it.

"It's a two-hour play," she said as we sat cuddled up on her parents' couch on an overcast Sunday afternoon, my first day off in over a week. "How can it take, like, fifty hours a week to make a two-hour play?"

"There's a lot that goes into it," I tried to explain. "It's not a high school play; this is a full-time job."

"But you memorized your lines, like, two months ago. What the hell takes so long?"

I smirked and shook my head. "It's not just about memorizing lines, Beth. That's a small percentage of what this is. There's dancing, singing, set, sound, all kinds of stuff that needs to be perfected. We're not just reading lines for ten hours every day."

"Sounds super gay, man," she said. Then, when I didn't say anything back, she looked at me and caught me glaring at her. She knew I hated when people used "gay" that way.

"Sorry. Forgot."

I decided I would try to shrug it off, so I put my arm around her and said, "You'll see when you come to the show how much work we put in. I'll get you and your family front-row seats so I can see you and give you a wink whenever I'm at center stage."

She gave me a half-smile and a kiss, then put her head down on my chest.

"I just want to be together, that's all."

"I know," I said. "It'll be over soon."

***

December 2003

Mrs. Forrester was right—the competition from the nine other schools at Pinkerton Academy that weekend *was* wicked fierce. I never thought I'd get to shake hands with a Hamlet reincarnate or learn about gambling and sports writing from THE Oscar Madison. Lesser thespians might've been intimidated, but to our delight, Mr. and Mrs. Loman materialized, on cue and bright as the Sirius star, and the boys and girls from Rockingham knocked it out of the proverbial park.

The standing ovation we got that morning under the luminous Stockbridge Theatre lights was humbling in that it wasn't just obligatorily heaped on us by loved ones. It was a friendly competition, but even so, any positive feedback—especially that of emulous teenagers from rival schools—was earned. We were third in line on Saturday—Day 1 of the two-day event—so we were able to get our show out of the way early and then just relax. But as well as we'd done, we wouldn't find out which school won the whole thing—or if any of us had won NHRTs (New Hampshire Regional Tony awards)—until the end of the day on Sunday. Mrs. Forrester was a member of the awards committee, but she wasn't allowed to say anything.

But Kaylin, a three-time NHRT winner, said our respected mentor had a bit of a tell.

"If she goes up to you and starts scratching the back of her hand like she's nervous, can't look you in the eye, and says all casual, 'D'you think you could get there a little early for the ceremony?' that means she wants you to get a good seat up front because you're getting an award," she said to a group of us during our post-performance lunch.

I told myself not to worry about it—I didn't join Drama Club for awards. I did it to try something new, to kill time until baseball season, and to get away from Ray. But it had turned out to be such a rewarding experience of making friends, discovering new things about myself, and even getting my first girlfriend, that I didn't need a certificate to tell me I was good.

But damn it, I wanted one.

Seeing all the talented kids from other schools in their element and working their magic, then getting a standing ovation from those very people, I'd enjoyed bathing in this Caribbean-like warmth of shared adulation. It was a special feeling of acceptance and love I hadn't found anywhere else. At the same time, I felt I belonged among their elite. I wanted a piece of paper with my name and the word "Excellence" printed above it. To be an outlier among these awesome people whom I now considered my peers would be nothing less than an insult after all I'd accomplished this semester. Right?

"Hey Mickey?"

I shook myself from the cross-eyed daze I'd slipped into, and I looked up. It was Danica.

"What's up?" I said. My eyeballs shifted back into focus.

She took a deep breath. "I think we need to talk."

My heart forgot it was a heart for about two seconds and decided to stop beating. I still didn't know much about relationships, but if Hollywood had taught me anything, it was that when a conversation starts with "I think we need to talk," it's never something small, and it's never something good.

"Uhh, sure," I said. Danica and I had kept a polite distance from each other since The Night She Didn't Say It Back. We awkwardly held hands for a few minutes the day after—our cold, clammy fingertips barely clinging to each other—but it no longer felt right. After that, we stopped sitting next to each other during rehearsals; when I wasn't onstage, I would sit toward the front of the auditorium observing my castmates at work, much less of a goofball than I'd been throughout the season, while Danica sat toward the back, quietly working on her homework or reading a book. It was as "over" as it could get—we just hadn't said it yet.

"So, I know we haven't talked much since—you know."

You mean since you tore my heart to shreds? Yeah, I DO know, I thought. But I didn't say it; I just shrugged and started chewing the inside of my cheek.

"I'm sorry I didn't give you the reaction you wanted," she said. "I just think—maybe we went a little too fast."

The right side of my face scrunched up. I always thought "too fast" meant sex on the first date or a Vegas wedding on a whim. But we hadn't had sex, and we weren't heading to Vegas, so I didn't think her phrasing applied here.

"What does that mean?"

She thought for a moment about how she wanted to word it.

"When you said you loved me, it freaked me out. I don't think you even know what love is; I don't, so how could you?"

She stared at me with those icy blue eyes and that upturned little nose, waiting for me to respond. But all I could think of in that moment was how gentle and patient she'd been with me when she taught me how to kiss, how adorable she'd looked in her little pink kitty costume on Halloween, and how she had to stand up on her tippy toes whenever she hugged me. I started looking around at the hard white bricks in the lunchroom walls as my own eyes began to water. I couldn't look right at her, and seeing all the kids in the cafeteria laughing and flirting with each other was even harder to stomach. But I finally spoke.

"I do know," I insisted, my voice cracking. "When I said it, I meant it."

"But you never even had a girlfriend before me," she fired back, as if it were a big red button on a control panel she couldn't wait to push. "And we've only been dating a couple months."

It all started to sound just like it had in our last conversation, but it didn't sting any less, and I didn't want to hear it again.

"I wouldn't have said it if I didn't feel it." I surprised myself with how urgent and desperate that sounded. Now was the time in the RomCom, just when it felt like it was all going to slip away, when Billy Crystal or Tom Cruise or Robin Williams or even fucking Adam Sandler would say something profound about love and what his female co-star meant to him to convince her to stay. And she always stayed. So, here was my last-ditch effort:

"Love isn't something you learn about in class or from a book. It's not something you can pinpoint on a map or solve with a math equation. It's not about whether you've been together for three months or thirty years, and it's not about whether you've had sex. Love is a feeling—the most amazing feeling I've ever felt. That's it. I felt it with you,

Dani, and I knew it when I felt it."

"Well—" Her bottom lip started to shake, and the rest of her body quickly followed suit. She began to tremble. Her face got pink. Then tears began to run down her cheeks as she blurted, "I didn't feel that, Mickey. I'm sorry."

She followed with the most gut-ripping sentence my young ears had heard yet.

"I think we should break up."

My heart forgot it was a heart again. This time, it stopped beating for four seconds, then six, then eight, then it sunk into my stomach and did a somersault. I'd known this was coming since The Night She Didn't Say It Back —but actually hearing those six words enter the atmosphere crushed every bone in my body. My chest felt heavy, but at the same time, empty. My legs were weak, like I'd been walking through the desert for thirty-seven hours. I couldn't get my hands to stop quivering. It was a weird feeling to have known this was coming but to have been blindsided by it all the same.

As Danica cried, I pulled her close, put her cheek against my chest, and wrapped my arms around her one last time. It was partly because I could tell this had been hard for her, and partly because I didn't want her to see me sobbing.

"It's okay," I whispered to her as I looked around the cafeteria. Hundreds of drama enthusiasts from ten different schools were looking at us and watching some *real* drama unfold. Maybe now they would all stop looking so fucking happy. "Thank you for telling me."

"I'm sorry." Her face was firmly pressed into my black Nike hoodie. "I didn't want to hurt you."

But she *did* hurt me. She hurt me more than I'd ever been hurt before. Danica was the first girl who ever smiled at me. The first girl who ever gave me butterflies. The first girl who ever held my hand. The first girl who ever kissed me. The first girl I ever thought I loved. And now, as she exhaled, shuffled away from me, and wiped the tears from beneath those big, sleepy-looking eyelids, she was the first girl who ever broke up with me.

I sat back down at the lunch table, and I could feel people gawking at me, wondering what I would do next. But I had no idea. My brain clicked and clacked like a hard drive that already had too much data to process and now had to deal with some crazy new virus. I couldn't figure out what I'd done wrong. I'd said all the sweet things they say in the movies, done all the nice things they do on TV, and told Danica that I loved her. And in spite of all that—or maybe, *because* of all that?—she dumped me anyway. I didn't get it.

I wished I had someone to talk to about all this, someone who could teach me a little more about women, relationships, even sex, so I wouldn't have to discover through trial and error what happened in those mundane moments between big, romantic scenes or after the credits rolled. Like what did Harry and Sally talk about on a random Tuesday two weeks after New Year's Eve? What was Sam and Annie's first fight about after they met atop the Empire State Building? How did Forrest deal with it after Jenny ditched him in D.C. to go to San Francisco? These were the kinds of things I needed answers to. But all I had was Raymond, and the last time I'd tried to share something big with him after the state championship, he showed me that his authority was more important than anything I had going on. So, he wasn't going to help me figure this stuff out. I'd have to do it on my own.

Maybe next time I got a girlfriend, I wouldn't come on

so strong. Or maybe come on stronger? No—next time I would let *her* tell me what I should do, let *her* tell me what she wanted, let *her* point me in the right direction. Maybe then I wouldn't get my heart broken. *Happy wife, happy life* was a thing I'd heard somewhere. Yeah, maybe next time I'd try that.

Next time.

I sat alone at that lunch table, navigating this maze of emotional confusion, long after the cafeteria had cleared out and the afternoon's series of plays had begun. I started wondering what the future may bring and daydreaming of kisses and snuggles and giggles with a woman who didn't have a face when I was startled back into reality by a slight tap on the shoulder.

Was it Danica? Had she changed her mind and come to tell me she loved me after all? Did she feel bad for making me cry and wanted to give it another shot? Were the long, lonely decades of darkness I was inevitably facing about to become a lifetime of laughter, love, and companionship instead?

It was Mrs. Forrester. She was scratching the back of her hand like she was nervous, and she was having a hard time looking me in the eye.

"Hey, Mick," she said all casual. "D'you think you could get there a little early for the awards ceremony tomorrow?"

11

I had never dumped anyone before. I'd been on the receiving end of a dumping exactly once, so that was the only first-hand experience I had to go by. How did that one go? Oh, yes, she avoided me for three weeks while she built up enough courage to do the dirty deed and then laid it on me in the cafeteria with eyes prying from every direction. Avoiding Beth for weeks, or even days, would be impossible; we'd become so co-mingled in each other's lives in just three months that if I went a day without seeing her, we'd be on the phone or on Instant Messenger for at least an hour that night. So, to suddenly "ghost" her (before that was a term people used) would be suspicious. I'd have to be more subtle about it.

I began my strategic withdrawal in the days following her "gay" comment. I started by dialing down my enthusiasm and affection. My laughs weren't as loud and my hugs weren't as tight. She didn't seem to notice for the first couple of days, probably because she was busy preparing for her graduation. But during her graduation party that Saturday, when I was sitting on her parents' back deck drinking a lemonade by myself instead of bouncing around from group to group making dorky jokes, she finally came up to me and asked, "What's wrong?"

"Nothing—why?"

She sat down next to me. It was warm and peaceful out on the deck, and the sky was clear and full of stars. The sound of crickets chirping nicely complemented the chatter and the hip-hop music rattling around inside the house.

"You sure, man? You've been weird this week."

I guess she had noticed.

"I have?"

"Yeah." She scooted closer to me and hooked my arm with hers. "Are you okay?"

"Of course." I sat up straight, looked her in the eye and said, with fake enthusiasm, "I'm good!"

I pulled her head toward me and kissed her on that freckle in the middle of her forehead I thought was so cute. It was important to act as normal as I could so she wouldn't suspect anything. But in the same way I had gotten to know the real Bethany Connelly over the past several months, she'd gotten to know the real Mickey Patrick.

"No, you're not." She tilted her head to the side and raised an eyebrow. "What's wrong?"

I flashed a cheesy, fake smile and said, "Hey—what's the difference between a bounced check and an angry jackrabbit?"

"Mickey! Stop!" She wasn't going to let me off the hook. "Are you gonna tell me what's going on? I'm supposed to just, like, pretend you're normal? I'm not stupid, man."

"I know." I broke eye contact and focused on the oversized spatula and meat thermometer on the grill table across the deck. Life was so much easier for inanimate objects. My right heel began bouncing up and down as it does when it's bursting with nervous energy.

"Then what?" She leaned closer to me with concern in her eyes, as if she'd begun to realize what I might be thinking. It wasn't the right time, though. Not during her graduation party. Not with all her friends and family around.

But she insisted.

"Tell me."

"Bethany, I just—"

"Beth," she interrupted. I wasn't going to miss *that* shit.

I took a breath and started again. "Beth, I just—I don't know if I can do this anymore."

"Do what?" she said. But when she saw my chin start to tremble, she knew what I was saying.

"Are you dumping me?"

After a long pause, I nodded. Her face reddened and her eyes welled up.

"No!" she blurted. "What did I do?"

"You didn't do anything." My voice cracked. "I just think we're two different people and we want different things."

"Is this because I called your play gay?" She was now in full-on blubbers. "I'm sorry! I didn't mean it!"

"No," I said. "I mean, yes, that did bother me, but this isn't just about that."

"Is it because we haven't had sex? I'll get on the pill right now! I just wanted to wait 'til school was over!"

"It has absolutely nothing to do with that," I said firmly. I hadn't once pressured her for sex because I never found her wicked sexy. Cute? Sure. Funny? Sometimes. Sexy? Meh.

"I'm just — I'm not sure we have a —" I thought about

how exactly I should word this. "I don't think we have a long-term future together."

"Why? Just because you're going to Boston for college and I'm staying here?" she said with garbled speech. "It's, like, an hour away, man! That's nothing!"

"No, no, it's not just that. Beth, you're a really cool person to hang out with. But with the directions our lives are going—where I want to go, where you want to go—"

"I want to stay here." She blubbered and buried her face in my armpit. "And I want you to stay with me."

She surprised me with how urgent and desperate she sounded as she embraced me with force. Her face was a radish, her eyes were clamped shut, and her mouth was cracked open and bellowing loud, desperate sobs, unable to form a coherent word.

As Beth held her body against mine, my heart forgot it was a heart, stopped beating, then sunk into my stomach and did a somersault. I'd known this reaction was coming since I decided to say it, but the thought of actually putting those six words—*I think we should break up*—into the atmosphere plastered me in a cold, shivery sweat I'd never anticipated. It was a weird feeling to have known this was coming but to have been blindsided by it all the same.

Then she hit me with, "You said you loved me."

She cried on me with those weepy jades and that cute freckle on her forehead, waiting for me to respond. All I could think of in that moment was how eager and anxious she'd been when I taught her how to kiss, how adorable she'd looked with the French braid draped over her shoulder at the basketball game, and how she mesmerized me with that bright, off-center smile packed with flashy white teeth whenever I gave her what she wanted. I started looking up at the soft, white clouds in the early evening sky as my own eyes began to water. I couldn't look directly at her, and seeing all the kids inside at the party laughing and flirting with each other was even harder to stomach. But I finally spoke.

"I do love you." Then, as I broke into full-on blubbers myself, I hugged her as hard as I physically could and repeated myself. "I do love you, Beth. I'm sorry. I'm being so stupid."

Maybe it was true this time. Maybe I did love her. Maybe the time we had spent together over the past three months in between basketball games and *Footloose* rehearsals and kissing practice and polite tugs-of-war had meant more to me than I'd thought. I guess I didn't really know because I'd been so busy with the show since we started dating that I never really gave her a fair shot. So, if I could just stick it out through opening weekend, I'd be able to commit the time and energy to this that Beth deserved.

We sat and cried together for a few minutes, holding each other close, quietly reflecting on the break-up that almost was. She rubbed the back of my head with her little string beans, then broke the silence with the inevitable question: "Does this mean you'll stay?"

I began chewing the inside of my cheek the way I do when I want to say something but can't.

"Yeah, I'll stay," I said in a huffy voice before sealing it with a kiss on her cheek. I was disappointed in myself that I couldn't go through with it but satisfied that I'd at least broached the conversation. It would prepare me for the next difficult conversation we would need to have. Now we could at least enjoy the summer together before I'd have to tell her I was going to NYU in the fall instead of Boston

University. And Beth probably looked decent in a bikini.

We stood up, wiped the tears from our eyes, gave each other a gentle kiss, and joined hands to walk back inside. Turns out the party was just getting started.

* * *

I got home around 10:30 that night, still drifting through a fog of uncertainty as I opened the door. I could hear the feint sound of *Roseanne* reruns coming from the living room; as the door clicked closed behind me, whatever Roseanne and Dan were bickering about was muted, and the only sound I could hear was Ray clearing his throat. He did that whenever he was about to say something he thought was important.

"Hi, Dad," I said cautiously, even though I had nothing to be cautious about. I was eighteen now and my curfew was 11 p.m.

"How are you?" That's what he would always say after clearing his throat. It meant he didn't care how I was; he had something to say.

"I'm okay. It was a nice little party."

"Good," he said with artificial enthusiasm. "Check the messages. There's one on there for you."

I walked into the kitchen and, sure enough, a digital "1" was blinking on our grungy old AT&T answering machine. Curious, I pushed the blue button.

The voice was familiar but a bit muffled by some light sniffles and feint weeping. But as soon as I heard "Mickey-Mack," followed by a tiny, sad-sounding giggle, I knew it was Luci.

"I'm sorry, I don't know who else to talk to. I just broke

up with Darius. He's been cheating on me with Danica. Can you call me?"

I looked at Ray as the machine beeped; he usually didn't like anyone on the phone past 8 or, at the latest, 9.

But this time, he nodded and said, "Go ahead, call her."

12

There was no reason to tell Beth about my phone call with Luci. Luci and I were just friends, and there was nothing flirty or filthy about the phone call. She'd discovered at her own graduation party that night that Darius, her boyfriend of three years, had been cheating on her for months with Danica, her best friend since kindergarten. Her brother was away at football camp, and her mother was on a date or something, so she called me. Besides, Luci had been there for me after my first breakup, so I owed her one. Beth didn't need to know that I stayed on the phone with this friend—who just happened to be a girl—until midnight the same night we almost broke up. The timing alone could be seen as incriminating to someone with Beth's fragile self-esteem, even though I knew it was totally innocent. It was just two pals catching up, making each other laugh until we couldn't breathe, and singing Mariah Carey songs in unison.

Things got better following the aborted breakup. Beth became more attentive, more flexible, more understanding of my time commitment to the show, and more support-ive. I began to accept that maybe I did love this girl, and all the little things that I'd seen Billy Crystal do or Tom Cruise do or Robin Williams do or even fucking Adam Sandler do—the deep gazes into her eyes, the gentle strokes of her cheek, the kisses on her knuckles, the passionate embraces—all started coming more naturally. I started looking forward to seeing her again, and I began saying yes to the things that she wanted with less debate, not just because I didn't want her to be upset, but because I really did want her to be happy. She started giggling at my silly jokes more often, and sometimes she would even ask about my day before she started ranting about hers. We were saying "I love you" to each other all day, every day, and not just when we said goodbye or goodnight. Finally, three months in, it felt like we were falling in sync. Maybe it took nearly ending our relationship for it to truly begin.

We had sex for the first time the afternoon before Opening Night. We told her parents we were going to Red Lobster for a celebratory lunch (and we did, so it wasn't a lie), but we didn't tell them that we were getting it to go so we could bring it back to my parents' house because nobody was home. We were on the big, bulky couch in the living room because it was much more comfortable than the creaky old twin bed I'd slept on since I was nine. It was Bethany's first time, and it was my first time since my first time. Neither of us really knew what we were doing, and I was worried about hurting her the whole time, but the look on Beth's face, though wide-eyed and cautious, told me she trusted me. Five minutes later, we were smiling nervously and munching on Cheddar Bay biscuits in our underwear.

"Are you okay?" I'd heard somewhere that sex could sting for girls the first time. I was sitting on the couch in my boxers and black T-shirt, and she was on the floor in her canary tank top and purple panties with her legs crisscrossed under the coffee table.

"Yeah, I'm okay," she said as she stared at her food. She didn't seem as happy as I thought someone who'd just had sex would seem.

"What's wrong? I didn't hurt you, did I?"

"No, not really—I mean, not bad," she said. "I was just thinking."

"About what?"

She glanced at me for a moment, then looked back down. "You said you've done this before, right?"

"Yeah, only once. Two years ago."

"Well—" she paused. "Now that we've done it, can you tell me more about it?"

I gave her a weird look. "I never said I wouldn't tell you, but sure. What do you want to know?"

"Like, what's her name? What did she look like? How did you meet her? Where did you do it?"

"Her name was Kaylin. I knew her from Drama Club in high school. She was a couple years older than me, and she came to see our play during regionals at Pinkerton Academy my junior year."

"She was *older*?" Beth's face popped in terror. "Fuck, Mickey!"

"What difference does that make?" I was genuinely confused.

"So, you go from banging a hot older girl to stupid me," she said. "I probably looked like a fuck-tard to you."

"Stop it. You're not stupid, and she wasn't hot. And you're not a fuck-tard. Don't say that."

"What did she look like, anyway?"

"She was—average. Short. Brunette. Kinky hair. Wicked big butt. Kind of a gross face."

"If she was so ugly, then why did you fuck her?" she said, half playfully, half sincerely. To my relief, my description of Kaylin made Beth a little less defensive.

"Why do you think?" I said, teasing myself. "I was sixteen and I'd never had sex before. I would've banged anyone!"

She paused, then smiled at me. She was coming around. "You horny little shit," she said. "Where did you do it, in her car?"

"Worse. It was on the floor of a handicapped bathroom. Not wicked romantic."

"Ew. Gross, man." She got up on the couch and nestled up to me. "Sorry, I just wanted this to mean as much to you as it did to me."

I pulled her head onto my chest and said, "It does, trust me. I loved it, and I love you. Besides, I never even talked to her again after that."

"Good," she said with a sweet little smile as she lifted her face up to mine and kissed me. "I love you too."

13

can't decide what's more fascinating—how your life can alter course in ways you never anticipated in the blink of an eye, or how lies and secrets can catch up to you the moment you let your guard down. If I hadn't played baseball, I wouldn't have become friends with Torey. If I hadn't made friends with Torey, I wouldn't have talked to Luci. If I hadn't talked to Luci, I never would have joined Drama Club. If I'd never joined Drama Club, I wouldn't be starring in *Footloose* at Silverman Theater on opening weekend, hustling with hope and conviction toward my dream of being a Broadway star—or maybe, with a little luck, a movie star.

And if Beth had gone to the show on Friday instead of Saturday, maybe I'd have kept pursuing that dream.

Opening Night went off brilliantly. The music and dance numbers were electric, our timing and blocking on point, and performing in this chic, modern auditorium packed with living, breathing humans fueled me with energy and pride. Mom was there in the front row, trying not to get caught snapping photos for the scrapbook; Raymond was there, applauding with a rare smile on his face; Mason was there making exaggerated Arsenio Hall-type whoops;

121

and Luci was there wearing a gray cardigan and a black undershirt sitting next to a chunky redneck-looking dude who couldn't have looked more bored. Beth wasn't there because she had plans to see *Superbad* with her friend Meg and Meg's brother Brad, but she came the next night with roses, a cute floral dress, and that flashy off-center smile I loved.

"Oh my god, Mick-a-Roni, that was sooooo good!" she said as she threw her arms around me and kissed my neck during the friends-and-family cast party after the show. "So proud of you, man!"

I smiled ear-to-ear and squeezed her. "Thanks, Bethy Bear. I'm glad you came."

"That was really good," said Brie. She was there with her dumb little skateboarder boyfriend, Preston, who gave me a fist bump and said, "Nice, man. Nice."

"Yeah, man, I didn't know you were so talented," Beth said.

"Well—" I shrugged, trying to stay humble. "They don't give the lead to just anyone."

"Not unless you're the great Mickey Patrick," I heard a familiar voice say. I turned around to see a tall, strikingly gorgeous blond girl—scratch that, blond *woman* now—with bright blue eyes, red lipstick, hair down to the small of her back, and the body of a supermodel.

"Oh my god, hi!" I said as I gave her a big hug. "It's great to see you! What are you doing here?"

"When you told me you were in *Footloose*, I had to come see this," she said. "This is one of my favorite shows—I knew you'd be perfect in it!"

"Thanks, that means a lot!" I said with a big grin. "Especially coming from the 'next Nicole Kidman'."

"Oh, stoppit." She tittered at my reference to an article from our old high school's newspaper, *The Hard Rock Life*, which was notorious for sensationalizing its students' successes (their sports editor once referred to me in an article as the 'next Pedro Martinez,' so it was obvious horseshit).

After a moment, I realized Beth and Brie were still there, giving each other looks and trying to figure out who the hell I was talking to.

"Oh, Bethany, this is—"

"It's Beth," she said.

"Sorry—Beth, this is Kaylin. Kaylin, this is my girlfriend, Beth, her sister Brianna—"

"It's Brie," Brie said. *Jeez, these girls and their names.*

"Sorry—Brie, and that's Preston."

"'Sup, girl?" Preston said, practically salivating over Kaylin.

Beth gave me a look. It started as confused but quickly morphed into pissed off.

"Wait—*this* is Kaylin?" she said.

My stomach flipped when I remembered how I'd described Kaylin to Beth the previous day during our post-coital conversation. She definitely wasn't short. Or brunette with kinky hair. And she definitely did not have a big butt or a gross face.

Beth shook Kaylin's hand apprehensively, her insecurities pulsating through her forehead. "Nice to meet you. Mickey didn't tell me how pretty you are."

"Aw, thanks—it's nice to meet you. Mick's a great guy," Kaylin said. Then she looked back at me and said, "I also wanted to introduce you to Isaac here. He's the head of the theater program at NYU. He wanted to come along and see the show, too."

Isaac was a well-dressed young-ish British chap wearing a navy-blue sport coat, perfectly pressed khaki slacks, and an expensive-looking gold Rolex.

"Wonderful to meet you, Mister Patrick—brilliant performance—Kaylin's told me wonderful things," he said as he shook my hand with vigor. "We'll certainly be blessed to have you come fall."

"I, uh—" That's when I knew I was busted. My only hope was that Beth wouldn't put it together until we got out of the theater. "Thanks."

No such luck. When I'd told Beth that she wasn't stupid, I'd meant it. And that lack of stupidity was about to bite.

"Come fall?" she said with a sneer. "Wait, you said NYU? Like, New York?"

"Yes. New York University," Isaac said, perplexed. "Your boyfriend here is joining us on scholarship come fall semester. Hasn't he told you?"

"Michael…" Beth looked at me with a new shade of vibrant fury. Her cheeks got red as fresh beets, her eyebrows descended, and her brow ridge protruded from above her eyes. A vein I'd never noticed popped to the surface of her temple, her chin lowered, and her bottom lip, instead of sliding out into a cute little pout, stiffened as she gritted her teeth and growled, "What. The fuck. Is going. On?"

The fearful pit that formed in my stomach was suddenly worse than anything I'd ever experienced on stage or on the pitchers' mound. It rivaled the feeling I got when Ray-Hole peered at me through his wispy eyebrows and with craggy teeth. My frazzled brain searched frantically for the right response while my eyes popped out of my face and my jaw hung helplessly on its hinges.

"Oh," Isaac said, realizing he'd let the cat out of the

bag. He put his hand on Kaylin's back and said, "Shall we?"

"Okay," Kaylin said as her pupils dilated and they skulked away. "Bye, Mickey. It was nice to see you."

"You too. Bye," I said, trying to hide my embarrassment. Beth and Brie were both staring at me with daggers. Preston was staring at Kaylin's ass.

"I'm going to go, too," Brie said. "You still want to ride home with him?"

"Yep," Beth said, maintaining fierce eye contact with me. "I think we need to talk."

14

The bus ride back to school from Pinkerton that night felt like it took ninety-seven years; it was probably only about thirty-five minutes. Normally I'd be bouncing from seat to seat, goofing off and acting like a tool for my own personal entertainment; this time, I stayed slouched in my own seat blasting Manson and Five Finger Death Punch into my headphones. Nobody checked on me or asked how I was doing, but anyone who'd seen the water works in the cafeteria already knew. Danica and Luci were a few seats in front of me, so I tried not to look in that direction. But every once in a while, I caught one or both of them looking at me and then resuming their wicked-secret conversation. *Gee,* I thought to myself, *I wonder what they're talking about.*

When we got back to the school, I jumped off the bus and didn't say goodbye to anyone. I just wanted to speed-walk home, tuck myself away in my bedroom, and do my algebra homework. Because algebra was easier for my brain to process. Algebra had distinct answers, and even if I got those answers wrong, at least my heart wouldn't get hurt.

My heart couldn't take anymore hurt after a day like this.

I could hear Ray yelling at my mom like an asshole as soon as I got within a hundred yards of my house. I couldn't make out the words yet, but I knew what it was about.

I'd missed my curfew again. It was 9:30 this time. And I hadn't called.

I slowed my pointy-elbowed speed-walk to a shoe-shuffling meander as I approached the house. When I got to the end of our pebble stone driveway, I could decipher the words "goddamn son of yours" before I stopped, tilted my head back, rolled my eyes, and took a deep breath.

I thought about how Danica had hurt me at lunchtime that day. I thought about how defeated I felt. How helpless. It reminded me of all those times Raymond had made me feel defeated and helpless. All those times I wanted to say something and couldn't, all those times I had just accepted what he said to me—what he ordered of me—because I didn't have the balls to stand up to him.

Show me what you were doing on the playground came bursting through the memory banks. That was the day he used his big voice to intimidate seven-year-old me and then a tree branch to beat me into submission.

You don't want to eat your cauliflower? Fine, spend the night in your fucking room. That was the day he clenched my ten-year-old arm from across the dinner table, dragged me through the house, and shoved me to my bedroom floor. I could still hear the sounds of the tendons in my shoulder popping.

Did you get your homework done? That was what he asked me the night we won states to remind me that my accomplishments—hell, my life—was secondary to the arbitrary contents of Ray's Rulebook.

Not today, Ray, I thought to myself. My life mattered. I was allowed to be heard, not just seen. I wasn't afraid of his big voice. His big muscles. I'd been awaiting this show-down—awaiting the right reason, the right moment. This felt like it.

I lowered my head and started marching toward the door with purpose. He wasn't going to intimidate me again. I wasn't scared of him anymore. *I'm going to walk through that door, brush off the shit he's going to throw at me, and throw it right b—*

"WHERE THE HELL HAVE YOU BEEN?"

He must have seen me coming. He'd blasted the front door open and pounced out onto the walkway, and he was storming at me like an enraged bull. And just like that, I was off my game.

"It is nine thirty. NINE THIRTY!" he snorted. "What is your curfew?"

"Eight o--"

"EIGHT O'CLOCK. And what are you supposed to do if you're going to be late?"

"Call—"

"CALL."

He took a moment to glare at me through his wispy eyebrows. Maybe he was giving it a moment to let his point sink in, or maybe he was waiting for me to give him some-thing else to interrupt. I was shaken, but either way, I just stared back at him, trying to show him he wasn't going to intimidate me just by looking at me and yelling in my face. His yellow teeth were looking especially craggy on this frigid winter night.

"Sorry," I said, not even trying to make it sound sincere.

"Yeah, you're sorry I bet." He knew I didn't mean it. If there was one thing that made an angry Ray-Hole angrier, it was sarcasm in the face of his authoritarian wrath. "We'll see how sorry you are in a month. You're grounded."

I had only been grounded once before, when I missed curfew because of baseball, and it was only for a week. But the timing of this particular grounding wasn't a big deal—baseball didn't start for a couple of months anyway.

"Okay," I said, accepting my fate. Until, that is, he said, "Tomorrow you can go with me to get wood for the garage."

Ray loved to tinker away in the garage. He loved working on his old '82 BMW (said it was an E30, 325-something, whatever that meant), he loved fixing things that didn't need to be fixed (he renovated and re-renovated the interior of his stupid garage about four times in six years), and he loved chopping wood for the little wood stove in the corner (it gave him time to "clear his head," he'd say). He would ask Mason and me for help sometimes, not necessarily because he needed it, but because to him it was some kind of bonding or whatever, even though we never talked about anything, and he answered all of our questions with "because that's just how it's done" or "that's just the way it is." But I hated helping him with that kind of stuff, and he knew it. So, he was going to use it as a punishment.

Normally, I would have just chewed the inside of my cheek and suffered through it, but this weekend was different.

"We have the awards ceremony at Pinkerton tomorrow," I said in meek protest.

"And?"

"And . . . I might be getting an award."

Ray stared at me, nostrils still flaring. I assumed he was working out a compromise. I was wrong.

"What makes you think you're getting an award?"

I didn't want to explain it to him.

"Mrs. Forrester just—said I should be there."

"I DON'T GIVE A SHIT WHAT 'MRS. FORREST-ER' SAID." He said "Mrs. Forrester" with such an acerbic tinge, as if she were as inconsequential to him as a crippled dust mite. He was wicked close to my face now; I could almost taste the cigarettes on his breath. "Have one of your friends bring it home for you."

That wasn't happening. I was going to that awards ceremony. A hard bubble of pain, fear, and repressed rage rose to the bottom of my throat. *Just a little bit further*, I thought to myself. *You can do this.*

Just then I noticed my shoulders, neck, and head had all been leaning backwards as this son of a bitch screamed in my face. It was probably a familiar sight to Ray-Hole. He worked hard to keep us all leaning away from him, off balance, and under his control, the way he wanted it.

Not today, Ray.

I straightened up my shoulders, and my neck and head followed. Then, I cleared my throat the way he always did when was about to say something he thought was important, and said, with as much authority as my post-pubescent teenage vocal chords could muster:

"No."

I couldn't believe what I had just done; it was the first time I'd ever stood up to him. I wanted to smile, but now wasn't the time. I knew, in that instant, that single, one-syllable word was about to change everything.

Ray stepped closer to me. Our foreheads were almost

touching. If I were in clown-mode, I would've kissed him right on the tip of the nose, just to break the tension. But this was a big moment—had to stay serious. My heart was pounding like a piston.

As powerful as the moment felt, a moment atop a pedestal of courage I'd been sculpting and building from deep down in my intestines since The Day of the Broken Tree Branch, it took Raymond mere seconds to demolish it. This wasn't his first showdown.

"You wanna think about what you're doing?" he said, taking the sharpness and volume out of his voice in a way he'd never done before. He continued to glare, but his voice sounded calm, controlled, and calculated.

He'd been waiting for this, too.

"I'm going to the awards ceremony." I wasn't asking his permission. "You can ground me all you want, but I'm going."

He chuckled. "You think you're just getting grounded if you leave this house tomorrow? You think I'm just going to tell you to go to your room and do your homework?"

I winced as I tried to discern his curious rhetoric; he clarified it for me pretty quickly.

"If you step one foot outside this door tomorrow," he said, "you will find everything you own—all your clothes, all your books, your toothbrush, your deodorant, your shoes—out on the front lawn. The locks will be changed, the alarms will be set, and you will not be welcome back in this house. You can take your little award, and take all your stuff, and find a new place to live. Maybe 'Mrs. Forrester' can help you with that."

I was fifteen years old. I'd spent my entire life watching *He-Man* and *Power Rangers*, studying History, Math, Science, and English, then playing baseball and joining Drama Club. I was naïve. I didn't know if he would actually go through with it, or even if he could (I knew nothing about child abandonment laws or CPS or empty threats), but I knew I couldn't afford to find out. And I knew I couldn't survive on my own.

My shoulders sank back down and the ice in my veins became puddles in my eyes, and Ray knew he'd won.

"That's right. You wanna take me on, boss? Learn how the world works, have a game plan, and come at me like a man, not like some fifteen-year-old shitbag who wants to prove you've got hair on your nuts."

I turned to walk away, tripped over a sprinkler head that was sticking out of the frozen ground, and stumbled into a muddy snowbank. It was the perfect way to punctuate this horrible, humiliating day. I picked myself up off the ground, wiped the grime off my jacket and pants, and trudged inside with dried boogers clinging to my nose hairs. Your nose produces a lot of snot when you've been crying all day.

***

An hour later, having finished blubbering and screaming my sorrows into my pillow, I was staring at the ceiling in my bedroom, reflecting on what had been the worst day of my life. There was a knock on the door.

"Yeah?" I said. Raymond let himself in and stood at the corner of my bed.

"Listen. Your mom thinks you should go get your award tomorrow."

I started to get excited, but I didn't want to show it.

"So, we're going to drive you over there so you can get it, and then you'll come home with us."

Oh.

"Thank you," I said, trying to sound grateful, even though this arrangement wasn't at all what I wanted. I wanted to be with my friends. I wanted to celebrate with them afterward. I wanted to ride the bus, goof off, and listen to my music—not sit quietly in the back seat of my parents' car listening to NPR and traveling 10 mph below the speed limit.

"You're welcome," he said, as if he were doing me some monumental favor. "But when we get home—you're mine."

Two days later, I was grounded for a month.

15

Clop-clop, clop-clop,
Clop-clop, clop-clop

The sound of Beth's high heels striking the pavement was all I heard as we walked to my car for what was about to be our first big fight. My heart was racing, my forehead slick with sweat, and I couldn't look anywhere but at the ground five feet in front of me. Whatever was about to happen, I deserved it.

Timidly, I put the roses she'd brought for me in the back seat, then I got in the driver's seat, closed the door, and looked out the windshield at nothing. She slammed the door, threw her jacket in the back seat on top of the bouquet (probably on purpose), then cranked her furious face toward me and said, "So, when were you gonna tell me about New York?"

I tried to soften it with another lie. "It's not for sure yet."

She knew I was full of shit. "It sure as fuck *sounded* like it's 'for sure,' man. Got a scholarship all lined up? People coming all the way up here to see you? Crocodile Dundee sayin' 'Aw we'll be glad to have ya come fall, mate.' Oh yeah, that's not 'for sure' at all, man, is it?"

"He's British, not Australian," I said, as if it were the right time to correct her.

"Who cares?" she said. "How long've you been sitting on this, Michael? You're s'posed to be going to Boston, man! New York is like four hours away!"

"I hadn't figured it out yet."

"When were you going to figure it out? Were you gonna pack your car to go to Boston and then as you're pullin' out of the driveway just be like, 'Oh, by the way, I'm really going to New York City and I'll never see you again, peace out!'?"

"Of course not. I wouldn't do that."

"How do I know that? How do I know what to believe now? You've been keeping this a secret from me—who knows when you were going to tell me?"

Then, her face melted in terror. "Is this why you wanted to dump me?"

"No, no, no." This was getting out of hand quickly. "That was me being insecure and stupid. I'm glad we stayed together."

"Oh yeah, 'cause at least you got to fuck me first," she said. "Wanted to practice up before you go down to New York to bang Kaylin again—who, by the way, is a fucking supermodel. Pretty sure you said she was gross. Another big fucking lie. What else've you been lying to me about, man?"

"That was it, I swear," I said, as if being caught in "only" two enormous lies would make this any better. "I have no interest in Kaylin like that."

"Mmhmm. Oh, and you said you hadn't talked to her

since. So, she just magically knew you were in this play? And she just happened to tell her buddy about you so you could get a scholarship?"

Shit, that's three lies. I had to course correct—fast. I sat in silence for a moment to try to figure out what my next move was. At this point, there was no way I could sugar coat any of this. I had to tell her the truth. The complete truth.

"Okay, fine. I have stayed in touch with her on and off since she graduated high school. I didn't get into NYU on my own my senior year, and when I told her that, she said she had a little bit of pull and could help me if I applied again this year. That's why I didn't go to Boston last year—I wanted to see if I could try to get into New York this year with her help. And I did."

"So, you were never going to go to Boston? You were just, like, stringing me along?"

"I was only going to go there if I couldn't get into NYU," I said. "But New York is an awesome school— their theater and film program is the best in the country. Lots of wicked famous people went there and then went on to be huge Broadway and movie stars. Getting in there is a big deal."

She wiped the tears off her cheeks with both hands while staring at the glove compartment. She didn't care about any of that. She could only focus on my lies. She sniffled, then asked, as if defeated, "When did you know?"

I hesitated, sighed through my nostrils, and came clean.

"About three weeks after I met you."

"SO WHY DIDN'T YOU TELL ME?" she lashed out at me. Her sudden eruption almost made me choke on the tears that were beginning to stream across my lips.

"I—I didn't want to upset you or cause a fight," I said, my voice trembling again. "Things were going so well with us, I didn't want to ruin it."

"So, you thought hiding this big secret from me and lying about it would just make it go away?" She used her index fingers to dab the corners of her eyes. "This just fucking makes it *worse!*"

A bubble of guilt rose from my throat and the inside of my nose started to sting. "I don't know what I was thinking."

"You were trying not to ruin it by pissing me off, man—but now you ruined it by lying! I don't know if I can ever trust you again after this!"

As those horrifying words rattled around inside my brain, the magnitude of my mistake started to crunch me under an avalanche of sorrow and self-hatred. My body shook from my shoulders to my knees as I tried with all my might to wrestle back my tears. Then, it felt like a big rubber band snapped inside my chest, and I collapsed onto the steering wheel and sobbed harder than I had in years. Harder than the day Ray broke my He-Man sword on my ass. Harder than the day Gammie died. Harder than the day Danica dumped me. I cried harder in that moment, in fact, than I had in all the years since the day my father went to work and never came home. Suddenly, I was five years old again, sitting on that stiff old tweed armchair, shifting for comfort as the mushroom cloud from my mother's atomic word bomb gushed toward the ceiling.

Daddy had an accident at work, Mommy said. I don't know why, but I remember it was a sunny October morning, and I could hear leaves swishing around on the pavement outside.

What does that mean? I asked her. *What kind of accident?* To me, the word "accident" was reserved for spilling my milk or peeing my pants. So, when she told Mason and me, with a look of devastation we'd never seen on her face before, that Daddy had an "accident," we were desperate for elaboration. Mommy had never sat us down like that before, just her and us, talking like regular people. The living room had always been reserved for fun activities like playing checkers on the coffee table, watching *He-Man* on the old Zenith, or unwrapping the colorful, cartoony gifts that Santa had put under the tree.

But it was different this time. There was no black-and-red board. There was no tree, and there was nothing colorful or cartoony about this. The TV wasn't even on.

The TV was always on.

It means that, even though he cared about you both very much, Mom paused as she wiped a gallon of tears from her eyes, the first tears I'd ever seen a grown-up cry, *Daddy is gone.*

And just like that, we didn't have a Daddy anymore. It happened so suddenly that I didn't fully grasp the magnitude of those words at first. Not during his funeral. Not during the mass, nor through all the inspired tributes his fellow firefighters delivered that day. But a few days later, when *Masters of the Universe* was on TV and Daddy wasn't there to mimic He-Man's booming voice or pick me up and toss me in the air with his big, heroic He-Man muscles, that was when the truth really hit me.

Daddy was gone for good.

For good.

The bomb that Beth had just dropped on me—that she didn't know if she could trust me anymore—was nearly as crushing. With that, every insecurity I'd tried so hard to mask, all the pain I'd tried to bury, and the fear of abandonment that had clung to my insides since my childhood broke, came rushing from deep within my bones all the way through to the surface of my skin, and as I bleated like a baby, all I could say was, "I'm sorry, I'm sorry, I'm sorry, I'm sorry."

Surprised by my sudden, urgent breakdown, Beth said, "Jesus, Mickey, are you okay?" She had never seen me like this. Hell, *I* had never seen me like this. She placed her hand gently on my back; I responded by throwing my head into her lap and wrapping my arms around her waist as hard as I could.

"I'm sorry," I said, still in full-on blubber mode, my words muffled by her stomach. I was sure I was getting mucous and drool on her cute little floral dress, but there was no time to worry about that. "Please don't leave me. Please don't go. I'll do anything!"

"Hey, hey, I'm not going anywhere," she said with a startled softness in her voice as she hunched over and put her arms around my head. "I just need you to be honest with me. I need you to tell me the truth, man, every time. Can you do that?"

Without hesitation I said, "Yeah," and nodded vigorously to make sure she knew I meant it. "I'm so sorry, Bethy Bear."

"It's okay, we'll figure it out." Then she kissed me on the cheek and said, "This isn't what I expected, but we'll figure it out as long as you're honest from now on. Promise?"

I sat up in my seat, put my big ol' bear paws on each side of her face, looked into her weepy jades and said, with conviction, "I promise. I will never do this again. I'll do anything to make this better, I swear. I love you, and I don't want to lose you."

"Okay, good. I love you too, Mick-a-Roni, and I don't want to lose you either—you're mine."

Two months later, I moved into my dorm room in Boston.

16

June 2007

To my sweet Michael,

I'm writing this because, like you, I'm terrible with face-to-face confrontation. So, please hear me out, hun. This is just because I care about you so much.

I'm sorry I did not react the way you wanted me to when you told us about your decision. Boston University is of course a good school with a great program for Sports Broadcasting, if that's what you truly want to do. I'm just concerned as your mother, and as someone who loves you and knows you better than anyone, that it is not.

Watching you onstage the other night was one of the most breathtaking things I have seen in my life. Not just because I was proud of you as your mom, and not just because of your excellent performance (By the way, I kept our tickets, the program, and the pictures I took. This will be a good one for the scrapbook!). It was breathtaking because I could see an abundantly talented young man living out his dream. When you took your bow at the end of the show, I knew that the smile on your face was not the cheesy showbiz smile we've picked on you about. It was your smile—your real smile. It's a beautiful smile of pure joy and genuine happiness, and those are the smiles a mother lives for.

I'm happy that you have found love, hun, and Bethany does seem to make you happy right now. I say "right now" because I'm worried this decision is going to hurt you. Not just your future but your relationship. You have talent and passion for acting, and as much as you care about Bethany, I'd hate for you to look back in 10 years and think "What could have been?" I don't want to see you go down the same path I did because, believe me, it's a path that leads to resentment, regret, and anger. I never got over it when Raymond asked me to leave The Penguin to be a full-time mom, and he's still bitter about his first wife convincing him to sell Raybeam Technology to Microsoft. My point is, be careful what you do for love, hun.

You're almost an adult now, and I know you'll do what you feel is best. In a few months, I won't be able to see you every day, so I won't be able to decide for myself whether the smile you're showing the world is real or if it's cheese, because even though you are a wonderful actor, I can still tell the difference. My only wish for you is that the path you choose is the one that makes it real. I wish this for your sake, for Bethany's sake, and for the world's sake. Because the Mickey I know and love, the real Mickey, the one who loves and respects himself and stays true to who he is, is destined to become a warm, glowing ray of sunlight on this cold, dark, mean little planet.

All my love,
Mom

Mom,

Thank you for your kindness and advice. I had to sleep on it a few nights, or else I might've written something nasty out of defensiveness. But I know everything you wrote in your letter was from the heart, so I wanted to respond with the respect you deserve.

You're right, though; this is my decision, even if you don't agree with it.

You may think I only did this because of Beth, but that's only part of it. I do love acting, but realistically, making a living at it is almost impossible, unless you have a whole lot of luck on your side (right place, right time, right agent). Meanwhile, there are thousands of television stations across the country, so the odds of me succeeding in that field are much better.

The other thing is, I haven't really made time for Beth since we met, and going to school closer to her will finally allow me to do that. Besides, people make sacrifices every day for the people they love. I don't need to hear about regrets or paths—everything will be fine. And yes, I am happy with her.

The part of your letter that bothered me most was when you said to be careful what I do for love. I love you, Mom, but this seemed hypocritical coming from you. You know how Mason and I feel about Ray (do NOT let him read this). It was bad enough when he used to beat our asses with tree branches and newspapers when we were little, then scream in our faces and threaten to kick us out of the house when we got older. I wanted to destroy him that time when he said he'd "bash your fuckin' skull in" if you called the cops, and "bash your kids' fuckin' skulls in" if you ever tried to leave him. And I'm still dumbfounded that you didn't press charges when he knocked a tooth out of your mouth. So, if letting your husband beat you and your kids into submission is what you did for love, then going to college a little closer to my girlfriend doesn't sound so bad, does it?

I'm sorry, that last part was mean. My point is, I KNOW you love me, and I hope you know I love you, but this IS my choice, and I wouldn't be doing it if I didn't think it could make me happy. I'm not going to make the same mistakes you did, I promise. So, please, just stay out of my love life from now on. Thank you.

Love,
Mickey

Catalina London, PsyD
Patient: Connelly, Bethany
Session 1.1 (Recording): July 14, 2007

"So, what brings you in today, Bethany?"

"Just Beth, please."

"My apologies. What can I do for you today, Beth?"

"I don't know, man. I didn't really even wanna do this."

"Then why are you here?"

"My mom and dad told me I need to work on my temper or whatever."

"Okay. Is your temper a big issue for you, Beth?"

"I thought I was fine. But then I was going through some stuff with my boyfriend, and I had this little road rage thing the next day. My parents told me if I didn't start talking to someone about my 'anger issues,' they weren't going to let me drive the car anymore."

"Was there a reason you used air quotes when you said 'anger issues'?"

"It's just—I'm sick of hearing it."

"So, this isn't the first time you've heard that phrase in reference to your temper?"

"No. And it's not just my parents. Teachers would always say it whenever I ran one of the snotty bitches into a locker for making fun of my teeth. My friend Meg said it after I dumped popcorn on some kid's head at the movies when he wouldn't shut up. Even the newspaper, whenever they wrote up my basketball games, said shit like, 'Oh, she should be the leader of the team if she could only control her temper, blah blah blah.' It gets pretty old after a while."

"I can imagine it does. Criticism is never easy to hear, and especially when it comes from people we care about. So, let me ask you this, Bethany—"

"Just Beth, please."

"Right. I'm sorry. So, this feedback you've gotten from all these people—your parents, your teachers, your friends—that you have a temper, that you have these, quote-unquote 'anger issues'—that feedback seems to be fairly universal, doesn't it?"

"I mean—I guess."

"Generally, when otherwise uncommon or unconnected sources—in your case, different people you know from different, separate aspects of your life—share a common opinion like this, it suggests there may be at least *some* validity to it. It would be one thing, for instance, if your family and friends expressed concerns about your temper but your teachers or co-workers said, 'Beth is always so pleasant and I've never even seen her frown.' But, from what you've said, there does seem to be a common perception that, maybe, you *do* struggle to control your temper. Can you tell me why *you* think all these people from different parts of your life make the same assertion?"

"I don't know. It's not like I *want* to lose my shit. But when people are assholes, it makes my blood boil. Next thing I know, I get this, like, bubble of rage in my chest, and the only way to pop it is to explode on someone."

"A 'bubble of rage'? That's very vivid, Beth. Tell me more about that."

"Ehh... I'm not very good at talking about feelings. It always feels so weird and unnatural. Makes me super uncomfortable."

"That's okay—a lot of people have a hard time expressing their emotions. Just do your best."

"It's like, when someone does something that pisses me off, I get this tight feeling in my shoulders and chest. Then my heart starts beating super fast, my face gets hot, my fingers and hands cramp up and I get this intense urge to smash something. Or someone."

"Sounds like a pretty powerful impulse, Beth. Is that what happened in the road rage incident you were referring to?"

"Yeah. I was already in a bad mood because of some stuff that was going on with me and my boyfriend, and some snotty bitch in her little Corolla honks her horn at me and cuts me off, so at the next red light I bumped her ass."

"You hit her on purpose?"

"Not like, *hit* hit her. Just enough to shake her up a little. Didn't even leave a dent. But she got out of her car squealing like I murdered her puppy, and then it was on."

"What does 'on' mean, Bethan-sorry — Beth?"

"I got right up in her face. 'You wanna scream at me? I can scream too, bitch! Maybe learn how to drive and not cut people off before you come at me like a psycho! I'll make sure your head hits the fucking steering wheel next time!' She got all flustered and threatened to call the cops. I said, 'Try it and see what happens,' but she just went back to her car and drove off."

"That must have made you feel pretty powerful."

"I mean, yeah—but that's not what it was about. I normally just flip people off or lay on my horn when someone cuts me off, but I was in a mood that day."

"Mmhmm. Some stuff was going on with your boyfriend? Tell me about that."

"He was just being weird and kind of sketch. And then I caught him in a couple of huge lies and I blew up at him."

"Oh no. What was he doing? Or saying?"

"Well, first he tries to break up with me right after my graduation. And that really hurt my feelings. I already have a hard enough time trusting people, and then when I finally do open up to a guy, he wants to end it because he says, 'I don't think we have a long-term future' or whatever. I'm like, 'Just because we're going to different colleges? You're only going to Boston—that's nothing. Then I start crying and go, 'You said you loved me,' and then *he* starts crying and says, 'I'm so sorry!' And I thought he meant it. He starts being really sweet and attentive all the time, we're finally grooving, and I decide to lose my virginity to him. Then literally the *next* day I find out he's been lying to me about going to Boston—pretty much for our whole relationship—and he has these big plans to go to New York he never told me about. Oh, and he's been talking to this girl he used to have a thing for who's super hot, and he told me she was ugly and they hadn't spoken in forever. It was one thing right after another all at once. So, yeah, I didn't really give a shit about Little Miss Corolla when that all went down."

"Wow, Beth. There's—That's a lot to unpack."

"Right? I was legit devastated. But you're right, Mom and Dad. 'It's just Beth and her 'anger issues' being dramatic again.'"

"No, your feelings are absolutely valid; I think anybody would be upset in that situation. And it makes me wonder—can I ask you kind of a hard question?"

"Go for it."

"Beth, why is it so important to stay with—what's his name?"

"Michael. Or, he likes Mickey."

"The break-up attempt, the lies, the omission of truths—honestly, these are all some pretty big red flags. Do you even want to stay with Michael after he put you through all of this?"

"Yeah, I do. I love him. He can be so nice. And he makes me laugh—a lot. He's the first guy who ever *liked* me. The boys in high school thought I wasn't 'girly' enough because I was tall and had these muscle-y arms and was good at sports and I didn't wear little pink crop tops or whatever. Then I met Michael after my championship game, and he was all nervous and stuttery, and I thought he was cute. And he wrote a really nice article about me in the paper the next day, so I was like, 'Wow, he's sweet, too.' And he *can* be sweet. Like, he brought me a stuffed bunny to add to my collection just because it was our one-month anniversary. And he always lets me pick what we're going to watch on TV or what game we're going to play. He treats me like a princess, and no one's ever done that for me before."

"Is being a princess something that's important to you, Beth?"

"I don't know. There's just so many thoughtless ass-holes in the world. Like the Corolla lady, or the kids who used to pick on me. It's nice to be treated like I'm special."

"You *are* special, Beth. You're an *incredibly* special person."

"I know. But so far, Mickey's the only one who acts like it."

17

It had been a somber four weeks since Pinkerton. Go to school. Slog through seven hours of classes. Go home. Sit quietly at the dinner table while Ray-Hole makes disturbing off-color jokes in weird, unsettling attempts to engage me. Go to my bedroom and do my homework. Stare at the NHRT award on my dresser with bittersweet pride, wondering where it all went wrong with Danica. Write angry, angsty melodrama in my journal. Go to bed. Repeat.

It had only been a year since I willingly hung out in my room studying state capitals and baseball statistics from the minute I got home from school until bedtime, but it may as well have been a lifetime since those lonely days. During this torturous month-long purgatory, I missed my friends. I missed the camaraderie. I missed the fun, energizing feeling of goofing off and making people laugh. I missed talking to people, whether it was about homework, movies, life, or twelve-pound guinea pigs with pickle toes.

The break-up and the grounding were a one-two gut punch that deflated me, and it showed. I shuffled lifelessly from class to class, avoiding eye contact with people in the hallways because I didn't want to catch pity glances when they saw the sadness smeared across my face. I sat quietly in classes, not responding to questions even though I couldn't believe no one else knew the answers. I barely talked to anyone at lunch, opting to just listen to other kids yammering on about trivial things and smirking to myself about how juvenile they all sounded. I ached for the freedom to be juvenile, too, but instead I kept my jaw firmly clenched as an angry voice in my head kept repeating, *I should be seen and not heard. Seen and not heard. Seen and not heard.*

Even Christmas couldn't cheer me up. Everywhere I looked I saw colorful lights and laughing children and happy couples sipping hot chocolate and making Eskimo kisses and all the other holly jolly bullshit, and all I could think about was how alone I was in this season of togetherness. But the holiday season had never done much for me since Dad died, anyway.

It was January by the time my punishment was over, and I was squirming to be anywhere outside my bedroom walls. So, Torey and I made plans to meet at his house and square off in some baseball video game where we could create players that looked just like ourselves. Video games were never really my thing, but I said I'd give it a shot because it was sixteen degrees out and we still had a couple months before we could play real baseball. So for the first time in weeks (thank God!), I went someplace else after school.

I knocked several times when I got to his house. Nobody was answering, but I knew someone was home because the windows were rattling to the soulful melodies of Mariah Carey. After waiting and knocking and waiting and knocking, I finally let myself in.

"Hello?" I said to the whole house. The volume suddenly drained from the stereo until Mariah's signature pitch was but a murmur.

"Mickey-Mack?" I heard from the living room.

"Luci Goose!" I said with vigor. I'd had plenty of down time over the past month to think up an adequate counterpart to her moniker for me. She giggled through the metal in her mouth when she heard it.

"Where's Torey?"

"He had to stay after school," she said as she walked on the balls of her feet into the kitchen. She was wearing hot pink socks, jeans, and a purple GAP hoodie. "He got in trouble for making fart noises in history class whenever Mr. Langford sat down. So stupid."

"Oh. When I saw him at lunch, we made plans to hang out." I wondered what I was supposed to do now.

"Well, OBVIOUSLY it happened AFTER lunch—DUH!" she said with the exaggerated sass I'd come to expect from her by now. She pulled a Tupperware container full of tuna fish out of the fridge and opened it. "Want a tuna melt?"

Luci and her damn tuna melts. She had one for lunch every day and a second one during rehearsals every night. It was just tuna fish cooked into a grilled cheese sandwich, but it was a weird obsession.

"I'll pass on the warm mayo this time," I said with a half-smile.

She put the container down on the counter and shrugged. "Fine, be a loser."

My half-smile grew into a full one with this light ribbing (nothing like what she gave to her big brother, though). Luci opened up the breadbox, grabbed a loaf of wheat bread, and leaned up against the counter. She took a breath and looked at me.

"Hey, so—it sucks what happened with Danica."

"Yeah." I suddenly found it hard to look at Luci without getting teary-eyed. "Well, she just—it just . . . I don't know. I thought it was good."

She kept looking at me with her big, round eyes. I could tell she wanted to say more.

"I mean, Danica's my friend, but—" she was choosing her words carefully. "I know she can be kind of a bitch."

I looked at her and began chewing the inside of my cheek. I never called Danica the 'B' word. I was afraid to even think it, because I knew it was one of the most horrific things you could call a girl. But something about the way Luci said it with such calm conviction told me she was in my corner.

Or maybe she was trying to get me to talk shit about Danica. And maybe she was going to go back to Danica and report whatever I said to her. And then there would be all kinds of teenage ex-boyfriend/ex-girlfriend drama. I didn't want that. Couldn't handle it. Didn't know what to say. Was this a set-up?

"Hey. Look at me," she said with a more serious tone than I expected. She was normally a ball-buster, a clown-around pal. Serious conversations weren't what I was used to with her. When I looked straight at her, I was nervous about what she might say next. But her eyes were telling me I could trust her. "Danica's my friend. But so are you. I know you're not going to talk shit about her—you're a good guy. But I'm allowed to say it.

"Danica can be kind of a bitch."

I relaxed my defenses a half-iota, let out a relieved laugh, and said, "Hey, YOU said it—not me!"

And with that, the sorrow and self-pity I'd wallowed in for the better part of a month began to wash out of my system, and I knew I was going to be okay. A big, metallic grin spread across Luci's face, and she declared proudly, "I don't care—I'll say it again! Danica's a bitch!"

As we laughed and low-fived, the dreamy opening piano chords of "Hero" dinged their way onto the speakers. *Ding. Ding-ding-da-ding, ding-ding, da ding.* Luci's face exploded with excitement. "I love this song!"

She squealed and made little, happy claps with her fingertips, then raced into the living room and spun the volume to full blast as Mariah began humming.

What I knew about Luci was that she was an incredible singer—easily the most talented freshman in the school chorus. And she knew it, too; whenever someone referenced a song she loved during rehearsals, she would show off her pristine pipes by belting out the lyrics with perfect pitch, just because she wanted to. So I wasn't surprised when Luci grabbed the television remote and started singing "Hero" into it like a microphone.

Luci knew I could sing a little bit, too. After hearing me sing along, half seriously, half mockingly, to her *Phantom of the Opera* soundtrack during rehearsals one night around Halloween, she tried to sell me on trying out for this spring's musical, but alas, my commitment to baseball wouldn't allow it. What she didn't know about me, though, was that I knew me some Mariah Carey, too; Mom had all her CDs and listened to them whenever I was in the car with her. So, Luci was surprised when I started singing along with her.

When the song came around to the chorus for the

second time, though, I decided to switch it up with some "Weird Al"-style nonsensical parody lyrics.

"And then DeNiro comes along, with the strength to wear a thong,"

Luci laughed, but then chimed in without missing a beat: "And then you cast your keys outside, and you throw a pecan pie!"

I got more animated, flailing my arms about as if possessed by cartoon Liza Minelli, while the footstool by the recliner became my own pint-sized stage, and I continued: "So when the preacher's hair is gone, and he's dancing with King Kong,"

She closed her eyes, put her hand on her heart, and punctuated our ridiculous duet with the perfect finishing line: "Then you'll finally see the proof—that a pizza cries for youuuuuu!"

I stepped down from my pedestal and we giggled and sang through the rest of the song with our arms rested around each other's shoulders, and as Mimi brought her ballad to its stirring conclusion, Luci turned toward me and gave me a hug.

"I'm sorry she hurt you," she said, just above a whisper. As we pulled apart and I looked at Luci's soft, sympathetic, brace-filled smile, my face didn't know what to do. My lips were curled in a tight smirk, my eyes started to sting a little bit, and my nose felt drippy.

"I'll be okay." I shrugged and looked at the floor, unconvinced. "Thank you for talking to me."

A comfortable silence hung between us before the next song began. Luci turned to walk back toward the kitchen and let out a shriek. "Jesus, you scared the crap out of me!"

"Sorry, Mecha-Mouth," Torey said with a childish chortle. "You and Mack-Pack wanna be alone?"

"Shut up," she snorted at him. I could practically see her invisible walls shoot back up. "He was here to see you, dumbass."

Two weeks later, she started dating Darius Duckman.

MASON PATRICK, Age 22
October 4, 2007

Hey Dad,

It was wicked nice catching up with my little brother the other day.

I guess I can't really call him "little" anymore; he's as tall as me now. You should see him. But Mick and I haven't hung out much since I moved down here, so I didn't mind driving him back to the city in exchange for a free meal (living in Boston isn't cheap). So, once we got back to BU, we hiked it over to the Tasty Burger on Boylston. It's like a block from Fenway Park—pretty sweet neighborhood for a big Sox fan like him (I'm more of a Bruins guy). Didn't really matter. It was just nice to see him. And you can't beat those burgers.

We spent the drive down shootin' the shit about sports and movies and surface stuff—you know, the stuff I'm comfortable jawing about. I've got my business and he's got his. No reason to mix it up. But something about the smell of grilled meat made Mick a little nosey.

"How's the cop thing going?" he asked.

"The cop thing?"

"Yeah, didn't you come down here to join the police force?"

"I did," I said. "But I gotta live here for at least a year first; it's been six months."

"Oh, right, right. Sorry, I knew that. The last six months have been crazy. I'm stuck in my own head. Sorry."

"Stop saying sorry. I know you've had a lot going on.

The newspaper, girlfriend, the show, the NYU thing. It's all good—just been doing my thing down here, working at the gym, training, trying to get ready for the academy when I can get in."

"The police academy?" He smirked. "You gonna be the guy who makes all the funny sound effects?"

I glared at him.

"From the movie? Police Academy? Get it? Michael Winslow? Remember?"

He tried to get me on his side with some weird laser beam sound effect like the dude in the movie. I kept staring, trying not to crack.

"Nah, you're more like the big Hightower guy," he said, still talking about those old, stupid slapstick flicks. "Big huge guy, all serious? Big caterpillar mustache? No?"

He waited for me to give him something. Some kind of nod, like I knew what the hell he was talking about. I held my stone-cold stare until Mickey cracked that grin of his, the one he flashes when he's pushing your buttons. I couldn't help it anymore; my sneer flipped into a full-on smile and I started laughing.

I could never keep up with Mickey in a battle of wits. And on the other hand, he's always leaned on me when it's time to get real. That's what we love about each other—I keep him grounded when his head's floating in the clouds, and he makes me laugh when I'm stressed out or pissed off. He's the yin to my yang.

Gotta admit, I was worried about the kid for a long time after some of the shit Ray-Hole put him through when we were kids. It changed him. Hell, it changed me. Wasn't a whole lot of fun growing up in a house where you felt like you had to be perfect all the time, or else you'd get screamed at, hit, or kicked out. Mick spent so long trying to make sure nobody (especially Ray) got upset with him that I think it became part of who he is. From the time he was in third grade all the way to ninth grade, you never heard him talk, let alone make a joke, especially if Raymond was around. I was worried he'd grow up to be a loner living in the basement whose only friend was a pet Betta fish named Krampus.

Watching his color come back the past few years has been an honest-to-God treat. You should see it. I missed his jokes, corny as they are (like the "mad bunny" one) and his goofy faces—I swear the kid came straight out of Toon Town from Roger Rabbit (speaking of old, stupid movies...). And it's been a kick to see how people are drawn to him now. After holing himself up in his room all those years, he loves the love he gets.

"So, Ma was pretty pissed about bailing on NYU?" I asked. We were both leaning back in our white metal chairs, waiting for our order. The smell of burgers and grease made my stomach groan.

Mickey looked at the wall behind me, and his right heel started bouncing up and down like it does when he's nervous. "Well, you know Mom. She never really gets pissed."

He was right. Ma never loses her shit like Ray does. She just chews the inside of her cheek and doesn't say much. Kinda like Mick.

"But she's not happy about it." He shrugged. "She thinks I'm giving up too much."

I kind of agreed with Ma, but I wanted to be supportive. "I think you'll be fine. Boston's an awesome town.

And I'm just glad you're getting out of that house so you don't have to put up with Ray-Hole anymore."

"Me too," he said. "And I'm still pursuing a good career. And I can see Beth more. And I'm closer to my bro!"

Mickey always tries to sugar-coat things. I took a beat to collect my thoughts as our burgers arrived. This was one of those moments I needed to pull his head down from the clouds.

"But Mick." I unwrapped my juicy meat sandwich. "Is that what you wanted?"

He fixed his eyes on mine and put a couple French fries in his mouth. "Of course. Why wouldn't it be?"

I took a big bite of my burger and put my hand up like, 'Can't talk right now, I'm chewing.' What I was really doing was thinking about what to say next. I kept chewing as I looked up at the ceiling, and then after pretending to chew for a long time after I had swallowed, I knew I had to say something.

"I just think," I stopped myself, but then decided to shoot from the hip. "I just think you're all-in with Bethany."

"Of course I am." He took a sip from his soda. "That's the way it should be, right?"

"I—I don't mean that in a good way, bud," I said with a mouthful of burger. I chewed for another few seconds, then added, "It's like you get super attached when someone likes you."

He squinted and jerked his head back. "What? No I don't."

"You do, Mick. You go so overboard trying to make them happy, to make them stay, that you kinda push them

away."

He munched on his fries and looked out the window at a middle-aged brunette with a ponytail who was feeding leftovers to her Dachshund. His heel was really going now.

"Think about it. That's why Danica dumped you. That's why Kaylin stopped talking to you for months after she took your V-card. It's like you get so excited when someone likes you that you're desperate to hold onto them, and that scares them away."

He stopped eating and began chewing on his cheek. I think he knew I had a point.

"I'm just saying, the wrong person might take advantage of you if they think you'll do anything—literally anything—to make them happy." I had fries stuffed in both cheeks. "If Bethany sees you'll go to a different college to make her happy, who knows what she might want you to do next? I think that's what Ma is worried about."

"Well, I'm not going to kill anyone for her, that's for sure," he said, a smile slowly creeping back across his face. "Well, unless she shows me her boobs first."

There's Mickey, always making jokes. That was his signal; it was time to drop it. There's always a fine line for Mick between cracking jokes and clamming up, and I didn't want the latter to happen. Nagging him about this would just push him further away from me and the family and into the arms of his precious girlfriend.

"So, what about you?" he asked. "How's the love life?"

"I don't have time for a love life," I said dismissively before taking a sip of my Sprite.

"Really? No prospects? Six months down here and

you haven't met anybody?"

"That's not what I said." I gave him a half-smile and a wink. "I said I don't have time."

That's one way Mick and I are different. When he's in a relationship, he's all-in. He clings so hard that people leave him. Me, on the other hand, I'm the one who leaves.

"Wouldn't it be nice to have someone to spend time with? Someone to hold onto? Someone to talk to?"

"I don't need all that, bud—I'm good."

Now it was me clamming up. I don't like talking about feelings, emotions, soft stuff. Mick needs to feel needed, needs to feel loved. He's always craved the affection he never really got from Ray. Me—I didn't need that. I earned Ray's respect. He was my hockey coach at RHS, so he helped me perfect my skating and my stick work, and he taught me how to run guys into the boards without getting penalized. He was the local Scoutmaster, too, so he helped me earn my merit badges and become an Eagle Scout. So I didn't grow up with a lot of the same neediness Mickey did. I wasn't afraid of Raymond like Mick was, either. I just thought the guy was a prick.

"But we're not talking about needs, Mace. You asked me if I'm doing what I wanted. Now it's your turn. Don't you want someone in your life?"

"I don't know, man. I don't put up with all the bullshit. The clinging, the constant touching, the need to spend every moment of free time together. I'm a busy dude."

"I know," he said. "That's why you've never had a relationship last more than a couple weeks, maybe a month."

"So?" I felt my lungs tighten as I grew more defen-

sive. But I kept it light. "I'm perfectly happy. I've got my buddies at the gym, I'm working on getting into the academy. I'm fine, trust me."

Mickey tilted his head to the side and looked at me with a skeptical wince.

"Are you?"

We both knew each other too well.

"Look—" I tried to think of something to say that would make him drop the subject; it was getting too touchy-feely for me. "I appreciate what you're doing, bud. I'm just not after a relationship right now. Flirting and making out is one thing, but I don't have time to debate what movie we're gonna watch or what we're gonna have for dinner every night. I've got bigger things to focus on."

"Fine." He threw his hands up in surrender. "You didn't push me, I won't push you. Just saying, if you ever want help in that arena, I know a lot of people."

"Appreciate it, bro." I sucked down the last of my Sprite. "Now can we talk about something else please?"

"By all means," Mick said with that grin of his as he ate his last two fries. He knew he'd pushed my buttons.

"Great," I shot back at him. "So, what's your boy Torey been up to?"

Forever yours,
Mason

18

We can finally relax," Beth said with a happy sigh as she put her head on my chest and wrapped her arms around me. I leaned back, kissed her on the scalp, and said, "It is, Bethy Bear."

An old, happy holiday movie was glowing from the television set—something black and white with Bing Crosby gazing romantically into the middle distance—and the lights from the tree filled the room with manufactured warmth. Our first Christmas together had been a nice one, but a busy one. We spent a couple hours at my parents' house for waffles, gifts, hugs, hellos, and goodbyes, then the rest of the day over at her parents' house watching movies I'd seen a thousand times, listening to her right-wing zombie of a father regurgitate Sean Hannity's latest rants, and trying to make Brie feel better about Preston dumping her so he wouldn't have to buy her a gift. But the night was silent now, everyone else had gone to bed, and Beth and I were curled up on the couch under a fleece blanket in her parents' living room.

"Did you have a good Christmas?" she asked. It was her

not-so-subtle way of asking if I liked what she got me for Christmas.

I smiled. "Of course I did. Now whenever I want to read *Zits*, I'll just crack open that book and think of you. And I can watch *Footloose* on DVD now!"

"Okay, good." She sounded relieved; first-Christmas gifts didn't need to be wicked extravagant. That's why I only spent $149 on a sterling silver Claddagh ring with her alexandrite birthstone in the heart.

"Did you like what I got you?"

She kissed me and said, "I love the ring, and I love you."

"Nice." I smiled and kissed her back. This time of year meant so much to Beth. She loved the whole season—the snow, the colors, the cold, the cuddling—it was the first time in months she seemed happy, and I wanted to make sure I did my part to keep the spirit of the season alive for her with a gift she would like. She hadn't adjusted well in her first semester at RSC, so I'd taken on the role of comforter over the past several months. I'd spent hours on the phone with her daily, listening to her cry about how tough her classes were, how she missed playing "real" basketball because intramural basketball was "stupid" and "pointless" because there was no one there to cheer her on, and how she couldn't make any friends because the girls at The Rocks were all "snotty bitches." A big part of my life had become telling her the classes would get easier once she adjusted, she didn't need fans in the stands for her to be the best player in the intramural league, and the snotty bitches were just being insecure. Rinse and repeat as needed.

We didn't talk much about what was going on with me at BU, because I was killin' it, and that made her jealous. I made the Dean's List, had already made an impression at

BUTV-10 with my sideline coverage of the BU/BC football game, and had found a pretty tight group of friends in my dorm. So, while Beth was sinking, I was soaring.

"Forget something?" she said, staring at me.

"I love you, too," I said with an embarrassed little smirk before I kissed her again. She smiled and put her head back on my chest.

"You guys are gross," a bitter Brie said as she walked through the room on the way to the bathroom. She slammed the door and we shared a laugh. Yeah, this felt nice. I put both my arms around her, gave her a little squeeze, and closed my eyes. I felt her breathing in perfect rhythm, taking a breath, then pausing. Then another breath, then another pause. *Breath. Pause.* I laid there, content and happy, listening to her breathing and feeling the weight of my arms draped over her back, and I started drifting. *Breath. Pause. Breath. Pause. Breath. FLUSH.*

I lifted my head off the arm of the couch, and Beth shook her head to wake herself back up. "I fell asleep," she said. "Did you?"

"For a second."

"You guys better wake up, or Dad will never let him stay this late again," Brie said as she walked back through the room and out.

"Shut up, Brie," Beth snapped. Brie didn't respond.

"What time is it, anyway?" I asked as I stretched my back and disrupted the perfectly cozy position we'd been in.

She glanced at her watch. "Ten fifteen."

"Oh, okay. I have to be home by eleven, so we probably shouldn't fall asleep. Ray gets all over my ass when I miss curfew."

"So stupid, man. You don't have a curfew in college, so why should you when you come home?"

I shrugged and threw my hands up helplessly.

"I still technically live with them when I'm not at school, and he still has his rules. And ol' Ray-Hole is all about his rules."

"I wish you'd stand up to him," she said. "You could kick his ass, man."

"It's not about size and strength with Ray," I said. "I mean, not physical strength. He knows I can't afford to live on my own yet, so he uses that to control me. He threatens to kick me out."

"He can't do that. He wouldn't do that."

"Yeah, he can, and yeah, he would," I said. "I'm nineteen, so he's under no legal obligation to keep me in his house. He knows I know that. And he also knows I know he would call the cops on me if I did kick his ass, even though I've never hit anyone before."

"But he's your dad."

"*Step*dad. He's my *step*dad. And he has never tried to pretend we were anything more to him than his wife's kids."

"Then you shouldn't have to listen to him."

She was not getting my point.

"Yes, I do."

"Dude, he's not going to kick you out," Beth said with a little more stank than I preferred in that peaceful moment with Bing Crosby and the Christmas tree lights. "Just get in his face. Your mom will have your back. I'll have your back."

That was easy for her to say; Beth was never one to back down from confrontation. I'd seen her scream at refs and slam the ball on the floor during basketball games, talk shit to waitstaff if she didn't like her food, roll her window down and spew vicious bile at other drivers when she was behind the wheel, and shoulder-shove other girls—and some shorter guys—when she was walking through crowded areas. It came from her deep-rooted mixture of competitiveness and insecurity, and it was one of the qualities that made her such a successful, cutthroat athlete. But in everyday, social situations, it was sometimes a little embarrassing. Also, intimidating.

"No way," I said with an incredulous laugh. "No, no, no, no, no."

"Why?"

"Because—" How could I explain this in a way she would understand? My right heel started bouncing up and down with nervous energy.

"Because—" I stopped again. I started to chew the inside of my cheek. But then I thought, *No, you should be able to talk to her about this. She's your girlfriend.*

"Because when he gets in my face and he starts screaming at me…"

Beth sat up and looked at me with a mix of concern and intrigue. "What?" she asked.

"My mind goes blank," I said. "I completely freeze up. I can't articulate my thoughts. I can't—I just…"

"He scares you." She started touching my face with the palm of her hand. "Jesus, you're sweating just thinking about it. Breathe, man, you're fine."

I exhaled, and my arms and shoulders started to tremble a little.

"No matter what I've done with my life, no matter how many friends I have or how old I am," I said as I glanced at her and then looked up at the half-melted snowman candle on the table. "When Ray gets in my face and screams, I feel like a helpless little kid again. I'll do anything he says, won't even question it—*can't* physically question it—to make him stop yelling."

"Does this happen when anyone yells?" She stroked my cheek with the back of her fingers. "Or just him?"

"So far, just him, thankfully. But no one else has ever really screamed at me. I've always tried to follow the rules, be friendly, be funny, and tried not to piss people off. It's gotten me this far."

Beth stopped stroking my cheek and put her hand on my shoulder. She got eerily quiet and began staring at the blinking lights on the tree. She shifted her legs underneath her into a cross-legged position, then lifted her head off my chest so she could sit upright. She looked at me and said, "Mick, can I ask you something?"

I sat up more, too, and kept my eyes on her. "Yeah?" I was a little nervous about what was coming next.

"You're not—" she stopped for a moment, looked at the tree, then back at me. "You're not just staying with me because you're scared to break up with me, are you?"

"Of course not," I said with as much sincere vehemence as I could muster.

"'Cause this summer you were going to break up with me, and then I got upset and you changed your mind." Her eyes started to well up. "And then the whole Kaylin thing, and then I yelled at you about New York. You're not just with me 'cause you're scared of me like you're scared of your stepdad, are you?"

"No—babe…" I grabbed her hands and weaved all our fingers together. "I *love* you, Bethy Bear. I'm with you because I *love* you."

"You mean it? For real?"

"For real."

"You would tell me if you didn't want to be with me?" She pulled a hand away and wiped her cheeks and nose on her sleeve.

"Yes," I said immediately. I knew if I hesitated, she wouldn't believe me, and I had to go home soon, so I had to convince her quickly. I wasn't sure I believed it myself, but I knew I had to make *her* believe it, or this would become a wicked meltdown, and then I'd be late for curfew, and I didn't want to spend the rest of my winter break grounded. I summoned my training as an actor to look deeply and convincingly into her jade green eyes and say, "I would tell you, I promise."

"Even if you thought I was gonna yell at you?"

This was getting exhausting. I squeezed her hands, said, "Yes, even then," and pulled her toward me to kiss her. "Promise."

"Good," she said. "Because I don't want those other boys from school. I want my Mick-a-Roni."

"And I want my Bethy Bear." I held her wicked tight, hoping I could hug away her fears and we'd never have to have a discussion like this again.

Then I ran my big ol' bear paws through her scarlet locks, narrowed my eyes, and said, "Other boys?"

"Wonderful to see you again, Beth. Have a seat."

"Thanks for meeting with me."

"How did your first year at college go?"

"Honestly? Not great. That's why I called you."

"You did sound a little down in the voicemail you left. What's been going on?"

"It's just—it's been a really hard year. I miss basketball. I miss my friends. The distance was a lot tougher for me and Mickey than I thought it was gonna be. So, I just wanted somebody to talk to."

"Okay, well, that's why I'm here. We can talk about all of that. Where would you like to begin?"

"I guess Mickey."

"Whenever you're ready, Beth."

"So, my mom and dad wouldn't let me stay home and commute to RSC like I wanted to. They said I needed to 'spread my wings' or whatever and they needed to 'cut the umbilical cord.' I was like, 'But you'll save so much money if I don't live on campus,' and my mom's like, 'Don't worry about us, we're fine, but you need to not be afraid to change things up once in a while,' which I think is bullshit."

"That's interesting phrasing your mom used—'afraid to change things up'. Do you find that to be true, Beth? Are you afraid of change?"

"Not *afraid* really. I just know what I like, and I don't really see the point."

"You don't see the point of change?"

"Not really. I mean, I know little things need to change. Like when my Jordans get worn out and I gotta break in some new ones. But why does the big stuff need to change? Like, why do I need to live on campus if all my stuff's in my room at home? Why should I get a new car if the motor on my Jetta still runs? Why do all my friends want to move away when they have everything they need right here?"

"Well—a lot of people are excited by change. For some of us, change means opportunity. For some, it means growth. Have you ever thought about it that way?"

"I don't need any more growth, man, I'm already six feet tall."

"Ha! I've always loved that sense of humor, Beth. But you know what I mean, right? Spiritual growth? Maturing from elder teenager to young adult? You're in a very transitional phase of your life right now, Beth, and the choices you make now and in the next few years can go a long way in shaping your future. I would hate to see you miss out on opportunities for spiritual growth—or for things of a more tangible nature such as jobs, education, friendships, what have you—because you haven't addressed your fear of change."

"I guess. But the thing I don't get is—if I'm already fine with everything, if I know what I like, I know what to expect, I know where I'm going—why mess with that? You start doing different things or going different places or hanging out with people you don't know, it's a crapshoot, man. You're *asking* for shit to blow up. I'd rather stick to what I know. Like, seriously—what's wrong with that?"

"I wouldn't say there's anything *wrong* with it. I

would just caution you not to limit yourself, that's all. Don't be afraid to seize an opportunity because you're reluctant to leave your comfort zone. For instance, what if you got a great job offer but you'd have to move away from home?"

"What kind of job offer?"

"Well—you tell me. What would pique your interest? What are some of your career aspirations?"

"I have no idea. I'm helping coach my sister's AAU team and I just got a job at Pizza Face for the summer, but I haven't really thought about a career."

"You said a minute ago that you know where you're going, so you must have at least some idea of what you want to do with your life."

"I just meant I know, like, what streets to drive down to get around town."

"Oh! I thought you meant you know where you're going *figuratively*—I'm so sorry!"

"No worries. But can we talk about that stuff another time maybe? I was trying to talk about me and Mickey."

"Of course. I did take us off on a little tangent, didn't I? My apologies. Go ahead."

"So, my parents basically forced me to live on campus so I could 'spread my wings,' but the opposite happened. My roommate was this smelly hoarder who just watched YouTube all day. Most of the other girls were just snotty sorority bitches who wore matching Uggs and skinny jeans, and any guy who talked to me just wanted to have sex with me. My friends were all away at their own colleges, I hated all my classes, the intramural basketball league was lame, and Mickey could only talk on the phone for, like, an hour a night because he was so busy with all his stuff. I just got really lonely."

"Sounds like it was quite challenging for you, Beth. A lot of people experience that the first time they leave home. It's certainly a big adjustment. It's unfortunate you didn't enjoy the intramural league—that's usually a good way for people to meet other students and make friends."

"It was dumb. You're playing in an empty gym with a bunch of weak-ass players who can barely make a layup. Even if you win the league, all you get is a shitty t-shirt, and no one cares."

"At least you got to play the game you love, right?"

"I guess, but it felt kinda pointless."

"Did you participate in any other activities? People try all kinds of new things when they get to college."

"I did. Rugby. Co-ed. And that's what got me in trouble."

"In trouble how, Beth?"

"So, my friend Meg's brother goes to the Rock. I've known him since I was a kid, but he's a couple years older so we never really hung out. But him and a couple of his friends were in my Anatomy class first semester, and they were looking for players for the team, so they asked me because Brad knew I was into sports."

"Brad is Meg's brother?"

"Yeah."

"Well, there you go, Beth! You said you didn't have any luck making friends!"

"I mean, that's how it started. I joined the team and met some people, and they were all pretty cool. Then I started bumping into Brad all over campus, so we started chilling between classes, shooting hoops, studying for our anatomy final together, and I finally felt like I had someone to hang out with…But then.."

"Just breathe, Beth, you're in a safe space. What happened?"

"Second semester, a bunch of us are watching the Syracuse game in his room. I got a little drunk, and after everyone else left, I—I stayed and fooled around with him."

"What does 'fooled around' mean? Did you have sex with him?"

"No, but—we did almost everything else. Like, he put his—"

"You don't have to elaborate; I get it. But the question I have for you is this: Why do you think that happened, Beth? Was it the alcohol, or do you think something else might have contributed?"

"I think—I think the loneliness had a lot to do with it. But, I mean, it wasn't the only thing. Me and Mickey hadn't been vibing since Christmas because I told him some other boys had been hitting on me and he didn't even do anything about it."

"What did you want him to do that he didn't do?"

"I don't know, just—*something*."

"Did you want him to confront the guys who were making passes at you?"

"I think, maybe? Mickey can be such a pushover sometimes. He hates fighting, he's scared of his stepdad, and he never really gets pissed about anything. So, when I asked him if he was mad these guys were hitting on me and he was just like, 'We're good, Bethy Bear,' I said, 'Fuck it, I guess he doesn't really care.'"

"I wouldn't say he doesn't care, Beth. You said yourself that conflict can be a challenge for him. Maybe it was easier in his mind to simply *say*, 'You know what, Beth, we're good,' so you two wouldn't have a fight. I'm not saying he was right to do that, I'm just imploring you to consider another perspective."

"Maybe *he* should consider *my* perspective. I'm not Mister Popular like him. I don't have a million college friends already, I don't have a big sports talk show on the college TV station, and I've never been the star of a big musical. I'm just this tall, weird chick with 'anger issues' and no friends, and all I do is go to my stupid classes, shoot hoops by myself, and sit in my room with my smelly hoarder loser roommate waiting for Mister Popular to find time to call me. Then Brad came along and started paying attention to me, and it felt nice to be treated like a princess again. Like Mickey used to."

"I see. So, some of the luster has worn off. That's not unusual after you've been with someone for a while, Beth. It doesn't mean anything is wrong with you, Mickey, or the relationship. Things change over time as you get a little more comfortable with each other, that's all."

"But it's kinda been this way since the beginning. He never has time for me. Like, as soon as we got together, he was all-in with his *Footloose* show, then he almost broke up with me, then we had that huge fight when he lied to me, and then things were finally good for maybe a month and a half, and then he went off to BU. Since Day 1, he's never made me a priority."

"There's a box of tissues there on the table."

"Thanks. So then Brad and I start kicking it, and he's right there with me at school, and he's always knocking on my door just to say hey, and then he starts inviting me to the dining hall with his friends, and then he starts spotting me at the gym, and I start feeling like *he's* my boyfriend more than Mickey."

"These are significant concerns, Beth. Have you and Mickey talked about any of this?"

"I told him a little about me and Brad making out. But I—left out a lot. He thinks we just kissed a little and I shut it down when Brad tried to go further. But actually, I was into it."

"So you *did* get physical with him."

"Yeah, I mean, like I said, we didn't have sex, but he definitely got to third base. A couple of times."

"How did Mickey respond when you told him you kissed Brad? I'm sure *that* must have gotten a reaction out of him, even if he didn't know the whole truth."

"He was just like, 'We're good, Bethy Bear.' Again!"

"That's it?"

"That was it! Seriously, I told my *boyfriend* I made out with *another guy* and HE FUCKING SAID 'WE'RE GOOD'. Like, for real—what do I need to do to make him act like he gives a shit about me?"

"Great question, Beth. We should explore that…"

19

June 2008

"What time are your friends coming over?" Raymond asked.

"Should be any minute now," I said as I pulled my arms through my Old Navy fleece.

"Make sure you build the fire pit at least fifty feet from the house."

"Already built it, and it's ninety feet away."

"Good. No drinking. No drugs. I'm not getting arrested for furnishing alcohol to minors."

"None of us do drugs, and we won't drink anything except soda and hot chocolate."

Chill out, Ray, I thought. *I'm having S'mores and a small pit fire with four other people. It's not a bonfire with the whole hockey team like you and Mason used to have.*

"Put the fire out by eleven. And watch it until it's completely dead. All the way."

"Yup."

"Watch the attitude, or you can tell your friends to go someplace else."

"Sorry. We'll watch the fire all the way."

"Don't make too much noise. I don't need a noise complaint from the neighbors."

"We won't."

Mace and his buddies used to keep the fire going until 2 a.m. and rarely lowered their voices to sleepable decibels, but I get it; Mr. Junior Firefighter and his crew are exempt from your patronizing "reminders."

"And pick up after yourselves."

"We will."

"Okay, have a good time. I'll be out later to check on you guys."

Good idea. A Dean's List Comm student, a Big-12 quarterback, and his Ivy League sister—that's a seedy concoction of evil and mayhem. Better keep us under your thumb.

"Yup."

"Michael…"

"Sorry. Yes, Dad. Thank you."

As soon as I got far enough into the back yard to escape the glow of the deck light, I huffed, shook my head, and rolled my eyes. For a lot of college students, returning home after their freshman year means reconnecting with their parents and exploring new familial dynamics. New freedoms are often granted during this transitional phase in which moms and dads learn to trust their new young adult and discover that, if they aren't watching their every move, they won't die. But Ray? He wasn't ready to loosen the reins. He still expected me to ask for permission to do anything or go anywhere and adhere to my 11 p.m. curfew. And as he put very plainly the night I moved back into my old bedroom for the summer, "If you don't like that, find another place to live, and find someone else to co-sign your student loans."

"Ray-Hole" was alive and well.

As long as I did what he asked, though, he left me alone. That's why I mowed our half-acre backyard, cleaned the pool, pressure-washed the deck, and washed his truck all by myself. That was the only way he would let me have my friends over. And now, as daylight began dimming to dusk, I could revel in a hard day's work and enjoy some time with a few of my favorite people.

Torey was bringing a buddy of his from the football team, and Luci was bringing her boyfriend, but it was a fractured version of the group I'd considered "my people" in high school because of the whole Danica-Darius scandal. And, to be honest, as much as I was looking forward to seeing the Rizzo kids again, I was nervous. We hadn't hung out as a group in almost two years, and in the past fourteen months, my relationship with Beth had begun taking up an enormous amount of real estate in both my heart space and my free time. Our lives were all much different than they were at Torey's "College Kick-off," a going away party that Luci and their mom held for him before he left for WVU. I was afraid our paths had already diverged irreconcilably and that we'd have nothing left to say to each other; I couldn't wait to see them, but I had some wicked butterflies.

I struggled to get the fire going. I didn't have that Eagle Scout training my brother boasted, so my fire ignition expertise was limited to word of mouth and a book I skimmed through once when I was ten. *Kindling, right? Stack wood in a spiral or something? Rub two sticks for friction? Maybe make a spark with a rock?* It started occurring to me that, maybe someone who's never started a fire before should've opted for a different kind of social gathering than a backyard pit fire. I didn't have matches, and I wasn't going to ask Raymond. *Maybe Mom has one of those fancy long-necked candle lighters or something.*

I turned to head toward the house when I saw her. The dark Italian complexion, the almost-black hair, the flared nostrils, the big round eyes. She was walking toward me with navy blue jeans rolled halfway up her calves, bright yellow flip flops, and an orange sweatshirt, the kind with the oversized neck holes designed to hang casually (or, maybe, suggestively) down on one shoulder. She had a bag of marshmallows in her hand, but I didn't give a damn about the marshmallows.

"Luci Goose!" I couldn't contain the big, doofy smile that instantly burst onto my mug. I opened my arms for a hug.

"Mickey-Mack," she said, but with a half-smile and considerably less vigor than I was used to from her. She walked into my arms, pushed her chest into my rib cage, swept her arms around my back, and squeezed as hard as she could—for a few seconds longer than I expected. "So nice to see you."

"You, too." I rubbed her back and breathed in. Her hair smelled like watermelon. "How have you been?"

Then a chunky redneck-looking dude in flannel came into the backyard and she let go without answering. He was the same guy who'd sat next to her looking bored beyond measure during my *Footloose* show the year before. But I was never formally introduced; I just remembered seeing him pull her toward the exit during the curtain call as she looked back at me and waved with an apologetic smile.

"Mickey, this is my boyfriend Carson—Carson, Mickey."

I extended my hand and said, with the friendliest tone I could fake, "Hey Carson! Great to meet you, man. Thanks for coming!"

Carson shook my hand for a single snap, nodded, and looked away. "W'kinda beer y'got?"

"Sorry, no beer," I said, off-put by his brazen disinterest in our exchange. "There's Pepsi, Diet Coke, and Dew in the cooler. Or I can get you some hot chocolate."

"Fuck," he said. He turned his head and put his hands in his pockets.

"Where's Bethany?" Luci asked. She looked around the yard and up toward the house. "I thought she was going to be here."

"She's coaching her sister's AAU team," I said. I turned back toward the fire pit and tried to squish the wooden sticks together, as if that would help. "I guess if they win, they'll qualify for some national tournament. She might be here later."

"Oh," Luci said. "Then I guess we have you to our-selves, tonight. It'll be like old times—kind of."

"Well, I don't mean to brag," I puffed out my chest, "but I AM pretty great all by myself."

"Yes, you are," she said. Her lips parted into a smile that was so surprisingly stunning that my jaw dropped and my eyes popped.

"Holy shit! Your braces! I haven't seen you since you got them off!"

"Yeah, last winter." She put her hand over her mouth and started to blush.

"Don't do that!" I said. "You're—"

I wanted to say you're gorgeous, beautiful, hotter than hell—but then I remembered Carson. He was standing there with his hands in his pockets, silent, giving me the side-eye.

"You're, um—you look really nice." I looked at the fire pit again, helplessly. I was going to need Mom's candle lighter. "I've got to go inside for a minute."

As I got closer to the house I could hear Carson say, slightly above a whisper and with an accusatory tone, "'Mickey-Mack'? Y'gotta pet name for'im?" to which Luci replied, "I told you, he's just a friend, and it's just a nick-name." Their low-tone-but-still-audible bickering faded out of hearing range as I got to the back door, and then I heard from the driveway, "Where the hell you think you're going?"

I yelped, "Dude!" then jumped over the railing and gave Torey a big man-hug, complete with the minimum-required two firm slaps on the back.

"What's up, dude?" he said. "How the hell you been?"

"Good, good. Awesome to see you," I said. I looked over at the towering, muscle-bound kid with a crew cut to Torey's right. "Who's this?"

"This is Vince. He's our starting center. Best blocker on the team."

"Vince! Welcome! So good to meet you."

"Same," Vince said as he shook my hand with authority. I'm not a wimpy person by most standards, but this guy just about crushed my hand—in a good way.

"Shit, dude—good grip," I said with respect. "You could be Torey's bodyguard or something."

"Something like that," he said with a light chuckle. "Salvatore's told me a lot about you, Mister Baseball. Four no-hitters in high school?"

"This guy came out of nowhere and threw smoke," Torey boasted. "'The Pedro Martinez of Rockingham.'"

Torey was always the go-to guy for reliving the glory days of high school sports, even though he'd moved on to bigger and better things as a Division I football stud for the Mountaineers and I hadn't played a sport in two years. Our championship baseball season freshman year was always a safe space when we had nothing else to talk about.

"I could play a little bit," I said sheepishly, and visions of opposing batters flailing helplessly at my heater danced through my head for the first time in ages. Then I gestured to Torey and said, "So could this guy. We batted three-four in the lineup our senior year. Just didn't have much supporting cast so we got bounced in the quarters."

"I could play, but you were the Mack-Pack."

"Shit, no one's called me that in a long time."

"Yeah, but I'm sure that arm still throws gas."

"Wouldn't know," I said with a passive shrug. "Haven't aired it out in a while."

"Ah, you never cared about ball that much." Torey smacked me on the shoulder. "You were all about hangin' with the hot theater chicks."

"Busted." I smirked. "Speaking of which, your sister's already here."

Torey blinked. "Did you just call my sister a hot theater chick?"

I didn't deny it.

"He didn't, but I think you just did," Vince teased. "Gross, you think your sister's hot."

I laughed and said, "I like this guy already. Be right back—gotta go inside and get a lighter to start the fire."

Torey scoffed. "You're using a lighter to start the fire? Dude, you're such a girl sometimes. Here, I'll do it."

Vince and I looked at each other, shrugged, and trailed Torey over to the fire pit, where he greeted his sister as he always did—by calling her "ass bag." Strangely, Luci didn't say anything back. In all the years I'd known those two, she never hesitated to respond to the ribbing she got from her decidedly less mature older brother. She always fired back with something equally brash like "fuck face" or "pube licker," and sometimes even emasculating like "toothpick dick" or "hamster balls." But this time, she just hung limply on Carson's arm, looked behind her, and said, joylessly, "Hey."

Torey had the pit fired up within minutes, and as we watched the waist-high flames dancing seductively under the stars on this warm June evening, a comfortable silence fell over the group. I stepped forward and let the heat seep into my skin, listening to the crackle of the fire in the foreground and the chirps of lonely crickets in the background, and my mind drifted back in time to simpler days. Playing He-Man with Mason. Making everyone break character during rehearsals. Flying into a sweaty hug with Torey after my first no-no. Talking about our fathers during Memorial Day barbecues. I hadn't thought about those days in quite a while. But Torey and Luci had been there with me through some of the best and worst times of my life, as I had been with them through some of theirs. So, even though my relationship with Beth had taken over my life, the bond I had with these two could not be broken or replaced. Or even matched.

A particularly loud pop from the fire brought me back to the present, and I looked around. Luci was roasting a marshmallow, Carson was looking at his watch, and Vince was leaning back in a chair with his hands folded, mesmerized by the blaze. Torey was on the ground, wedged between Vince's calves, his arms sprawled out on Vince's lap. It took me a moment to realize what I was witnessing.

"Wait a second." I started pointing at Torey, then Vince, then back at Torey, and then asked, "Are you two…."

Torey tilted his head back to look at Vince, then smiled at me. "Yeah, man. We're together."

Luci looked over at them, and then looked at me, confused. "You didn't know that?"

Embarrassed at how blind I must've looked to them, I chortled and said with an excited grin, "NO, I didn't know that! How long?"

"'Bout ten inches," Vince chimed in.

Everyone except Carson laughed, and then Torey smacked his boyfriend on the thigh and said, "Yeah, you wish."

"No, but how long have you known?" I asked, ardently interested in what was, to me, a brand-new development in my best friend's life. "When did you come out?"

"I've always known, man," Torey said. "I never had any girlfriends in high school—don't you remember that?"

I took another trip down memory lane, this time with much more purpose, and strained to remember any time he ever hung out with a girl or even talked about one. When I was dating Danica, he mentioned the size of her boobs once, but now that I thought about it, it was mostly to point out that a lot of guys would think I was lucky; he never said he was one of them. Other than that, we never talked about girls together. I was never wicked comfortable talking to other guys about dating when I was in high school, and apparently he, as I'd just found out, had his own reasons. Torey didn't go to our senior prom, either, because he said it was "gay," and I never knew how ironic he was being until this moment.

"You never had any boyfriends either, so how was I supposed to know?" I said with a laugh.

"Well, the only other gay guy in our grade was Bryson Moreover," Torey said. "He had a face full of zits and didn't shower, so I wasn't exactly dying to date him. Pickings were slim."

"What about other grades?" I said. "You should have told me sooner, I could've—"

"I know, man—it's all good," he said as he rubbed Vince's knee. "Don't worry about it. Vinny's a great guy. I'm happy."

Vince started playing with Torey's earlobes and said, "Me too, babe."

An audible huff blew out of Carson's nostrils as he looked at his watch again and then off to the side. Luci smacked him on the bicep and whispered, through gritted teeth, "Stop."

"This makes me so happy," I said. I raced over to Vince's chair and threw one arm around him and the other around Torey. "Vin, this guy's one of my best friends, and I've never seen him smile like this. Keep it up, buddy."

"I will," Vince said. "He makes me smile, too."

Torey shook his head and looked at me. "Dude, you really are a girl sometimes."

20

Torey's revelation by the firepit was just the tip of the iceberg in what would end up being a pivotal summer.

For the first time since Christmas break and only the second time since we'd begun dating, Beth and I were spending most of our free time together. There were breaks, of course; coaching Brie's AAU basketball team kept Beth occupied on many nights and weekends, and I was earning some extra cash covering American Legion baseball games for the *Daily Record*. But we still had plenty of time in each other's company, and fifteen months into our relationship, Beth and I were again trying to get in sync. We'd reached the point where the polite games of tug-of-war from the previous summer had progressed into something more like stare downs between a pair of Doberman Pinschers. We hadn't started squabbling over every little morsel, but there was definitely a little tiff, almost daily, about how we were going to spend our time together, and I was the one who most often flipped on my back and showed my belly. So, for anywhere between four and fourteen hours per day, I was at her house watching bland sitcom reruns, swimming in the muddy river behind her house, getting embarrassed in 1-on-1 basketball, or listening to her dad's latest monologues about the Grand Old Party's "traditional values."

It was a welcome reprieve when Brie's team qualified for the national tournament. That meant Beth, Brie, and their parents were all going to Orlando for three nights, and I was off the hook for a weekend. I could do what I wanted and go where I wanted, and I wouldn't have to debate about it with my girlfriend.

The problem with that? I had no idea what to do or where to go when Beth wasn't around.

My first thought was to give Torey a call. Since the conversation about our baseball glory days, I'd been itching to go to the field and throw the ball around, something I didn't know I missed until we'd talked about it that night. Some of my favorite teen-hood memories were the days when we would toss round after round of batting practice to each other under the sizzling summer sun, then go to his house, glug down Gatorades, snarf cold turkey sandwiches, and taunt each other while battling it out in *MVP Baseball*.

"Vince could come, too. It'd be nice to have someone there to shag fly balls for a change."

"Sorry, man—wish I could." He sounded genuinely bummed that he couldn't take some hacks with me. "We're heading down to Virginia Beach for a week. His parents invited us."

Then I called Mason up and suggested a spontaneous "Bro Weekend." I offered to get Red Sox tickets for us and then maybe go see the new *Incredible Hulk* movie. But he just said, "Sorry, bud. Training all weekend. Maybe another time."

My remaining options for the weekend were limited. I

hadn't realized until then how spending all my spare time with Beth over the past year-plus had prevented me from nursing other tertiary relationships. And it occurred to me for the first time how much more difficult it could be to make and maintain friendships as a quasi-adult. I was about to resign myself to three days of weeding the garden with Mom, re-reading old books in my bedroom, and politely tittering at Ray's crude jokes during dinner when I got a call from Luci.

"Hey…" I said, trying to mask my confusion. I didn't know much about Carson, but I knew he hated when Luci talked to other guys. Torey told me he bought his sister a new phone for Christmas because Carson smashed hers on the sidewalk after she talked to her male lab partner about an assignment during Thanksgiving break.

"Mickey-Mack!" she said in a much more exuberant tone than she'd had when her boyfriend was with her at the campfire. "What's new, chicken poo?"

An uncontrollable grin broke across my face. This was the Luci I was used to. "Not a lot, polka dot!"

She giggled. "What are you up to? Torey said Bethany is out of town and you're sad and lonely."

I snickered at the mocking, droopy way she said "sad and lonely." Then I said, "Sad and lonely? Nah. Between my crossword puzzles and Backgammon with Mom, I've got a full weekend."

"Shit. Well, I was hoping you'd be down for a matinee at the Silverman on Saturday," she said. "Y'know, if you can tear yourself away from all the Backgammon."

I rolled my eyes and smirked, knowing that if she'd been next to me, she would've jabbed me with her elbow to say "I gotcha."

"Yeah, I saw *Phantom*'s playing," I said. *Phantom of the Opera* had been Luci's favorite musical since she was nine, and back in high school drama rehearsals, when she would burst into spontaneous opera with her booming mezzo soprano simply to startle people and laugh at them, *Phantom*'s theme song was her favorite with which to do so. "I figured Carson would take you to that."

"He said he would take me, but then he made plans with his buddies to go to the Speedway in Loudon," she said. "But it's fine, he hates going to shows anyway."

I recalled the scowl I could see on his face from center stage. "I remember that from last year."

"Yeah, sorry about that. Anyway, wanna go? No point in both of us sitting around doing nothing all day."

"I'm down to clown." I was hoping my subdued-but-silly retort would disguise how surprisingly excited I was at the prospect of some quality time with the ol' Goose.

"You *are* a clown, Mickey-Mack," she said with a smile in her voice. But before I could burn her back, she said, "Show's at three. See you Saturday!" and hung up. I shook my head and laughed.

***

It was unseasonably cool when I knocked on Luci's door two days later. The sky was gray, the ground still damp from fresh rain earlier that morning, and the wind was chilly and erratic, so it felt a lot more like mid-March than mid-June. I wore my navy blazer, a checkered blue button-up shirt, khakis, and dark java-colored oxfords instead of the polo shirt and cargo shorts I normally wore when I wanted to look "summertime nice." I looked respectable, but I didn't want to look like I'd put too much effort into my outfit, because this was just a hangout with a friend, and not a date.

Luci didn't get the memo, though, because when she opened the door, my jaw dropped. Her bright yellow sun dress popped dramatically against her deliciously brown summer tan. Her shoulder-length hair was up in a top knot that looked both effortless and elegant, and her face, with those big eyes and that gorgeous new smile of hers, was strategically framed by an adorably sexy pair of wispy tendrils. She accessorized the ensemble with a pearl necklace, a matching bracelet, and a twisted leather anklet. I'd never seen Luci look this way before, and as we hugged hello, I could smell citrus in her skin, and something stirred inside me. This wasn't the same brace-faced freshman girl that hugged me in her mom's living room a few years ago. This wasn't my friend's mouthy little sister. This was a woman. A stunning young woman.

"Luci Goose," I said, trying not to gawk, even though my eyes were drawn to every curve and crevice of her body. "Oh my god."

She beamed and said, "I know! I look pretty hot, right?" She spun around with her leather clutch in her hand and then did a curtsy.

"You really do." I closed my eyes and gave my head a quick shake to release myself of this trance.

"You look nice, too." She pretended to hold a camera and click a picture of me. "Now let's go. The Phantom waits for no one."

The fifteen-minute drive to the Silverman was the most fun I'd had in a car in years. Luci and I caught up on each other's first year away at school, talked about the friends

192

we'd made, reminisced about those simple, silly days in the Rockingham High Drama Club, rehashed and laughed at old jokes we thought we'd outgrown, bashed Danica and Darius for their betrayals, and talked a lot about Torey. I asked her why he never told me he was gay, and she said he didn't want things to get weird between him and me because, even though he always acted too cool to admit it, he loved me like a brother. Also, she said, he didn't like me "like that," which kind of hurt my feelings, I said with a modest chuckle, even though I didn't like him "like that," either.

One thing we didn't get into was our current relationships. She didn't tell me why she stuck by a guy who had no personality and no sense of humor but did possess a mean jealous streak. And I didn't tell her why I stuck by a girl who I had nothing in common with, had no real direction in life, and had made out with another guy. There was an unspoken understanding between us that this was just a light, fun little friend date, so we wouldn't burden each other with our respective relationship issues. But throughout the evening, I couldn't help but notice some of the contrasts between her and Bethany. When I told her my "75-pound chipmunk wizard" joke, instead of rolling her eyes, she guffawed. When we were in the lobby observing strangers before the show, instead of making fun of them, we made up love stories about them. ("The guy in the striped polo shirt—he put on a little weight after his divorce, but the lady in the purple dress next to him recently confessed her long-standing love for him; they're getting married in the fall. The guy in the black V-neck met the guy with the red necktie in college. They dated on-and-off for a few years before Tie Guy moved to L.A., but he gave up the posh life to come back to New Hampshire because he couldn't live without him."). Luci, I discovered, had a big, romantic heart. And I loved that.

We took our seats, and as I looked down at that big, beautiful stage, the same one from which I had roused a monsoon of applause with my Ren McCormack backflip in the *Footloose* finale a year prior, I felt admittedly odd looking on from the third row of the loge. Sure, I'd watched shows from the seats before, but having fallen so deeply in love with the theater over the past five years, it was a weird, wistful feeling this time—like watching someone else drive away in my car.

At the same time, though, something told me I was in the right place.

Luci and I joined in the murmurs reverberating through the house as anticipation for the show built, and when The Goose put her lips close to my ear to whisper, "Thank you for coming with me," my head dangled there, drifting involuntarily toward her cheek until it brushed against mine. I turned my chin toward her ear and whispered, "My pleasure," and it was all I could do to not graze her earlobe with my lips.

That tender moment, whatever it meant, was interrupted by Andrew Lloyd Webber's iconic show-opening "Overture" as it exploded from the electric organ and blasted through the auditorium. I couldn't help but smile as Luci squealed and made little, happy claps with her fingertips; I'd always thought that was wicked cute, and it showed me that, despite her physical, emotional, and intellectual maturity from young teenager to young woman, she was still the Luci I'd always known. And there was something refreshing about that. Something that told me I didn't have to be in "impress-my-date" mode. I could just relax and be myself. I could always be myself with her.

As brilliantly as this Broadway classic was being performed in front of me, I was struggling to focus on it because of what was next to me. I looked at Luci several times throughout the evening, and each time, she was watching the show with a gleeful, focused smile, as if she were seeing *Phantom of the Opera*—which I knew she'd seen at least eight times—for the first time. She was like an adorable little girl watching fireworks on a warm summer night—mesmerized by the sights and sounds, completely engaged, unable to focus on anything else in the world. So, she never caught me. She didn't catch me studying the symmetry of her face and the color in her cheeks. She didn't catch me ogling her big, beautiful eyeballs and wondering what it would be like to lose myself in them. She didn't catch me watching every move her body made, from the tiny breaths that made her stomach billow in and out to the way she tapped her left wrist to the beat of the music with her right index finger. And she didn't catch me staring blankly at the receding hairline in front of me as I tumbled, heart-first, into a hazy void of self-reflection.

I didn't know what was bringing about this sudden infatuation with my old buddy from Drama Club, or what was making it so intense. Maybe it was the sights, the sounds, the story, the stage; maybe it was that some of the happiest times of my pubescent years and beyond had happened in theater; maybe it was the feeling of sharing a sensory experience with someone I cared about who was sitting so close to me our arms were touching. Or maybe I hadn't gotten over the fact that my girlfriend had made out with another guy. All I knew was, that afternoon in the third row of the loge, there was nothing I wanted on this planet more than to pull Luci close to me, kiss her with the passion of a triumphant voyager reunited with his long-lost lover, and rest her head on my shoulder until the curtains came down.

But I didn't do that. Halfway through the second act, I forced myself to stop looking at her and pay attention to the show. I was dangerously close to the edge of a reckless emotional rabbit hole; Mason once told me I got so attached to people that I pushed them away, and I couldn't bear to do that with Luci. So, as I watched the Phantom pine for Christine, a love he'd have to force himself to accept he could not have, I knew I had to do the same with Luci Goose. I was with Bethany and she was with Carson— simple as that—so I would have to keep half of my face covered, too, and just be her friend and nothing more.

The show came to its dramatic conclusion and drew a standing ovation. The curtain call was prompt and showered in whistles and cheers. The patrons in the audience, dressed overwhelmingly in black and white, rocked toward the end of each row like penguins, then trickled toward the exits like slow streams of syrup. Luci and I were finally able to escape, and as soon as we got through the rotating doors and onto the sidewalk, we both took big breaths of fresh air. I stretched out my arms and back, and Luci got up on her tiptoes to stretch her legs.

"Did you have fun?" I asked with the same fake smile I'd give the mailman. I didn't want her to know about the journey I'd traveled through captivation, curiosity, desire, realization, sorrow, and acceptance that had nothing to do with the strife between Raoul and the Phantom.

"I had a great time—thank you, Mickey!" She threw her arms around my neck for a big hug. I smelled citrus again.

Wonderful, wonderful citrus.

"Awesome. Me too," I said. We released each other and started walking toward the parking garage. "But I have a question for you."

"Shoot."

"What do you call the bartender from *Cheers* who hides under the stage and gives singing lessons to girls?"

She smiled skeptically and looked at me out of the corner of her eye. "What?"

"Danson of the Opera!" I laughed with my belly, proud of myself for my clever, if cheesy, little joke.

"Wow! That's so bad," she said, though her face told me she appreciated my quip in spite of its corniness.

"Get it? Ted Danson? I just came up with that!"

I giggled, not just with pride, but with joy that I could share this dorky side of myself with Luci, and that was enough for me. We'd always been friends, and we always would be, because she'd always liked me for who I was. And that's all I needed this to be. The inner torture I'd put myself through during the show was amplified by the enamoring atmosphere of the theater, that's all, and now that we were back out in the sunlight, life could resume as normal.

"Now I have a question for you," Luci said as she slowed her pace down.

"What's up?" I fished for my car keys in the pocket of my blazer.

She stopped and clicked her heels, then I turned to look at her as she said, "Why were you staring at me the whole time?"

21

I didn't know what to say. I was stunned. My frazzled brain searched frantically for the right response while my eyes popped out of my face and my jaw hung helplessly on its hinges.

"Staring at you?" It was the only thing I could come up with to break the uneasy silence. My eyes darted in every direction while my mouth and vocal cords continued to grasp for more words. Nothing.

"You were looking at me the whole show." The way Luci said this wasn't accusatory—it was more observational—so that helped me relax a little. "Was something bothering you?"

I still couldn't think of any original material, so again, I just repeated what she said. "Bothering me?"

She tilted her head and smiled. "Hey. Look at me," she said with a more serious tone than she'd had all day, and I was nervous about what she might say next. Serious conversations weren't what I was used to with Luci. But when I looked straight at her, her eyes told me I could trust her. "I know something's on your mind. Talk to me."

I exhaled and relaxed a bit. I couldn't believe how easily this woman could coax me into opening up to her with a head tilt and a soft tone.

My lips were wedged in a tight smirk, my eyes started to sting, and my nose felt drippy. I looked down at the sidewalk and said, "I mean—being here, with you, at this show, and the ride over here, with all the stuff we were talking about, just felt—I don't know …"

"Natural," she said. Alarmed, I immediately looked up to catch her gaze. She knew exactly what I was talking about. Her eyes were misty and looked worried. She wiped the corners of both with the tip of her thumb.

I nodded lightly and paused. "Yeah."

Luci took a step toward me. "I felt it, too, Mickey-Mack."

My heart rate began to pick up. "You've always been one of my best friends, Goose." I smiled. "But I never knew how much you meant to me until—"

I hung my head again. Luci took another step toward me and took my hand.

"'til what?"

I looked around wondering how far down the rabbit hole I might be willing to go; I saw a blue jay in a pine tree, a yellowed sheet of newspaper blowing across the crosswalk, and a black lab barking at a kid in a *Power Rangers* shirt. Bethany and I had been dating for over a year now—she was my first "real" girlfriend (Danica barely counted). But we were never in sync—hadn't been from Day 1 when she thought my lame jokes were too lame and then we shared that weird kiss. And there were signs all over the universe that I probably shouldn't be with her. But Luci and I had a history together. We'd gone to high school together. We were in theater together. We'd been to each other's houses for snowball fights, Whiffle ball games, Sweet 16s, and graduation parties. We'd helped each other study, helped our moms with bake sales, and helped our fathers' memories live on. We were solid. So, I wasn't about to find a bush to beat around. I had to just tell her.

"I never knew how much you meant to me until I saw you with Carson."

"With Carson?" Now she was doing what I'd been doing before.

"Yeah." My chest began ballooning with courage. "When I saw you with him the other night, you were just—different."

Luci's eyes fell toward my shoes. "I know."

"You weren't yourself at all. You were wicked quiet. Like you weren't even there."

She nodded. "Carson and I haven't been getting along lately."

"What do you mean?"

"He just gets super jealous whenever I even talk to another guy."

"Yeah, Torey told me he wrecked your phone."

She inhaled. "Yeah. And he knew I was going to your house, and even though Toto and Vince were going to be there and your parents were around, and I'm with him and he knows you have a girlfriend, he didn't want me to go."

"Wow," I said. "But he knows we're just friends, doesn't he?"

"Doesn't matter—you're a guy. So, he would only let me go if he was there, too, and he could only go if he skipped the demolition derby he wanted to go to with his buddies that night. So, he was pissed about that, too."

"Guess that explains why he was in such a chipper mood." I tried not to insult him in front of Luci, because he was her boyfriend or whatever, but I was starting to dislike the guy more and more.

"Yeah, he can be kind of a bitch when he's pissed."

I tipped my head back to let out a laugh and said, "Hey, YOU said it—not me!"

A big, gorgeous grin washed across Luci's face as she recalled the same thing I just had. She declared proudly, "I don't care—I'll say it again! Carson's a bitch!"

With that, we shared a laugh and a high-five. But it was different this time. Because this high-five wasn't like the one we shared in her mom's living room as "Hero" came through the speakers. It was something more. Something meaningful. As the palms of our hands connected, our fingers involuntarily melted together. Luci took a step closer and looked up at me. Our hands interlocking felt so… natural (there's that damn word again), almost as if they were cut from the same mold. Like puzzle pieces. Like round pegs in round holes. Or, I guess, hand-shaped hands in hand-shaped holes. No other girl's fingers and palms had ever melded to my fingers and palms so effortlessly—not Danica's, not Kaylin's, not even Bethany's. There was no way this could be real, was there? I had to find out, so as my heart began to rattle the inside of my ribcage, I took Luci's other hand with my empty one, and instantly, effortlessly, they clung together, as if drawn to each other by— something like static electricity, but stronger. An industrial magnet, maybe.

The silence between us this time was not uneasy. It was comfortable. We were communicating, not with words, but with eyebrow twitches, relaxed smiles, and racing pulses.

My mind could only think one thought while I stood there on the sidewalk, just outside the parking deck, holding Luci's hands and looking at her like I'd never looked at her—or anyone—before. It wasn't about how Bethany would probably flip out, even though she'd made out with Brad that one time. It wasn't about how Carson would probably get all his redneck-hunter-demo-derby buds together and beat the shit out of me (and then I'd never see Luci again). It wasn't about how much shit Torey might give me for messing with his sister. It was about Luci, how much we had in common, how well we got along, how much she made me laugh, how I loved the way she did those little happy claps, how gorgeous her big, beautiful eyeballs were, and how I wanted to kiss her perfect mouth more than I'd ever wanted to kiss anyone's mouth in my life. Every first kiss I'd known to that point had been pervaded by nerves and my deeply embedded insecurity. But it wouldn't be like that with Luci. A kiss with her would be easy. It would feel right. It would feel—

"Natural," Luci said. Her lips drooped and her eyebrows arched. I nodded—she knew what I was thinking. She knew how I felt, and she felt it, too. So, she knew what had to happen next.

"But we can't," I said.

"I know." She shook her head, rolled her eyes at herself and said, trying to make it sound like she was half-joking, "Sorry, I'm just being stupid."

We let go of each other's hands—but not in a bad way—in a 'let's-just-be-friends-because-that-makes-more-sense-right-now' way. Then I put my arm around her (because it was chilly for a mid-June day) and said, "You're not stupid at all, Luce. You know, if we were both single, I could totally see this being a thing."

"A 'thing'?" she said with a pompous laugh. "I'm so honored that I could be your 'thing'!"

"You think you could qualify as anything more than that?" I teased, pretending I didn't find her scorching hot. "I mean, look at you. A baboon in a yellow dress is still a baboon!"

A shocked laugh exploded out of Luci's face before she came back with, "Oh, I'm a baboon?"

"Yup!" I said with a smirk.

"Well then I'm the hottest baboon you've ever seen!" She jabbed me with her elbow and gave me a cocky grin.

I held my smirk, looked at the ground and said, after a half-beat of hesitation, "Yup."

***

We dropped comfortably back into the Friend Zone on the drive back to her mom's house. We joked, we teased, we laughed, we reminisced. We didn't acknowledge the conversation we'd had outside the parking deck because there was no point; she was with Carson and I was with Bethany—Beth, whatever—and we were friends, just like we had always been. In fact, if there was one thing we'd gotten out of our not-a-date, it wasn't the revelations we'd made to one another, it was the growth our friendship had endured because of them. We were on the same page about our feelings, and we were on the same page about what we were going to do about them—nothing—so no further discussion was needed. But sharing a secret so significant and, at the same time, so intimate, made me feel closer to Luci than ever, even if we weren't going to do anything about it.

Right?

I asked Luci if she wanted to stop and get something

to eat before I dropped her off. My stomach was growling and, truth be told, I didn't want to let her go just yet.

"Nah," she said. "I don't really have the money—my car payment is due soon."

"Okay." I tried to mask my disappointment. "I can pay for dinner, it's no prob—"

"No thanks!" she said cheerily but firmly. She was probably worried that me taking her to dinner would turn our "not-a-date" into a date, so I didn't fight her on it. But then she added, "Why don't you just come in when we get to my house and I'll make tuna melts or something?"

"You and your tuna melts," I said with an obnoxious snicker. "What are we, five?"

"Shut up—they remind me of my dad." She slapped me on the arm. "Ass."

"I know," I said. "Just playing."

"For real, though, if you want to come in I can make something. If not, then you can go fuck yourself!"

"Wow!" I laughed at her boldness. Of course I wanted to come in.

When we got there, I noticed her mom's car wasn't in the driveway and wondered if Luci had known we'd be alone if I came in. With this observation, I hesitated to get out of the car until she said, "Are you coming? I thought you were hungry."

The house hadn't changed much in all the years I'd known the Rizzo kids. There were a few more pictures on the living room walls documenting their slow metamorphoses from babies to gawky teens to young adults. Luci's valedictorian speech was framed and hung next to her senior photo; Torey's medal from our freshman year baseball title hung next to a photo of him and me grinning ear to ear and flashing "Number One" signs with our index fingers; an 8-by-10 of their dad, sporting the flared nostrils and snaggled grin his children both inherited from him, proudly holding a certificate that read "Superintendent of the Year 1982." The one photo, though, that really snatched my attention was the one from Luci's freshman year. In it, she sported the same hopeful, cocky smile full of metal I remembered from that first autumn in Drama Club my sophomore year. Her smile, albeit without the perfect teeth she now donned, was one of the warmest I had ever seen, and her eyes in this photo declared to the world, "Nothing can hurt me, and no one can stop me." It was taken before Darius and Danica smashed her heart to smithereens, and before Carson shoved her personality into a jar to be opened at his will only. Now, even though Luci's smile was still stunning, the fearlessness in her eyes had been flushed away and replaced with caution and mistrust. The youthful self-assurance in ninth-grade Luci's face had been whittled down to guarded semi-optimism bordering on cynicism.

But, damn was she sexy now.

Luci came back downstairs after changing out of her dress, but even in her bright pink Adidas soccer shorts and oversized Dartmouth crew neck sweatshirt, she looked incredible. I summoned every speck of will power I could to avoid looking at her butt as she walked by and said, "You can turn the TV on if you want."

"Cool. Thanks." I picked up the remote and sat down on the brown beanbag-style love seat. "Hey, where's your mom anyway?"

"I think she went to the beach with her boyfriend Bill and his kids," she said over the buzz of the electric can opener. "She'll be back tomorrow."

"From Hampton Beach? That's ten minutes away." I flipped to NESN to see how the Red Sox were doing.

"No, she stays over at his house, dumbass," she said in a condescending tone. "They're not like, 'Oh Em Gee, Hampton is soooo far away, we should probably get a room.'"

I said, "You're a dick," to which she replied proudly, "I know!"

I turned my attention to the Sox, who were leading Cincinnati 4-3 in the ninth inning. Jonathan Papelbon was on the mound, and I sat at attention in hopes that my silent prayers from two hundred miles away would be the magic spell Boston needed to close it out. Jerry Remy was meandering on in his distinctively shrill Boston accent about Papelbon's pitch selection or whatever when Luci came in with my tuna melt, plopped the plate and a glass of water on the coffee table and then plopped herself down—right in the love seat with me.

It was a bold move, for sure, but a welcome one, if I'm being honest. Because a lot of things were clarified for me with that move; despite my best intentions to keep this above board and firmly planted in not-a-date territory, Luci was clearly interested in moving toward something that wasn't typical of two people in the Friend Zone. Friends don't sit this close to each other on a small couch with their thighs touching.

Luci crossed her legs and turned toward me, propped her head up on her fist and gave me a seductive smile.

"Hey," I said with an airy tone and a little smile as I looked at those big brown eyes.

"Hey," she said back with a tinge of sweetness in her voice. Friends don't say "Hey" to each other the way we had just said "Hey" to each other.

I knew she wanted to say something to me—maybe even *do* something to me—as we studied every captivating fleck of texture in each other's irises. Her eyebrows were arched but she looked relaxed at the same time—even happy—and our chests were not only touching but inhaling and exhaling lightly, comfortably, and in unison. I smelled citrus emitting from her baggy Dartmouth sweatshirt—she must have re-applied when she changed—and I felt tiny breaths coming from the flared nostrils of her cute, rounded-off nose. There was so much I wanted to say to her—even *do* to her—in that quiet, beautiful moment between us. But I didn't dare, even though friends don't study captivating flecks in each other's irises like this.

"Thank you for the tuna melt," I said. Friends thank each other for tuna melts.

"You're welcome." She smiled and brushed her fingers down my cheek. Friends don't brush their fingers down each other's cheeks.

So much was spoken in the silence between us. As we stared at each other for centuries, she continued touching my face, and I began to stroke her outer thigh with my hand. Intense stares like this make most people uneasy, and normally I was no exception; but with Luci, it felt right. Natural. In fact, I never wanted her to stop. I could suddenly picture her at age forty with crow's feet embedded by her eyes from years of laughter and happiness; at age sixty, with grey hair and a gleeful twinkle; and at age eighty, sleeping peacefully after a fulfilled life of making the world brighter each day and then coming home to nestle up with me—just like this—each night. I pictured children running through sprinklers, golden retrievers chasing tennis balls, vacations in the Caribbean, reading books in identical rocking chairs. I pictured watching the sun set from our lush suburban backyard and making love under the moonlight until dawn. It was some of the sappiest, cliché bullshit I'd ever envisioned, and I never knew how badly I wanted all of that sappy, cliché bullshit until I envisioned it with Luci.

"What are you thinking about, Mickey-Mack?" She rested her head on my chest and put her arm around me.

I wanted to say it. We were both thinking it. I knew I shouldn't say it, though, but I knew if I waited too long to respond I would ruin the moment altogether. So, I put the ball back in her court.

"I think you know."

She took a sad breath. "Yeah."

I looked at the television for the first time in twenty years, and it was all tied up. I wondered if the Sox would still pull out the win. Or if they could.

Or if they should.

"I think—I think I have feelings for you, Luce," I said. "And not just friend feelings."

"I think you do, too," she said. "And—I know I have those feelings for you."

So, it was finally out there. After dancing around it all day, the ambiguity was gone. I just didn't know where to go from here. Because, when the strings of your heart are pulled in different directions, the decision must be outsourced to your brain, which pulls you toward what you know, not what you want. I knew what my relationship with Bethany was. It wasn't perfect, but it was familiar. Luci was a different kind of familiar—I'd known her for years—but these feelings for her were new. Weren't they? My brain and my heart were having a hard time sorting this one out.

"So, what the hell are we gonna do?" she asked sincerely. She wasn't implying anything. She didn't say it salaciously or flirtatiously. She genuinely wanted to know how we were going to deal with this. I didn't know what the right answer was, but I knew what the safe answer was, so I went with that.

"I don't think we can do anything." I looked away and sulked. "We're both with other people, and unless that changes, we can't."

I paused for a second, then added, "Or at least we shouldn't."

"I know." She played anxiously with my shirt collar, then she sniffled and wiped her cheek. "I just—"

She wanted to say more but stopped herself. I was both afraid of and intrigued by what she was going to say, but I didn't pry, because I knew we were heading back toward the safety and sensibility of the Friend Zone, if I could just keep us on this path.

"Besides, Luci Goose, we're friends. Really good friends. I wouldn't want to screw anyth—"

"I just know we'd be so much happier if we were together," she blurted out. "Both of us."

She began pushing hard on her eyes and nose with her hand, as if she were trying to muscle her tears back into their ducts.

I looked at her gorgeous, near-crying face and clenched my jaw as hard as I could to hold back my own tears. "I think you're right."

I took a deep breath and added, "Actually, I know you're right. I've been thinking about it all day. That's why I was staring at you in the theater."

She laughed through her sniffles and nodded. "I knew it."

"But we both know what it's like to be cheated on." I stopped rubbing her outer thigh and put my hand on her waist. It felt so nice to just hold her. "I mean, you more than me. And if we do anything now, we're just as bad as them."

She nodded and sniffled. As much as I loved the wit, intelligence, and confidence Luci typically showed the world (when Carson wasn't around), I had to admit, seeing her vulnerable side was even more gripping. Because she didn't share this side with just anybody, and I knew that, which made her even more attractive to me. But that only made it worse.

"I know, Mickey-Mack, I know." Her voice cracked. She was pushing on her face again, this time so hard she looked like she was going to break her own nose. "I'm just— I'm just so fucked up."

"What? No, you're not!" I was not going to have someone insult my friend like that, even if it was my friend herself.

"Yes, I am!" she insisted as she blinked away the waterworks. "I was such a blubbering mess when I found out Darius was fucking Danica. I was desperate. You were with Bethany, so then I made out with Carson at some stupid pig roast thing, and now I feel like I'm stuck with him."

"Stuck with him?" I didn't know what else to say, so I was back to repeating her last few words.

"Stuck with him." She wiped her nose with her Dartmouth sweatshirt. "He treats me like shit, he gets mad when I even talk to other guys, he never laughs at my jokes, he hates it when I sing, and we have nothing in common.

All he ever wants to do is hang out with his hick friends, and for me to be his arm candy and never say anything. He thinks women should be s—"

"Seen and not heard," I said. She paused, straightened up, and looked at me with her mouth hanging half open.

Luci nodded as her eyes connected with mine in a whole new way, as if she were looking at herself in the mirror. "So, you know what I mean."

I nodded back assuredly. Carson was her Ray-Hole.

"So, why don't you just dump him?" I asked. But I knew the answer. She couldn't stand up to her boyfriend any more than I could stand up to my stepfather. She'd been beaten down and defeated by what happened between her, Darius, and Danica in much the same way that I'd been beaten down and defeated by Ray and his explosions. She couldn't escape her situation with him for the same reasons I couldn't let Raymond kick me out of the house when I was fifteen. She didn't know what she would do with her life if she were alone and single in the same way I didn't know at fifteen what I'd do if I were alone and on my own.

"Because. Like I said—I'm fucked up."

She didn't need to explain it any further. I got her, probably better than I had ever "gotten" anybody. And she got me, too. But she didn't have to be so hard on herself.

"Stop saying that! You're not fucked up!" I tried to laugh it off to lighten the mood. It worked a little, because she responded with a laugh. A defeated-sounding laugh, but a laugh, nonetheless.

"Yes, I am!" She sat up on my lap. "It's like, psychologically—actually, even physiologically—I need a man in my life. I haven't been single since I was fourteen, and the thought of not being in a relationship makes me literally feel like I'm going to puke. That's fucked up, dude!"

"I'll tell you something that's fucked up," I said. "I'm bigger and stronger than both my stepdad and my girlfriend, and I'm scared to death of both of them because I hate getting yelled at."

"That doesn't make you fucked up, that just makes you a pussy," she said with a blubbery giggle as she jabbed me with her elbow.

I said, "You're a dick," to which she replied proudly, "I know!"

It got quiet again as I watched the Red Sox win it in the 10th, 6-4. It took them a little longer than they wanted to, but they prevailed, nonetheless.

Maybe we could, too.

I looked back at Luci, who was staring blankly at the arm of the couch with streaks of dried tears on her cheeks, contemplating something. "Hey," I said to her with the same airy tone as before. She looked at me with a little smile and said, "Hey" with much more than a tinge of sweetness this time.

"What if we make a deal?"

"'What kind of 'deal'?"

I took a slow, deep breath and said, "We give each other one week. I break up with Bethany. You break up with Carson. And then…"

She sat up at full attention. "Mickey—"

"… and then I'll meet you back here, look you in the eyes…"

"Don't break up with your girlfriend for m—"

"—and I will kiss you the way I've wanted to kiss you since we sang Mariah Carey together."

She looked at me with her head tilted. I could tell she

wanted to smile. But she was nervous.

"What do you think?" I asked.

She looked at my tuna melt. She stole the glass of water she had brought for me and took a sip. She put the glass back down. My stomach churned as I awaited her answer. She looked at me. "You'll really do it?"

"Yes," I said emphatically. And I believed with my whole heart that I was telling the truth.

"I know confrontation is hard for y—" she paused to re-word. "For both of us. So, if one of us goes through with this and the other one doesn't, things will never be the same with us again. You know that, right?"

"But if we do both go through with it, things will never be the same with us again, anyway. They'll be better—better than they've ever been. And I'm willing to risk what we have for what we could have."

Luci looked at me with an uneasy but hopeful smile, touched my face again, and said, "Me too."

We held each other in a peaceful silence for a few minutes, enjoying the moment, anticipating the sun-soaked meadow we'd be able to enjoy together on the other side of the treacherous mountain we would first need to scale separately. Breaking up with Bethany and Carson was going to be tough and it was going to be terrifying, but we would have each other once it was all over. We just had to power through what would inevitably be the biggest fights of our lives, but it would all be worth it in the end.

We agreed to meet back in this very living room at noon the following Saturday. We sealed it with a handshake and a hug. Luci squealed and made little, happy claps with her fingertips. My right heel began bouncing up and down like never before.

22

I'd still never successfully dumped anyone before. I'd bailed on my only attempt the previous summer when Beth started crying and begging me to stay, and I was prepared for that this time. But I also had to expect that it could go in a different direction entirely. Because I didn't have the power I once had—the power of being the only guy who'd ever given her affection—a power that had made her so desperate that she'd vowed to do anything to keep me. The dynamics between us had shifted dramatically since then, and the power in our relationship had not merely balanced but tilted decidedly in Beth's favor. So, this would be a tough situation for any guy to tackle, let alone one who notoriously froze in the face of confrontation.

But it was Friday night already, and my time was almost up. I hadn't heard from Luci all week, per our agreement, but I was supposed to be at her house to give her that kiss in less than seventeen hours, so it was now or never. *I'm willing to risk what we have for what we could have,* I'd told her. I'd said it out loud—said it with conviction—to show Luci I meant it, but also, to convince myself I could do it. I just had to power through. It would all be worth it. Just power through.

It was a humid, rainy day, and we'd been cooped up in Beth's house watching *King of Queens* and *Seinfeld* reruns with Brie all day. Sitcoms were never my thing—too low-brow and predictable, and canned laughter made me cringe—but they'd become a big part of my life since the Connellys had. Most days like this—sitting on the couch with Beth while she and her sister cackled about George Costanza's latest meltdown about nothing—were quite mundane. But not this one. At least not to me. Because I spent all day staring blankly at the television set, trying to summon the intestinal fortitude I would need to break up with her.

I had a built-in excuse for most of the day; I couldn't do it with Brianna hanging around, and then her parents got home from work, so I couldn't do it in front of them. But after dinner, Brie went off with her friends, and Beth, who was as tired as I was of being stuck inside, said, "You wanna go out back?"

"Out back" was code for "to the muddy river for a swim," and "a swim" had grown to mean more than one thing to Beth and me. Sure, we swam sometimes. But the muddy river, which was two hundred yards behind her parents' house and shielded in every direction by bushes, oak trees and tall banks, had also become a place where we would flirt, splash each other, flash each other, make out, and sometimes have sex. So, it was a location that held many fond memories for us as a couple. Was that really where I was going to try and end things with her?

I nodded. "Sure."

Power through.

She changed into her bikini—mint green with little pink

stars—I stripped down to my charcoal grey boxer briefs, and we walked through the rain until we got to our spot. We were already drenched, and we hadn't even gotten in the water yet. The riverbank was extra sloppy, too, which made Beth all giggly because she loved playing in the mud. I hated it. But there was that bright, off-center smile packed with flashy white teeth. How could I take that away from her?

Power through.

After getting sufficiently caked in mud, Beth slid down to the river as if by boogie board, then belly-flopped into the waist-deep water. She stood up, wiped the wet hair out of her face with both hands, and looked at me. She reached around to her back, untied her bikini top, and threw it onto one of the giant boulders protruding from the stream, grinning at me the whole time. She gestured to me with her string beans. This was going to be even harder than I'd imagined.

Power through?

I stepped gingerly down the riverbank, looking down at my feet and, alternately, at her "come hither" smile as I made my way to the edge of the water. I oozed into the river, cringing at how ice-cold the water was as it rose above my ankles, then knees, then groin, then stomach. I finally got to Beth, who threw her arms around me, pushed her naked boobs up against my chest, and planted a steamy open-mouth kiss on me. She lifted one of her long legs up, wrapped it around my back, and started grinding herself against me; there was no question what she wanted. But as her hands trailed down my chest and my stomach, and her fingertips slipped underneath the waistband of my briefs, one big, important question slipped into my mind: What kind of asshole was I going to be?

Was I going to be the kind of asshole who had sex with his girlfriend and then dumped her? Or was I going to be the kind of asshole who told his half-naked, horny (but very insecure) girlfriend he didn't want to have sex with her right now, then dump her, making her feel both unattractive and unworthy of love at the same time? Or would I be the kind of asshole who wanted to dump his girlfriend but didn't, had sex with her instead, and then strung her along for ten more years as both of us grew more and more miserable and resentful of one another? None of those sounded like good options, but in that confusing, lustful moment, when Luci's face was in my mind but Beth's body was in my face, they felt like they were my only options. So, I went with the first one.

And then, later, the third one.

***

"Are you fucking serious right now, man?" Shock, incredulity on her face. "We just had sex, like, ten minutes ago, and now you're dumping me?"

"I—I've been thinking about it for a while." I couldn't make eye contact.

"How long is 'a while'?" She stared at me with anger, anticipation.

I shrugged. "Since—at least since the whole Brad thing."

"Brad?" She looked to the sky, fake-laughed, then looked back at me. "I told you I shut that shit down, man."

"You still made out with him, though." My eyes dipped to her muddy feet. I still couldn't look at her face.

"Yeah? And I told you about it and said I was sorry. Like, a hundred times."

"Still doesn't make it okay."

"Fine." She shook her head to try to find a solution. "Then you go make out with another girl, and we'll be even."

I shook my head. That's not what I wanted. "This isn't just about making out."

"Then what?"

I didn't immediately respond. I began chewing the inside of my cheek. *Not now, Mickey*, I thought to myself. *Power through.*

"Then WHAT, Michael?"

"I just—think we want different things. In life."

"What 'things'?" She looked genuinely confused. She really hadn't thought of this before. "You said you wanted to stay here. With me."

I shook my head.

"Were you lying about that, too?"

"I never said I wanted to stay here. I was gonna go to New York, remember?"

"Yeah, and then you didn't go because you fucking lied to me and got caught, remember?"

Despite the way she mocked my use of the word "remember," that wasn't the way I remembered it.

"I didn't stay because I lied. I stayed because you were upset."

"I was upset because you fucking lied!"

"Whatever. My point is, I w—"

"Yeah, whatever is right." She rolled her eyes. I re-started.

"My point is, I wanted to go to New York, L.A., Chicago, wherever. You don't want to go anywhere. You just want to stay here."

"So? What's wrong with here? I like Rockingham. My friends are all here. My parents and my sister are here."

"There's nothing wrong with it. But that's my point. We want different things."

"But I thought you wanted me. You said you loved me."

"I did. I do. I do love you, and I do want you. But I want other things, too."

I felt like I was winning, so I was finally able to look at her face. It was crimson with rage, though her eyes were saturated with sadness. But I'd forgotten who I was talking to. This wasn't some random girl named Beth with a nice smile and pretty red hair. This was Bethany Connelly, superstar athlete and ultimate competitor. As if a switch had been flipped, she began to single-handedly deconstruct my defense. With her back against the wall, she morphed into an invincible beast. She was a sleek, gray wolf, I was a common household mutt, and she went on the attack.

"So, you're saying I made you give up New York. That's bullshit, man. You said on our first date that you dreamed of being a famous actor, but it was, like, a million-to-one shot, and YOU said that going to Boston and being a *SportsCenter* guy made more sense. It was more realistic. YOU said that, man. Not me. And when you found out you got into NYU, you were the one who didn't tell me about it, then lied about it, and let me find out about it from fucking Forrest Gump."

"Forrest Gump is southern, not British…"

"I don't care! But YOU were the one who cried to ME when you got busted. YOU were the one who decided not to go. It was YOUR decision, man. Don't put that on me."

"What was I supposed to do? Just go to New York and say, 'Bye Beth, fuck you. I don't care about your feelings'?"

"You tell me, man. You've known yourself your whole life. You knew me for, like, three months when that went down. If going to school to be an actor was so important to you, if it was such a big dream, why the hell would you let some girl you knew for three months stop you?"

I hung my head. I had no answer for that one.

Beth knew she was on a roll, so she kept going.

"And now you're dragging my ass through the mud, like I forced you to do something you didn't want to do. YOU chose to stay here. YOU chose to stay with me. And now you want to dump me for something that happened a year ago? You're full of shit, Michael. Now WHAT the FUCK is going on?"

My frazzled brain searched frantically for the right response.

"Come on, Mick. What is it? It's not Brad. It's not New York. Why all of a sudden? Why today?"

My eyes popped out of my face and my jaw hung helplessly on its hinges.

"Is there someone else?" I shook my head no. "Did something happen when I went to Orlando?" I shook my head no.

"Then WHAT?"

My continued silence was making her more animated. More agitated. Her face was getting redder, and her brow ridge was protruding from above her eyes. She was pissed. But I couldn't come up with anything else to say.

"Fine. Let's do it," she said.

"Do what?"

"Let's break up. I don't want to be with some gay little

fuck-tard who can't even form a sentence when he gets scared. I'll find a real man who can stand up for himself."

Now she was just being mean. She knew I hated when people used "gay" that way, she knew I hated the term "fuck-tard," and she was definitely pushing my buttons about standing up for myself. But if I didn't take her bait, this would be over soon. I just had to power through.

Then Beth stepped toward me, lowered her chin, and peered at me through what suddenly looked like very wispy eyebrows. In an instant, her pointer finger looked meaty, and her teeth looked yellow and craggy and were inches from my nose. I couldn't tell if I was staring at Beth or Raymond, but I was frozen, speechless, and unable to do anything but listen to what she said next.

"But I swear to God, man, if I find out you've been seeing someone else, I will fuck you up, and I will fuck her up. I will knock her ass to the ground, kick her until her ribs snap, then I will smash up her car, smash up your car, and then wreck your house."

"C'mon, Bethany, you're not going to—"

"It's BETH. And go ahead, try me, man. Let me find out you've got another girlfriend. See what happens. You don't think I know how to deal with people who hurt me? Maybe I wasn't one of the cool kids, but I knew how to stand up for myself. Unlike you. Gay little fuck-tard."

The Red-Faced Banshee had pierced my defenseless soul with its horrific shrieks.

I looked at her for a few moments with shattered nerves and a palpitating heart. My breaths were short and frantic, tears rose in my ducts, and my bottom lip started to tremble. Beth had rattled me to my core, worse than Ray ever had, and all I could do was crumble. I fell to my knees in that mushy bank by the muddy river and, with every muscle in my body heaving with remorse, began bawling.

"There's no one else, Bethy-Bear, I swear," I glogged. "I was just being stupid. You're right about everything. There was no reason for this."

She stood in front of me with her hands on her hips and a smug expression on her face, as if she'd expected me to do this. I pulled her toward me, wrapped my arms around her waist, and pressed my face up against her stomach.

"I'm sorry," I said in a pitiful, desperate tone. "You're everything to me. Don't go. I love you."

She scratched the back of my head as if I were an obedient little schnauzer. "I love you too, Michael. I'm not going anywhere. You were."

"No," I said with my nose buried in her belly button. "No, no, no, no. I'm not going anywhere."

She looked down at me, put her fingers under my chin, and tilted my head up to look her in the eye. "Promise?"

"I promise. I'm sorry. So, so sorry."

Beth nodded. "Never again?"

I shook my head vehemently. "Never again. I swear."

"Good," she said with the smile of a victor. She knelt down in the mud with me, kissed me on the forehead and added, "that's the right answer."

Bethany always *did* have a flair for the dramatic.

***

I went to Luci's house the next day at noon, just like we'd agreed. I told Beth I had to help my mom with some gardening and I'd be over later (I knew Beth wouldn't offer to help, so I'd be in the clear for a few hours). This was

222

going to be rough, especially since Luci would be an emotional wreck after dumping Carson. Maybe even a physical wreck. I wasn't sure if she'd have a black eye, cuts on her face, or a fat lip. But he hadn't come to my parents' house looking for me yet, so maybe he'd decided to bow out gracefully (sure, Mickey). It didn't matter, though, because I was about to break Luci's heart and destroy our friendship forever.

I took a deep breath, rang her doorbell, and waited for her. She was going to say "Mickey-Mack!" and look at me with that heartwarming smile and those big, beautiful eyeballs, make those adorable little happy claps with her fingertips, and then throw her arms around me. And then I was going to devastate her. But how could I explain that I had to do it in order to protect her from literal bodily harm? How could I explain that Beth was a bigger bully than I ever thought, and that somehow, I knew she was serious about those threats? Luci will have just escaped an abusive relationship with her asshole redneck guy, and I didn't want to subject her to abuse from my asshole redneck girl. She didn't deserve that. This was for her own good, even if I never got to see her again.

She opened the door, put her hands on her hips, and said, "Hey." She was wearing a long-sleeved black NASCAR t-shirt and bright salmon-colored yoga pants. Her hair was in a high ponytail and messy. She hadn't showered yet. There were no bruises. No black eyes. No scratches. So that was good. But there was no "Mickey-Mack," either. There was no smile, and no happy claps. Had she already heard somehow?

"What's up?" she asked. This wasn't the Luci I took to *The Phantom of the Opera*. This wasn't the Luci who giggled at my Ted Danson joke. This wasn't the Luci who practically sat in my lap and told me how happy she knew we could be together. No, this was the Luci from the bonfire. Subdued. Quiet. But she knew why I was there, even though she was pretending not to.

I took another deep breath, shook my head and said, with a resigned expression on my face, "I couldn't. She said no."

"Well—" Luci looked at me, then through the frosted front door window, then out into her front yard, then down at her left hand. She slowly lifted that hand in front of her cheek and turned her knuckles toward me so I could see the cushion cut diamond on her ring finger.

She looked at me and winced. "I said yes."

INTERMISSION

MASON PATRICK, Age 32
October 4, 2017

Hi Dad,

It's weird being called "Sarge." The boys started calling me that last week after my promotion. I'm wicked pumped about it, and I know I earned it taking my lumps for eight years in D-4. But when they call me that, all I can think of is that fat, google-eyed idiot from Beetle Bailey. But this promo, and the fat stacks that come with it, will definitely help us pay for this big, crazy wedding we're planning.

I know. I never thought I'd tie the knot, either. Said it a million times—I don't put up with other people's bullshit. I don't care what movie we're gonna watch or what's for dinner. And if your feelings get hurt because I'm too blunt or whatever, that's on you. But once you find someone whose bullshit you'll not just put up with, but you actually kinda love, your attitude changes. You wanna spend as much time with them and their bullshit as you can. And the thought of them kissing anyone else the way they kiss you makes you want to puke. So you want to put a ring on that shit. Sorry, I don't have a way with words like Mick does.

We actually got together at Mickey's wedding. Long time coming, I think. I wasn't sure if the hand touch at the bar during the rehearsal dinner the night before was on purpose, but it got my attention. Then, when we caught eyes during the first dance, the smile and eyebrow twitch removed all doubt. I got a few laughs with my best man speech, we clinked glasses, and when Savage Garden's

"Truly Madly Deeply" started playing, I asked him to dance.

I'd had a thing for Salvatore for so frickin' long. Probably since he started hanging out with Mick way back in high school. I loved his perfectly imperfect smile. His big, cocky laugh (I knew he wasn't as cocky as he pretended), and a wicked tight body that got even more ripped when he went to West V. But they were freshmen and I was a senior, and being "out and proud" wasn't a thing at our school in the early aughts. The only known gay person at RHS was Bryson Moreover, and he had a face full of zits and didn't shower, so it wasn't worth coming out for him. Then I graduated, moved to Boston, met some guys here and there. But there was always some kind of drama. Either their daddies didn't accept them, or they didn't accept themselves, or their feelings got hurt when I told them they gained a couple pounds. It was just bullshit here, bullshit there, bullshit, bullshit everywhere.

When Torey got with Vinny, I knew I didn't have a shot. Those two seemed to have the real thing. They made each other laugh, looked at each other like there was no one else in the world, seemed to really love each other. I saw them together a bunch of times, and the more I did, the more I wanted what they had. I wanted someone to look at me that way. I wanted someone who could make me laugh (because I'm not that funny). I wanted the real thing. Plus, they were a fucking hot couple. But after five years, Vinny signed a huge contract to drill oil in Iraq, and Torey didn't want to give up his job as o-line coach at Boston College. So they split. He was still a little broke up from that, so when I asked him to dance and he said, "You sure?" I just gave him a little smile, reached my hand out to him, and said, "Yeah. Come on."

A few people gawked when we took the dance floor together. Mostly we heard whistles and cheers. "I'm older; I'll lead," I told him with a smirk, even though he's a little taller than me. He nodded and looked at me like I've never been looked at before. Other people were on the floor when we got there, but as we rocked back and forth, Salvatore put his cheek on my forehead, and I closed my eyes. When the song was over, I opened them, and everyone (except the Connellys, of course) was in a circle around us looking on with their hands over their hearts or wiping their cheeks. That shit would normally embarrass me—I hate being the center of attention—but I had waited too long for this. I didn't care.

I wasn't trying to steal Mick's thunder. But when I looked over at him to say sorry, he was smiling at us—a real smile. Not the fake, show-bizzy one he used to make when he was still on TV. Not the one with the sad eyes he makes whenever Bethany's around. It was a genuine smile. A happy smile—the kind he used to make in the "B.C." times ("Before Connelly," me and Ma call it).

We've gotten used to Mickey not smiling by now. I don't think he ever expected his life to turn out like this. The kid had star potential. Charisma, confidence, and commitment. He coulda done anything he wanted. He coulda brought down the house on Broadway. He coulda gone to NYU, then L.A., then went on to star in movies with fuckin' Rachel McAdams and Anne Hathaway and Jason Bateman. He coulda't least taken that ESPN job. He didn't, though, because Bethany wanted to stay in Rockingham. So he turned it down, figurin' he still had his gig with NESN SportsDesk to fall back on. But when NESN found out he had an offer, they brought in Peter Gammons. And even Mickey isn't going to compete with a Boston sports media legend like Gammo. So he doesn't do much these days. Doesn't act anymore, even in the local theaters. Doesn't play ball, unless you count the local rainbow-pitch leagues against old guys with bad knees. Doesn't read, not even the old plays he used to love that no one's ever heard of. He just works at Charlie Mart, then goes home to that paint-chipped little two-bedroom house two miles from where we grew up.

The charisma we all used to love is pretty much gone, too. Sometimes there's a flash of it for a second when we're talking about something that reminds him of who he used to be and he makes one of his old jokes (they were cheesy, but I miss them). But his confidence is shot. When I saw him on Christmas, he told me that, after a brutal day on register dealing with assholes, he thought about the decisions he made that led him to wearing a green vest with a name tag on Black Friday. I don't think he's stood up to Beth once in all the years they've been together; definitely not in the two years since they got married. But now he doesn't like to make decisions anymore because he says he always makes the wrong one. So he never commits to anything, except to Bethany and whatever the hell she wants. Because she has no problem making decisions for him. She likes it that way, actually.

He almost never visits me and Torey here in Boston anymore. When he does, Bethany never comes because she's "not really into it," she told him once. Said he asked her what she meant, and she just said, "Like, the gay thing." I pretended not to notice the sneer she shot us when we danced at their wedding, but it's sand-blasted into my brain. Just like the image of her fucking mustache-faced father shaking his head and avoiding eye contact with us; I never liked that goddamn family. I keep the peace, though, because Mickey says he's happy. He just tries to laugh it off (or justify it, I guess) by saying, "Happy wife, happy life, right?" Bullshit, bullshit everywhere.

Ma never really sees him, either, which is weird. I figured, with Ray out of the picture, Mick would hang out with her a lot more. At least so he wouldn't have to spend every single moment of his free time with the Connellys. But, I guess by the time Ma got the balls to leave, Mick was so sucked into the Connelly culture that it became his way of life. No time to hang out with lonely old Ma. But Ma won't say anything to him about it—she's almost as afraid of confrontation as he is. That's why it took her so fucking long.

She was so scared to do it, even after she found those long brown hairs on the wall of their shower about six months back (Ma's got a blonde bob now—you should see her!) that she called me and asked me to be there for the conversation in case he flipped. I couldn't get there right away, so Ma had to sit on it a couple days until I could come up from Boston and mediate. I was out of my jurisdiction, of course, but she knew I had the training to handle Ray if he went ballistic. Which he can do sometimes.

Sure enough, when he knew he'd been busted, he started yelling and throwing shit. I've seen it a million times in domestics—woman kneeling and crying, man screaming and denying—I know how fast this shit can es-

calate. But when it's your own parents, it's hard to check your emotions. Watching Ma sob made my eyes water up a bit, and when Raymond stepped toward her, I intercepted and pushed him up against the fireplace mantle, probably a little rougher than I should have. I got in his face and said he needed to calm down. His response was classic Ray-Hole: "What are you gonna do? Arrest me? Or kiss me, you little bitch?"

He never brought up my sexuality before. Didn't say "congrats" (or even "get the fuck out") when I came out. Just, nothing. And then, for fourteen years, nothing. I guess he figured if he didn't mention it, it wasn't real. But when he thinks someone's got something over on him, he attacks their weaknesses. That's why my brother has always been afraid of him. To this day, Mick doesn't know how to stand up to Ray (or anybody, really). But being gay is not a weakness. It's just a part of who I am—as much as being a cop or a hockey player is—except I didn't choose it; it chose me. So I kept him pinned against the mantle and looked directly through his bushy eyebrows while he stared back at me, anticipating my reaction like he'd got under my skin or something. I didn't say anything back; I just tilted my head and gave him a gentle kiss on the neck.

"Aw, come on, Mason!" Ray said while he flailed loose and started rubbing the spot I kissed like he'd been stung by a wasp. "Not funny, man!"

Ma disagreed. She couldn't contain her wide-eyed laughter when Ray's face got all red. I started smiling at how uncomfortable I'd made him. He looked back and forth between the two of us, but couldn't think of anything nasty to say (a first for him). With Raymond dis-

armed, Ma was able to gather her composure, stand up, and say, "I'm leaving you."

I put her up at the Best Western for the rest of the week, then came back up from Boston the following weekend to help her look for a place. We found a decent little one-bedroom apartment on the nice side of town, and the following weekend, I helped her move out of the place she'd called home—the place where Mickey and I grew up—for twenty years. And where was Mick during all of this? You know, the guy who lived two miles away (as opposed to me, who lived an hour away)? The guy who could've come, helped move shit all day, and been home to his precious Bethany in time for Modern Family?

He was hiding.

I've been waiting for Mick to stand up to Ray-Hole for years. He's always let Ray push him around, walk all over him, and I think that's affected the way he is with everyone. Even his own wife. So I figured if it was ever going to happen, this would be the time. Especially now that Ray didn't have a leg to stand on. Instead, Mick just kept avoiding him, even when Ma and I coulda used an extra hand. Ray was only there for a couple minutes in the morning when I went to move her out, but Mick wouldn't even come around then because he was "exhausted from standing on my feet all day" at Charlie Mart. No shit, bro, we're all tired. But this is big and we could use your help.

"I know, but when we have a late dinner, Beth gets a little hangry."

Oh, shit. Wouldn't want Beth to get hangry. Fine, then have her come help, too. Oh, that's right, Beth hangs out with this family even less than Mick does because she hates Raymond and she knows I hate her.

"I can come help tomorrow while Beth's at work."

Forget it, Mick. We've got it. Even Torey came to help for a little while. And we got almost everything—all Ma's clothes, her eighteen pairs of shoes, her photo albums, her Kitchen Aid mixer, her laptop, her collection of Tom Clancy hardcovers, most of her makeup, her Julia Child cookbook, her Will and Grace DVDs, her Mariah Carey CDs, her favorite dishes and silverware, her feminine products, some blankets, sheets, and towels, and the urn. We got all the necessities and all the important stuff. Except for one thing.

We didn't get the scrapbook. I couldn't believe it. That thing is Ma's frickin' crown jewel. She's put everything into that book ever since Mick and I were kids—my Straight-A report card from second grade; the Christmas ornament he made out of beads in fourth grade; my merit badges from the scouts; the programs from all his plays; newspaper clippings from my hockey games and his baseball games; the pressed pennies we made on our trip to Niagara Falls; my acceptance letter to the police academy; his acceptance letter to NYU—everything. She started it right after the accident, and we look at it every New Year's Day to review what happened the year before, take a dive deep into the good ol' days, and put in new, blank pages for the upcoming year.

But it wasn't in the safe with all the family albums when we went to grab those, and Ma and I didn't think to look for it because we were busy trying to remember everything else we had to pack up and ship out. It wasn't until two weeks after the move, when Ma had finally fin-

ished unpacking, that she called me to tell me she didn't have the damn scrapbook. I asked her where the hell it was, and she started to panic. She thought Ray might have hidden it or destroyed it. But even Ray wouldn't do something that messed up and vindictive. I hoped.

I called him up the next day, and before I even got a full sentence out, he blurted, "Yeah I have the fucking scrapbook. It's in a box with all your brother's shit. If he wants it, he can come get it; I'm not his delivery boy."

And then I remembered.

After we were done looking through it as a family this past New Years, Mick grabbed it off the kitchen table and said he wanted to "give it another look" for some reason. I guess he was going through one of his bouts of depression, so he lugged the thing to his old room to re-member his glory days. He holed himself up in there for two hours while the rest of us watched Hacksaw Ridge (he hates war movies). When he came out all misty-eyed and distracted, though, he forgot to put the book back in the safe. Then we all went home and got on with our lives, until three months later when they split. Ma and I got our stuff out, but Mick hasn't been back there since January.

So, there it sits—my mother's heart and soul—col-lecting dust in the same closed-off space as my brother's pride and joy—his acting awards, his baseball medal, old newspaper articles he wrote, his Excellence in Sports Journalism award from BU, pictures of a young and con-fident Mickey smiling, loving life, and looking ahead at things to come, and clothes that haven't fit him in years. I don't have time to go up there between working my new job and planning a wedding, and Ma doesn't dare go back. So, if Mickey wants any of those keepsakes, so he can remind himself who he was and who he still could be—or if he wants to at least help his mother out for once—he's going to have to grow some balls and go get them.

I don't know. Maybe you could give him the strength he needs.

Forever Yours,
Mason

"It's nice to see you again, Bethany. What brings you back?"

"Just Beth please."

"Of course—my apologies, it's been a few years. How can I help?"

"I just—I feel like everything's falling apart. I don't know what to do."

"Can you tell me what's been going on, Beth?"

"The anger. The rage. It's back. I thought I finally had a handle on it. But I've been going through some major shit with my husband, and then I lost my temper at work, and I got fired."

"I'm sorry you're going through such a difficult time, Beth. I know your anger has been a concern for you for a long time, so let's start with that. What happened at work?"

"So, I already had a write-up in my file because I blew off a couple of shifts to go to some—unexpected doctor's appointments. But then a customer started riding my ass, and I already wasn't in a good head space. But I put up with his shit for like an hour and then I dumped his cocktail sauce on his lap and told him to fuck his mom."

"Was that the first time you've responded like that to a customer?"

"I mean, I've never dumped food on someone before, but sometimes if I'm in a mood, I talk shit back at them when they talk shit to me."

"What was it about this particular interaction that

prompted you to elevate your response to a physical one?"

"He just, I don't know, kept pushing my buttons. Like, on purpose."

"Let's talk about buttons. What are some of your 'buttons' and how was this customer pushing them?"

"It—It's gonna sound stupid."

"Nothing you say is going to sound stupid, Bethany."

"BETH."

"I'm so sorry—Beth. Thank you for the gentle reminder."

"And that's the button he kept pushing. My name tag even says 'Beth'. He asked if it's short for Elizabeth, and I told him it's short for Bethany, but I prefer Beth. But he kept calling me 'Bethany' all night—on purpose—like, he was putting extra emphasis on it. 'These shrimps are a little undercooked BETHANY, can you send them back?' 'Hey BETHANY, get me another beer.' 'You just gonna just stand there with that look on your face, BETHANY?' That's when I lost my shit."

"That's when you dumped his cocktail sauce in his lap."

"Yup. I knew I was gonna get in trouble, but I didn't think they'd fire me."

"How did you respond when they had that conversation with you?"

"I was livid. I was like, 'Dude, that guy was an asshole! You should ban *him* for harassing your waitstaff instead of firing *me* for standing up for myself. They were like, 'You can't act like that in a professional setting,' and I said, 'Professional setting? This is the fucking Shrimp Bucket.' That's when they told me to leave."

"You used 'harassing'—a pretty strong word. Was this customer pushing other buttons, too?"

"He just had this shitty condescending attitude all night. He kept saying BETHANY with this fucking smile on his face, like he thought he was funny. I think he was trying to get a laugh out of his girlfriend or wife or hooker or whatever she was. He's lucky it was just cocktail sauce. If I wasn't working I legit would've punched him."

"I don't think we've ever explored this name choice of yours, Beth, and now I'm curious. I always assumed it was just a strong preference, but it's clearly a very potent trigger for you. So, I'd like to know—what is it about people calling you Bethany that makes you so upset? That is your legal name, yes?"

"Yeah, but I hate it."

"Why do you hate your name?"

"I—really don't want to get into it."

"Beth, I promise you can trust me. We're here to figure out what triggers your temper, and how you might be able to curb it so things like this don't happen."

"I don't give a shit about this job. I'm still coaching basketball and teaching CrossFit. I'll find some other bullshit thing to do in between. It's fine."

"Okay. But if your track record suggests you're unable to hold down jobs—even jobs you don't care about—it may hurt your chances at getting a job you *do* want someday."

"There are no jobs I want. But obviously I need money, so I have to work somewhere."

"What about coaching? You've been doing that for a long time. That must be important to you."

"Yeah, I've been coaching the girls varsity team at my old high school for five, six years now. But that's just a seasonal thing."

"Well, what if you had an opportunity to get a full-time coaching job? That seems like something you'd be passionate about."

"I mean, yeah, I'd love a job like that."

"So, wouldn't it make you upset if you were denied such an opportunity because you had a reputation that you couldn't control your temper? It's hard to get a job like that without some strong references."

"Fine. I'll talk about it."

"Whenever you're ready, Beth."

"So, when I was a kid, the other girls made fun of me a lot. I was the tallest girl in my class, but I was really skinny. And lanky, too. So they called me 'Baby Bambi Bethany.' The red hair and freckles didn't help. I was just a freak. And my teeth were crooked, so they called me 'Buck-Toothed Bethany.'"

"I see—you associate the name Bethany with name-calling and bullying. That must have been difficult for you."

"Yeah. I didn't really have any friends when I was little, so I shot hoops every day after school, sometimes by myself, sometimes with my dad, and I started learning all kinds of moves under the hoop and making shots from all over the driveway. When my little sister was old enough, she started playing with us, too. We both got really good."

"And basketball gave you a sense of value."

"Sure, I guess. But then when I got braces in seventh grade to fix my fucked-up face, they started calling me

'Bionic Bethany' and making fun of the way I talked. And when I got to high school, this one guy started calling me Beth-Anal and telling everyone I was a lesbian. So, even though I was good at hoops now, people still wouldn't hang out with me. So I figured, fuck it, if you're gonna be shitheads to me no matter what I do, I don't need to pretend I'm nice anymore. Then I started beating the shit out of girls whenever they said shit to me and I smashed that one guy's face into his locker. Then they started leaving me alone."

"So, you began using intimidation and violence as a defense mechanism, because hurting the people who hurt you gave you a sense of control you didn't feel you had before."

"I don't know—I just didn't wanna be fucked with anymore. Once I put a few of those snotty bitches in their place, people saw I wasn't just gonna take it. You fuck with me, I'll fuck you up. Been that way ever since."

"A pretty strong philosophy to live by, Beth. I remember way back when you first came to me, these hair-trigger responses were a concern for some of your friends and family. Now, I haven't seen you in quite some time, but when you came in today, you said that rage was 'back.' Tell me—where did it go? And why is it back now?"

"I think it was a combination of—you were helping me by giving me someone to talk to who wasn't snotty and judgy, and at the same time, things were starting to get better with my boyfriend. Like, I totally blew up at him that time he tried to break up with me right after we had sex. But after that fight, things were good for a really long time. He was sweet and funny and cool again, and he was treating me like a princess, just like when we first started dating."

"So, this is Michael then? You're still with him?"

"Yup. We got married a few years ago."

"Oh. Well, congratulations!"

"Thanks, I guess. But like I said, we've been going through some major shit."

"Let's talk about it."

"Things have just changed a lot. For the last few years, he's gotten really—I hate to say whiny, but that's what it feels like. All he ever talks about is the jobs he never got, how he missed his 'big break' or whatever and how he's 'stuck in Rockingham.' He blames *me* for his fuck-ups, and now he just sits around playing video games all the time won't even look for a decent-paying job."

"Do you ever discuss this with him?"

"Not much anymore. We had a fight after the ESPN thing where he was like, 'I wish you were more supportive of the things I want,' and I was like, 'You're a grown-up, Mickey. You don't need my permission. Do what you're gonna do, man.'" But it hasn't been bad since then.

"I'm not familiar with 'the ESPN thing'. Can you tell me more?"

"So, a couple years ago, he got this offer from ESPN to be some kind of sideline reporter-whatever thing and said, 'We have to move to Connecticut,' like I should be all excited or whatever. But I was like, 'I love you, Mickey, but I am *not* moving to Connecticut.'"

"Still not a fan of big changes, are you, Beth?"

"Nope. Still don't see the point. So, we had this huge fight, probably the biggest one we've had since the after-sex breakup thing, and I finally said, 'Fine. Go to Connecticut if that's what you feel you need to do. But just know if you go, you've made your choice.' And things were way better for a while after that."

"Way better how?"

"He stayed. And we haven't really had a fight since then. He does his thing, he lets me do my thing, and we're cool. Happy wife, happy life, y'know?"

"And he's okay with 'Happy wife, happy life'?"

"He's the one that taught me the expression."

"Interesting. Does that concern you at all?"

"Why would it? Michael hates fighting, and this way, there's no fighting. It's win-win."

"Well, in my experience, Beth, couples who never fight often have underlying issues that don't get addressed. That can lead to problems later on. Problems with anger, resentment, communication, things like that. Often, when one partner maintains that level of control for a long period of time, the other eventually grows unsettled with that arrangement. I'm just saying be careful, that's all."

"He says he's fine with it."

"How would you know if he wasn't?"

"Because he knows if he lies to me ever again, I'll crush his nuts."

"I know you're kind of saying that as a joke, Beth. But can you see how that angry, confrontational response might make someone reluctant to approach you? Especially someone like Michael who you've noted doesn't like fighting? I'm just concerned that you and your husband might be heading down an unhealthy road if he doesn't feel he can adequately express his concerns to you, or that you can't express your concerns to him without anger."

"What the hell? I thought you were on *my* side."

"I can see you're getting upset, and that wasn't my intention. I'm sorry. But I *am* on your side. You came in here today because you said your temper has been resurfacing, and I want to help you manage that so it doesn't continue to have negative implications on your life—whether it's your romantic relationships, your family and friends, your career, what have you. So, I'm using the example you provided of what some may view as a skewed dynamic between you and Michael to illustrate how a relationship like yours may become strained over time if both parties don't feel they are on equal footing."

"I mean, I think it's already pretty strained."

"I'm sensing that. You two have had a somewhat rocky history since—well, really since the first time I met with you. Have you guys ever considered marriage counseling? Of course, I can provide feedback on your personal journey based on the things you tell me, but I'm only hearing one side of the story."

"Yeah. If Mickey told this story, he'd probably make it into a book and make me sound like a heartless, narcissistic bitch who uses 'like' every other word and can't tell the difference between Crocodile Dundee and Forrest Gump."

"What?"

"Nothing. Go ahead."

"So, as I was saying, for a lot of couples, it's beneficial to have both people involved in a mediated conversation with a neutral party. That way, both sides can be heard, and you can begin the healing process as a team."

"I don't know. I think it might be too late for that."

"I don't think it's ever too late if both of you approach it with an open mind, ready to listen, ready to love each other, ready to do the work, and ready to revisit and honor the commitment you made to each other."

"Maybe. But there's some stuff I haven't told you yet…"

ACT II

23

Kay: Wait, r u serious?!?!

MP: Yep. And you were the first person I thought of :)

Kay: I'm flattered, Mickey :) but I worry for u sweetie.

MP: You don't need to. We have an agreement. She can't get upset—she "owes" me (HER words, not mine).

Kay: Ya but that's not what I mean.

MP: ???

Kay: I just mean…

MP: She said it's okay. You can text her yourself if you want. Here's her number:

Kay: do NOT give me ur wife's phone number!!!!

MP: Just saying, if you don't believe me

Kay: I believe u, Mickey. And that's what worries me.

MP: ???

Kay: u let her get away with cheating on u :(And she's trying to make it OK by letting u sleep with someone else. That's mega messed up.

MP: I guess, but it's not cheating if we're playing by the same rules. We both get a piece on the side and it's all good.

Kay: But u weren't playing by the same rules when she had sex with that guy. OR WHEN SHE GOT PREGNANT with his kid. She's changing the rules in the middle of the game so she can win.

MP: Well, we'll be tied at least :)

Kay: No, sweetie. If she gets away with this, she wins. U always told me she's super competitive. What makes u think this is any different?

MP: I think you're missing the point.

Kay: I dn't think so, but go ahead..

MP: You and me. We can finally do what we've always talked about ;)

Kay: Come on Mickey I'm being serious RN

MP: Me too ;) that weekend in the Poconos is calling. Wine, whiskey, lingerie, pizza, laying around naked watching rom coms. It would all be above board now.

Kay: Not 4 me lol.

MP: I'm sure Isaac could handle the kids by himself for the weekend..

Kay: lol I'm sure he could. He's an awesome papa.

MP: ... and you deserve a break...

Kay: It would be nice 2 not wear clothes all weekend lol.

MP: Then come on, let's book it!

Kay: haha sorry Mickey, u know I love u sweetie, but I don't have a hall pass like u. You'll have to find some other lucky girl ;)

MP: But this is our chance! We've always talked about it!

Kay: Ya but sexting and sending pics isn't the same as actually sleeping with someone. Nm how cute ur :)

MP: Awww blush* And you're not wrong, but I think

we both know the sexting and pics are, at best, a morally grey area

Kay: Ya but ur forgetting, Isaac takes all the pics and gets to approve or veto the ones I send 2 u. And I get the best angles of his johnson to post.

MP: Gotta keep those OF subscribers happy

Kay: Ya and that's something we do together. And usually when u and I are doing our thing, Isaac is right in the same room sexting other girls too.

MP: You guys have a weird relationship

Kay: Maybe lol but it keeps it fresh, & keeps us from cheating, so it works for us

MP: Well maybe that's what Beth and I are trying to do. Just keep it fresh.

Kay: …

MP: What does that mean?

Kay: Just—I think there are more issues with u guys than just sex.

MP: …Go on…

Kay: u really want me to get into this RN?

MP: You brought it up, so now I need to know WTF you mean

Kay: OK. So, I think she tries to control u. And I think u let her. I think she knows u don't stand up 4 urself so she steamrolls u. I think she knows if she gets in ur face and screams, you'll give her what she wants. I think ur unhappy and u know ur unhappy, but ur too scared to do anything about it. And I think she's unhappy too but she likes having someone she can push around and who does whatever she wants.

MP: Wow.

Kay: I kno. Sry :(

MP: Well this conversation didn't go how I thought it would.

Kay: Ya. I'm sry Mickey. I'm not the girl 4 u. I couldn't do that to Isaac and the kids.

MP: I know. I get it, but now I'm more concerned with what you said about me and Beth.

Kay: Well, if it helps, ur one of my BFFs and I just want u 2 be happy..

MP: A little.

Kay: And we'll always have the Pinkerton bathroom >:)...

24

What's the difference between a bounced check and an angry jackrabbit?" I asked the fair-skinned brunette with a cute little overbite and a black thong peeking out of her low-risers. I leaned on the bar with both elbows, cupped my glass of scotch like a mug of hot chocolate, and smirked at her in anticipation of—something; a smile, a laugh, some acknowledgment that I was a human being who had spoken to her. Instead, she grabbed her Genesee by the neck, slid her elbow across the polished oak bar top, and turned her back to me in one fluid motion that she'd clearly practiced and perfected.

I looked down at my drink and smiled to myself. Then at the corner of the bar, I spotted a half-person gap by a curvy blonde with a low wavy updo, a white tank top that was only a little too tight, and salmon lipstick. I slid into that opening (as smoothly as a tallish, overweight ginger dude can slide) and said to her, "Y'know, behind every great man is a great woman. And you look like a great woman."

She raised an eyebrow, put down her phone, and shot

me a skeptical smile. "Oh yeah?"

"Yes," I said, proud that I'd at least gotten her to respond, even if it was with a face that said, "This better be good."

"And of course," I added, "behind every great woman is a sleazy man checking out her ass."

She raised her other eyebrow but broke eye contact. Her attention was back on her phone. "And which of those men are you?"

I gave her a sheepish shrug. "I—I could be both."

Her eyes widened as she began texting someone. "I'm actually all set. Thanks."

Ouch. It stung more when they *did* talk to you. So, I limped back to the table where I'd been sitting with Mason and Torey and said, "Welp, 0-for-2 so far. Not a good start."

"No worries, man," Torey said. "The night is young. Have another scotch."

"Yeah, plus you're wicked old compared to these girls, bud," Mason said.

I laughed. "Thanks for the vote of confidence, Mace."

"And don't forget fat," Torey said with a snide grin.

"Hey, it takes a big man to admit he's obese," I joked as I jiggled my gut with both hands. Then, with fake confidence: "Besides, if Kevin James can land a hot piece of tail, I can, too."

"Yeah, but K.J. is rich and famous, dude," Torey said with a nod and a wink. "You're no Kevin James."

I tightened my lips, downed the rest of my drink, and slammed my glass on the table. "I know! I fucked up, okay? I didn't follow my path, I married someone I shouldn't have, and that's why I'm in this fucking mess to begin with."

They both took uncomfortable sips of their beers as we all sat in silence and scanned the young, vibrant college students there inside the Cask n' Flagon. They all flashed flirty, flawless smiles at each other. They all brimmed with confidence and hope. They were all building lifelong friendships and celebrating what it meant to be free for the first time. They reminded me of my college days, when life was simple and it was easy to make friends. I used to flash smiles, not so long ago, and I used to brim with confidence and hope. But there was one distinct difference between these horny, happy kids and me, even the 'me' who used to hang around this boppin' little sports bar with my friends until 2 a.m. and then ace my Biology final at 8 a.m.: I had never really experienced the kind of freedom they all enjoyed—true freedom. I'd always been under Raymond's thumb growing up, and then I went right from that to the underside of Bethany's thumb all through college and into adulthood. And living under thumbs my whole life had me crushed, crippled, and weak. So what the hell was I doing here at some bouncing Boston bar trying to hit on young women who still smiled, still brimmed, and had no reason to be interested in a chubby, thirty-year-old Charlie Mart cashier?

"Steffiana de la Cruz is a scorcher though," Torey said, mercifully breaking the silence to show us a Google image search of oval-headed chunker James and his gorgeous Filipina-American wife. "You know, for a girl."

"I know, right?" I said as he and I shared a polite chuckle.

Torey shifted in his seat and said, "Sorry, Mack-Pack. We're just messin' around."

"No, no, I'm sorry," I said, regretful of the way I'd

lashed out. "I guess I'm just wicked sensitive these days. You guys didn't do anything wrong. I'm glad you came out with me."

"Of course, man." Toto grabbed my shoulder and squeezed it. "You can still talk to us about whatever, y'know."

Mason verified his fiancé's assurance with a nod.

"I know. Thanks," I said as I signaled the waiter over to order another drink. "Just—life choices, you know? You never know how things are going to work out; you make a decision and hope it's the right one. But it seems like every one I've made has been the wrong one. And now I'm stuck in this rut I can't get out of."

"Yeah. Not gonna lie," Mason said as he paused to take a sip of his Heineken. "You haven't been yourself in a long time, bud. You're this—fucking muted version of yourself. Like you were for all those years after Ray beat the shit out of you when we were kids."

"Mickey the Mouse," Torey said. He hadn't called me that since our little baseball practice dust-up in ninth grade.

"Hey, don't make me throw you down and put my knee in your back," I said with a half-smile.

"Please—you're such a girl," he said with a playful scoff. "You wouldn't have the balls to do that nowadays, kid."

All I said back was, "Ouch, man."

It hurt because he was right.

"You know I'm just playing," Toto said. "We just miss you, that's all."

"The real you," Mason chimed in. Then he gestured a hand-scan from my face to my feet. "Not—whatever this is, bud. It's like, is the real Mickey ever coming back? Or is he gone for good, like Dad?"

He broke eye contact and looked up at the Bruins game on one of the televisions. My head dipped a bit.

"Both our dads," Torey said with distant eyes; he and Mason joined hands and began stroking each other's wrists.

I never knew our father as well as my brother did. I was only five when the accident happened. But I saw the aftermath of it—how much it affected Mace his whole life—what he believed in, who was important to him, the way he walked around with the slightest slope in his back from shouldering the weight of loss, abandonment, premature responsibility, and flawless integrity for the last twenty-five years. He never really got over it—that's why he notoriously bailed so quickly on relationships—he always left them before they could hurt him. But Torey's a different story—his family and ours have been connected in one way or another since way back in the day—so I guess Mason figured he was a safe bet to stick around. And I didn't want him to think I was going to be the next one to leave him.

"I miss you guys, too. I mean, you're only an hour away, but it might as well be three time zones with how often I see you these days."

"Whose fault is that?" a strong-voiced but misty-eyed Mason said.

"I know," I said as the waiter clopped my drink down on the table in front of me. "You guys are down here living your dreams, and I'm stuck there in the Land of Beth getting older, getting fatter, and just—dreaming about my dreams. I wish things were different."

"So," Mason said. He paused, looked at his fiancé, then looked back at me and said, "Make things different."

I looked up from my scuffed-up gold wedding ring. It was less than three years old but looked like it had collected a lifetime's worth of tarnish. "What?"

"Just move to Boston," Mason said, like it was just that easy. I laughed. He didn't.

"I'm not kiddin,' Mick. Leave that clam and move down here. We'll help you find a place. Toto could help you get a job at the local station—It's not ESPN, but it's not Charlie Mart either."

"No joke, man," Torey said. "I'm still buddies with our old Sports Info director. She's at News 7 now. She remembers you from NESN."

I leaned back in my chair, stared at my scotch, swished it around in a slow clockwise motion, and started chewing the inside of my cheek. The thought of moving to Boston was intriguing. Torey had been coaching at B.C. for years and had tons of connections in the Boston sports media landscape (I used to be one of them), so I knew he wasn't just blowing smoke to get me interested. I could have a second chance at a career. It wouldn't be Broadway or Hollywood or ESPN or even NESN, but it would be a chance to start anew. I could get the hell out of Rockingham. I could be close to my boys again. Maybe I could find a cute little Boston honey to hang on my arm. And then she'd introduce me to her friends, and they'd introduce me to their friends, and then I'd have all kinds of friends, like I did back in the day. And then we'd all live together happily in the same apartment building in the city, having coffee in the middle of weekdays, engaging in off-the-wall antics and snappy banter with a live audience (or at least a convincing laugh track) rooting for us and "woo-"ing whenever we kissed and "aww"-ing whenever we were sad. And best of all, I could be the star in my own life again.

It was a beautiful, rose-colored fantasy.

"That sounds great, guys." I stared at a random dark smudge on the corner of the table. "But let's be real—I'm not going anywhere."

I threw back the last of my scotch as they looked at each other and, at the same time, looked back at me and demanded, "Why not?"

I shrugged and flashed a defeated smirk. "She's happy where we are. We have a little house down the street from her parents. She loves coaching her old high school team. She gets to see her family and sister and friends whenever she wants. She lets me do my own thing most of the time, and now she's giving me a free pass to get some strange, so it's all good. 'Happy wife, happy life,' right?"

"Is it?" Torey said without hesitation. "Sorry, kid, but that sounds pretty pathetic."

"I agree," Mason said. "That's the dumbest fuckin' thing I ever heard. That bitch steamrolls you, and you just let it happen, bud. That's not 'Happy Wife, Happy Life,' that's 'Bethany is a Spoiled Brat and Mickey is Miserable.'"

"It's tough love time, kid," Torey said. He leaned in and pointed straight at my chest. "You don't drive your own car anymore."

"Dude, what are you talking about? I drove all the way down here."

"Metaphorically, dipshit," he continued. "*You* decided to play ball, *you* decided to be an actor, and *you* decided you were going to work your ass off to be awesome at both of those things. *You* were in the driver's seat back then."

Mason folded his arms and nodded at me. Toto went on.

"Then you met *her*, and something changed. It was like you forgot how to drive. Or you were afraid to, so you just quit."

I narrowed my eyes and looked at my brother for translation.

"You don't make decisions Mick," Mason said. "You talk about all the bad decisions you made, and now you're stuck in this rut—at least you used to *make* some decisions. Now you just freeze up 'cause you're afraid."

"Well, yeah," I conceded. "I don't need to fuck up my life any more than I already have."

"But you can't be so afraid of the bad things that might happen that you don't give yourself a chance for anything good to happen," Torey said. "You'll live your life stuck in neutral, and when you're in neutral, people can push you whichever way they want you to go. You'll have no say in it unless you shift into gear and pick a direction."

"That's exactly what happened with Bethany," Mason said. "You didn't pick a direction on your own, and now she's driving your car."

I sat quietly for a moment, processing what they just said. And they were right. Everything they said made sense, and it was all completely true. The thing was, though, it wasn't anything I hadn't already thought of on my own. I knew I was unhappy. I'd known for a long time. And I had thought a lot—A LOT—about where I might be in my life if Herb Fitz hadn't gotten stuck in the snow and I hadn't gone to Plymouth State to cover that game all those years ago. Or if I'd told Beth the truth back in the beginning. Or if I'd powered through. But that's not how it went down. Instead, I'd shoved a decade of my life down the garbage disposal, and now I was old, awkward, chubby, five scotches in, and trying to save my marriage by trying to hook up with other women.

"You know what, boys? You're right," I said. I stood up a little too fast, stumbled for a beat, and then puffed out my chest. "Fuck neutral. Time to take the wheel. I'm gonna make another play, and I'm gonna go get laid. See you guys later."

"Go get'em, Slugger," Torey said.

"Good luck, bud," Mason added. They raised their beer bottles at me, then leaned toward each other with subdued smirks and shared a kiss as I sauntered away.

And with that, I approached a tall, slender girl with dark brown skin, fuchsia lipstick, and a drawstring weave and said, "Excuse me—that blouse looks great on you." She gave me a cheeky look as I scanned up and down her blue sequin top and motioned my empty scotch glass to the bartender. I added, with a grin, "It would look even better *off* of you."

25

I walked through the door and put my keys on the little cedar table to the left. The raucous cheers of some overzealous college basketball crowd screeched from the television in the living room. I scuffed my boots across the doormat to loosen the mud and slush I'd collected, took off my jacket and my hat, and hung them on one of the barren chrome hooks to my right.

The basketball game was muted, and suddenly, I heard a cheerful "Hey!"

"Hey," I said with a glint of artificial warmth as Beth shuffled in, hugged me around the neck, and said, "How'd it go?"

I knew it would be the first thing she asked as soon as I walked through the door, and even though I'd been thinking all weekend about how I would answer her, I still wasn't sure what to say. She'd given me a free pass, an opportunity to "even the score," as she kept putting it, and I'd blown it. Mason and Torey were my wingmen, there to plug me back into the Boston social scene and help me get some action. But other than those pitiful "flirts" with women I wouldn't have had a shot with if I *had* been on my game (and sixty pounds lighter), I'd spent most of the weekend lamenting my marriage, regretting my life choices, and dreading my return to the world that had been built for me. After those humiliating (but unsurprising) rejections on Friday night, I decided not to subject my ego to further bruising. So, I hung out with the boys at their apartment on Saturday, and after they went to bed, I watched *Family Guy* reruns and jerked my half-hard dong to MILF porn for an hour. I couldn't even finish, though, because all I could think about was how much of a failure I had been at the Cask the night before, how old and gross I must have looked to those blistering hot college girls, and how no one would ever have sex with me again. Even my wife would rather fuck someone else.

But I knew Beth wanted me to tell her it went well, and that I'd found a cute little (but not too cute and not too little) gal pal. She wanted me to say that my corny little jokes had won the affections of a lovely lady for a night, and I'd spent an evening wrapped in the sweaty embrace of another woman, that we'd pounded each other sore, that she gave me a phone number I would never call, and that all would be forgiven and Beth's wrongs would be righted. Hell, maybe if we were lucky, I'd meet someone with whom I could meet for a casual encounter on a semi-regular basis, thereby opening the door for Beth to hook up with Brad or Chad or Tad or Flad or whomever she wanted, because we'd both be getting some on the side. We could just live as platonic domestic partners, each with our assigned chore list during the week and our assigned whore list on weekends, and we'd never have to fuck each other again. We would be roommates who kissed sometimes and said they loved each other (but not, like, LOVED each other) so we could save on taxes and have someone to go look at Christmas lights with. I couldn't think of a better way to nurse a starving marriage back to health than that.

"It was great!" I said with a little smile. "Mack-Pack is back in the ballgame."

Beth's face lit up. "Really?!"

"Yup! Friday night wasn't so great—still getting my feet wet, y'know—but last night was fire."

"Ooooh, tell me what happened!" She clutched my two index fingers, led me into the living room, and sat down on the couch with me, closer than she had sat to me in months.

"So, I saw this girl at the corner of the bar, no one really talking to her, but she looked cute enough from where I was."

"Oh yeah? What did she look like?"

I knew I had to make this mystery woman believably average-looking, maybe even below-average-looking, or else Beth's insecurity might morph into jealousy and ruin this whole thing.

"Kind of chunky-ish. Not fat, but definitely a spare tire."

"You little chubby chaser." She snickered.

"Whatever," I continued. I couldn't sound like I was too excited by—or turned off by—girls with a few extra pounds, just in case Beth put on a few someday. "Dark skin, wide nose, eyebrows could've used a trim. But other than that, not bad looking. Said she was from Brazil or Bolivia—some place in South America."

"So, a chunky little Mexican," she said.

"Mexico is North America, Bethany."

"Just Beth."

I rolled my eyes. "Anyway, we had a couple drinks, got a little flirty, and I gave Mace and Toto the signal."

"The signal?" She raised an eyebrow. "What's 'the signal'?"

"Oh, you know—" I had to think fast. "Just, like, a quick salute and a little nod or something."

"Okay, so then what?" She sat up straight and was more interested in this than anything we'd talked about in years. "You took what's-her-name—little Dora or whatever— back to their apartment and, like, had sex on their couch?"

"Nah, got a cheap little hotel room," I said. "And her name was Lacey."

I hoped Beth wouldn't notice how much the name of my fictional fling partner sounded like "Luci." She didn't.

"I bet you didn't last long with Lacey," she teased. "It's been what, like three months?"

"Seven." I was quick to correct her because, if there's one thing guys keep an ongoing internal audit on, it's frequency and quality of sex. See, filed deep in every guy's cranial hard drive is a spreadsheet detailing every sexual encounter he's ever had. It can be accessed at any time and sorted categorically by date of session, physical attractiveness of partner, interpersonal chemistry scaled from 1 to 10, boob size, underwear style, intensity of male orgasm, number of female orgasms, and the inclusion (Y/N) and quality (scale of 1 to 10) of oral sex. So, I knew exactly how long it had been since Beth and I had had sex with each other (seven months, two weeks, four days, and fourteen hours), and it was important to me that she knew I knew.

And I didn't find her jab about my coital brevity due to our sustained dry spell all that funny considering her personal dry spell hadn't been nearly as long. So, even though my date with Lacey (as well as Lacey herself) was completely fabricated, I had to make it sting for her, at least a little bit.

"I mean yeah, it had been a while, so the first one was a quick one," I said. Beth snorted back a sophomoric giggle. Then after a moment, she realized what I'd said, so she cleared her throat and said, "The 'first one'?"

Like a lot of guys, I had always been a single-batch slinger. A one-load wonder. A solo-cum conundrum. Over the years I had honed my stamina so I could build slowly toward a single, momentous conclusion, and once I was spent, it was over. Sometimes Beth was fine with that and just wanted to turn over and go to sleep. Other times, when she wasn't ready to be done, she'd do anything she could—kissing, licking, stroking, poking, teasing—to get me hard again so she could have one more go at it. And most of those times, I couldn't deliver (shit—maybe that's why she cheated). So it definitely got her attention when I hinted that I might've been able to get the engines revved up for a second go-round with an outsider.

"Well, I wasn't going to pay for a hotel and be done after five minutes," I said. "I wanted to make it worth my time. And hers."

"Uh huh," she said with stone in her eyes. "So you went again?"

"We did—and THAT one was crazy." I tilted my head back and closed my eyes, pretending to think about how hot my second round of sex with 'Lacey' had been. "Mmm! When she started teasing me with her big, juicy double-D's, I was ready to go in like a minute."

Beth always hated her small breasts, so I knew the image of me getting aroused by someone with bigger ones would get under her skin.

"Oh yeah?" she responded, her interest and enthusiasm a little more forced now. "I bet your chubby little Dora dyke rode you like a stallion, didn't she?"

I had her right where I wanted her.

"Nah, she didn't have to. We did it doggy-style."

Beth hated doggy-style, always said the angle didn't do anything for her. She knew I liked it, though, so if 'Lacey' liked it that way, too, that might mean I liked sex better with her. Another way to make Beth antsy, and another point for me.

"I guess if you want to stare at someone's fat ass." She wasn't sitting as close to me now as when we first sat down. "If that's what gets you going, man, whatever."

"I won't lie, it was pretty damn good." Time to put the nail in the coffin. "I didn't think I had much left, but then the third time—"

"You did NOT do it three times!" she said with her face all twisted up.

"Dude, I had seven months built up! And she was super into it, so even though we were sweaty and tired, we went at it one more time and damnnnnn that was the best one all night. I've never come so much in my life."

"I call bullshit, man. That didn't happen."

"Oh, it happened alright," I assured, trying to figure out where the line was and if I had crossed it yet. Beth seemed to be trying to calculate the same thing as she sat there staring at me. Her eyebrows sunk downward in anger, her eyes were wide with confusion and concern, and her mouth hung half agape with disbelief.

After a moment, she huffed and looked sideways and said, "Well—glad you finally got some strange, man. And glad we're finally even."

But that's what Beth didn't understand. We would never be 'even.' Even if the Lacey story were true, there was so much boiling under the surface for both of us that none of this would ever feel right. Because she never had a "free pass" from me. She did what she did without my knowledge or consent, and it was only when she thought she might have herpes or something that the truth came out. She thought it was about sex. She thought it was about the abortion. But she missed the whole point. This was about honesty, respect, and trust. This was about her deep-seated insecurity and my deep-seated fear of confrontation. This was about the weak foundation upon which our relationship had been built—the lies I'd told, the secrets I'd tried to keep, the explosive reaction she'd had when I was busted and the way I crumbled when she got in my face back then, and every time since. This was about Beth having feelings for Brad, whether she wanted to admit it or not. And this was about the fact that we were both miserable in our marriage.

Nevertheless, being "even" in Beth's mind sparked something inside her as she yanked down my pants, pulled her shirt up over her head, and started kissing my chest.

"Now that we're all good," she said, her eyes looking up at me as her lips started working their way downward, "time to get that skank's stank off my husband."

Before I knew it, Beth was all over me, just like when we were teens. Before I knew it, her underwear was on the floor and her breasts were pressed against my neck. Before I knew it, she was on top of me and holding me tighter than she'd held me in years. And before I knew it, I was having sex for the first time in seven months, two weeks, four days, and fourteen hours.

It would be just three weeks, six days, nine hours, and seventeen minutes until I had sex again.

***

I woke up that night to a peculiar light on the ceiling and an odd trembling coming from the other side of the bed. I rubbed my eyes and shook off the sensation that I'd been singing showtunes in a pink thong on 5th Avenue with Wilma Flintstone, and I looked over at Beth. She was on her phone with a gawky smile, shaking the whole mattress trying to suppress her laughter so she wouldn't wake me up.

"The hell?"

"Hey," she said without looking away from her phone or softening her goofy grin.

"It's almost 12:30, who are you talking to?"

"It's only, like, 9:30 in Cali," she said as she typed who-knows-what to who-knows-who.

I knew who.

"Why's he talking to you right now? He knows it's late here."

"Whatev." She shrugged. Still typing. Still smiling.

I didn't have the energy to fight it, so I turned over and dropped my head back on the pillow. As I dozed off, Mrs. Flintstone was nowhere to be found, but I was enjoying the view from atop the Gateway Arch with Jennifer Lopez and the tiger from *The Hangover* when I was awoken again, this time by an audible giggle. Apparently, because I had turned over and said words before, she didn't need to be quiet anymore. I tried to remain still and pretend I was sleeping in hopes that she might take the hint. She didn't. More giggles. More light on the ceiling.

Finally, I turned over and said, "WHAT is so funny?"

"I'm just telling Brad about your little adventure with Dora."

"Why are you telling him about that?"

"He wanted you and me to be even because he felt bad."

"If he felt bad, he wouldn't have had sex with my wife to begin with."

"You know what I mean."

Actually, I didn't. Did he feel bad for me because I'd been cheated on? That didn't make sense coming from the benefactor of the cheat. Did he feel bad that he'd gotten my wife pregnant? If so, how would my extramarital sex make things "even" between him and me (which was a separate issue from me being "even" with said wife)? Did he empathize with me because Beth went ahead with the abortion without considering how I felt about it? Again, that would make no sense coming from him because it was his kid. So, no, I did not know what Beth meant.

"So, what the hell is so funny about my quote-unquote 'adventure?'"

She looked at me and snickered. "He called you—" she looked away. "The Dora Explorah."

I rolled my eyes. "That's so fucking stupid."

"Get it? Instead of Dora the Explorer?"

"Yes, I get it." I shifted my weight and pulled the blanket up over my shoulders. "It's stupid. Her name's Luci, so it doesn't even make sense."

My eyes popped back open as I realized my Freudian slip. "Er, Lacey. Whatever."

"Lacey, Luci, Lilly, it doesn't matter, man," she said as

she laid her phone face-down on the bed. Finally, darkness. Now maybe some peace and quiet would follow.

"But Brad did point out one thing."

"Yeah? What's that?" I was only half-listening now because I really just wanted to go back to sleep and see how J-Lo and Hangover Tiger were getting along.

"So, him and me only had sex that one time."

Yeah, right, I thought. *And Seth Rogen only smoked weed that one time.*

"And you said you had sex with Dora three times."

It was too dark for her to see the side-eyed scowl I was shooting at her. I knew what she was about to say.

"Uh-huh?"

"So, I mean, it seems to me that I should be able to do it two more times now."

I turned over on my back and huffed. "Jesus Christ, Bethany."

"Just Beth," she said. "And what's the problem with that?"

I looked at her silhouette through the darkness, my mouth agape and my palms turned up. I couldn't force myself to say a single word, even though my mind was suddenly crawling with questions. Like, *Is she fucking kidding me? Is it really more important for her to screw Brad two more times than it is to get our marriage back on track? Is having fun with him really more important than doing the work with me? Does she really not get it?*

Or was it I who didn't get it? Was I ever going to learn that lying to Beth would always come back to bite me in the ass? She hadn't even found out the truth this time, and still I was going to pay for it. Of course, telling the truth now—that there was no "Lacey" (or "Dora"), and that I only told her I'd gotten lucky so this whole "getting even" thing would go away—would set her off like a crate of dynamite. And I wasn't about to have a big, emotional fight with her about this at 12:30 a.m. Or—let's be real, Mickey—ever, because it was just easier to let it go.

"Whatever, it's fine. Go for it."

I turned back over on my side and accepted my fate as I began to doze off. I was now complicit in Beth's affair—so much so that I was going to knowingly allow (hell, even encourage) it to happen again. And again. And, probably, again.

"For real?" she said. Beth had a way about her when she got angry, sad, or disappointed. Her eyebrows would descend, her chin would lower, her bottom lip would slide out into a cute little pout—her face would almost shrink—her arms would fold, and she'd avoid eye contact. It was the most dejected, child-like look I'd ever seen on a twenty-nine-year-old woman, and I had learned early on that all I had to do to erase that face was say yes to whatever she wanted. And that little, harmless, three-letter word would magically transform that gloomy, heartbroken scowl into the sunny, heartwarming smile I said I loved.

I couldn't see her face in the darkness, but I could hear the smile in her voice.

"For real," I said. "Just do me a favor and don't get pregnant this time. We can't afford another abortion right now."

"You got it, man," she said excitedly as she sat up on her knees and touched my back. "So, you're really okay with this?"

"Go nuts," I said. "I just want to go to sleep."

My brain said I shouldn't be okay with it. But then,

strangely, a warm tranquility began to melt through me. Maybe I really was okay with it. Or maybe I was still enjoying my first post-sex glow in months, so the surges of anxiety and jealousy one would typically experience given the nature of this discussion would remain dormant until I woke up and had my caramel latte the next morning.

But then again, maybe it wouldn't bother me as much if she wasn't doing it behind my back. Or maybe—maybe—it truly wouldn't bother me at all, because I just didn't fucking care. It was hard to love someone who clearly didn't love me anymore, and accepting that would make everything that followed a hell of a lot easier.

She made a gleeful squeal, her phone lit back up, and that goofy grin returned to her stupid face. Five minutes later, she interrupted my ski trip to Nova Scotia with the Fairly Oddparents with, "Alright, man, all booked!"

"That was fast," I monotoned with one eye open and the other half shut.

"Yup. I fly out to Cali on March 2nd. Back on the 4th."

I sat up and turned on the light. "Are you serious, Beth?"

She looked at me, confused. "What? Dude, you just said it was fine! You said you were okay with it!"

I glared at her and said, "That's the weekend of Mason's wedding."

26

My heart had forgotten it was a heart again, but this time, I feared it might be permanent. It stopped beating for four days, then six, then eight, then by around Day 9 or 10, it had sunk into my stomach (as usual), but instead of doing a somersault, I felt it slowly retreating into my colon, from whence I might never retrieve it. But maybe at this point, I just needed to remove it from the equation entirely.

"Phil Collins!" Mom blurted as the slow-rising intro to "In the Air Tonight" seeped its way across the radio waves in the old black Jetta.

"Damnit, you beat me to it!" I said while she put another hash mark under her name. She was beating me by three in "The Radio Game" as we approached the Boston skyline the day before the wedding.

"You'll never beat me to any Phil Collins songs," she said with a laugh. "He's my boy."

"I wouldn't want to," I grunted as I switched stations. "I

can't stand Phil Collins."

"Oooh! I know this one," Mom said with her fingers on her temples, prodding her recall to move a little faster. "Kryptonite! This is Kryptonite! Another point for old mom!"

"Actually, 'Kryptonite' is the name of the song. The band is Three Doors Down. So, who gets that point, Mother?"

She knew the rules. You have to get the name of the artist, not the name of the song. She sighed and snarked, "Crap. You do."

"That's right." I pointed both thumbs at my own cheeks. "This guy."

"Both hands on the wheel, Michael," she said. "This traffic makes me nervous."

"We're fine, Mom, don't worry." As I returned my hands to 10-and-2, I spotted a plane in the distance ascending toward the clouds, and I wondered which landmark, city, or patch of farmland Beth was flying over at that moment. She left before I'd even opened my eyes that morning, but it was a seven-hour flight to LAX from Manchester, so I knew she had at least a few more hours before she'd be back in the hulking arms of her California lover.

We never really had it out over her decision to miss Mason's wedding. That night, after I pointed out that she'd booked her fuck-date weekend (her "fuck-end?") with That Brad Guy the same weekend as my brother's wedding, her response was to stare at me with her mouth open for thirteen seconds, shrug and shake her head, then shoot me a disingenuous, "Sorry?" like she was trying to guess the socially appropriate reply for this situation.

"Right words. Wrong tone," I said as I shook my head

and turned the lights back off.

"I already booked the tickets, man, what am I s'posta do?"

"The invitation's been on the fridge since October, but whatever; you do you, Bethany."

I laid there next to her in the dark, immersed in a state of anger and exhaustion that had grown so familiar in recent years. It used to fight against itself, keep me up all night, and make me even more tired the next day. It used to twist my gut into knots while I tried to figure out how to get her to change her mind, to see things from my perspective, to look past the end of her own nose. But something had clicked in me—or, maybe snapped is the right word—in the two months since that drive to the clinic. Since that cold January morning when three "harmless" cysts pulled the curtain back on the earth-shattering truth, and I learned that we had much bigger problems than I'd ever considered, the cracked foundation on which we'd built our rocky relationship had begun to crumble, piece by piece. And now, knowing how little she thought of me (at least in relation to how much she thought of herself), how unaffected she seemed by the devastation her words and actions caused me, and how blatantly unimportant repairing our marriage seemed to be to her, it felt like the final avalanche was inevitable.

That night, I wept quietly and stared at the ceiling as I grieved the sad state of our decaying love in the same way an expectant widower grieves a brain-dead spouse whose organs haven't failed yet. I knew the end was coming, I just didn't know when or how. I wiped the dampness from my cheeks, took a deep breath, and tried not to let her hear my sniffles.

But I guess she did. So, there in the darkness, I felt her fingers touch my arm as she said, "Hey."

"Hey," I said back, wondering with one last shred of hope if this was the olive branch I'd been waiting for for two months—nay, eleven years.

Instead, and of course, she reminded me, "Just Beth."

In the two-plus weeks that followed, words between us were sparse. We were cordial with each other, but the tension that typically saturated the air we shared whenever we had a fight had slowly dissipated to nothing. It hadn't been supplanted this time by any semblance of peace or joy, nor sadness or dismay, nor anger or angst. Even the lingering discontent that had accumulated over the years and grown into unspoken resentment for each other was absent now. It was just—nothing. Just my heart retreating into my colon, never to return.

"Marilyn Manson!" Mom shouted. "Point for me!"

"What?" I said, suddenly throttled from my melancholic stupor. I refocused on the road in front of me.

"I can't believe you didn't get that one; you used to love Marilyn Manson."

"Yeah, sorry; wasn't paying attention."

"I'll let you steal the point if you can tell me who originally did this song in the 80s," she said playfully.

"I don't need your charity," I said confidently, "but I'll take it. Soft Cell."

"Good job, hun!" She put the point under my name. "How'd you know?"

"Mom, everyone who listens to Manson knows that." I changed the station, heard the ominous acoustics of "Radioactive," and blurted out "Imagine Dragons!"

Now we were tied.

"You're making that up," Mom protested. "I've never heard of that."

"Dude, this song's been out for like six years. Everyone's heard of it."

"Well, I haven't, but I guess I'll let you have it. But I'm keeping an eye on you, young man."

I snickered. I had to admit, being with Mom and playing "The Radio Game" was a comfort food I hadn't tasted in far too long. Way back in the beginning, before Raymond, before Bethany, when decisions small and large were made for me and I hadn't begun to hate myself for every bad one I'd ever made, I enjoyed our Mommy-and-Me time. She understood me better than anybody else, and she always knew just what to do to make me feel better. Even now, she still knew how to brew that magic formula that only moms are qualified to concoct. She knew I was having issues with my wife, and she knew I was feeling low, defeated, maybe a little broken. But she knew I would only talk about it with her if and when I wanted to, and in the meantime, she knew playing "The Radio Game" was just what I needed to distract me from the fact that Bethany was bailing on my brother and best friend's wedding to be with another man in California.

Mom scanned through a few stations trying to find one that didn't have sports analysts arguing about sports, political analysts arguing about politics, or commercials from local used car salesmen and Old Spice. Finally, she landed on the local Soft Rock station and we both jumped at the familiar hums of our favorite pop diva.

"Mariah Carey!" we said in unison as Mimi sang to me about casting my fears aside, looking inside myself, and being strong.

"Damnit, a tie—no points for anyone," Mom said. She reached for the scanner again, but I put my hand up and said, "Wait."

She looked at me curiously and sat back in her seat as my brain shifted to auto-pilot. I'd taken Route 1 through Chelsea and Isaactown so many times on the way to and from BU, it was just muscle memory now. Meanwhile, as Mariah's brilliant soprano entranced me in her sweet, sweet fantasy, fond memories fluttered forth from my hippocampus. DeNiro in a thong. Crying pizza. Bald preachers dancing with giant gorillas.

Luci.

I wondered where she was. I wondered how she'd been. We hadn't talked in a few years, and she didn't have Facebook or Instagram or even Twitter. I couldn't remember the last time I'd seen her, but singed irrevocably into my memory bank was our not-a-date, the hopeful conversation we had afterward, and how, the following weekend, the universe had yanked us apart, right when we thought it was pushing us together. I wondered if she ever thought about that, ever thought about me, or if she was happy with the divergent paths we took after that weekend. I never asked Torey about her because, whether she was happy or whether she was miserable, it would hurt too much to know. But I wondered what she was doing right now.

And then reality came flooding back when it occurred to me that Luci was probably heading to the same place I was; her brother's wedding rehearsal.

"Shit," I said out of nowhere.

"What?" Mom shot back with concern. "Mickey, what's wrong?"

My stomach flipped. "I just realized—Luci's gonna be

there."

Mom tilted her head, and her face relaxed into a knowing smile. "Of course she is."

I drove in silence for a moment before Mom reopened the conversation.

"Is that a bad thing?"

"No, not at all. I just—I haven't talked to her in a long time."

"You'll see a lot of people you haven't talked to in a long time," she said, pretending she didn't know exactly what was going through my mind. "Why are you so worried about Luci?"

"You know it's different," I said, still dancing around the real issue. "She used to be one of my best friends."

Mom wasn't in the mood to dance.

"Is it because you wish you'd gone out with her instead of—sorry. Is it because you used to have feelings for each other?"

I sneered. "What? Where'd you come up with that?"

She folded her arm and tilted her head. "Come on, Mickey, I know the deal. You were going to break up with Bethany, Luci was going to break up with what's-his-name—"

"Carson," I said with a scowl.

"Carson—and you both chickened out."

I put my hand up to stop her. "Okay, first of all—it's not 'chickening out.' You of all people should know how hard it is to go through with something like that. It took you forever to leave Ray."

"Sorry, poor choice of words," she said. "And I do know, hun. It's not easy. That's why I never said anything. Plus, remember, you asked me to stay out of your love life."

"Right, and I appreciate that," I said. "So, on that note — how the hell do you know this?"

"Please. Dana and I talk all the time," Mom said. "Especially since our boys got together."

"I know, but—" True, Dana Rizzo (actually, Dana Craven since she got remarried) and Virginia Slater (actually, Virginia Adams since she got divorced) had been friends even longer than Torey and I had. But that was no excuse. "How does she know this?"

Mom shrugged. "I guess Luci isn't as shy about talking to her mom about her love life as you are."

"Ouch. Sick burn." I switched the station on the radio. Mariah's majestic ballad was over, and Amy Lee was belting out the captivating refrain of "Bring Me to Life." "Evanescence! Point for me!"

Mom put another hash mark under my name. "I'm just saying, she's always been a little more open with her mom about everything. And there's nothing wrong with that."

"Luci always did have a big mouth," I said with a smitten little smirk. "I just never knew you knew."

"Of course, honey, we all knew," she said as she scanned to the next station. "Michael Bublé! My point!"

"Who's 'we'?" I commanded.

"Well, me. Mace and Salvatore. Dana and Bill. Raymond."

I tightened my lips at the thought of everyone I knew knowing something I thought was private and personal.

"And we all know everything else, too, sweetie," Mom continued. But "everything" could mean so many different things.

I glanced at Mom out of the corner of my eye, hesitated, and asked exactly what I knew she wanted me to ask. "'Everything else'?"

"With Bethany. The affair. The abortion. Her friend in San Bernadino (she put air quotes around 'friend')—we know he's a boy, and we know he's not just a friend."

Then she put her hand on the back of my neck as my bottom lip slid outward. "And we know how hurt you are."

With my mother's gentle, reassuring touch, I felt like a frightened, vulnerable little boy going to the dentist for the first time. I began breathing heavily and blinking rapidly. My eyes were stinging and I felt sweat on my lower back. As I began chewing the inside of my cheek, I noticed how fast the pavement was passing underneath the tattered wheels of my battered old Jetta. My right heel, instead of anxiously bouncing up and down, had shoved the accelerator to the floor.

"Slow down, sweetie," Mom said.

So I did. I slowed all the way down. All the way down and then all the way over to the side of the road, where I shifted into Park and sat in a stunned state of overwhelm, humiliation, and panic. Suddenly, my body shook from my shoulders to my knees as I tried with all my might to wrestle back years of tears. But then, it felt like a big rubber band snapped inside my chest; I collapsed onto the steering wheel and sobbed harder than I had in years. Suddenly, I was fifteen years old again, my first girlfriend had just dumped me, and Ray-Hole had grounded me for a month after threatening to kick me out of my home.

As I wallowed in desperation from the enormity of the hole I'd dug for myself with all the bad decisions I'd ever made and all the failures that had come as a result, I needed Mom to be Mommy again more than ever. And in this harrowing moment, she delivered the magic formula I didn't know I needed. She embraced me with all her might and confirmed that she loved me, and so did everyone else who knew about my harsh reality. Then she sat next to me in my car, gently rubbing my back without saying anything, and saying so much at the same time.

Then, "You Can't Hurry Love" shimmied through the speakers, and Mom broke the silence.

"Phil Collins."

I smiled, hugged her even harder, and said, "You win."

27

Mason Patrick, do you take this man to be your husband, your partner in life, your most trusted and cherished friend, and the keeper of the key to your heart from today forward and forsaking all others?"

"I do. I mean, yes. Yes, I do."

"Great. And Salvatore Rizzo, do you take this man to be your husband, your partner in life, your most trusted and cherished friend, and the keeper of the key to your heart from today forward and forsaking all others?"

"Yes, I do."

"Then if anyone here today, present in person or in spirit, can speak to any reason that Mason and Salvatore should not join hands and begin this journey down the path of eternal love, laughter, faithfulness, and forgiveness, please do so now, or honor these two lovers with peace and respect until the end of days."

"Good God, that's sappy," I blurted, maybe a little too loud. "I'm gonna get a toothache from this shit."

Mason and I, along with a couple of his cop buddies and one of his old hockey teammates, stood shoulder-to-shoulder at the head of the aisle on the second-floor overhang of the Waterfront Weddings Ballroom, a glorious two-story modern dance hall atop a posh four-star hotel cradled by City Hall Plaza, Faneuil Hall, and the New England Aquarium. Everything about this place screamed luxury, from the cherry wood dance floor to the sparkling broad pane window walls to the illuminated floating staircase to the breathtaking panoramic view of the harbor. I'd already teased Mace and Toto about the venue ("you guys wouldn't know class if it bit you in the ass"), and disrupting this tender moment during which they were reciting their vows was icing on the cake. So, I wasn't wicked shocked when Mason elbowed me in the stomach while everyone else looked at me with a mix of amusement and surprise.

"Really, Mick?" Torey said, peering at me over my brother's shoulder. "Right now?"

I grinned and said, "You really are a girl sometimes, you know that?" Torey had always teased me about liking Drama Club more than baseball, and he was always quick to call me a girl whenever I couldn't start a fire or didn't know how to use a socket wrench or said something with the mildest tinge of sentimentality. So I had been waiting years for the right moment to say that to him, and this was obviously it.

He rolled his eyes, chuckled, and said, "Well played, Mouse. Well played."

Mason smirked and said over his shoulder, "Get it out of your system now, bud; try that tomorrow, and I'll tag you in the sack."

I flashed a proud smile and squeezed his shoulders. "No worries, brah, I'll behave during the *real* wedding."

Mason shook his head and re-focused on his husband-to-be. Then, as the Justice of the Peace was about to continue, I heard from behind Torey's back, "He's not wrong though."

Torey turned to his side. "Now you're gonna start too?"

It was Luci. She was wearing a royal blue skirt and a black blazer, and her hair was tied back in a bun that looked like a big black pom-pom. She hadn't aged a day.

"Well, he's right," she said, glancing at me from across the aisle. "I mean, a pink tie and cummerbund?"

We'd been in the same room for the last hour, but the expansive layout of this extravagant dance hall—half the tables were on one side of the dance floor, half were on the other—had enabled us to conveniently avoid each other (and the uncomfortable small talk obligated between long-lost former friends). That is, until we had to come upstairs for rehearsal in the smaller, more intimate overhang where the ceremony would be held. The awkwardness we'd both tried to eschew was plopped directly into our laps when, as the best man and the maid of honor, we were paired up for the practice run and made fake titters as we walked down the aisle with our elbows interlocked. We'd gotten away with just a polite "Hey" to each other, and I thought that might be the end of it. But now, she was just across the aisle from me, picking on her brother (like the Luci I used to know), and she'd looked at me with those big, beautiful eyeballs.

"Bitch, it's a hot pink, and I look fantastic," Torey replied as he confidently tugged at his jacket.

"And those vows?" Luci said with that "I gotcha" smile I remembered so well as she jabbed Torey with her elbow. "So girly."

"You helped us write the vows, ass bag." Torey never backed down when challenged by his feisty little sister, even on the eve of the biggest day of his life.

"Well, I *am* a girl, dumbass," Luci shot back.

"Psh. A stupid girl, maybe," Torey said as he stuck his tongue out at her. He knew the quickest way to push her buttons was to belittle her intelligence, something she took great pride in.

"Whatever, dork," Luci said as she slapped him on the arm. "How many Ivy League diplomas do you have? That's right—zero."

I smirked because it was always entertaining to see Luci shut her older brother down like that. She looked at me again briefly, but looked away when she noticed me gawking wistfully at her. I dropped my head and blinked with embarrassment, but it was too late.

Then, Torey came back at her with, "Well, you're still an ugly little troll."

No.

No, she wasn't.

***

So many wonderful memories and pivotal moments in life are tied to tentpole events—graduations, funerals, childbirth, weddings—things like that. I couldn't wait to find out what little and large things Mason and Torey would be smiling about years and years down the road, because despite what had happened between Bethany and me since our wedding, there are memories from that day I wouldn't trade for anything. Little, funny things like my excited new wife catching her dress in the door of the limousine and laughing it off, or Mom spilling red wine all over her buttermilk-colored blouse and slipping in the puddle while dancing to "I Gotta Feeling." Big, significant things like the scowl Bethany shot Brianna when Brie announced she was pregnant, or the look of nervous wonder Mason and Torey gave each other when they danced together for the first time. Now, those boys would have a day of their own to remember with fondness long after the hair in their ears turned gray, and I wouldn't dare do anything to rob them of that. But the day *before* their memorable day, this seemingly insignificant Friday in March, would secure itself for all eternity as a day I, personally, would never forget.

It wasn't just because of what happened that day; it was a feeling. An emotion. A wave of serenity. Because that day was the first in many, many days—the first in many, many years, in fact—when I didn't have either a red-faced banshee pinning my legs to the ground or a hungry mountain lion with craggy yellow teeth roaring in my face. Instead, I was surrounded exclusively by people who'd shown me love, encouragement, and support my entire life. Mom. Mason. Torey. Luci. Even Mrs. Craven (Mason's cop/hockey friends and Torey's football buddies were there, too, but they didn't count). And Kay was there in spirit; she called me "Stud" (with semicolon-and-closed-parentheses) when I sent her a picture of me trying on my tux. So, I had warmth, energy, and confidence surging through my veins with every movement I made.

What had started with silliness during the wedding rehearsal carried throughout the afternoon while we were decorating the big, glitzy ballroom with splashes of navy blue and hot pink. I was bouncing around the room helping put centerpieces on tables, tacking streamers and rope lights to ceilings and walls, prepping the head table, and finding nooks and crannies throughout this massive venue to put up cute (and only slightly embarrassing) photos of Mace and Toto as adorable children and doofy teenagers. I was having the time of my life playfully pestering both my brother and my best friend and drawing eye rolls and groans from my captivated (well, captive) little audience with some of my signature jokes. Even the typically stoic contingent of cops/hockey/football dudes who were there helping out gave me a few chuckles, and when one of them asked Torey, mid-laugh, "Who is this nut?" Torey smiled at me, smacked my shoulder, and said, "This guy right here? This is Mickey Patrick. The *real* Mickey Patrick."

Despite my fantastic mood and the shenanigans related thereto, I'd kept my distance from Luci because I still didn't know what to say to her. I heard her a couple times from the opposite side of the room, where she was arranging flowers with her mom, listening to Spotify, and singing shamelessly (but beautifully) whenever a song played that she knew. And I did catch her glimpsing at me observationally once or twice, like when I made my chipmunk wizard joke or when I jumped from a chair onto Mason's back and said, seductively, "Take me in, officer, I've been a bad, bad boy." But there had been no conversations, no looks with big, beautiful eyeballs, and no wistful gawks since the practice ceremony. I guess whatever magic had once bubbled between us had officially worn off.

And then, it happened.

I'd just finished putting all the place cards on Table 6 while Torey and I were telling the story about our championship baseball season to one of the other BC football coaches. I was locked in on the details about my shutout in the semifinals and Torey's leaping catch against the backstop in the finals when I heard, from way over at Table 22, *Ding. Ding-ding-da-ding, ding-ding, Da Ding.*

"Wait, shut up," I said. My eyes popped open and I turned toward the center of the room.

"Dude, you were the only one talking," Torey said.

I put up my hand and shushed him as the volume elevated and Mariah began humming. My eyes darted around the room as I tried to figure out who had turned it up, and there she was, beaming at me from sixteen tables away.

Mariah sang through the first verse as I began making long, slow strides toward Luci. When Mimi reached the chorus, I began to sing along. Well, in a way.

My way.

"And then DeNiro comes along…"

Luci began strolling in my direction and sang, "…with the strength to wear a thong…"

I picked up my pace and put my hand on my heart: "And then you cast your keys outside, and you throw a pecan pie!"

Luci continued toward me with one hand on her diaphragm and the other dramatically in the air: "So when the preacher's hair is gone, and he's dancing with King Kong…"

I grabbed an empty champagne glass by the stem and sang into it as if into a microphone: "Then you'll finally see the proof…" We were only a few steps away from each other now.

She put her hands together, palms up like a plate, and shuffled into my invisible bubble with an unsure but genuine smile: "… that a pizza cries for …" then she extended me the proverbial olive branch in the form of an adorable little hand plate, and punctuated this ridiculous (but profound) farce with, "youuuuuuuuu."

I grabbed her hands and pulled her toward me, then wrapped my arms around her. She squeezed me with all her might and, with a happy sigh, said simply, "Mickey-Mack."

As I held her there in the middle of the ballroom with twelve other people staring at us, many wondering what the hell they'd just witnessed, her wonderful citrus scent trickled into my nose, and I said the only thing that needed to be said.

"Luci Goose."

Luci pulled away, squealed, and made little, happy claps with her fingertips, and my heart suddenly emerged victoriously from my colon and remembered it was a heart again. Then, with warm red blood coursing through my veins with exuberance and life for the first time in ten years, I heard Torey chime in from Table 6.

"Wow, Mick. You really are a girl sometimes."

28

We spent the rehearsal dinner at Legal Seafoods seated next to each other at a huge table with Mason, Torey, the moms, and the rest of the wedding party. But it felt like it was just the two of us. We were laughing and poking fun at each other from behind our menus, teasing our brothers, and making up fake love stories about couples around the restaurant. ("The guy with the glasses and the sweater vest was always kind of shy, but he met the girl with the low ponytail and the schoolgirl pumps on OKCupid, and they connected over a mutual love of dwarf hamsters."). By the time dinner was over, my cheeks ached from smiling so much and I had a stitch in my side from cackling like a hyena all night. Also, I couldn't believe dinner was over. I wasn't ready to call it a night, so, as everyone was getting up to leave, I panicked.

"LuceLuceLuce," I said as I touched her forearm. She had one arm in her jacket but stopped and said, with fake concern, "MickMickMick! What?"

"Can—can you hang out for a bit? We haven't really had a chance to catch up."

"Dude, we've been hanging out all day," she said as she put her other arm in her jacket and loosened her bun a little. "What do you want from me?"

"Uh... " I hadn't expected that response. My frazzled brain searched frantically for the right response while my eyes popped out of my face and my j—

"Kidding." Her face softened into an "I gotcha" smile and she jabbed me with her elbow. "I'd love to."

I breathed a sigh of relief and said, "Ass," as everyone started funneling toward the exit. "Hey Mom, I'm gonna hang back for a bit. I'll be back later."

I was a little embarrassed that, at a few months shy of thirty, I was sharing a hotel room with my mother and thus felt the need to "check in," but then I remembered Luci was doing the same thing.

"Me too," she told Dana.

"Okay, sweetie—don't be out too late," Mom said with a wink.

"Have a nice time, kids," Dana said with a knowing smile.

We both rolled our eyes at the insinuations our mothers were not-so-subtly making. We were just two old friends catching up, and that was it—another harmless not-a-date. So, we went to the bar and ordered drinks (friends have drinks at bars together), and then we started talking. She told me how things went down with Carson. He started being an asshole to her a month after they got married ("Started?" I said), and she recounted some of the horrible things he used to call her. Lovely things like "Fat Bitch" (she wasn't fat or a bitch) and "Stupid Clam" (she wasn't stupid or a clam) whenever she would disagree with him. He told her once that she was lucky he didn't have a temper, "'cause most guys would put you in yer place fer run-nin' yer mouth." *Yeah, such a lucky girl,* I thought to myself. Then, when they were trying to have kids, he finally did "put her in her place" when he discovered she'd secretly been taking birth control because she didn't want to bring children into the world with someone who might abuse them. She said as soon as her brother saw the bruises on her neck and the cut on her lip, he "went ape-shit on Carson and busted up his face," and Mason made sure Torey didn't go to jail.

"After I divorced that fucking hick, I finally—FINAL-LY—figured out that I didn't need a man in my life."

I looked at her cheek as she stared off at the aquarium on the other side of the room.

"I had never been on my own, and I needed to be," she said. "There were some shitty days at first; I cried a lot, felt really lonely. But Mom and Bill took really good care of me until I felt better. Toto, too."

I looked down at my own hands. They were wrapped around my little glass of scotch. A bit of condensation trickled into my palm. Pangs of regret began floating around at the bottom of my throat. I wished I could've been there for her when she was going through all of that. Or that we had followed through on our pact all those years ago, so she and I could've avoided all the bullshit we'd been through since then.

"So, I did some traveling—London, Paris, Singapore, Sydney—all by myself. And I was in a much better place," she said. "I can't tell you how, just, transformative it was to realize how much control over my own life I really had. Once I figured that out, I promised myself I would never, ever get into a relationship again unless I knew with my whole heart that it was with the right person."

"Should've called me," I said with a smirk.

"Please, you've been up Bethany's ass since you were nineteen." She threw back a buttery nipple. "I've heard wonderful things, by the way."

When she noticed me looking at my half-empty glass and chewing the inside of my cheek, her eyes tumbled downward and she said, "Sorry."

"Sorry for what?" I began stirring my drink with the little red straw. "You're totally right—it's been horrible." Then I talked about everything that had gone wrong over the past three months. Or eleven years. The misery. The depression. The affair. The abortion. The free pass. I knew she already knew about all of it because our moms were besties. But she listened anyway because she knew I needed to talk about it. Friends let each other vent about their marriages. So, she let me ramble, looked at me with kindness, patted my leg when I seemed upset, and laughed at the funny parts (like the lame lines I used to try and pick up younger girls at the Cask). With my eyes stinging, I finished my third scotch and decided I'd had enough to drink for the night. Luci downed her last buttery nipple, turned to me, and got all serious.

"Hey. Look at me," she said, holding my face with her hands and looking wicked intense. "I'm saying this as your friend." I was nervous about what she might say next. But her eyes told me I could trust her. "We all care about you, Mickey-Mack. Me. Torey. My mom. Your mom. Mason. Even Bill. We just want to see you happy."

I nodded and felt my lower lip twitch. Then Luci added, "And we all wonder if Bethany really does."

I broke eye contact, exhaled, and glanced down at the

bar. She put her index finger under my chin and said, "Hey." I looked into those big, beautiful eyeballs again.

"I know you're not going to talk shit about her. You're a nice guy. But I'm allowed to say it. Bethany can be kind of—"

"A bitch," I cut her off.

"Well, I was going to say, like, domineering, narcissistic, childish." Luci smiled. "But, yeah, that works too."

"I don't care—I'll say it again!" I cleared my throat, stood up, and cupped my hands around my mouth so the whole restaurant could hear it. "Bethany's a bitch!"

"Hey, YOU said it—not me!" she said.

And with that, the sorrow and self-pity I'd wallowed in for the better part of a decade began to feel just a little bit lighter. Luci always seemed to know just the right thing to say. She was a wonderful friend.

I could be okay with being just friends with Luci. Now that our brothers were getting married and we were back in each other's lives, I could look forward to seeing her at various family gatherings over the next half-century. I'd catch up with her once in a while at Christmas parties or Memorial Day cookouts or funerals of old teachers, find out how her music teaching career was going, meet the new man in her life who treated her right and filled her heart with happiness, and watch her mature and grow old—from a distance. It would be a pleasure enjoying her company on those rare occasions, and it would give me something to look forward to once or twice a year. And that would be just fine, because I had Bethany—Beth. Whatever. And Beth was a cool person to hang out with.

As we strolled back toward the hotel where everyone was staying, we enjoyed a happy silence. I didn't think about the woman I was married to who was out in California and probably having sex with That Brad Guy. I thought about the woman I was friends with who was four inches to my left. I didn't think about the broken road I'd wandered aimlessly and hopelessly down; I thought about where it had brought me—to this wonderful night surrounded by people who cared about me, sans the wife who didn't, and it had granted me an opportunity to re-nourish my relationship with one of my oldest, closest friends.

It was nice to reconnect with Luci. But "reconnect" wasn't really the right word, because I realized that night that we'd never truly disconnected. Despite the miles and the years that had kept us apart, our friendship was as strong on this night as it was the day we'd sang Mariah Carey in her living room, or the time she called me when she found out about Darius and Danica, or the time she sat with me in the love seat after *Phantom of the Opera*. There had always been something palpable between Luci and me, something warm and toasty, and ten years had done nothing to dull it or dampen it. It was something I craved. Something I relished. Something that had taken up permanent residence in my limbic system, and hung there, glowing, gleaming, growing, no matter where I was, whom I was with, or what I was doing. It felt right. It felt pure. It felt familiar. It felt… it felt…

29

atural," Luci whispered to me as we hooked elbows and watched our mothers walk down the stairs in front of us. We were next in line—the last to be announced before Mason and Torey took center stage—but as she wrapped her arm around mine, I looked at her and lost my ability to breathe. Our post-rehearsal dinner not-a-date meant so much to me that I didn't want it to end. It reminded me that, despite all the mistakes I'd made, the wrong turns I'd taken, and the desolation that had caked my soul in hardened mud, I still had people in my life who cared about me and loved me for who I was. And one of them was a beautiful, irreverent divorcee with big, beautiful eyeballs, and the warmest smile I had ever seen.

She looked gorgeous. Her jet-black hair was tied back in a low rose bun with long wavy tendrils on either side of her face, and her hot pink dress popped dramatically against her deliciously tanned skin. The pearl necklace and matching bracelet she was wearing reminded me of what she wore to *Phantom of the Opera* (I wondered if they were the same ones), and her feet, toenails painted to match her dress, were decorated with open-toed ivory heels. Something definitely stirred inside me.

The wedding ceremony was magnificent. Both of the guys snorted back tears as their mothers walked them toward each other with love and pride. When they joined hands and looked at each other, Mason was red as a McIntosh apple and flashing the biggest smile I'd ever seen on his typically deadpan mug, and Torey was giggling with glee and making little, happy claps with his fingertips—just like his sister. I kept my promise and didn't crack any jokes during their vows, but as soon as the JOP formally announced their union, I shot my hands into the air, let out a guttural "Woo!" then threw my arms around my brother from behind. Luci did the same with her brother, and before the two of them were allowed to walk down the aisle together, the four of us stood at the front of the room with hundreds of eyes on us and applause showering over the newlyweds. We huddled together in a group hug, paid tribute to those who couldn't be there with us, and told each other we loved each other.

We slogged through the cocktail hour and family photo formalities, and then everyone in the wedding party took our places at the top of the floating staircase to descend into the main ballroom in grand fashion. Then, with "Moves Like Jagger" thumping through the subwoofers, a DJ with two chins and curly gray hair introduced the guys from both sides of the party, one by one. Some tried to bust a move as they worked their way down the stairs and through the banquet room, some waved sheepishly as they scuttled to their seats and tried not to look like they hated every second of it. As I awaited my turn in the spotlight, the thought of busting out some of my finest footwork from my Ren McCormack days did cross my mind (I hadn't had the opportunity to entertain a crowd like this in years!), but then I remembered I wasn't flying solo. I was, of course, paired with Luci for the introductions, and that (as well as the extra sixty pounds on my former *Footloose* frame) was enough to dissuade me from attempting one of Ren's legendary backflips. And as we waited for our names to be called, there was no awkwardness or fake titters between us like there had been at the rehearsal.

But when Luci took my arm, smiled at me with her perfect face, and said, "Natural," just before we entered the ballroom, it grabbed me. All I could do was stare at her, stunned, study every captivating fleck of texture in her irises, and wonder if something had stirred inside her as well. Friends don't study captivating flecks in each other's irises.

Then, over my shoulder, I heard, "Guys! Go!"

It was Torey and Mason, holding hands and looking at us impatiently.

Shit, we missed our cue. We looked at each other again (but with more of an "Oops" look on our faces) and entered the spotlight at the top of the stairs. We began waving at all the exquisitely dressed people in the room, and D.J. Doublechin greeted us with, "Here they are! Ladies and gentlemen—maid of honor Luciana Rizzo, escorted by best man Michael Patrick!"

We got to the bottom of the stairs and started dork-dancing to our seats as Adam Levine's buzzy falsetto cranked on about taking each other by the tongue and moving like Jagger. And as I separated from her and watched her move through the crowd, smiling, bopping around, and spreading her unique brand of electricity throughout this massive and enchanting auditorium, it was at that moment I knew that being just friends with Luci would be impossible.

30

The night was better than perfect. The lights were low—save for the fuchsia-tinted up-lighting splashed across the walls and Boston's brilliant evening skyline smiling at us from across the harbor—and spirits were high. The feint smell of buttered lobster lingered in the air long after the waitstaff had cleared the tables, and DJ Doublechin had the place popping with wicked beats like "Born This Way," "Shut Up and Dance," and that one about apple bottom jeans. Everywhere you looked there were women with red lipstick and long earrings jumping up and down in high heels, men with buzz-cuts and broad shoulders bobbing about in tuxes, and half-dressed children with cake on their faces playing with squirt guns (great wedding favors, Mace). The colorful, sprawling ballroom was packed to capacity with all the glitz and glamour you'd expect at an event of this magnitude (nuptials between a big Boston police sergeant and an ACC football coach sure drew some fanfare) and the evening was brimming with laughter, love, and joy. And in the middle of it all, my brother and my best friend were looking at each other with tender smiles and soggy eyes.

I'd been carving up the dance floor for two straight hours—two-stepping in triangles, dropping the dopest Dougies, and whipping all the nae-naes—when I decided to take a breather (my Dad-bod belly and grandpa knees could only take so much). So, with my chest still huffing and puffing, I grabbed a glass of water and sat down with Mom.

"Kesha!" I said as "TiK ToK" thumped through the room.

"Like I would know any of this modern hip-hop stuff," she said, trying to defend herself. "And we're not even playing right now anyway."

"Oh, we're always playing," I teased as I leaned back in my chair. "And now I'm winning."

She smiled and rolled her eyes. "Having a good time, hun?"

"The best." I took a sip of water and began crunching on a piece of ice. "I haven't had a night like this since—" I couldn't think of a time. "Since my own wedding, I guess."

"Well, good. You do seem much more relaxed. Much more—yourself."

"Myself?" I quipped.

"Yourself," she repeated with an understated smile. "You're my Mickey."

I looked at her and crunched on some more ice. "It's been forever since I was your Mickey, Mom. Or anybody's Mickey. I'm just 'Beth's Husband' because I've got nothing going on. But she isn't here tonight, so I'm just trying to enjoy it."

"I know, hun, and that's what I mean. Tonight you've been Mickey B.C.—the Mickey we all knew—from before."

"Before what?" I was curious about what exactly she was implying.

"Before Connelly," she said with a familiar smirk. "The Mickey who's sensitive, funny, and sweet. The Mickey who lights up a room. You always make people feel good about themselves. You're a warm, glowing ray of sunlight on this cold, dark, mean little planet."

Mom pointed at her temple, then to my chest. "I knew that Mickey was still in there."

I felt my face heat up; I hadn't felt like "that Mickey" in a long time. So, I did my best to deflect every compliment Mom was throwing at me.

"Light up a room—right. I haven't done that since I was a teenager."

"Are you kidding?" Mom gestured out to the dance floor. "You've been doing it all night! Your best man speech had the room in stitches! You had a crowd circled around you clapping when you were doing the 'Poker Face'! You led the conga line!"

I smiled. "Mason hated the conga line."

"At first maybe, but he was laughing like a toddler by the end of it," Mom said. "And that was all you, Mick! People gravitate to you—they always have—you have a way about you that puts everyone in a good mood."

"Well, it's his wedding—he should be in a good mood anyway," I said. Then, as "Truly Madly Deeply" by Savage Garden slowed things down, I watched all the happy, sappy couples merge together on the dance floor and morph into a soppy blob of swaying hips and swooning eyes. I thought about Bethany for the first time all weekend and wondered if her hips were swaying or her eyes were swooning over

That Brad Guy, and I felt a tinge of resentment toward her for not being here with me. Not because I wanted her with me, per se, but because I felt like an outsider during the slow stuff with no one to sway hips with and swoon over.

"You know what I mean," Mom said.

"Well, thank you—that means a lot to me," I said with a reluctant smile as I raised my glass to her. "More than you know."

"Sure, hun," she said with a wink.

After a moment or two of contemplative silence, I decided it was time for a subject change.

"You must be getting tons of good stuff for the scrapbook," I said. "Programs you can highlight, flowers you can press, place cards, favors—well, the squirt guns might be tough to tape to the pages. But this is a goldmine for scrapbook stuff."

"It certainly would be." She turned her head and took a sip of the champagne she hadn't touched in three hours.

"'Would be?'" I said with a funny look. "What's that mean?"

She started with a wimpy "Well…" before I interrupted her, aghast that she would ever stop working on that thing.

"Are you not doing the scrapbook anymore?"

"Not as much these days, hun. But it's okay, really."

"Wait," I said. "My whole life, any time we'd go any place or do anything, you'd say, 'Oh, take a picture of that—This'll be a good one for the scrapbook.' 'Hey, hold onto that—it'll be a good one for the scrapbook.' That thing is your life's work."

"Well, you boys are grown up now." Mom rested her chin on her fist. "Maybe it's time to retire the ol' scrapbook. It had a good run."

I squinted and stared at the side of her face. This didn't sound like my mom. She was obsessed with that goddamn scrapbook. What wasn't she telling me?

"Mom?" I leaned toward her. "What's going on with the scrapbook?"

"Nothing, hunny, I just think it's time to move on." Her eyes drifted. "I left Raymond, so we can close that chapter, and we can start a new thing. Like a photo album on Instagram or something."

"Raymond?" I said, squinting. I thought about it for a second, then I sat up and said, "Wait, does Ray have the scrapbook?"

She hesitated, then nodded.

"Mom! Why does Ray have the scrapbook?" I was getting irritated. "I thought that would be the one thing you'd make sure you grabbed!"

"Well," she said, "it wasn't in the safe where it belonged, so we missed it."

I remembered then that I hadn't been there to help Mom, Mason, and Torey get her stuff out of the house when she'd finally gotten the courage to leave him. My stomach suddenly imploded with guilt when I remembered where it was.

"It was in my old bedroom." I covered my face with both hands.

"Right. And Raymond said if you wanted your 'crap,' you'd have to come get it. Remember? He texted you about it, and he said you ignored him."

My right heel started bouncing up and down.

"Well, I didn't want my stuff," I said. Which was only partially true. Most of it was old school supplies and text-books I didn't need, clothes that didn't fit anymore, and photos I could get re-printed. But there were a few things—my Drama awards, my baseball medal, theater scripts with my lines highlighted, yearbooks with handwritten messages from friends—that I wouldn't have minded having. The truth was, I'd convinced myself I didn't want any of it because I didn't want to have to ask Ray if I could come and get it. "But I didn't know the scrapbook was still in there."

"Well," Mom said with a shrug of her shoulders and resign in her voice, "what's done is done, hun. I have no desire to see him again, and Mace won't even talk to him anymore. And you and he never really got along, so I'm not surprised he's—"

"'Never really got along'?" I said. "He beat the crap out of me. And you, too. He was a miserable fuck, and I hated him. I know that's not your point, but still."

"It kind of is, actually," Mom said. "That's why we don't have the scrapbook, Mickey. Because you and I—neither one of us has ever been able to stand our ground with him. I'm so thankful Mason was there to help me get out, or I might still be in."

"I should have been there, too. I know," I said. It was something that had nagged at me for months, but I just couldn't bring myself to go into the belly of the beast and take a stand with the rest of my family. Or, what did I say before? I had something going on with Beth. That was it.

"No, honey. That's the thing," Mom said. "I never expected that from you after what he did to you."

"What about all the horrible shit he did to you?"

"Oh, you don't need to—"

"Like your bruised rib." I looked at the sweat on my glass. "Or the broken tooth. Or when you had to wear a turtleneck in August to cover the choke marks."

Mom put her hand on her cheek. "I know, hun. I'm sorry."

"What?" I took a confused sip of water. "Why are you saying sorry?"

She looked at me with weepy eyes. "Because—" she exhaled. "If I could've stood up to Raymond when he… you know… to me…"

I nodded, still curious.

"Then he wouldn't have gone after you boys." Mom sniffled. "And if he hadn't made it so scary to speak up for yourselves when you were little, then maybe you'd be able to stand up for yourself now. And then we wouldn't have lost the real Mickey. And you wouldn't be lonely and unhappy and feeling like you're stuck in this horrible marriage with no way out."

We'd never really talked about it, but growing up, I never understood why she didn't leave Ray when the abuse started. But as I got older and learned more about relationship roller coasters (and horror shows), I learned that things weren't always that simple. After the accident, she did everything in her power to support two young boys for two years. She tended bar at the Penguin until 2 a.m. five nights a week and worked as a cashier at Charlie Mart five days. When she wasn't working, she was often pinned to her bed with a debilitating migraine. More often than any of us wanted, our dinners came from little plastic trays and our entertainment from crayon boxes and coloring books, as she just couldn't summon the time or energy to engage us. She was miserable, exhausted, and scared. So, when a bearded entrepreneur with a BMW showed interest in her, then invited her and her two boys to move in with him, she was understandably intrigued. And, like me, once she was in, it was hard for her to get out, because it was familiar. And when a decision is outsourced to the brain, the brain pulls toward what is known, and she knew what her relationship with Raymond was. It wasn't perfect—on many days it was the antithesis of perfect—but it was familiar.

"Mom. I cannot emphasize this enough." I took my mother's hands in mine, kissed her on the thumbs, and looked at her with depth and sincerity. "My shitty marriage is not your fault."

She smiled a teary smile and sighed. "I love you, hun."

"I love you, Mom."

Then I felt a tap on my shoulder, and everything changed.

31

I gave Mom her hands back, turned around, and there she was.

"Hey Mickey-Mack," she said with that incredible smile. Then she looked over at Mom and said, "Sorry to interrupt, Ms. Adams, but I was wondering if your son might join me in a dance?"

"Luci, I've told you a million times to call me Ginny," Mom said, dabbing her cheek with a napkin and waving her other hand as if she were wiping Luci's over-politeness out of the air. "Or Virginia. Or even Mom, seeing as we're family now. And yes, he's all yours, hun."

I liked the sound of that.

"I promise I'll take good care of him," she responded with a side-eyed grin. I liked the sound of that even more.

Then, as Savage Garden hummed on about standing on mountains and bathing in seas, Luci and I twirled out onto the dance floor. I dipped her playfully, and she giggled, but when she came back up, our eyes met, and it was no joke. We looked at each other, our noses inches apart, without saying a word. We were communicating, but with eyebrow twitches and relaxed smiles. Swaying hips and swooning eyes. So much was spoken in the silence between us.

She draped her arms over my shoulders, and I wrapped mine around her back; we fit together perfectly.

"What took you so long?" I asked with a smile. "Didn't think you were ever going to ask me to dance."

"I was waiting for you," she shot back. "You've been Mister Dancing Queen all night, and then you were talking to your Ma. When exactly was I supposed to cut in?"

"Fair point," I said. "But I s'pose I could've asked you."

"Meh," she shrugged. "You've been busy with other things."

I couldn't help thinking she was talking about more than just tonight.

"Well, I'm all yours now, Luci Goose. My mommy said so," I joked. "I guess she's giving away two sons tonight."

"Hey, don't count your chickens, Mister Man. You're mine for this dance, and that's all."

"Song's almost over though." I tightened my lips. "I'm not ready for it to end."

"Welp. Guess you'll have to make yourself available for the next one, Mister Popular."

I chuckled through my nostrils and gave her a weird look. "Why do you keep calling me 'Mister' everything?"

"I just like the sound of it," she said with a dash of dalliance. "Mister Mickey-Mack."

I settled my face into a hazy gaze and enjoyed the moment, not yet realizing it was one I'd been waiting for my whole life.

"I like the sound of you saying it," I said after a moment. "I like the sound of anything you say."

"You do?" she teased. "Would you like hearing me say, 'Hey Mickey, I slaughtered a village of innocent children and ate their corpses with mustard'?"

I smirked and asked, "I mean, where were their parents? They should've been there protecting their kids from the carnivorous goose on the loose instead of snorting jelly beans and licking fidget spinners."

"Oh, is that where they were?" she asked, playing along. "I thought they were having an orgy with Count Chocula and Marty McFly."

"No, that's only on Tuesdays. But he has a time machine, so I guess he can just show up whenever."

We were both guffawing at the absurdity of this conversation when another slow one melted through the speakers. "Ocean Eyes" by Billie Eilish. The silliness quickly faded away as we began listening to the lyrics, still swaying but more slowly and rhythmically, swooning again but more intense and focused, and it was sometime during that song that I decided that I never wanted to sway or swoon or make jokes about Count Chocula orgies with anyone else. Maybe it was when we pulled each other closer, so we were no longer dancing but embracing on the dance floor. Maybe it was when our foreheads touched, and I found myself not just studying the flecks in her irises but entangled in them, and I could imagine our foreheads touching when they were both wrinkly and gray and bedecked with liver spots. Maybe it was little Billie's seductive vocals oozing through the room.

Or maybe it was when I kissed her.

Anytime I'd ever imagined kissing Luci, I'd pictured it being playful and fun, but exciting at the same time. I'd pictured tongue teasing, face touching, nose booping, and heart racing. I'd pictured giggles and tickles and pokes and little moans.

This was better.

It wasn't playful and fun—it was electrifying. Our tongues weren't teasing each other, they were dancing together. My heart wasn't racing, it was radiating in my chest. We weren't touching each other's faces, we were feeling each other's fire. It all felt so natural with Luci—just like everything did with her—and I never wanted it to stop.

We paused for a moment to catch our breath and check with each other to make sure we were both okay with what was going down. All I could get out was, "Are you—" before she nodded assuredly, whispered "Yes," and started kissing me again. I brushed one of her wavy tendrils back behind her ear and settled my thumb gently on her cheek as our lips played together and our tongues caressed each other. The sweet scent of citrus filled my nose, and the bare skin on her shoulders and back felt like velvet at first. But the more I touched it and the longer we kissed, the more I could feel the goose bumps up and down her spine. Luci Goosebumps.

She pulled away slightly, looked at me with worry in her big, beautiful eyeballs, and said, "What about you? Are you okay?"

My bottom lip quivered, my eyes began to moisten, and I took a deep breath.

"I've never been more okay in my life."

32

The tone of the evening changed dramatically for us after that. There was no more dance floor carving from me; I spent the remainder of the reception sharing everything with Luci. We shared laughs. We shared looks. We shared drinks. We shared chairs. Now that our walls had finally collapsed, we wanted to spend as much time together as we could, as if we were trying to stuff fifteen years' worth of repressed love into a two-hour session of hand-holding and lap-sitting.

We tried to ignore the looks of intrigue we were getting from my mom on the other side of the room. We tried not to see Mason and Torey whispering in each other's ears and glancing in our direction while they ate their cake. We pretended not to notice Dana and Bill pointing at us and making not-well-hidden thumbs-ups to each other while we danced to "Thinking Out Loud" by Ed Sheeran. But when our brothers grabbed us each by our forearms and pulled us to opposite sides of the room, we couldn't turn a blind eye. Because they were about to make sure we knew they hadn't.

I looked back at Luci with widened eyes as Mason

pulled me toward the lobby, and she shrugged at me as Torey dragged her over toward the ice cream bar by the stairs. Mason released me when we got outside the ballroom, straightened his bow tie, and said, "Mick, what are you doing?"

I knew what he was asking, but I decided to be a smartass and say, with fake naivety, "Not much, bro, what are you up to? Big night, huh?"

"I don't know, is it?" he said with an edge in his voice.

"Yeah!" I said, with perhaps a smidge too much enthusiasm. "It's my brother's wedding!"

He put his hand on the wall behind me, got uncomfortably close to my face (something I'm sure he pulled from his suspect-interrogation bag of tricks) and said, "Enough. What are you doing with Luci? You're married."

Mason never did put up with bullshit.

I dipped away from him, flung my arms outward, palms up, and looked around with exaggerated motions. "To who?" I blurted. "Where is she? I don't see anyone I'm married to in that room."

"That doesn't make it okay to make out with someone else all night." His eyes were intense and fixed on mine.

"Oh, shove it, Mason. What do you think Bethany is doing right now? She's probably fucking him right this minute." I looked at my watch. "Actually, it's only like seven in Cali right now. She's probably having dinner with him right this minute, and she'll fuck him later."

I felt a catch in my throat and the corners of my mouth suddenly pulled downward. Mason's glare began to soften. He put his arms on my shoulders and said, "Look. I know things have been rough with your wife lately. But this isn't—"

"Lately?" I said. "Mason, I haven't been happy in years. *Years.* What happened 'lately' is just the goddamn culmination of everything I've let her get away with for the last decade. I gave everything up for her. *Everything.* She wanted to stay in Rockingham fucking New Hampshire with her redneck parents and her bitchy little sister, so she could coach her little basketball team and get drunk every weekend with her friends. I did that for her. And how did she repay me? By using me as a doormat for years, then getting dick behind my back, getting pregnant, getting an abortion, and getting away with all of it because I'm too much of a pussy to do anything about it."

Mason looked downward in thought. I wasn't done.

"And now I'm stuck in that shitty little town with nothing going on. People don't go to Rockingham to live, Mace, they go there to die. That's why you left, isn't it? That's why Torey and Luci both left. And that's why all of Bethany's friends left. So, now she's miserable because she can't leave town, and I'm miserable because I can't leave her, so we're both going to be miserable fucks until we die miserable deaths and get buried in a plot in Rockingham fucking New Hampshire with her redneck parents and bitchy little sister. So, if I want to spend one night here in Boston having a good time with people who care about me, kissing someone I've loved since high school and pretending we're more than friends, then just let me have it, Mace. Please. Just let me have this one."

He took a step back, looked at me with arched eyebrows and said, "You—love her?"

I hesitated for a moment, not because I was unsure of my feelings, but because I was nervous about how Mason would respond. He'd always kept me grounded when my head was floating in the clouds, and I'd always been able to make him laugh—he was the yin to my yang. And since I'd done my thing by bringing him out of his shell with the conga line, it was his turn to do his thing and bring me back down to Earth with some tough love. So I nodded in response to his question and braced for the reality check.

"You love her." He said it as more of a statement this time. "Luci."

I looked at the ground, sniffled, and nodded again. "I've never said it out loud before. But yes. I always wonder where she is, what she's doing, who she's with, and if she's thinking about me. I wonder what life would have been like with her if we had gotten together after *Phantom of the Opera* like we wanted to. And I wish it had been me who knocked the shit out of Carson when he hurt her."

Mason put his hands in his pockets. "If it helps, he yelped when Torey ripped into him."

"Yelped?" I cracked the slightest smile. We sat down next to each other in a couple of overstuffed lounge chairs.

"Yeah, each time he blasted him in the stomach, he made this high-pitched squeal." He pantomimed a head-lock and a series of gut punches. "Like a dolphin or something. Yeek! Yeek! Yeek!"

"Wish I could've seen that," I lamented, "or done that."

"Mick, you don't have a violent bone in your body," Mason said. "Even if we had told you we were gonna go mess him up, you woulda stayed a hundred miles away."

I hung my head. He wasn't wrong. Because that was Confrontation—my arch-nemesis.

"I just wish I could've helped in some way," I said. "Been there for her or whatever, y'know?"

"Ehh, you've got your own demons, bud." He looked at

me with softness. "You need to conquer those before you start helping other people with theirs."

"Yeah? How do you suggest I do that?" I was honestly asking. Because almost three decades of hungry mountain lions and red-faced banshees had effectively browbeaten me into a permanent state of submission.

"You can start by standing up for yourself," he said. "Maybe don't shrink the second someone raises their voice at you."

"That's easy for you to say, Mace. You're not afraid of anything. People scream in your face all the time, and that's never bothered you a bit."

"No, it hasn't," he granted me. "I've never been afraid to stand my ground, and that's one reason Ray always respected me; I wasn't scared of him, and he knew it. So, he didn't walk on me like he did you."

"And I'm sure he still would be walking on me if he were still in our lives. But now I have Bethany for that."

"But he still *is* in your life."

I gave him a side-eyed look. "What? No, he isn't."

"Oh yeah?" Mason sat up and tilted his head. "Tell me, where is all of your stuff from high school, Mick? All those awards and trophies and shit? Where are those exactly?"

I sighed and pursed my lips. He knew I knew. That stuff was all still at the house where we grew up. With Ray. With Mom's scrapbook. And he knew I knew why.

"I don't need that stuff," I said, deflecting his point.

"Maybe not." He shrugged. "But there is one thing you do need."

"What's that?"

"You need to be able to square up to Ray and tell *him* that," Mason said, "not just ignore his text messages and avoid him because you're scared of him. You need to be able to look at him with his jagged eyebrows and jacked-up teeth and say, 'Ray-Hole, I don't need that shit. Throw it to the curb for all I care.' Then you need to get in your wife's face and say, 'Beth—I don't need *your* shit. I'm gonna throw *you* to the curb.' You need to face the fire. Just like Dad taught us."

"Taught *you*." I looked my brother squarely in the eyes. "And let's be real. You and I both know that's never going to happen."

"Oh yeah?" Mason folded his arms. "Why not?"

"BECAUSE OUR FATHER DIED FACING THE FIRE!" I shouted. "He *died*, Mace! You remember that, right? *Died*. I know you think I was too young to remember him, but I do. Bits and pieces, but enough to know who he was and what he meant to our family. Then Raymond came along when I was already wicked messed up from that, and he pounded me into an amorphous pile of mush. And Beth molded that mush into a spineless little Yes Man who lets her get away with anything she wants."

"You think you have no personality?" Mason said. "You spent the first half of this night getting all these people—people you've never met in your life, hundreds of them—to laugh with you, dance with you, clap for you. You lit this place up, Mick."

I shrugged as my eyes began to sting. He continued.

"You think you have no passion? You spent the second half of the night making goo-goo eyes at Luci, dancing with your foreheads touching, kissing her face and holding her hand like you never wanted to let her go."

I tilted my chin away from him and tried not to let him see the salty stream on my cheek.

He put his elbows on his knees and leaned forward. "And you think you're spineless? You used to point a tree branch at the sky and tell the whole universe, 'I have the power.' You stood up to your bully in second grade and told him and the whole world to kiss your ass. Then you threw a high and tight one at that same dude during baseball practice and pinned him to the ground when he came at you."

With each example Mason delivered, my chest swelled a little bit. At one time in my life, I *did* stand up to people. I *did* hold my ground. I *did* push back. And I, too, didn't put up with bullshit. But that was a long, long time ago.

"I was a kid back then," I said. "I'm a different person now."

"Are you? Because that kid grew into the man sitting right here. The man who just stood face-to-face with a Boston Police Sergeant and told him to shove it because he's in love with that girl in the other room."

I smirked.

"So stop making excuses, Mick. Stop being a victim." He knew he was on a roll. "Yeah, Ray can be a loud, proud asshole. Yeah, Bethany can be a selfish, screaming bitch. But they didn't choose your path for you. *You* did. You did that by letting them push you in whatever direction they wanted, when you could have stood up at any time and told them to shove it, like you just did with me."

He got out of his chair, bent at the waist, and with his hands on his knees, put his nose fifteen centimeters from my cheek and said, "And, Mick. You—only you—have the power to change your path. It's no one else's fault your life hasn't turned out the way you wanted, and no one else is going to fix it for you. It's *you*, bud. It's all you."

He was right. He was a thousand percent right. This wasn't about my stepfather, no matter how many times he'd gotten in my face with his meaty pointer finger and craggy yellow teeth. This wasn't about my wife, no matter where she was or who she was banging or how many times she'd steamrolled me into doing what she wanted. This was about me, and it always had been. It was about me and how, when faced with a pushy person, I never pushed back. It was about the hardened callus that had formed inside my cheek from years and years and years of chewing the skin raw. It was about me and how I'd buried my own ambitions, needs, and desires beneath everyone else's because I didn't want them to yell at me. This was about me and how I responded to bullies.

I'd spent twenty-five years stuck deep inside this dark and lonely crater of sorrow, blaming others for my broken spirit, and looking skyward for help. But the solution had been so simple all along. My He-Man sword wasn't some broken tree branch Ray threw in the garbage, never to be found again. It had been with me the whole time.

I inhaled through my nose, nodded, and blew out through my mouth. *I have the power*, I thought to myself.

"So, I'm going to ask you one more time," Mason said. "What. Are. You. Doing?"

I felt a sudden surge of passion sear through my chest; it felt both brand new and strangely familiar at the same time, like driving a newer model of your favorite old car. "I'll tell you what I'm doing," I said, invigorated.

I stood up without warning, almost bashing my brother in the face with my skull. "I'm gonna go get that fucking scrapbook."

"Yes," Mason said with the second-biggest smile I'd

ever seen on his normally deadpan mug. He threw his arms around me and squeezed so hard it almost knocked the wind out of me. "You've got this, bud. Go tell Ray-Hole to shove it.

"And when you do, give him this for me."

Mason slipped an envelope into my breast pocket and told me not to worry about it. Then we turned to go back into the reception hall with our arms on each other's shoulders, both grinning like school kids plotting to egg the principal's house, and there was Luci. She was leaning in the doorway with her blazer on over her dress and her clutch strapped to her wrist, smiling at us.

"Hey Mickey-Mack," she said, lightly brushing one of those wavy black tendrils back behind her ear. "Think that could wait until morning?"

33

We made out three times before we even got to the room, a tornado of twirling tongues, bursts of breath, and meandering hands. First in the Uber on the way to the hotel; then in the lobby while we waited in line to check in; then in the elevator up to the tenth floor (whomever was monitoring the elevator cameras got to see some neck action and some good old-fashioned dry humping).

By the time we locked the door behind us and plopped down together on the big, cushy bed with the squishy white comforter and the pillows as hard as concrete, we were both ready to go. Fifteen years' worth of ready-to-go. My tux fell off, piece by piece, and gathered in a crumpled pile by the faux cherry desk next to the television we wouldn't be watching. She tossed her blazer in the corner by the heater we weren't going to need, unzipped the back of her fluffy hot pink dress, and stepped out in a black strapless bra and a bright orange thong. We reconvened in the center of the king-sized bed, she in her thong and I in my bold blue boxer briefs. We tossed the pointless pillows off the bed with a laugh and then pulled each other close. I kissed her sweet lips as she ran her soft hands up and down my back, and as I smelled that wonderful citrus scent on her collarbone, a rush of excitement surged through me. I kissed down her neck, put my arms around her back, and lifted her up off the bed so I could get my fingers on the clasps of her bra. She squeaked out an encouraging giggle, and as her bra slid off her beautifully tanned breasts, I shifted in between her legs and kissed down to her cleavage and then back up to her mouth. My hands, meanwhile, traveled up and down the silky skin on her ribs, waist, and thighs, then back to her neck and cheek.

Luci's kisses were invigorating; I couldn't get enough of them. Her lips brushed and stroked mine so gently, so lovingly, while her tongue flicked around in my mouth with purpose, telling mine it wanted more. No matter what our almost-naked-and-fully-heated loins and limbs were screaming at us, we couldn't keep our lips off each other's lips or our hands off each other's faces. Because this wasn't about sex or passion or lust, or even your garden-variety, late-night drunken fireball of hormones. For Luci and me, this was about finally letting each other completely and totally in, allowing ourselves to feel our long-lingering feelings for each other, and be who we'd always wanted to be with each other. Regardless of whether or not we went any further, we were making love in its purest form.

But—we went further.

She pulled her lips away from mine and began kissing my cheek, then my neck, then my ear. Her hands, after sifting through my crunchy, hair-sprayed hair, began trailing down my spine, and then she tucked her thumbs into my briefs. I slipped my hands behind her back again, but this time they made their way southward. After I squeezed one of her butt cheeks and pulled her up against me, I grabbed her thong with both hands and yanked it all the way down her smooth, caramel-colored legs, and as I got up on my knees to toss it vaguely in the direction of her piled-up dress, she scooted closer to me and pulled my shorts down.

I sucked a cubic yard of nervous air through my nostrils and blew it out through my mouth as my heart slowed to a beat per century. I couldn't remember the last time I'd felt this desired or this attractive to someone, nor could I pinpoint a time when I'd felt such a magnetic force thrusting me toward another human with such extraordinary ferocity. And as Luci looked at me with that perfect smile of hers, the one that looked so grown-up since the days of braces, Drama club, and tuna melts, I scanned her curvaceous and radiant naked body with voracious eyes, and then pulled her up onto my lap.

As we melted together, her breasts against my neck, her arms around the back of my head, my hands supporting her back and buns and squeezing her up against me, her eyes connected with mine. It was a hazy look, her eyelids half down, her eyebrows half up, and her mouth open as if she were surprised or in pain.

"You okay?" I whispered.

"Yeah," she said in a husky voice I'd never heard her use before but that I instantly loved. "Just … finally."

With that, we began kissing again, our tongues, lips, and teeth all exploring one another in a mess of vigorous passion. As our rhythm increased, our sweat began to run together, and at one point when she was lying on her back and I was hovering over her, a bead of moisture ran off the tip of my nose and landed in her eye. I apologized immediately, but she just laughed about it hysterically, which made me laugh hysterically. I'd never laughed during sex before—always thought it was supposed to be serious and sacred. But soon after the giggles dissipated, I had five fingernails digging into each of my butt cheeks, a long, melodious groan in my left ear, and the most intense orgasm of my life. Leave it to Luci Goose to show me how much fun it could be.

***

I laid on my back the next morning, staring at the ceiling, replaying in my mind everything that had happened over the past thirty-six hours. The drive down with Mom, when I pulled to the side of the road and cried in her arms like a five-year-old. The rehearsal, how distant Luci and I had been at first, and how one Mariah Carey song melted the ice and set the stage for everything that followed. My brother and his crimson-red grinning face as he married the love of his life, a guy who also happened to be one of my best friends. Dancing to "Truly Madly Deeply" with that friend's sister, joking about Count Chocula orgies, and kissing her during a Billie Eilish song. The room full of strangers joining me in the Conga line and then cheering me on as I danced to Lady Gaga. Mason telling me to stop blaming others for the path I'd chosen for myself. The resignation on Mom's face as she accepted that she couldn't put anything from this memorable weekend into her prized scrapbook. And the vow I made that I would go get that fucking scrapbook and butt heads with Ray-Hole if I had to.

Then I thought about what happened after that. Wavy tendrils. Invigorating kisses. Tanned boobs. Giggles and sweat droplets. I thought about Luci making fun of me afterwards for calling it "making love" and asking if I was an effeminate thespian from the 1850s. I thought about how much that made me laugh—how much she'd always made me laugh—and I thought about the early-morning moment when the sun began peeking in through the heavy cotton curtains when I kissed her on the nose and said, "I think I'm in love with you, Luce."

"I think you are, too," she'd responded with a happy sigh and a bleary-eyed smile. "And … I know I'm in love with you. Mister Mickey-Mack."

And now, Luci's head was resting on my chest, her hair tickling my nose, her arm draped over my stomach, and I couldn't wipe the smile off my face.

Luci's head. *Luci's* hair. *Luci's* arm. Was this even real?

I had no way of knowing, because the sensations that had pulsated through my cardiovascular situation all weekend were so foreign to me, it was almost like they were happening to someone else. It was energy and optimism I'd forgotten I had. It was warmth and support I didn't realize I'd been missing. It was freedom to be the person I used to be, the person who everyone had missed seeing, but not nearly as much as I had missed being.

It was happiness.

It was life.

And when Luci turned her head, settled her chin on my chest, looked at me with those big, beautiful eyeballs, and said, "Hey you," I knew it was real. Very real.

Call it a re-birth. Call it a renaissance. Call it a revival. Call it whatever, but I knew something else, too. I knew there was no turning back. I knew I couldn't be what I had been for the last eleven years. Not anymore. I knew I couldn't lose these long-buried pieces of me—not again—that I'd unearthed with the help of the people who loved me the most. I knew I couldn't go back to being a doormat in Rockingham fucking New Hampshire, working at Charlie Mart, playing video games in oversized sweatpants, and living in constant fear of hungry lions and red-faced banshees.

And most of all—best of all—I knew Beth's Husband was dead.

34

om and I spent the drive home from Boston playing another round of "The Radio Game," but she slaughtered me this time. I was too distracted by the glorious slideshow of memories from the previous two days that kept replaying through my mind, as well as the unsettled feeling sloshing around in my stomach as I anticipated what would come as a result. I had a vow to fulfill.

I didn't tell Mom what I was planning on doing. I'd been trying to build the courage to confront Raymond for the eleven months since she'd left him. Or maybe for the twenty-five years since she'd met him. I knew myself well enough to know I had to take advantage of the momentary burst of fearlessness I was gripping with all my might, and I couldn't risk Mom trying to talk me out of it; it was all I could do to not talk myself out of it. But it needed to happen. Right now.

We pulled into the parking lot outside her apartment building, and I helped Mom bring her luggage inside. She invited me to stay for an early dinner, but I couldn't afford to let some delicious chicken Alfredo, no matter how creamy and delightful, derail my mission, so I told her I had some errands to run. Bethany's flight would be in in about three hours, so I had to do this before I went to pick her up, because once she got home, the dead weight of my depressing reality would threaten to drag me back down to Earth and keep me anchored there for another ten or thirty years.

Before I left, Mom said thank you, hugged me, and then added, "I'm so proud of you, Mickey."

I scrunched my face up and said, "For what?"

"It was just—so nice to see you…" She started chewing the inside of her cheek. "Never mind."

"Mom." I dipped my head down to her eye level and gave her a look that told her she could trust me. "Just say it."

She looked back at me, sighed, and grabbed both my hands.

"You looked so happy this weekend, hun," she said with the tiniest smile. "You were yourself again—like the old Mickey."

I looked downward and smiled. "You keep saying that."

She gave my hands a squeeze. "I just don't want to lose that Mickey again, hun. And I don't want you to lose him either."

"I know." I stood up straight. "Neither do I."

I gave Mom another hug, then kissed her on the cheek and said, "I'll be back later, okay?"

"You will? Why?"

"Can't talk—gotta go—bye!"

I didn't have time to explain. It was now or never.

***

I drove across town with the music cranked, preparing for the biggest battle of my life.

"Not Afraid" by Eminem. *Yes.*

"Enter Sandman" by Metallica. *Fuck yes.*

"You're Going Down" by Sick Puppies. *Let's fucking do this.*

As I weaved through traffic, probably faster than I should have, running yellow lights, cutting people off, and honking at people who honked at me, I thought back to all the times Ray-Hole ruined everything. He broke a tree branch on my ass. He pulled my arm out of its socket. He grounded me on baseball championship day. He threatened to kick me out of the house the same day I'd been dumped. He'd screamed in my face. He'd pushed me around. He'd hurt me. He'd hurt my mother.

It was useless at this point to contemplate what our lives would have been like if he hadn't flirted with my mom at The Penguin all those years ago. If she'd had one of her debilitating migraines and called out sick that night, or if he'd gone to another bar to drown his sorrows that night, things might have turned out vastly different. Who could say where I'd be, what I'd be, who I'd be? But then I thought about what my brother said, and he was right; that's not what this was about. It was about how I played the cards I'd been dealt, not about the cards themselves. And I was about to tear up the deck.

I pulled into the old pebble stone driveway, shifted "The Jet" into Park, and took a deep breath. It was a gray March afternoon, sunlight was peeking out from behind the clouds, and it was chilly, but not unbearable. There was a mix of snow and mud in the front yard, and the house where I'd grown up, where I'd spent so many days—happy days, devastating days, memorable days, horrifying days—sat colorless. Lifeless even. I turned off my headlights and stepped out of my car, and there he was.

I cringed when I first saw him; not out of fear, but out of surprise. He looked so much more wilted and gray than I remembered. Had he aged that much in just a year? Had Mom's departure torn him down that quickly? Or had the ferocious mountain lion I'd always pictured in my head just been a cranky old house cat the entire time? Maybe this wouldn't be the heroic battle I'd anticipated. Maybe this wouldn't be much of a fight at all.

Scratch that. The truth is, seeing him like this—his shoulders not looking so broad, his fingers not looking so meaty, his angry eyes looking more tired than anything—just fueled me. I felt more strength in my frame and more courage in my chest than I ever had in Ray's presence.

"Michael?" he said as he stepped out onto the porch. "The hell are you doing here?"

"You have some stuff that doesn't belong to you," I said, matter-of-factly.

"Ah," he said. A shit-eating grin crept up his cheeks. "I was wondering if you'd ever grow some balls and come get it."

There's The Ray-Hole I knew.

"I was going to take it to the dump or have a yard sale if I didn't hear from you soon."

"Well," I put my hands on my hips and looked at him leaning on the porch railing. "I'm here now. Can I please come in and get it?"

"Do you still have your keys? I was just heading out the door to go to San Fran, and I won't be back for a week."

I tilted my head. "Of course I don't; I haven't lived here in six years."

He shrugged and said, "Guess you'll have to come back another time then. Maybe call or text first—if you're not too busy blowing me off."

He'd clearly been waiting for this. Preparing for it even. He knew exactly what he was going to say to me if I ever showed up. He knew I didn't have the keys, and he wanted to pretend he was teaching me one last lesson about responsibility, even though he could just open the door and let me inside. But this wasn't a lesson; this was Ray being a prick, just because he could. And the Mickey he knew—the Mickey he groomed—would have chewed on the inside of his cheek, gotten back in his car, and called it a day.

But, to his surprise, the Mickey he groomed was nowhere to be found.

"I'm not coming back another time, Raymond," I said, staring directly through his wispy eyebrows. "Please let me in."

He seemed momentarily stunned as he worked up a response. He hadn't prepared for that. "Wow. Someone's got hair on his nuts today." He started making his way down the porch steps.

"Just open the goddamn door," I said as he got closer. "I'll get my stuff and get outta here, and then we'll never have to see each other again."

"You want your stuff? Doesn't really seem like my problem."

My pulse began to pick up. I knew this wasn't going to be easy. And he knew he was pushing my buttons. He was practically begging for some kind of confrontation—a screaming squabble, a fist fight, a battle of wits—anything.

It was as if he'd been waiting for this as long as I had. He stopped about six feet from me, glared at me with his arms crossed, challenging me, awaiting my response.

I could push buttons, too.

"Y'know—I'm sorry I didn't bump into you at the wedding." I kept my shoulders relaxed and my hands in my front pockets to show him he wasn't going to intimidate me. "There were just so many people there, I didn't get a chance to talk to everybody."

Ray continued to glare at me. I knew that one would sting.

"Nice try. Now get off my property. Go."

"I'm just saying, it was a really, really nice wedding." I cracked the slightest little smirk. I'd found over the years that a passive-aggressive approach to angry, aggressive people made them even more angry and aggressive, and that always made me laugh. But I never dared try it with Ray-Hole until now. "And the reception—oooh, that was lit. Absolutely incredible. Everyone Mason cared about was there. Literally hundreds of people. I thought maybe you'd—"

"YOU KNOW I WASN'T INVITED," he barked. Yeah, I knew. And he'd just taken my bait. "He's just as much of an ungrateful little dick as you are after everything I did for you guys growing up. Your mother, too."

"Psh," I scoffed. "Everything you did for us? Like 'Children should be seen and not heard'? Or teaching us that treating people you love like dogshit shows them you care? Or that hitting and shoving is how you teach people to respect you?"

"I never hit Mason. Not once."

"I know. You saved that for me and Mom," I said, "because we didn't fight back. Wow, what a hero you are, Raymond. You should be so goddamn proud."

"I offered to pay for *all* of it," he said, ignoring my snide remark. "I told him I'd pay for the wedding, reception, hotel rooms, rehearsal dinner—all of it. And he basically spat in my face and said, 'Fuck you, old man.'"

"Because he doesn't need you," I said as I took a step toward him. It was the biggest step of my life, because it was the first time I'd ever actually closed the gap between us during a dispute instead of cowering away from him in terror. There were no popped-out eyes or hanging jaws or frazzled brains searching for the right response. I knew exactly what I wanted to say.

"None of us do."

With that, I took an envelope out of my pocket, snapped it toward him, and said, "Here."

He took another step toward me and snatched the envelope out of my hand. He recognized it immediately. It was the $10,000 check he'd sent to Mason and Torey as a wedding gift. He opened it, and inside was a handwritten note on a torn sheet of notebook paper:

Cheaters and wife beaters should not be seen OR heard.
Rot in hell.
—Mason

"Real nice," Ray said, his voice a bit uneven as he crumpled up the note and put the check in his back pocket. And for the tiniest millisecond, I actually felt bad for the guy. Regardless of the issues between him and me, he'd always liked my brother. He was Mason's hockey coach and his scout master, and an argument could be made that he'd helped Mason become the man he was today. So, as Ray's eyes dropped and his mouth drooped, I could see he was shaken by the rejection.

But as soon as I tried to take advantage of his weakened state and step past him to go into the house, the mountain lion roared back. He grabbed my shirt and shoved me back toward the driveway. Then he stepped straight toward me, and there it was. The wispy eyebrows. The craggy yellow teeth. Even the meaty pointer finger.

"YOU DON'T NEED ME? HUH? YOU DON'T NEED ME?"

I knew he was winding up for one of his big speeches. Or threats, or whatever. He was going to try and take control of the situation by getting in my face and screaming mean things.

"That's not what you said when you begged me to co-sign your college loans. That's not what your brother said when he begged me to pay his security deposit for his expensive Boston apartment. You selfish little assholes needed me THEN, didn't you?"

I stared at him, unimpressed. I'd thanked him via full-page ad in my BU senior yearbook and had long since signed the loans into my own name. And Mason had paid him back for the security deposit within three months. So, I looked at Raymond as if to say, *Are you finished?*

He wasn't finished.

"You weren't saying you didn't need me when you wanted to learn how to drive, or when you wanted to borrow the truck to go to a basketball game. Mace wasn't saying it when he wanted to learn how to make a bean hole for scouts or do a snap shot for hockey."

Oh, you mean regular 'dad' stuff? I thought. Then I shrugged and said, with blatant insincerity, "I'm so sorry we didn't make you feel more validated, Ray-Ray. Maybe you can beat that into your next family."

He wasn't getting to me, and I think he suspected it, so he started changing up his tactics. He dropped his meaty pointy finger, lowered his brow, and raised his shoulders.

"Well, your mother sure needed me." The shit-eating grin returned to his face. "She needed someone to rescue her from the hell she was in, trying to support her two dumb-shit little fucks because their dumb-shit father was too stupid to get out of a burning building."

I had never hit anyone before, but there was nothing I wanted to do more when that contemptible venom oozed out of his mouth. I was bigger than Ray now. Stronger. And one fist to the side of his hairy fucking skull would be enough to knock him on his ass like I'd always dreamed. But then, I sucked some of the early-spring air through my nostrils to cool the angry ball of fire that suddenly rumbled around in my ribcage, waiting to explode in a fit of flying fists. And with that crisp, clean air came clarity. After spending years trying (and failing) to avoid the wrath of this reprehensible monster, I finally saw Raymond for what he was—what he'd always been—there in his front yard on a dusky March afternoon. He was nothing more than a mouthy little troll, so desperate for the respect and love that his own parents never gave him that he had no idea how to earn it. So, he had to force it from people; he used money to buy love and fear to buy respect. And when that love and respect inevitably dissipated (because it wasn't real), he would try to hurt people worse than he'd been hurt.

He'd never made the slightest disparaging remark about my dad before; it was an unspoken understanding in our family that, no matter what the fight was about, no matter how upset he was, that was a line that should never be crossed. But as this moment (and all the control he'd ever had over me) began slipping away from Ray, and he had nothing more to lose anyway, his audacity ballooned to levels of sacrilege.

So, I puffed up my chest and stood above him. For the first time, *I* got in *his* face. *I* looked at *him* through my eyebrows. *I* pointed my chunky finger at *his* nose.

"I don't care how much money you've given us, what you've taught us, or what you've done for us," I said in a slow, measured tone. "You will *never* deserve our respect. You will *never* be a hero. And you will *never* be my father."

"Good," he said as he slapped my finger out of his face. "Now get the fuck off my property." As soon as that finger went down, my other hand went up in a tight fist, as if by trigger, and hung in the air above my shoulder, waiting for him to say one more thing about my dad. Just one.

He snorted and said, "Oh, what are you gonna do? Hit me?" Then he tapped his hairy chin with his index finger and said, "Right here. Go ahead. I'll give you a freebie."

I gave it a half-second of thought—like, *really* considered it—but I concluded that, as powerful as that might feel for a second or two, hitting him was exactly what he wanted me to do. Because then he'd have the control back. He could call the cops and have me arrested for trespassing and assault. And, knowing Ray-Hole, he would. So, I put my fist down and said, "No, I'm not going to hit you."

He chuckled and said, "That's what I thought. Same old Mickey the Mouse."

Then, without warning, I grabbed him by his shirt with both hands and pulled him toward me. I clenched his rusty old plaids with fists of rage and peered with seething barbarity into the cold, evil eyes that used to terrify me to my core. And as I studied his expression, I saw in those eyes something that had never been there before.

Fear.

He didn't know what I was going to do. He couldn't figure out what was going through my mind. He had no control. He was afraid. For that beautiful split second, I was doing to Raymond what he'd done to me my entire life—intimidating him; scaring him—and the rush of adrenaline I was getting from this momentary tipping of the scales made me feel invincible.

I have the power, I thought to myself.

But, at the same time, it made me feel disgusting. And as he stared back at me, shocked and wondering what was going to happen next, I couldn't imagine hurting someone so defenseless and vulnerable.

"I'm not like you, Ray," I said to him, our eyes still locked. "I never will be."

Then I gave him a gentle kiss on the end of his nose and released him.

"Ugh, come on, man!" Ray-Hole said as he flailed backwards and started rubbing the spot I kissed like he'd been bitten by a horsefly. "The hell's wrong with you and your brother?"

Then, as he backed away, he tripped over a sprinkler head that was sticking out of the frozen ground and stumbled into a muddy snowbank. A burst of laughter popped out of my mouth faster than I could even try to muffle it, and as he flopped around in the mud, shouting obscenities and trying to regain his footing, I pulled out my phone, opened the camera app, and said, "Hold on, hold on—this'll be a good one for the scrapbook."

35

For the last eleven years, whenever Bethany would lean toward me and sob on my shoulder, my throat would fill with mucous and my achy eyes would begin to water. My fragile heart would tumble back to simpler, more innocent times, like when she covered her face with a pillow after she told me she loved me for the first time, or when we shared our perfectly imperfect first kiss. We'd grown up together and discovered as a young couple how this insane world could be both magically uplifting and heartlessly cruel at the same time, and all I ever wanted to do in those tender moments was protect her and make her smile.

But a lot had changed since those early days.

In the beginning, I would do anything in my power to bring that bright, off-center smile packed with flashy white teeth to her face. All I had to do was whatever she wanted me to do, and her face would light up like a freckle-faced Jack-O-Lantern. Later on, though, I taught her that all she had to do to get her way was get angry, get in my face, and get mean, and I would fold like a collapsible tent. But, after years of submission and complicity, during which she'd grown accustomed to getting what she wanted with little regard for what was important to me, my long-ingrained instinct to protect her, to make her feel better, to make her smile, was gone.

So, this time, as Bethany blubbered on my shirt and told me what happened, I stared straight ahead, motionless, emotionless, waiting for her to shut up.

"Brad dumped me."

Brad couldn't deal with the distance, she said—even told her she should move to California. Brad wanted more than a cross-continental fuck buddy. Brad was tired of being "the other guy." Brad wasn't sure how he felt about her decision to terminate the pregnancy without talking to him first, but Brad was sure he wanted something real with her. Brad, Brad, Brad, Brad.

The longer I remained stoic and unaffected, the more Bethany's blubbers reduced to sniffles, the more her red face faded to pink, and the more she realized I wasn't going to pull her close, wrap her in my arms, and tell her everything was going to be okay. Not this time.

"Why are you so quiet?"

I shrugged and set my sights on one of our wedding photos on the wall. There was a crack in it, but we'd never bothered to fix it. "I don't have anything to say. I'm sorry your boyfriend dumped you and you're stuck with your husband."

The drive home from the airport had been pretty quiet. We met in baggage claim, exchanged a loose hug and light peck, and smiled at each other with our mouths but not our eyes. I carried her bag to the urine-scented parking garage and put it in the back seat of the car next to Mom's scrapbook and the box of mementos I'd snagged from my old bedroom after I jimmied the door open with my Charlie Mart card. I opened the passenger-side door for her. She gave me a little nod and said, "Thank you."

There was something in the air between us. It wasn't tension, not this time. It wasn't anger. Or even sadness. It was the indescribable but palpable presence of, maybe, words that needed to be said. Or maybe it was the last, wheezing breath of love on life support. Or maybe it was just pollen. Either way, she didn't ask about my weekend, and I didn't ask about hers. She'd made it clear when she booked this trip that she didn't care about my brother's wedding, and I didn't care about her screwing That Brad Guy. Strangely, in fact, I'd made peace with it. *The quickest way to get over someone is to get under someone else* was a thing I'd heard somewhere. And maybe, after my night with Luci, there was something to that. But it wasn't that simple. After eleven torturous years of broken dreams and two turbulent months of broken promises, this weekend away from each other proved something that I'd considered for a long time but wasn't sure of until now: We didn't love each other anymore.

It was a tough pill to swallow at first, but once I lubricated it with a weekend surrounded by people who did love me, it became fairly easy to digest. What further eased it was the realization that it didn't happen overnight, and it didn't happen because of the weekend away. It didn't even happen because of Brad. Or the abortion. Or the open arrangement. The erosion of our love had been going on for years—probably since the very beginning. And all the things that had happened between us recently were just bright neon signs that we didn't belong together anymore, and I'm not sure we ever really did.

So, the silence between us that would normally ratchet my anxiety up to eleven provided, instead, a soothing calm. It gave me a chance to think things over. I thought about what I was going to say to her. How I was going to say it. When I was going to say it. *If* I was going to say it. I'd gotten to this point before—the point where I was clenching my bowels, tightening my heartstrings, and trying to summon the courage to have this conversation. To power through. It had blown up in my face before, and quite spectacularly. Or, rather, she had.

Bethany was in a weakened state this time, though, already vulnerable because Brad dropped her. But for once I could see things from his perspective (not that he deserved that from *me*). Bethany had led him on; he was nothing more than a plaything to her. She'd used him as an escape from her monotonous marriage, and when things got too real, she quickly and unabashedly aborted that reality so she wouldn't have to take responsibility for anything—a child, her actions—nothing. And once she'd gotten away with all of that (because I didn't do anything about it), it was back to Playtime with Brad. But he was apparently tired of being a toy to her. So, I had a newfound respect for that adulterous motherfucker, because unlike me, he had the balls to tell her he'd had enough.

"I'm not 'stuck with' you," she said with a stuffy nose. She was on the far-right side of the couch wearing chunky fleece pants and one of my old sweatshirts; I was on the far left in jeans and a long-sleeved polo, and there was a random NCAA basketball game playing in low volume on our old 32-inch Samsung. "It was just fun to, like, have a little something on the side, you know?"

"I guess… " I said. I thought about Luci.

"But now that that's done," she said, "I think I'm ready to start working on us again."

I gave her a blank stare for what felt like ninety-two years; it was probably only about eight seconds. But it was long enough for Bethany to get antsy.

"What? That's what you wanted, isn't it? That's what we needed, right? Talk to me, man."

"I—I…" I struggled to put my scrambled emotions into words. But then, I took a deep breath, collected my thoughts, and said, "I never thought I'd hear you say that."

"Of course, man." She scooted over to my side of the sofa. Then she rested her head on my shoulder, weaved her fingers through mine, and said, with a sad smile, "Big ol' bear paws."

That one caught me in the throat. She hadn't said that since our honeymoon. The urge to respond with "Little string beans" gallivanted to the tip of my tongue, but I clamped down on it with my teeth. Then she gently pulled my hand toward her lips and began sucking on my fingers.

"Bethany…"

"Shhhh…" She pulled my hand down to her neck, then her collarbone, then her breast. "Just Beth."

I tried to pull my hand away, but she caught it and put it between her legs. I couldn't feel much because of the chunky fleece pants, but I suppose that wasn't the point.

She began to slowly unzip her (my) hoodie and said, "Just you. Just me. Nobody else." She tossed the sweatshirt aside to reveal her black Calvin Klein sports bra, which she always wore when she wanted to feel sexy. That meant: a.) Either she'd worn it to feel sexy with Brad all weekend, or b.) she put it on after he dumped her so she could try to manipulate me. I didn't like either scenario, but since she hadn't changed clothes when we got home, I had to assume it was Scenario A—Brad. It had always been about Brad. But he apparently wasn't in the picture anymore, so she had to make sure she still had me wrapped around her finger. So maybe it was Scenario B. Option B. That was me.

"Whaddya think?" She climbed on top of me, started kissing my neck, and reached down toward my waist with both hands. Just as her fingers began playing around with my belt buckle, I looked over her shoulder and saw the wedding photo on the wall again. I squinted. Yep, still cracked. We could try to put a piece of tape or something on it, but it would always be broken.

I grabbed both of Bethany's forearms and took her hands off my belt. This needed to happen. Right now.

"What do I think?" I squirmed out from underneath her, stood up, and looked her square in her perplexed face. "I think you don't really want to be with me."

"What? Yes, I do."

"No. You. Don't," I said in a controlled tone. "Because if you really wanted me, you never would've had sex with him in the first place."

She rolled her eyes and sighed as she shoved her arms back into the sweatshirt and yanked the zipper back up. "I said I was sorry, like, a million times, man. Even gave you an out. I said you could divorce me if you wanted. You chose to stay."

"I thought maybe you'd want to work on things with me after that—like you were actually sorry," I said. "But you couldn't wait to get back out there and fuck him again."

Her voice began to rise. "What do you care, man? You got to fuck fat little Dora! You should be happy!"

"Her name was—" I couldn't remember the name I'd

made up for my fake hook-up. "Not Dora."

"Well, whatever, you got to fuck her, like, three times—this mind-blowing sex or whatever," she said with a healthy dose of mockery. "That's the only reason I went out there to be with Brad this weekend."

I shot her a look. "Please, that is not the only reason you went out there. You've had a thing for him forever. You don't even try to hide it anymore."

"Who cares? At least Brad still tries. He doesn't just sit around playing video games all the time."

I raised my eyebrows and jerked my head back. "Wow."

"Wow what, Mickey? You don't do anything anymore, man. You work at Charlie Mart, then you come home and watch TV and do PlayStation all night. Brad works out, like, every day, plays sports, runs his own store. He never just sits around. Sorry, Mick, but you've gotten really fat."

I had to break eye contact; the Sleek Gray Wolf was definitely baring its teeth. I sat down slowly in the recliner. "Ouch."

"Sorry. That was really mean," Bethany said, softening her voice as she sat down on the couch and put her elbows on her knees. "But, it doesn't even matter now. Brad is out of the picture, so now we can work on us. We can join a gym together, get you back in shape, and—"

"That's not what I want; that's what *you* want," I said. "It's always about what *you* want."

She sneered. "So, you *want* to be fat? You just want to keep getting fatter and fatter until they need a crane to get you out of the house? Is that what you want, Michael?"

I scowled at her, and for the first time ever in our relationship, I said "Fuck you" to her.

Her mouth dropped. "'Scuse me?"

"Fuck you, Bethany. The only reason you—"

"Just Beth."

My whole body tensed up when she said that this time; it was more important to her that I used her preferred moniker than for her to hear what I had to say. I understood why it was important to her, and I had always tried to respect her wish to be called "Beth." But in times like this, when she wasn't being respectful to me, I couldn't force myself to give a shit. We had bigger things to discuss.

I took a breath and started again.

"The only reason you want to work on things with me now is because Brad dumped you."

"That's not true!"

"Oh, it's not?" I said. "Let's revisit our discussion from a few weeks ago."

She rolled her eyes; I continued.

"If you, me, and Brad all lived in the same place, who would you be with?"

"You, man. Obviously. We've been together for eleven years."

"Being together for eleven years isn't a reason to be together *now*."

"Well," she considered my point and thought about her response. "It doesn't even matter, man, because he lives in California."

"It matters to *me*. Why would I want to be with someone who's only with me out of convenience?"

Bethany remained seated with her elbows on her knees, fidgeting with her fingers, looking at the floor. Her bottom lip was scrunched up and her eyebrows were curled upward. As I waited for some kind of response, my right heel began bouncing up and down as it does when it's bursting with nervous energy.

She sat back and folded her arms. "Well, what am I supposed to do? Move to California? I'm not doing that, man, so I guess *you're* stuck with *me*."

I shrugged. "Well, then I guess you're making the same choice I did."

She looked at me, puzzled. "The fuck does that mean?"

"You're unhappy with the life you chose for yourself, but you're blaming everybody else for it," I said. "You wanted to stay in Rockingham, remember? Because that's where all your friends and family were. Then your friends moved away, your parents got old, and your sister had kids, so all you had left was me. You were bored with your life, and then your old college crush came to town for Thanksgiving, so you had a little fling, and then you blamed me for your affair because I 'don't do anything anymore.'"

"I didn't blame you for the affair, Mickey," she protested, trying to save face.

"Yes, you did—you *just* did, like five minutes ago! But it doesn't even matter because—curveball!—your little fling became more than just a little fling, didn't it? You caught feelings for him, Beth. And now you're blaming *me* for your misery in our marriage, and you're blaming *him* for living far away. But guess what? *You* have the power to change both of those things."

She gave me a look I couldn't quite read. Was she angry? Was she sad? Confused? Inspired? I had seen her make so many faces over the years, but this was a new one—a Bethany driven by thought and contemplation rather than raw emotion, perhaps? A rare sighting that would be.

"So—what—you want me to break up with you?"

"That's *not* what I'm saying."

"That's what-the-fuck it sounds like you're saying!"

"I'm saying you're never going to be happy if you never leave your comfort zone. You've stayed in Rockingham your whole life because it's familiar and comfortable. That's why you never went to Syracuse. And it's why you're still with me—familiar and comfortable—even though you clearly want someone else."

"There's nothing wrong with me wanting to be around my family."

"You're absolutely right," I said, thinking again about the unbridled freedom and happiness I'd felt all weekend. "There's nothing wrong with wanting to be around the people who love you."

I smiled to myself because I could suddenly relate to Bethany in a whole new way. She just wanted family. And that's all I wanted, too. But even though we were married to each other, we had wicked different ideas about who our family was.

"Then why are you giving me so much shit about it?"

"BECAUSE I SHOULD BE ONE OF THOSE PEOPLE!" It was the first time I raised my voice, and it began to tremble on the word "people."

"YOU ARE!"

"No, I'm not." I was trying to keep my cool, but I was losing my grip on it. "Maybe I was, but I'm not anymore. You want Brad."

"BRAD IS OUT IN CALIFORNIA!"

"But if he wasn't—" I could feel my nose starting to run. My eyes began to blur. I wiped the moisture and the mucous away with my bare hands. A sharp-edged ball of frustration, resentment, and pain that had spent a decade growing and churning in my chest began to rise into my throat. "If he wasn't, you'd already be with him."

Bethany didn't say anything, just shifted her feet underneath her and folded her arms again. The faint sounds of sneakers squeaking and whistles whistling on the television were beginning to grate, so I muted it, then sat forward in the seat of the recliner and hung my head between my legs. She didn't deny what I'd just said, and I didn't expect her to. The three minutes of silence that followed not only confirmed that her feelings for Brad were very real, they gave me time to breathe, reflect, swallow the sharp-edged ball in my throat, and pull my He-Man sword out of its sheath for the final push.

I have the power, I thought to myself.

"I don't want to live the rest of my life feeling like I'm someone's second choice," I said. "And you shouldn't either."

She looked at me with a raised eyebrow. "I shouldn't either? What?"

I'd tried so many times over the years to circumvent conflict with Bethany by lying, omitting parts of truths, or covering things up that might upset her. I was afraid of her anger, her wrath. The Banshee. But every time I'd lied, omitted, or covered, it had backfired. When she did find out, she would explode like an atom bomb, obliterating anything within a fifty-mile radius and reducing me to ashes. And when she didn't find out, karma would somehow find a way to leave an indelible bite mark on the juiciest part of my ass. Maybe she was smarter than I thought; or maybe I wasn't as savvy as I thought. Either way, my lack of transparency had always made things worse. So this time, I decided, I would tell her the truth. The entire truth. Because that couldn't be any worse than being caught in another lie.

"I had sex with someone in Boston."

She was still confused.

"Yeah. Dora. Fat Mexican chick. I know," she said. "Why are you bringing that up now?"

Then her eyes widened with intrigue.

"Wait, was she at the wedding? Did you hook up with her again?"

"No—No." I put my hand on my face. "Let me start over."

The entire truth.

I proceeded to explain how badly I'd struck out when I went out with Mason and Torey a few weeks prior, and that I'd only made someone up so she'd think we were "even," and then we could get on with trying to repair our broken marriage.

Her face hardened. Her eyes narrowed. Her brow began to protrude. She looked like she was gearing up for an explosion.

"You lying motherf—"

"That's all I ever wanted to do, Beth. Fix things," I said, matter-of-factly. "I just wanted to get back to normal. Just you and me. Making fun of strangers in restaurants. Mick-a-Roni and Bethy Bear. Us. I could almost forgive the Brad thing. Even understand it a little. But I just wanted that whole thing to be over. And you just wanted us to be 'even.' That was more important to you than getting us back on track."

"So, you thought lying to me would be a good way to—" she threw up air quotes, "'get back on track?' That's fucked up, Mickey. How many times do we have to have this conversation about you lying, man?"

"I know. That's why I'm telling you now."

"I mean, I know I fucked up big," she sat up and crossed her legs. "But I never lied to you about anything."

"Oh, you didn't?" I sat up straight, too. "I seem to recall someone getting home at 4 a.m. one morning and telling me she was just at Goldy's with Meg."

I began tapping my chin and looked to the ceiling, trying to solve this "mystery."

"And I seem to recall that same person bawling about some little white spots, only admitting her affair because of those little spots, and then finding out she was carrying some other dude's baby."

I looked at her with squinted eyes. "Does that ring a bell to you, Bethany?"

She just peered at me, still as a statue, and said, "Beth."

"Right." I looked back up at the ceiling. "Because that's important right now. Our marriage is crumbling beneath us, but as long as I call you 'Beth,' we can work through anything."

I'd found over the years that a passive-aggressive approach to angry, aggressive people made them even more angry and aggressive. But I'd never dared try it with Bethany until now.

Her face filled with fury in an instant. She shot up off the couch, stomped her foot, and shrieked, "FUCK YOU!"

It was all I could do to stop myself from flashing a smug little smirk at the red-faced banshee hovering over me. But smirking wouldn't get my point across. I had to play her game. I got out of the recliner, stood up, and met her at eye level.

She stared at me with ferocity and fight in those jade green eyes—the ones that had always been able to make me feel weak, either by flirt or by fire. This time, though, as I peered back at her, not budging, I looked a little deeper and saw something in them I hadn't ever picked up on before.

Fear.

I suppose it had always been there. That was why Bethany never backed down—her fear of failure, rejection, and loss, was stronger than her fear of the fight. But if you could survive the fight with her, you could expose the weeping, insecure little girl she kept buried deep in her brittle soul. It was that little girl who used to get picked on and pushed around on the playground, just like me when I was "Mickey the Mouse." But unlike me, who had always wilted into a dead possum in the face of confrontation, Bethany had learned to thrive on it. She would morph into the invincible beast—the Sleek Gray Wolf—and devour anyone who tried to defeat her, reject her, or hurt her.

If I was going to do this, I had to be a wolf, too.

"So? Who's the little slut?" she asked, point-blank. "Who's the little bitch who I'm all-of-a-sudden 'second choice' to?"

The entire truth.

"It's—"

"Was it that 'K' girl?"

"Kay?"

"Oh, don't play stupid, Michael. I've looked through your phone. I've seen the naked pics she sends you. Your slutty little fuck buddy from Drama. Lucky the Leprechaun's girlfriend."

"Okay, first of all, he's British, not Irish—"

"I DON'T GIVE A SHIT!"

"Second of all—you went through my phone? Jesus

Christ!"

"Yeah, like ten times. Why do you think I hooked up with Brad on Thanksgiving?"

I paused, looked to the side, then back at her, thoroughly confused. "What?"

"Yeah. I saw pictures in your phone of that girl in a slutty Catwoman costume," she said. "Then I scrolled through a few, and there was one of her with your dick in her mouth. I figured, if you had a side piece, I should, too."

I threw my hands over my face and said, half-laughing, "Good God, Beth—that wasn't even me."

"Yeah right, man. Another lie."

"For real," I said. I pulled my phone out, opened the OnlyFans app, and went to Kaylin's page. "It's her husband. They make amateur porn and they post it here. People subscribe, and they get money. It's their side hustle."

She scrolled through some of their photos, half disgusted, half intrigued, and recognized the photos she'd seen on my phone—including the one of Kay performing oral sex on Isaac.

"Gross." She handed my phone back to me. "But why're they on your phone if you can just go to this app?"

"I just take screenshots and save them to my phone so I can look at them whenever," I said. "But I never had sex with her. Well, not since the one time back in the day."

"Fine," Bethany said, apparently satisfied. "So, then, who did you have sex with?"

"Wait—" I said, suddenly not satisfied. "If that's why you hooked up with Brad on Thanksgiving, why did you insist on this open arrangement thing? If you thought I'd already slept with someone else, we already should have been 'even.'"

As I stood in front of my wife, staring at her, waiting for an answer, I noticed a few things. I noticed the slouch in the lips that once kissed me with lust. I noticed a crease that had formed between her angry eyes after twenty-nine years of hateful pouting and sour scowls. I noticed the way that crease pointed toward that freckle in the middle of her forehead I used to think it was cute, but that now I just thought looked hairy and gray. I noticed she was starting to breathe unevenly. I noticed a glistening of sweat forming at her hairline. And I noticed the Sleek Gray Wolf's evil eyes had puddled up like a puppy dog's.

That's when I figured it out.

"That wasn't the first time you had sex with him, was it?"

She shrank. Her shoulders sunk. Her face collapsed. She shook her head "No," and the tension that had been building throughout this strange and horrible afternoon suddenly exploded from every fiber of muscle in her body. She collapsed on the couch and began sobbing with the innocence of a three-year-old who'd broken her two favorite toys.

For the last eleven years, we'd grown up together and discovered this insane world could be both magically uplifting and heartlessly cruel, and all I'd ever wanted to do in these tender moments was protect her and make her smile. Now, as I looked down at her and watched her cry uncontrollably, I accepted that she, Bethany Connelly, my own wife, was one of this insane world's heartlessly cruel people.

My long-ingrained instinct to protect her, to make her feel better, to make her smile, was gone.

"How many times?" I pressed as tears dribbled down

her puffed-out cheeks. Her eyes were clamped shut and her mouth was cracked so wide open from her loud, desperate sobs that she couldn't form a single coherent syllable, let alone an intelligible sentence. She just turned her palms up and shrugged.

I cleared my throat and kept my eyes fixed on this pathetic, weeping pile of deceit.

"How long?

I watched. Waited. I looked over at the cracked wedding photo on the wall again. In it, she was showing her bright, flashy, care-free smile, and she had her hair tied back in a braided bun and decorated with little white floral pins. I remembered thinking she looked really beautiful that day, but now, looking at the picture, she kind of looked like a selfish whore.

Her sobs eventually settled into coughs. The streams of tears dried into droplets. She caught her breath. She sat up. She didn't make eye contact. She cracked her knuckles one at a time with her thumb, shifted her weight, and wiped her nose on her (my) baggy old sweatshirt.

"The whole time," she whimpered.

I took a moment to choke down the cement block that was suddenly lodged in my throat as blood-boiling anger blistered my veins. There was no heel-bouncing this time; I wasn't nervous. There was no cheek-chewing, like when I want to say something but can't. There were no popped-out eyes or hanging jaws or frazzled brains searching for the right response. I knew exactly what I wanted to say, and it was time to say it.

"I'm leaving you," I said. Then, as her lips began to quiver and her face began to get red, I leaned toward her with my hands on my knees, looked deep into those jade green eyes for the last time, and said, with jagged stone in my voice, "Bethany."

I stared at her ugly face, challenging her to say "Just Beth" one more time. I couldn't wait for her to say it, because that would be just the trigger I needed to unleash my atomic bomb of incarcerated fury—the massive, super-charged one I'd been nursing and growing and feeding since the day my stepfather broke a tree branch on my ass. Instead, she flipped over, buried her face between the couch cushions, and bawled.

I straightened up, walked over to the cracked wedding photo, and picked it off the wall.

"By the way," I said as I studied the photo that captured the day I became 'Beth's Husband.' I held it by the bottom corner, cocked my old pitching arm back behind my head, and smashed it on the hardwood floor, shattering the glass and the sterling silver frame into eleven million pieces—a million for each year I'd wasted trying to make Bethany Connelly happy.

"It was Luci. And I'm in love with her."

I turned, walked away, and grinned.

CURTAIN CALL

Hi Dad,

Feels like it just happened yesterday.

I remember I woke up that morning all crusty-eyed and stumbled toward my dresser, trying to shake the grogginess out of my head so I could gear up to tackle another wild week of third grade. It was bright for October and pretty warm out; we'd spent the weekend putting up Halloween decorations, but we ran out of time to carve pumpkins, so we were gonna do that when you got home from work that night.

Mickey had already been up for an hour watching his He-Man tapes. He was at the kitchen table eating a peanut butter sandwich and sporting a wicked milk mustache because he was five. I'd just opened the cupboard door to grab a bowl for my Frosted Flakes when Mama wandered out in her purple bathrobe with a lost look on her face. She asked us to come sit with her in the living room. I gave her a weird look because we never sat in the living room before school, and when Mickey asked where Daddy was, her face broke and she started bawling.

After telling us about some "accident" and then dancing around our questions, I guess she figured out that there was no easy way to say it. So, with tears running down her cheeks, she told us our daddy did a very brave thing. She said there had been a fire at our school principal's house, and that the firefighters were able to save his family, but Mr. Rizzo himself didn't make it. And neither did Daddy.

I remember feeling flabbergasted—that was the only word I knew to describe that feeling back then—at the thought of our school principal being dead. Dead wasn't something that happened to people in real life. That only happened in like Robocop movies and Stephen King books. And if it did happen in real life, the first dead person I knew definitely wasn't going to be our school principal, the guy with the rough voice and raspy laugh and the big belly who dressed up like Santa Claus every December and could make even the shyest kids smile. And the other first dead person I knew definitely wasn't going to be my dad, the guy who'd come home smelling like sweat and burned hot dogs every day, give Mama a big happy kiss and usually some flowers or candy, and read us bedtime stories in that perfect Homer Simpson voice. No. Not him. Not my dad.

I can't believe it's been twenty-five years.

Torey and Luci never talk about their dad much. They were so young when they lost him—just like Mickey was when we lost you—that they don't remember him all that much. But I do, just like I remember you. Dana always said you guys had been good buds ever since the early 80s when you were roommates at The Rocks. She said that's why you tried so hard to save him after the roof caved in on him. Ma always said if you'd gotten out a few minutes sooner, the smoke and fumes wouldn't have filled your lungs. They both said Chief Duckman found you guys on your stomachs—Mr. Rizzo in his pajama pants under a pile of charred debris, and you in your helmet and turnout gear—gripping each other's forearms, looking like you were napping. And they both agree that, if the old stove top hadn't thrown sparks when Mr. Rizzo was making tuna melts for the kids, both of you would still be around.

I still wake up every year on this date and wonder what time you're gonna be home, just like I did when I was eight years old. I wonder what adventures you're gonna take me on, what cool things you're gonna teach me, and what corny dad jokes you're gonna tell us. And every year on this date, it hits me in the gut when I realize again that I'm not eight years old, you're never coming home, and I'm never, ever going to stop missing you. That's why these letters are so damned important—I'm sorry I don't write every year, but no matter what's going on in our lives, when October 4 rolls around, that's when I feel you the most. That's when I need you the most. And this is the only way I can think of to keep you in my life. In our lives. You're our hero.

You both weighed heavy on our hearts at the wedding. We combined our last names in tribute, and it looked cool in writing. But then, when the J.O.P. said out loud, in front of all our friends and family, "I now pronounce you, Mason and Salvatore Patrizzo," it literally took my breath away. Right after that, Mickey and Luci huddled up with us and told me and my new husband how proud our dads would be of us. We all hugged real tight, squirted a few tears, and said we loved each other. And Dad, I think that might have been the best moment of my life.

Things only got better after that. Torey and I spent two weeks down in Cape Town, and I already wish we could go back. We spent days on their beautiful beaches, nights in some sick nightclubs, hiked up and down Table Mountain, and went on a Safari (didn't catch any lions but saw a wicked huge rhino). When we got back, Torey interviewed for the head coaching job at BC, and I got a raise, so things were going well for the Patrizzos. But the real exciting stuff was happening up north, 'cause it seems like something ignited in Mick during our wedding weekend. Or woke up or whatever. Because he's been a new man since then. Well, maybe a newer version of the man he used to be, back in the day. The man we only saw flashes of for a long-ass time. He finally—and I mean finally—told Raymond to shove it. And, maybe even crazier, he finally—and I really mean finally—left Bethany. He's been staying with Ma for the last few months, which sounds a little sad on the surface, but honest to God, he's truly the happiest I've seen him in years. You should see him. Still working at Charlie Mart, trying to save up money to move out on his own, but he's also picked up an evening gig directing RSC's production of The Homecoming. When that's done, he says, he wants to "take some time." When I asked what he meant by that, he just shot me that trademark grin of his and said, "For me."

I was just as surprised as anyone when Mick didn't get together with Luci after he had it out with Bethany. But I guess it makes sense. Dude hasn't been single in eleven years; I'm sure he wants time to breathe. I was on my own for a long time before Salvatore and I finally got together. By then, I knew exactly who I was and what kind of bullshit I was and wasn't willing to put up with. And all signs pointed to Torey. He's fun, outgoing, sweet, and thoughtful, and he's passionate about everything he does. But he's also emotionally strong—probably even stronger than me. And between staying strong for Ma and Mickey my whole life and spending fifty hours a week in the Beantown streets looking out for other people now, it's wicked nice to go home to someone who wants to take care of me; he's the real deal.

And those two have something real, too. Something you can feel whenever they're together. Something most people never find. The way they make each other laugh with their dorky jokes (his sense of humor is so much like yours, Dad), the way they light up whenever they hear that damn Mariah Carey song, it's just, I dunno—magnetic. So it will happen when the time is right, just like it did for me and Toto. In the meantime, it's nice to see the kid smile and laugh again. I'm talking about his real smile and his real laugh. He seems way lighter on his feet, like he's not lugging around this big boulder of angst anymore. Got a little more pep in his step. Oh, and I mean that literally, too. He's lost about twenty pounds since March and he's working on shedding a few more. So, he's heading in the right direction; you'd be proud of him. I sure am.

Which brings me to my last thing, and this one's got me a little choked up. Before I fold this little write-up into a paper football and put it in the lockbox by your urn with all the others from over the years, I wanted to share one last little tidbit. See, Torey wants to adopt. He's been saying it for years. Me? I've been on the fence about it. And not 'cause I don't like kids. I do—I love them—and he would be a great dad. What I worry about is that I'd be a shitty one. Even though I couldn't have asked for a better dad when you were around, Ray was the one who brought me up the rest of the way. And I'm afraid I'll have a tough day at work sometime and I'll lose my shit and do permanent psychological damage to a kid like Ray-Hole did with Mick. That would be the last thing I'd want to do, but as Mickey says, the brain pulls you toward what you know, not what you want. And I know short tempers and child abuse.

I told Mick and Ma that over Labor Day weekend, and they gave each other a weird look. And then, you know what those bastards said to me?

Mickey said, "Mace," all serious. And this kid is hardly ever serious anymore (I mean that in a good way). "I barely knew our father. All I had was Ray. And he wasn't someone I looked up to. He was someone I avoided. You know who I looked up to?"

I said, "Who?"

"You. You were the one who was always there for me and Mom. You were the one with the courage and strength I wish I had. You were the one who pulled my head out of the clouds and gave me tough love when I needed it. But you were also the one I could talk to about anything, the one who always knew the perfect moment to give me a hug, and the one who always laughed at my corny jokes. So, if anyone's qualified to be a dad, it's you. Because you've been doing it for most of your life."

Then Ma tossed in the kicker.

"You have so much of your father in you, hun," she said. She looked sad and happy at the same time, if that makes any sense. Like I said, it gets me all choked up. "You walk like him, you talk like him. You have his eyes and his smile. But most of all, you have his heart. It's coated in steel sometimes, but it's big and warm for the people you let inside. You're one of the most honorable men I've ever known—just like him—and you would never hurt anyone you love. Just like him. You're nothing

like Raymond, hun. You're everything like Jason. And you would be an incredible father. Just like Jason."
So, we submitted the application today.

Forever Yours,
Mason

"I've got to say, Bethany—I'm a little sad this is our last session."

"Me too—but I feel like it's a good thing."

"It absolutely is. You've come a long, long way since I first met you. Even more so since your divorce. I'm really proud of you."

"Thank you. I feel really, like, energized, you know? I mean, I'm nervous, too, but I'm ready."

"I never thought I would hear you say that. Are you all packed up?"

"Just about. My dad's gonna leave with the U-Haul tonight, and my flight takes off at 6 tomorrow morning."

"So, you're really doing it! I'm so happy for you."

"I—I couldn't have done it without you, Cat. I know I was a bitch sometimes, and I'm sorry. But taking this job, moving so far away, getting Brad back, I'm just— this is the happiest I've been in a long time, and I owe you everything."

"You don't have to apologize, and you don't owe me a thing. *You're* the one who decided to go to anger management. *You* decided when it was time to leave your comfort zone and interview for this huge coaching job on the other side of the country, and *you* decided to follow your heart to a place—I think we both agree—it wanted to go all along. You're the one who did the work, Bethany. I was just your guiding hand."

"When I think about stuff, I can't believe how, like, pig-headed I was being for so long. I feel like I wasted so much time and energy being angry and intense about everything, and I could've been happier a lot sooner if I had a little more chill."

"Well, remember—that was a defense mechanism you developed from being bullied as a child; nobody would expect that to completely go away as an adult. Sometimes it takes a long time to learn how to manage it, and some people never do. That's why I'm so proud of you."

"Thank you. But I do wonder if things could've been different if I'd figured it out earlier. You know, before I messed up jobs, friendships, my marriage. I burned so many bridges."

"It's all part of growing up, Bethany. We all have our crosses to bear, and this was one of yours. That being said, I also feel compelled to remind you that the problems in your marriage were not all on you. That's one thing you were correct about from the beginning, so don't you dare start taking on all the blame for that now, because you're in a great place. It's been really fun the last few sessions listening to you talk about the things that make you *happy* instead of the things that make you angry—like spoiling Brie's kids and becoming their favorite aunt or coaching your girls to another championship—how many is that now?"

"Three in a row, man! And, yeah, I love Danny and Abby, those hilarious little shits."

"See? So, I can tell you're finally at peace and looking forward to the next phase of your life. So there is absolutely no sense in reliving your past mistakes. Because that's not you anymore. That's just Beth."

"But that *is* me. *I'm* Beth."

"You know what? I'm not so sure about that. Because I've called you Bethany three times in the last five minutes and you haven't corrected me once."

"Wait—Really? You did? Ha! I didn't even notice!"

"Yep! You see? So, you're not 'Just Beth' anymore. You're so much more than that. You're Bethany. *Beautiful* Bethany."

A Mariah Carey sing-along with the love of my life isn't even the best part of my day.

The drive to the clinic flies by. It feels like it takes about five minutes; it's probably closer to twenty. Blinding rays of sunlight fill the city skies, the warm wind slashes through our hair, and "Dreamlover" is blasting through the speakers. Gobs of traffic ooze their way into intersections and under overpasses, typical of any busy weekday afternoon in Boston. But there is nothing typical about the kooky couple in this bright orange Jetta.

As we sing at the top of our lungs and dance around in our seats, we wave fervently at somber-looking folks heading home from their depressing jobs. Some of them flip us off, some turn away and pretend they don't see us, some laugh and wave back. We even lock eyes with a couple of little brown-haired girls, probably no older than six, in the back seat of a RAV4. One of them bops along with us, and the other giggles and gestures at us with her stuffed Moana doll.

"We're gonna be great parents," I say as I shift my focus back to the road in front of me.

"'We'?" Luci says as she rubs her little baby bump and gives me a look. "Oh, you think this kid is yours? I think I should tell you about this guy Brad..."

I shoot her a dirty look. Her face softens into an "I gotcha" smile and she jabs me with her elbow.

"If that's true," I say, pausing for suspense (and for a sip of my caramel latte), "I might have to 'put you in yer place'..."

A shocked laugh explodes out of Luci's face. "Bring

it! Maybe you can get your ass beat down by a cop and a football player!"

"Nah. At least one of them would be on my side."

"Right," she says. "Like they'd have time for those shenanigans these days."

She has a point; Mason and Torey have been quite busy since they adopted their little boy thirteen months ago. It took them about two years to get through the process and find the right fit, but they stayed plenty busy in the meantime; Torey was promoted to head coach at B.C. right after their wedding, and Mason remains on the fast track to Lieutenant at the BPD. But all that took a back seat when little "J.C." came into their lives. They named him after our fathers (Jason Carlo Patrizzo), and Luci and I named him honorary ring bearer at our wedding a few months later.

It wasn't a big wedding—and it didn't need to be. When it takes you as long as it took us to get together with your P.E.P. (your "Perfect Effing Person," as we call each other now), you don't want to spend months of your life or millions of dollars shopping for expensive clothing or elaborate venues or DJs with double chins; you just want to look at each other and say your "I do's" in front of the people you love. So, that's exactly what we did. It was an outdoor wedding on a bright September day in Christopher Columbus Park, just a few blocks from where Mason and Torey tied it up, and we held a small private reception around the corner at Legal Seafoods. And although it wasn't a big, flashy event, it was full of little and large things we will remember with fondness long after the hair in our ears turns gray: Luci's deliciously tanned skin popped against her bright white Mermaid-style dress, her gorgeous black hair cascaded onto her shoulders, and her big, beautiful eyeballs wept as she walked toward me. We referred to each other as "Mickey Mack" and "Luci Goose" in our vows (as in, 'I, Mickey Mack, take you, Luci Goose, to be my wife'). Our First Dance song was "Hero" (because of course it was). We studied captivating flecks of texture in each other's irises for the first time as a married couple. And we honored both our brothers and our fathers by adopting the Patrizzo surname.

But more important than that, everyone we cared about (who hadn't died in a house fire when we were children) was there. Mace, Toto and little J.C. were front and center with us. Dana and Bill were there, of course; they welcomed me into their family with open arms but told me I'd "always been a member of our clan." Mom was there with her new boyfriend Jimmy, and it warms my heart every day to see her with someone as kind and loving as he's shown himself to be. Some of my co-workers from News Channel 6 and a few of Luci's fellow teachers from Berklee College of Music were in attendance as well, and Kaylin even made a "special guest" appearance with Isaac (they've become minor celebrities having written, directed, and starred in the popular Netflix dramedy *Drama Club Confessions* since 2019).

Then there were the people who weren't there. I read a while back in a *Rockingham Daily Record* sports column that "former Saint Mary's basketball superstar and one-time SMCS coach Bethany Connelly" had gone to California to coach at UCLA or Cal State or USC or something. I didn't really pay attention to the details, but I remember thinking how bizarre it was that the only thing I knew about Bethany's life now was what I'd read in the *Daily Record*—just like when we first met. She used to be a real person to me—a real, flesh-and-blood, fury-and-tears human being with a freckle in the middle of her forehead and a flashy, off-center smile—a real person who'd had me in such an emotional stranglehold for eleven years of my life that I'd lost my own identity and my own sense of purpose. And now, after all that, after all those years, after all the fun times and hard times and happy times and painful times I'd endured with her, she was just another name in the newspaper. Just black ink on cheap paper that would be tossed haphazardly into a green bin or used as piss pads for someone's puppy. It's kind of surreal. Oh well. I just hope she was able to find happiness with Brad.

Ray, meanwhile, started anger management (finally) and has begun trying to make reconciliations (I guess the prospect of being old and alone after two failed marriages was daunting, even to that arrogant asshole). He leaves Mom alone, but he texts Mason and me each once a month, always very friendly and courteous, as if he's trying to pretend he wasn't a complete dick to us (well, to me) for twenty-five years. Sometimes Mace texts him back; usually I don't. He knows the basics of what's going on in my life—my divorce, my job, my move to Boston, my marriage to Luci—and I know the basics of what's going on in his (he got enough money to retire to a beach house on the Cape after he sold some kind of fact-checking algorithm to Facebook during the 2020 Presidential race). He did apologize to me once for "everything I put you through," and said if Luci and I ever needed anything, call him. But we don't need anything from him, and we never will. So, I call him on his birthday, and I call him on Christmas, and if that's not enough for him, I don't care. Because I won't let other people's emotional responses—no matter how explosive or aggressive—dictate what I do anymore.

***

Everyone in the bright yellow waiting room is the same as before, but somehow different: This turtle-shaped lady isn't so wrinkly, her hair not so stringy—in fact, she looks a little younger and a lot more vibrant. The twenty-year-old fuckboy in this waiting room is sitting upright with his Celtics hat on straight, and his neck tattoo is much splashier. The fourteen-year-old blond girl here has more certainty in her eyes, more color in her face, and no visible bun in the oven. And then there's us—an early-30s couple comprised of a tall-ish but brawny strawberry blond dude with a chinstrap beard and a He-Man tank top, and a curvy, bright-eyed brunette wearing a tight-fitting *Phantom of the Opera* T-shirt. Our paths, as disparate as they are, have all led us to the same waiting room to sit in quiet solidarity, exchange hopeful, wide-eyed glances as we listen to the Sox game on the radio and think, *I hope they beat the Yankees today.*

As Luci fills out her paperwork, I pull out my phone, show her the latest freebies Kay sent us, and Google "popular baby names." The number of websites that flood my feed fills my stomach with nervous excitement—there are so many options!—but since Mason and Torey hogged both our dads' names, Luci and I will have to get a little more creative. If it's a boy, we were thinking about another 'M' name like Marvin or Miles or Mickey Junior. Or maybe we'll just name him Mason Salvatore after his uncles. If it's a girl, it will either be an 'L' name like Lydia or Laney or Lisa, or she'll be named Virginia or Dana after one of our mothers. Or maybe we'll scratch all that and just go with a versatile, gender-neutral name like Cameron or Taylor or Morgan or Jamie. We don't know yet; hopefully this appointment will help us decide.

"Mr. And Mrs. Patrizzo?"

My heart pauses as Luci Goose and I look at each other, stand up, and walk toward an auburn-haired nurse with glittery eyelids and shiny pink lip gloss. Excitedly, we approach the shiny metal door that leads toward the little room with the exam table and the crinkly sanitary paper that will seal our fate. I hadn't been too nervous before, but the moment we hear our names, my mind begins to race: *What if I'm a terrible father? What if I have no idea what to do? What if I fail my child in every conceivable way? How do I keep Luci calm when I'm here freaking out?*

But just as we get to the door to go out back, Luci looks at me, squeals, and makes little, happy claps with her fingertips. Then she takes me by the hand and asks, "Are you ready?"

I look at the door we're about to go through together, smile at my P.E.P. and say, "I've never been more ready in my life."

THE BEGINNING

Acknowledgements

First off, I'd like to extend a sincere thanks to Andrew Valenza at Valenza Publishing for taking a chance on me and my literary love child. I hope this novel will be one of the seeds that feeds this fledgling publishing house as it grows the wings it needs to fly. And to Dr. Stephen Hull, whose editorial expertise helped me elevate this from "decent manuscript that needs another set of eyes" to "publishable novel I'd be excited to put on any shelf."

Many of us want to write a book. Some of us even start. Few of us get here. I'm one of the lucky ones, and I could not have done it without a cast of characters throughout my life that has supported me, influenced me, taught me, and believed in me. It would be impossible to list every single person who helped to put me on this path, but I will name some of the standouts.

Mom, you always believed I could do whatever I wanted. I know now you didn't mean that literally (I never discovered how to time travel), but your steadfast support and belief in me, even when I didn't believe in myself (and not just in my writing) has carried me through many good and bad phases of my forty-plus years.

Justin, you have never hesitated to try something new – whether it's a new hobby, a new job, or a new craft. To you, that might mean you're always trying to "find" yourself. To me, it served as an inspiration, and it gave me the guts to do something I've always wanted to do – write a book. It's safe to say I wouldn't have even *started* this if it hadn't been for the example you set.

Lisa, so much of this story was inspired by what I have learned through our relationship – the importance of finding *the* person, not just *a* person, of showing each other love *and* respect, and of respecting yourself as much as you respect others. And as much as we like to pick on each other, when I told you I wanted to go down this path, you took me seriously and encouraged me to go for it. I love you for that – and for many, many more things.

I've enjoyed writing stories for as long as I remember. But it wasn't until high school, when I met Mrs. Dana Cray, that I began to take writing seriously. She introduced us to books like George Orwell's *Animal Farm* and William Golding's *Lord of the Flies*, and she taught us that a story isn't just about what *happens*, it's about what it *means*. But Mrs. Cray was also the first teacher to suggest I had any kind of talent for writing. Up to that point I knew that I was good at math, and I liked baseball. But I *hated* math, and I hadn't yet discovered that I was not Nomar Garciaparra (90s Red Sox All-Star shortstop for you youngsters). So, to find out from a respected teacher that I was good at something I enjoyed – writing – that gave me the sense of direction I needed.

I also owe a lot to now-retired sports editor Bob Fredette. He took a chance on a completely green 19-year-old and gave me my first opportunity to write professionally when he granted me a seasonal internship at my hometown newspaper, the *Rutland Herald,* in Rutland, Vermont. There I learned from a veteran team of local sports writers not only how to generate readable sports copy and interesting features, but also how to conduct myself in a professional setting (do I *still* need reminders about that sometimes? Well…). So, thank you to Bob, Tom Haley, Chuck Clarino, Carlton Laird, and Dennis Jensen for providing me with a solid and enduring foundation on which to build my writing career.

Then there's Craig Beck – you think I'd forget about you, Mr. Beck? Craig gave me my first full-time sports writing job when he hired me fresh out of college at the *Caledonian-Record* in St. Johnsbury, Vermont. He helped me grow by allowing (or, to be more accurate – encouraging) me to hone my voice as a writer and develop my style. He also taught me (or, tried, at least) to take things in stride and helped me learn how to brush off criticism (am I *still* working on that little bit? Well...).

My years at the *Brattleboro Reformer* in Brattleboro, Vermont, were some of the best of my life. Thank you to Kevin Moran and Ryan Wondercheck for the opportunity, and I will never, ever forget the kick-ass, award-winning team I formed with Jonathan Howard and Brian Rumsey. Seriously, working with you guys remains one of the highlights of my career.

Lastly, I want to thank the people whose advice and insight helped me transform this book from something I liked a lot into something I loved. Thank you to Lyle J., Maddy D., Kim, Nikki B, and Kathleen Foxx for putting in the time and grunt work, and for meeting these characters and reading their stories long before they were unleashed on the rest of the world in a much more polished, streamlined capacity. Your feedback was more than invaluable. It was transformative. And to Kristina Conatser, who used my shoddily self-made design and mishmash of vague descriptions as a baseline for what became a fantastically cool cover for this book. It's everything I wanted it to be.

And now, dear reader, I pass the finished product on to you, and I hope it's everything you wanted it to be. But if it wasn't, please don't let that discourage you from giving another independent author a try. Because you won't find an author more proud (or more exhausted) than an indie author, someone who puts *literally* everything – the writing, the editing, the proofreading and revising, the design, the layout, the networking, the damn marketing and selling – into their book. Don't get me wrong; keep reading your Stephen Kings and your John Grishams and your Colleen Hoovers and your Liane Moriartys and your Abby Jiminez-es, too; but once in a while, make sure you give a K.T. Car-lisle or an Andrew Valenza or a Thea Landen a try as well. Chances are, it will mean more to one of them than anyone you'll find on the *New York Times* Best Sellers list.

Oh, that reminds me. My final acknowledgement goes to you, dear reader. Thank you so much for reading my book.

About the Author

Jamie Norton has written for various daily and weekly newspapers in Vermont, New Hampshire, and upstate New York, including (but not limited to) the *Rutland Herald*, the *Brattleboro Reformer*, and the *Caledonian-Record*. He now lives with his wife Lisa and their five "fur-babies" near Saratoga Springs, New York. Jamie loves English bulldogs, St. Louis Cardinals baseball, and slow-pitch softball, and he believes whole-heartedly that writing about himself in the third person is weird. *The Second Act Comeback* is his first novel. To read more of Jamie's stuff (or to see what he's up to next), go to www.jamiescreamsintothevoid.com. Jamie would also love to follow you back on Threads/Insta or TikTok at @jamiescreamsintothevoid or X/Twitter at @jamiescreamsITV.

Please leave a review on Amazon or Goodreads!

Follow us on social media!

Jamie Norton
@jamiescreamsintothevoid - TikTok/Instagram
@jamiescreamsITV - X

Valenza Publishing
www.valenzapublishing.com
@valenzapublishing - Instagram/Facebook/Threads
@valenza_publishing - TikTok

And support indie authors by checking out these
incredible books!

"Fate's Tether" by Jade Nioma

"Goodwill's Secrets" by Christopher Mele

"Witness to the Revolution" by Kiersten Marcil